On the Side of Good

On the Side of Good

Published by The Conrad Press in the United Kingdom 2021

Tel: +44(0)1227 472 874
www.theconradpress.com
info@theconradpress.com

ISBN 978-1-913567-73-6

Copyright © Iwo Załuski, 2021

The moral right of Iwo Załuski to be identified as author of this work has been asserted in accordance with the Copyright, Designs and Patents Act 1988.

All rights reserved.

Typesetting and Cover Design by: Charlotte Mouncey, www.bookstyle.co.uk
Cover designed with images of Iwonicz-Zdrój, the Zaluski spa from a mid-1880s print in the author's possession and *Battle of Vienna*, a sketch by Rybkowski, Tadeusz (1848-1926) at National Museum Warsaw.
The Conrad Press logo was designed by Maria Priestley.

Printed and bound in Great Britain by Clays Ltd, Elcograf S.p.A.

The Carpathian Cradle
Book One:

On the Side of Good

Iwo Załuski

POLISH PRONUNCIATION

a – *u* as in but
ą – as in French *en*
c – *ts*
ć – *tch*
ch – hard *h*
cz – *tr* as in train
dź – *j*
dż – *dr* as in drain
e – *e* as in get
ę – *in* as in French vin
g – *g* as in go
i – *ee*
j – *y*
ł – English *w*
ń – *n* as in Tanya
o – *o* as in got
ó – *oo*
ś – *sh*
u – *oo*
w – *v*
y – *i* as in it
ż – deep *zh*
ź – *zh*

To Lorna

Prologue

Theo Samojarski looked up at the television set and for a few moments watched the convoy of Trabants making their epic journey from East Germany to the Hungarian border with Austria. The volume was turned up too high, and was making conversation difficult. What was it about Poles and noise pollution? The previous morning, breakfasting at the Orbis Hotel in Kalisz, Theo had been hypnotised into a senseless stupor by two television sets, placed side by side on their wall brackets overlooking the dining room, one purveying the news while the other simultaneously ran a video of *Simply Red* in concert. Both were turned up high. The day before that, in a grubby roadside restaurant somewhere in the Częstochowa region, he had managed to consume a plate of *bigos* so well-stewed that it no longer qualified as *bigos*. That was bad enough, the bottle of excellent *Żywiec* lager served at a decent temperature notwithstanding, but he ate to the strains of rap from a transistor radio with flat batteries placed on the counter, turned up full. Opposite the restaurant, on the other side of the road, was a graffiti scrawled wall. *Fuk the Comunists* stood out like a beacon of international aspiration. *What the fuk am I doing in this God-forsaken hell-hole of a country,* he thought to himself.

Theo was actually covering the events in Poland for a London broadsheet: the ascendency of Solidarity during the summer of 1989. They had sent him because he spoke Polish. He had learned the pre-war version of the language, now tinged with an educated English accent, at his mother's knee. The Poles found it quaint. 'How well you speak Polish,' they all said, 'considering…'

Considering he had left Poland aged three months. Now the Communists, who had stolen his rightful inheritance forty years previously, appeared to be losing control. The Hungarians had flung open their borders with Austria and the Free West, the Russians were panicking beneath their rhetoric, and the East Germans, whose borders were still strictly controlled, were seizing their chance by packing their Trabis with as many belongings as they could fit in, and making for Austria by a circuitous route, verging on the epic, through Czechoslovakia and Hungary. It all seemed as if the Gorbachev era was about to have an apotheosis.

The Polish head of state, General Jaruzelski, appeared on the screen, but his words were drowned out by *Simply Red*. Red. How apt! Whatever it was, Theo had heard it all before anyway. He had reported most of it, anyway. He cast his mind back to the winter of 1981, when Jaruzelski had crushed the charismatic Trades Union electrician Lech Wałęsa's *Solidarity* movement, proclaimed martial law and threw him into jail.

And now, by a totally unexpected quirk, the government had permitted free elections, with *Solidarity* in ascendency at every level. On June 4 1989, *Solidarity* won every seat of the new *Seym*, or Parliament, except for one, which went to an independent.

Is this the end of Communism in Poland? was Theo's brief.

'I tell you this is the end of Communism in Poland,' said Stefan Samojarski, his attention concentrated on the blaring television set. Theo emerged from his reverie and returned his attention to dinner. Earlier that hot August afternoon he had arrived at his nephew's tiny flat, which he shared with his wife Bożena, seventeen-year-old Karolina, Ździch, aged 12, in the grey and featureless town of Gorzów Wielkopolski, in north western Poland.

Stefan was the son of Theo's older brother, Czesio, the last owner of the spa estate of Sarenki, situated in the Carpathian

Mountains of south eastern Poland. The day after the Nazi invasion of Poland, his grandfather Bogdan had whisked his family, including six-month-old Theo, out of the country, and, eventually, to Great Britain. Czesio, however, had chosen to stay and see the war through as best he could. In 1948, after the Communist take-over of Poland, Sarenki was confiscated and taken over as a state health centre. Such Samojarskis as remained at Sarenki, were expelled and not permitted within 100 kilometres of their estate under pain of arrest. Czesio had weathered first the Nazi storm, then the Soviet 'liberation', despite the fact that the love of his life was picked out and shot by the liberators in cold blood for not showing enough joy at the prospect of liberation. In the dead of night, he 'burgled' his own manor of anything that might be of use, including silver and jewels, and a wooden chest of papers and documents, all of which he piled into his elderly Tatra. He then drove in a north westerly direction, and eventually ended up in Gorzów, diametrically opposite Sarenki on the other side of Poland. He never saw Sarenki again.

Czesio married Hania Trawnik the following year, and they managed to live off the sale of some of the salvaged family silver, while Czesio earned extra money by doing translations: he was fluent in Polish, German, French and English.

Stefan was born in Gorzów in 1950, plain Comrade Stefan Samojarski. Not only had all titles been abolished by the Communists, as irrelevant relics of the long defunct Austro-Hungarian Empire, and former aristocrats suffered discrimination as far as jobs were concerned. When Stefan left school, he found work as a car mechanic in a garage on the outskirts of the town, and was thus able to support his parents in his tiny, two-bedroomed flat in the centre of the town. Eight years previously, at the height of the Solidarity movement's initial gains, Czesio died, a bitter and disillusioned old man. His widow Hania, being of peasant stock, did not find it necessary to instil in Stefan any feeling for family history or sense of heritage. She had, after all, missed out on being a Countess, and saw no reason for any regrets, and even made a point of acting as proletarian as possible. She died shortly after her husband. Stefan had little or no curiosity as to his own background or history. Such residual interest as may have survived at the back of his mind had been pretty thoroughly eradicated by a 'peoples' education in the local schools, where he learned that his family had made millions from exploiting the peasants for over a century. 'We jumped from Counts to Comrades in one go,' he told Theo wryly. 'More *buraczki*?'

Bożena had prepared an excellent meal, traditionally Polish for Theo's benefit. 'I don't suppose you get much of a chance to have *wieprz pieczony z kminkiem* with *kasza gryczana* and *buraczki*, in England,' she had said.

She was right. Theo had virtually forgotten all the Polish dishes that his mother used to make when he was a youngster in post-war London.

Bożena seemed to read his mind. 'You never married, Teofilku,' she said, recalling that he had been christened Teofil.

Theo toyed thoughtfully with the *buraczki*. 'It's...' he concentrated intently on the colour of the beetroot streaked with strands of freshly grated horseradish.

Stefan came to the rescue. 'You never met the right girl?' he said.

'Yes. No, it's not that,' Theo replied. 'It's just that – yes, there was one – but – it's a long story, and – and really I prefer not to talk about it.' Then his stance changed and his face lit up. 'But this is wonderful, Bożenko! My favourite Polish meal, just like *Mamusia* used to make.'

He was familiar with this one: roast pork with caraway seeds, buckwheat and creamed beetroot with horseradish. All washed down with a dumpy bottle of table Chianti in its basketwork wrapping, a present from visiting relatives from Britain twenty years previously. They had been saving it for a special occasion. It should have been undrinkable, but was, surprisingly, extremely good after thirty years. But Theo would still have preferred *Żywiec*. Polish food doesn't really go well with wine.

'Thank you,' said Theo, proffering his plate.

'Leave some for me!' cried Ździch in what appeared to be panic.

'Ździsiu!' cried Karolina in a mock shocked tone. 'Where are your manners? Is that the way to talk to our rich bourgeois capitalist uncle from England?'

Theo looked fondly at his nephew and niece: two such handsome and charming youngsters it would have been hard to find. They were very much alike, both had the poise and elegance inherited from their broken grandfather, as well as the blond hair, blue eyes and simple, folksy-pretty peasant looks of their mother. But why, thought Theo, was the boy christened with such an awkward name to pronounce? His friend, also a journalist and Polish-born, had the same name. Ździch short for Ździsław Sidorowicz, but all the Brits pronounced it Jeek. A silly name, which loses everything in translation. He had a thing about the name, which preyed on his mind. Theo the journalist and frustrated poet and writer had a love of language – any language – and all its quirks, puns, and suggestion. To him Jeek sounded like a detergent. Or the Polish for wild boar: *dzik*. Or a South African saying 'Jack'. Impossible to pronounce for an English tongue. He wondered how it would be spelt phonetically. *Zh-jeech?* Short for *Zh-jeesswahv*. Whatever. A split second of change of concentration. 'Wouldn't dream of robbing my starving little nephew of his beetroot,' he grinned, accepting only a small helping from Bożena.

'Thanks,' said Ździch, in English. 'You're cool, *Wujku*. No problem.'

'Now you're showing off!' said Karolina superciliously. 'Anyway, no one says *no problem* any more! It's *passé!*'

'Stop it, you two!' said Stefan. 'They're always at it, those two.' Stefan took a hefty swig of Chianti. 'But, as I said, the days of the *Komuna* are coming to an end...' he continued in full flow, but Theo was not listening. Three months in Poland being told that Communism was at an end at every turn, with Solidarity in the ascendancy, and with events moving along with the Trabis to match the theory, Theo thought his head would burst. He had interviewed every politician from Wałęsa down, and was amazed at the number of rampant communists who had experienced a Pauline conversion to rampant Thatcherism over the past weeks. The quarter-of-a-century-old *'I speek Eenglish. Bobbee Charltonn!'* suddenly became *'I speek Eenglish. Margarett Tut-chairr!'* He had interviewed the whole spectrum of delirious priests, bishops and cardinals – with the exception of the Pope. That would no doubt come later. After all, they were already saying that it would be two Poles, Lech Wałęsa and Pope John Paul II, who will have brought down Communism. The former had already made a start: in July. Wałęsa and his trades union, Solidarity, were on the brink of forming the first non-communist government in Poland for forty years. The catch being in partnership with communist premier Wojciech Jaruzelski.

Theo did not like Poland. The outdated plumbing, the ubiquitous weeds growing between the acres of uneven paving stones, the tiny, drab flats in the endless, ghastly townships of grey tower blocks. Some of them, like the one Stefan and Bożena lived in, were built along the highway in the middle of nowhere, like a village compacted into one cluster of concrete blocks by the roadside. Above all, he could not stand the surliness of the people. The young copied all the worst attributes of the West: baseball caps worn back-to-front, foul language, insolent attitude and mis-spelt graffiti; and the older generation, cold, private, uninvolved in anything outside their thoughts and monosyllabic in their replies to the simplest questions. What God-forsaken agency had turned a once outward-going, crazy, passionate, resilient, warm and friendly people into an anaesthetised nation of mindless zombies, each man an island unto himself?

Except, Theo had to admit, in the privacy of the tiny flats in the grey tower blocks where, behind locked doors, flowers, tidiness, warmth, love, friendship, culture, the cut-and-thrust of lively conversation and the heady debate of enquiring minds could still be found if you knew where to look. Like among the Polish crowd back in London, of which Theo had been an active member since his arrival there as a refugee after the War: new Britons every one, primarily English-speaking but also bi-lingual, yet still retaining, in some way, an essential Polishness that they would never lose. He had found it hard to associate or reconcile the Polish *émigré* community in Britain with the grey masses inhabiting this grim, traditionally torn, polluted, devastated, flat and featureless land.

And, of course, the shortages, as exemplified by the ubiquitous *'Nie ma!'* There isn't any. The standard shopkeeper's reply to any question about availability of anything from food to television sets. *Banany? Nie ma.* Milk? *Nie ma!* Bread? *Nie ma! Baterie do radia? Nie ma!* To obtain such basics as fruit and vegetables, milk, butter, and this in a basically agricultural land, you had to know the right people. Which most people, including Stefan, somehow did, hence the *buraczki* with horseradish sauce. And, in Theo's case, petrol for his Volvo. He filled up at every petrol station he came across for fear of landing in the lurch.

At a whim, Theo had decided to get away from politics and reporters and his job for a few days and check out his roots. 'Thought I'd take a look at the land of my forebears,' he had telephoned Bożena. 'It would somehow be wrong not to.'

Towards the end of August, he drove in his British-registered, right-hand drive Volvo to Sarenki. After all, he was born there. It turned out to be quite a pretty dump. The health centre and its immediate surroundings were well-maintained, with flowers everywhere. The forest walkway to the spring was uneven and needed some attention, most of its cobbles having been removed. The carved, wooden statue of the Virgin overlooking it had been vandalised – someone had applied an axe to her shoulder and had rent her whole side off. There was a story behind that, he was told. Old carved timber bathhouses and new concrete blocks clashed in appalling disharmony, although the Manor, which was the Hotel *Przy Wodzie* – beside the water – the *Pałac Szpilberga,* the administrative centre, the Villa de Villiers, the medical centre, as well as the clock tower and the ballroom – now doubling as the cinema – were well-kept, even though a coat of paint was more than somewhat overdue. But the whole lot was surrounded by grey concrete blocks, enormous blots on a beautiful, natural, unkempt landscape of the undulating forested foothills of the Carpathian Mountains. Sarenki lay in a valley, like a cradle, and could have been so beautiful. Probably was once. The cradle of my family, thought Theo. A seething rage welled up in his heart. And look what the *fuk* they've done with it, the *Komunist* bastards, he muttered out aloud, surprising himself at the strength of his feelings.

On the evening of Theo's arrival there was a punk-rock band in concert on the *Muszla* – the oyster-shell stage overlooking the flower-bedecked central square. Theo wondered what administrative idiocy considered a punk-rock band as suitable evening entertainment for the elderly, sick and wheel-chair bound *clientèle* of the health centre, for whom there was no escape within a radius of three decibel kilometres of the village.

As it was high season, Theo could only find a room at the small Hotel *Pod Dwoma Grubasami* – The Two Fat Boys – once no doubt a pleasant little hostelry close to the centre. He wondered where the name came from. Theo had been around, and stayed in some dreadful places, and compared The Two Fat Boys to a cockroach-infested dive he had mercifully spent only one night in, in downtown Caracas when he was a junior reporter for a tabloid newspaper at the start of his career. Its Polish equivalent was filthy, cockroach-infested, had no running water during the day, and at night the taps all came alive noisily spurting black, brackish water in all directions. A surreal situation for a spa. The curtains needed only the slightest tug to bring them down, thus covering the carpet of dead flies on the floor beneath. The unshaven proprietor, clad in shirtsleeves and braces, was drunk, but, having noted the name Samojarski in the register, himself registered the fact that it was the Samojarskis who had originally owned Sarenki. For a good minute confusion reigned in his glazed eyes as his befuddled mind tossed up between whether this Samojarski was Beloved Master and Lord of the Manor Returning unto the Bosom of his People, or Bloated Capitalist Landowner Come Back to Drink the Blood of the Peasant Children, and Rub the Faces of the Proletariat into the Mire. In the event, the hapless man read the portents and opted for the former, fell on his knees, hugged those of Theo, and let loose a diatribe of invective against those who had expelled *Pan hrabia* – Sir Count – from his rightful inheritance, and what a disgrace it was that this same *Pan hrabia* had to put up with a place as dreadful as this. He ended by kissing Theo's hands, praising his goodness and understanding – where on earth he got that impression from Theo could only guess – and apologising for his fellow-countrymen's appalling behaviour and lack of respect, and that God in his goodness and mercy would surely repay in the end.

Theo breakfasted in the gloomy half-light of the restaurant, watching the rough diamond at the next table breakfast off *żurek* soup with lots of bread and a total of eight bottles of beer – he had lined up his empties on his table in a neat row – while perusing a very explicit hard-porn magazine, grunting his approval at regular intervals.

Then there was the damsel in distress. What was an obviously English girl doing trying unsuccessfully to explain to the po-faced woman behind the bar that she would like milk for her tea?

'*Nie ma!*' barked the woman. '*Nie ma!*' That phrase again. It had, Theo recalled the Shakespeare quote, a dying fall!

'Can I help?' asked Theo coming up.

'You're English!' she said with a sigh of relief.

'Yes, but I was born here. Only just.'

'Oh, right! What a bit of luck! What does *Nie ma* mean?'

'This is Poland, love. It's an expression you must learn. It means there isn't any. There ain't none! Besides, Poles don't drink tea with milk.'

'Oh, I didn't know that! Thanks ever so much! *Nie ma!* My first and only words in Polish!'

With that Theo gave her a big smile and returned to his seat to contemplate his next move. He had booked in for four days, but could not stand the prospect of a second night there. So, having learned the basic fact that Sarenki was one of the perks enjoyed by fully paid-up, card-carrying Communist Party members, he left in his Volvo for the comparative civilisation of Kraków, where he telephoned his cousin Stefan, and asked if he could come that weekend. The invitation had been an open one, as Stefan specifically wanted Theo to look through some boxes of old papers, photographs and music.

'Apart from some silver and jewellery it was all my father could salvage when the Communists kicked him out in '48,' Stefan had told Theo. 'I haven't really got time to go through it all, and I'd like to bin the lot, being as we need the space. You're a journalist, Teofilku, a writer, a man of letters. Educated, like.

I don't want to bin what might turn out to be important, and I wouldn't really know.'

From Kraków it took Theo three days to reach Gorzów, with stopovers in Kalisz and Poznań.

After dinner Bożena and Karolina cleared the table in the sitting room of dishes, while Stefan and Ździch went to fetch the wooden chest from the garage.

'Here it is, Teofilku,' said Stefan, placing it on the table. 'Shall I leave you to it, then?'

'Yes, that would be best. Thank you.'

'Shall I leave the TV on?'

'No. No, that's all right,' said Theo politely.

As it was past ten o'clock Bożena unfolded the bed-settee and left a duvet and a couple of pillows for Theo for when he was ready to retire. Then the family all excused themselves and, after lots of kissing and hugging, went to bed.

'I'm feeling very tired,' said Bożena.

'Got work tomorrow,' said Stefan. 'And Bożenka's been helping out at the *Gmina* with a bit of cleaning.'

'And I've got my ballet,' said Karolina.

'And I've got my Youth Brigade,' said Ździch the Wild Boar.

'Bit of a joke these days, your Youth Brigade,' said his father.

'Only this one's actually funny,' laughed Ździch, adding in English, 'We learn English from pop records! Good night, *Wujku,* stay cool and rock on!' He raised his fist at his uncle.

When they had all gone, Theo poured himself a glass of *Wiśniówka,* took out his reading glasses, placed the standard lamp above the table, and opened the chest. It was a small, nineteenth century walnut trunk with rosewood inlay, and brass fittings dulled colourless with lack of polish. It was covered in scratches. At first, he heard the other televisions of the block, all turned up high, through the thin walls, but as the evening gave way to night, they dropped out, one by one, until the night yielded the blessed silence that Theo craved. He then spent virtually the whole night rummaging through the contents.

It became evident that someone had arranged these in some semblance of order. Firstly, there were numerous letters, many of them tied with ribbons or stuffed into a larger envelope. The greatest letter writer appeared to be Julek Samojarski. A cursory glance at his spidery handwriting, almost illegible to twentieth century, word-processor-oriented man, meant many prospective hours of poring and transcribing. There was two-way correspondence, in Polish, French or English – fortunately Theo spoke all three – with his parents from his English public school. There were more letters to and from a place called Nibork, and correspondence with his sister Franciszka in Frontillac. Somewhere in France. There seemed to be some trouble there. Anyway, the galleys were mentioned. He would have to find out where these places were. There were letters by Julek's wife to some cleric on the Isle of Skye. Scotland? Julek certainly seemed to have got around a bit. There were a few letters from France signed by someone called Maurice, as well as Adam, probably Julek's brother although he could not be sure. There was a document signed by Metternich. Surely, not the famous Congress of Vienna Metternich? He would have to verify the signature. There was considerable mention of Teofil Samojarski, the founder of Sarenki. Theo had been named after him. Would be interesting to see what kind of a man he was. He appeared to have died twice. There was a document signed by a Father Józefowicz describing some local mass murder, but the scrawl was almost illegible, and would need careful study. Then there were the diaries of a Jolanta. Theo read the signature because he could read Cyrillic. He had taught himself to read Russian and Greek just for fun, although he knew neither language. Jolanta's diaries were all in Russian. No problem. His journalist friend Jeek the Unpronounceable Wild Boar Sidorowicz back in London was fluent in Russian, and would surely help out.

More interesting in some ways were some music manuscripts and published works contained in a scratched old leather case at the bottom of the trunk. Most of them by someone called Daniel Meadows. English? Theo, who liked classical music well enough and listened to Classic FM but no further, had never heard of him, but he had a friend who was professor of pianoforte at the Royal College of Music. Not only was Tom Wilkins a brilliant pianist obsessed with introducing the piano sonatas of Carl Czerny to the tone-deaf world (unsuccessfully, as it turned out), but he was also a heavy-duty industrial-strength dusty archive/yellowing manuscript history buff who liked rediscovering long lost compositions and imposing them on the afore-mentioned tone-deaf world. This little lot will be gold dust for him. A Piano Concerto in D flat, published in London in 1820, and another, in C minor, still in manuscript. There was a dedication written in on the first page. *Dédié à Jolanta Barnicka, de la part de son admirateur, Daniel Meadows Saint-Petersbourg le 12 avril 1818.* There was also a Meadows piano solo in manuscript, *Romance in D*, inscribed *souvenir d'une nuit d'amour* under the title. There must be a story in there somewhere. He had a momentary vision of a couple doing it at a grand piano. But then there was a composition by Jolanta herself, entitled, in English, *The Legend of the Golden Pumpkin,* beautifully hand-scripted on finest quality paper, bound in leather and embossed in gold. On the inside of the front cover was a small window containing a slip of paper with the words, in Russian, *To Arkady, with all my love, Jolanta. Christmas 1821*. Ah, reflected Theo. Roman Christmas, or Russian Orthodox Christmas? A three-way affair? Did she ditch Arkady for Meadows? Or did she take up with Meadows on the rebound from Arkady? Theo wished he could understand Russian.

Music featured strongly in the chest. There was a folder

of press cuttings chronicling the career of concert pianist Jan Prosper Samojarski. The cuttings were from enough foreign-language journals and papers to testify to a brilliant international career, which included the United States of America as well as Europe and Russia. The last cutting, in a French journal, caught Theo's eye. An obituary. 'Pity,' he thought. 'Such a brilliant career cut short. Absolutely senseless!'

There were lots of other press cuttings from Austrian journals, which Theo put off for later. His eyes could not cope with the Gothic script at that hour. Only the headline words *Riot, Revolt, Uprising, Dead, Peasants, Landowners* and such like pointed to the overall topics.

Two albums of photographs held Theo's attention as he tried to guess who some of them were of. Whoever compiled them failed, inexplicably, to label them all.

He then came to a batch which seemed to be an accountant's chronicle of expenditure in the development of Sarenki as a health centre during the latter half of the nineteenth century. It lacked the innate drama of the previous batches of letters and music. He began to be aware that his eyelids were becoming heavy. The first light of dawn was breaking when Theo, finding himself staring inanely at sets of figures in columns, finally gave way to utter exhaustion, not to mention boredom, and fell asleep on the settee, not even wrapping the duvet around him.

The following morning, Bożena woke Theo with a glass of strong, black, sweet tea. Theo drank it gratefully, as he did tea of any kind anywhere. When in Britain, milk and one sugar. When in a Chinese restaurant, Jasmine straight, and before it gets too stewed. When in Poland strong black with lots of sugar. No lemon, or course. That's for the Russians.

Stefan called briefly before going to work. 'Any use?' he asked peremptorily. 'If not, I can put the stuff in a bag and take it to the dump on my way. We can keep the chest. Could be worth a *grosz* or two.'

'Don't you dare!' said Theo with mock strictness. 'To do so would be an act of wanton vandalism!'

'You mean we should keep it?'

'It's a gold mine, Stefan. And the chest's quite nice, too,' said Theo. 'English. Victorian. I think it must have belonged to Julek.'

'Who's Julek?'

'Julek Samojarski.'

'Oh, that Julek!'

'What other Julek could it be?'

'Look, Teofilku, I must go or I'll be late for work,' said Stefan. 'We'll talk about it later. Are you staying?'

'I should be back in Warsaw by tonight, but this is far too important. I'll phone them and tell them I'm unavoidably delayed.'

'So, you'll stay?'

'Try to stop me!'

'Wow! Cool!'

Theo grinned and ruffled the thick blond hair of his nephew. Jeek the Unpronounceable. Sounds like some mediaeval warrior. Maybe I'll write a children's story one day. Jack and the South African Wild Boar. The Unpronounceable Meets the Illegible. We Did It On A Grand Piano: Confessions of a Concert Pianist.

Maybe I'll put the lot in a bag and take it all back to London with me.

Stefan can keep the chest. It's the only heirloom he'll have to pass on to Ździch. He can use it as a cradle when he grows up, gets married and has kids. It's about the right size.

'I'll pick it all up on my way back to England,' said Theo. 'I don't know how much longer I'll stay in Poland, but I've just got to see it all through.'

Book 1

The Side of Good

Part One - 1813

I

The snort of horses momentarily attracted the attention of a grey wolf. He had feasted off a piglet taken from a farm, so his interest in the two exhausted riders making their way through the snow-covered forests of the Beskid uplands was purely academic. It was night, and the cold penetrated every defence against it. There was no moon, and the horses picked their way by the eerie glow of the snow that managed to reflect itself enough to make the ghostly outlines of the trees visible.

A colourless dawn had long been established when the riders emerged from the southern edge of the forest to safety, leaving behind the dangers of the wolf's domain. He and his pack seldom braved the open spaces, except to raid the farms in the night. The taller of the two men reined in his chestnut stallion and looked up. He was dressed in an army greatcoat covering the tattered remains of the uniform of Napoleon's Grande Armée. His unkempt hair, which would have proved fair under scrutiny, was matted and dishevelled. His face was a colourless mass of sallow blotches. His lips, not quite concealed by the many days' growth of mangy stubble, were cracked. He should have been a handsome man in his mid-thirties, endowed with the proud and elegant poise of a high-born Slav; but his height and slimness now gave him the appearance of a living cadaver, despite some weak signs of life in his pallid blue eyes, the only specks of colour in an otherwise colourless facescape. He raised his hand with an effort, and pointed ahead with fingers blue with frostbite.

'Sarenki!' he croaked.

His companion, mounted on a dun Kladruper stallion that he had bought a week previously from a dealer near Zamość, was a small, dapper man in his thirties, who had managed merely to appear tired. Despite the intense cold his face still retained a swarthy vigour beneath his fur hat, and his brown eyes were alert but unconcerned. His moustache, although streaked white with frost, was black and neat, with its attendant stubble giving him the casual look of an adventurer. 'About time too, *mon brave*,' he said, managing a charm-charged grin, which in better times - seduced maidens - and made enemies by the score.

'I used to come here with my father to hunt wolves,' continued the taller man. 'On a clear day you can see the high Carpathians to the South.'

'At the moment, *mon ami*,' replied the other, 'it is an obscure day, and I am more interested in seeing a log fire blazing in a hearth, a leg of pork roasting within aroma range, a large jug of whatever passes for a *liqueur intoxiquant* in this place, and a wench in boots with a touch of the gipsy in her heart, eh!'

'You dream like a Pole, Maurice! Come on, then, and we shall see what we can find for you!'

The horses snorted into action, and they set off again. The hill sloped steadily down towards a wide, winding valley. There was a small river flowing northwards, eventually to join many other rivers for their assignation with the Vistula – and eventually with the Baltic Sea. On the hillside beyond, there were groups of white-washed farmhouses, cottages and barns. They would have been well-camouflaged were it not for their distinctive thatched roofs, which were so enormous as to almost swamp the buildings themselves from view. Every chimney yielded plumes of grey smoke, each proof of a warm hearth below. In the midst of this settlement a small onion dome surmounted with a cross pointed surreptitiously at the sky, a testament to Christian values. A dirt road followed the approximate course of the river, linking the farms and cottages of the village to a large, two-storey Manor set in a cluster of copses. The whole settlement was overshadowed by a large forest draped across the high ground beyond.

'Sarenki means deer,' continued the taller man, pointing in the direction of the building. He had hardly spoken for the past two days, but now the sight of the village in the valley – his village – had made him almost garrulous by comparison. 'When my grandparents first came here, there was nothing except the ruined Manor and a couple of woodman's hovels. My grandfather hoped he might be left alone to paint and farm, and rebuild his life.'

'Ah, the pioneering spirit, that one!'

'More of an escape from reality into a dream, Maurice.'

'A Polish trait these days, *mon ami*, to dream!'

'My grandfather Mateusz was an artist. All artists dream. When he first arrived, he stood on the riverbank at that bend where the bridge is now. It was winter, and dusk was closing in. There was that mysterious grey light that you find in these hills in winter. You can see it – feel it, now. On the hillside above, just below where the forest begins, he saw a pair of deer. They had come to drink from the spring there, because all the streams were frozen. He gazed at them, as they stood against the clean black and white of the forest. He used to speak of the cold perfection of the scene. An artist has an eye for these things. He loved animals so much. Suddenly, without warning, three wolves emerged from the forest, and the vision turned from a winter idyll to a scene of horror as the wolves attacked. He built the Church on the spot where the killing happened, beside the spring. He called it the church of St Francis of Assisi, the patron saint of animals, and he renamed his domain SARENKI.'

They had reached the bottom of the valley and joined the

dirt road. It was deeply rutted, churned up and hardened. Fresh tracks suggested that ox- and horse-drawn carts had been this way recently. It was easier to ride in the frozen fields beside the track.

'Over the next twenty years my grandparents farmed the land. They were joined by others, and Sarenki village was born.'

'Did he ever paint the picture?' asked his companion.

'The deer? Oh, yes. It used to hang above the mantelpiece in the drawing room at the Manor.'

'Used to?'

'My grandfather was arrested by the Austrians in 1792. There was trouble in the Russian and Prussian sectors which spilled over into Galicia, and he had been harbouring dissidents at the Manor. The soldiers stripped the house of everything. The paintings, furniture and anything of value were carted off, and they made a bonfire of the rest. Mercifully, the Manor survived.'

'*Voilà*, the Austrians, the Russians and the Prussians, your three wolves and the Polish deer!'

A tear trickled down the other's face and froze. 'One day, Maurice, there will be no more wolves in Poland!' he sighed. 'It's what we've been fighting for, you and I.'

'It's what you have been fighting for, *mon ami. Moi*, I know no other way. They tell me to fight, I fight!'

'Napoleon's finished, Maurice,' said the other. 'Who will you fight for now?'

'*Voilà la question!*' said Maurice. 'You fought for France, maybe I return the complement, and fight for Poland? But then, maybe the time is come to stop, *hein?*'

The village seemed deserted, although the two men felt that many eyes were fixed on their progress. The sound of pigs grunting and the cackle of geese behind closed barn doors suggested that life went on despite winter, war and pestilence. They came to the timber church, an octagonal central domed tower with four wings. Icicles hung like decorations from the high-gabled, snow-clad roofs. 'The Church of St Francis of Assisi,' said the tall man.

The two men dismounted, tethered their horses, and made for the entrance. 'I was baptised here,' continued the tall man. Inside, both men bared their heads. The interior was starkly simple and very dark. The only decorations were wooden artefacts and statues. Many empty vases of crude, peasant manufacture suggested that in summer the church was full of flowers. Two solitary candles glowed on either side of a wooden crucifix on a white-clad altar. 'My grandfather's paintings used to hang here before the Austrians came. There was also an altar-piece.'

His companion was silent. He gazed at the bare walls and imagined how it must have looked before the wolves came. The sound of the door opening made them start. A coarse-featured, elderly man with near-Asiatic high cheekbones, piggy eyes, a crooked mouth and a close-cropped tuft of grey hair stood in the doorway. He was wearing a black soutane. He peered into the darkness of the church.

'Who's that in there?' he barked. 'What do you want?'

'Father Józef?' said the taller man. 'It's me, Teofil!'

The priest came closer. His gait was awkward, and he moved gracelessly. 'Teofil? Teofil Samojarski? Surely not!'

'The same, Father, except a little the worse for wear!'

Father Józef strode up to Teofil, grabbed him roughly by the arm, dragged him into the daylight outside and stared uncomprehendingly into his face. Maurice followed.

'May the good Lord Jesus be praised for all eternity!' he thundered in a guttural voice, waving his fist at the sky. 'And where the Devil have you been for the past God only knows how many years?'

Despite his cracked lips, Teofil managed a grin. 'Same old Father Józef!' he laughed. 'You haven't changed a bit, you old

Ukrainian villain! Still taking the names of both God and the Devil in vain, all in one breath. I sometimes used to wonder whose side you were really on!'

Father Józef grabbed Teofil in a bear hug. 'I may curse and swear like a Russian, Teofil, but you know damn' well I'm on the side of Good! We all thought you'd be dead by now! Welcome home!'

'I'd like you to meet my companion-at-arms, Maurice Chavelet, Father,' said Teofil, disentangling himself from the priest's grip. 'Maurice and I met in Italy in '97. I owe him my life, and he owes me his.'

'A Frenchman?' grunted Father Józef, avoiding Maurice's eye. 'What did you want to bring even more damned foreigners into our blighted country? Haven't we got enough of the bastards already?'

'*Enchanté, Monsieur le Curé*,' said Maurice with a grin, ignoring the priest's xenophobic outburst. He had met bombastic clerics before.

'You see, he doesn't even speak Polish!' cried the priest, staring at Teofil. Then his coarse face turned to the Frenchman and exploded into a radiant leer, making it look like the sort of face that frightens children. 'Any friend of Teofil's is welcome in my parish, provided he brings something to drink, but in your case, I will make an exception as I can see how low you have sunk! Welcome to Sarenki, *Monsieur* Maurice!' With that he embraced Maurice heartily.

A few minutes later, Teofil and Maurice were seated at the wooden table in front of a blazing hearth in Father Józef's cottage next to the church. *Pani* Marynia, the priest's elderly and bad-tempered housekeeper, was forcibly dragged from her cottage on the hillside to come and prepare what passed for a fatted calf in one of the poorest regions of Europe, Galicia – the Austrian sector of partitioned Poland. A continuous mumbling diatribe of curses and complaints issued from her lips as she shuffled about with bad grace preparing the table and stoking up the fire.

'May lightning strike you dead, you wizened old bag, if you don't shut your bearded face and get on with your work!' cried Father Józef, waving a large wooden ladle at her threateningly.

Then he turned to his guests. 'First you eat...' he growled. The *bigos*, a seething cauldron of boiled soured cabbage imbued with pork fat and such apples as were still fit to be cooked from the year's harvest, was suspended over the fire. *Pani* Marynia augmented it by the addition of some sausage left-overs and potatoes. A large loaf of rye bread with caraway seeds and a poppy-seed cake appeared on the table.

'...then you drink!' Father Józef poured out three cups from a large, earthenware jug. 'It will help dispel the cold. It's a vodka made with water from the spring outside by Old Pankracy – surely you remember Old Pankracy, he's been Old ever since I can remember, and I'm sixty-four – he claims he knows three hundred and forty-seven things to do with potatoes, and this hooch is one of them. Personally, I don't believe him, even though he won't admit to telling lies in the confessional, the lying hound! Now tell me what you have been doing for the past fifteen years, fornicating around Europe instead of fornicating right here in the bosom of your own!'

According to Father Józef, *bigos* with vodka was the second greatest combination known to Man – he never divulged what the first was, and speculation among his parishioners was rife as to what it could be. For all that, as a conversation lubricant *bigos* with vodka was very effective.

'So how did you get here in the first place, anyway?' said Teofil.

II

Maurice decided to retire and leave Teofil and Father Józef to reminisce into the night.

'I was born in 1757 in Swir, a small village near Lwów, an only son. My mother and father were Catholic Ukrainian peasants, and, as a boy, I saw the Church as the only escape from the grinding poverty of the steppe. When I was eighteen, I entered the seminary in Lwów, with my parents' blessing. It was there that I first put on a pair of shoes!'

I didn't understand the complexity of politics then, or the Commonwealth's first partition of 1772, but my good friend Leonid explained that instead of having our faces ground into the mire by the Poles, we were going to have it done by the Austrians.' Father Józef opened another bottle of vodka and poured two glasses. 'In 1774,' continued Father Józef, 'I was ordained as a priest without anyone grinding my face into anything more sinister than a bowl of *kasza*!' Teofil laughed as he sipped his vodka. 'So, I set off westwards on foot for Kraków in search of a parish. I'd heard a lot of good things about Kraków, especially about the Mariacki Church and that trumpeter fellow who's been trumpeting to God from the topmost spire…' Father Józef raised his fist and head at the ceiling, '…for hundreds of years.'

'But you didn't get that far?'

'No.' Father Józef belched profusely, 'I lost my way and blundered upon this small village with a manor in the foothills of the Carpathian Mountains. Way off course for Kraków. I went up to investigate, and discovered that the village was called Sarenki.' Father Józef tapped his forefinger on the arm of his armchair. 'This very village, here. The local landowner,' he continued, 'was your father Ksawery. He inherited Sarenki after Mateusz, his father, had taken off for America to follow Kościuszko, and fight in that American War.' Father Józef emptied his glass and had a coughing fit. 'So, I sneaked into the village and immediately chanced upon Count Ksawery himself, along with a dozen villagers, building what was going to be a small timber church close to a spring that was gushing merrily out of the ground. I took in the scene before me, rolled up my sleeves, shook my fist at the sky and invoked God's strength and courage to help complete the building of the church, blessed the site with the sign of the Cross, and got stuck in.'

Father Józef had found his parish.

*****

'So, you never wanted to leave Sarenki and move on?' said Teofil late the following morning as he, Father Józef and, holding back so as not to intrude on their conversation, Maurice rode out onto the icy lower grasslands behind Sarenki.

'How can I leave a church that I helped build with my own bare hands?' he growled. 'I shall die and be buried here. You shall see to it, Teofil.'

Four years after his arrival in Sarenki, Father Józef had married Mateusz's son Ksawery to Princess Świetlana, daughter of Russian Prince Leonid Sczasny, who had an estate at Czarne Lasy, near Kraków. The following year Ksawery and Świetlana produced a son, Teofil.

'I swear before Almighty God, the Virgin Mary and all the Saints, if they're listening…' He shook his fist at the ceiling '…you were the noisiest little son-of-a-bitch I've ever had to baptise, Teofil! You howled all the way through the ceremony, until I almost gave up and abandoned you to the Devil, because I thought if anyone could drive him to distraction, you could!'

'I wouldn't have put it past you, Father,' laughed Teofil. 'Why didn't you?'

'Because I'm on the side of Good!' He sat back and gazed into the fire. It was getting low. 'They were good days, those days,' he muttered. Suddenly he straightened. '*Pani* Marynia!' he bellowed. 'This damned fire's going out! Get your fat backside moving and fetch some more logs, or we'll freeze to death in here!'

For the next few minutes, the only sound was that of the housekeeper shuffling backwards and forwards fetching logs, while keeping up, under her breath, her monologue of invocations for harm to visit those present. The murmurings increased in volume as the old woman finished with the fire and contemplated her further duties with displeasure.

'Since your mother's gone to Kraków to live with her parents at Czarne Lasy,' continued the priest, 'the Manor's stood empty.'

'Maurice and I were with Napoleon at the gates of Moscow last winter, and there certainly was no room at the inn,' chuckled Teofil. 'I daresay we'll survive!'

When *Pani* Marynia was gone Father Józef drank another glass of vodka, straight down after which he threw the glass into the dying embers in the fireplace. 'I've always wanted to do that!' His piggy eyes watered momentarily, then went mellow, glowing gently by the light of the flickering candle on the table, for the day had drawn in and it was already dark outside. Somewhere a wolf howled. 'Yes, they were good days,' continued Father Józef in contemplative mode. 'The land yielded twenty years of good harvests, and food was plentiful. Your grandfather Mateusz's paintings hang in a number of wealthy houses in Kraków and Vienna. He and Ksawery restored the Manor and filled it with beautiful things, paintings, rugs and fine furniture. What elegance! And no one ground anyone's face in the mire!'

'Until '92,' muttered Teofil. 'I remember I was just fourteen.'

*****

The Summer of 1792 was a significant year for the Polish nation, both in what was left of her territory and among those living under foreign domination. Twenty years after the First Partition Empress Catherine of Russia did a deal with a cabal of Polish nobles to annexe a further enormous tract of Polish territory to Russia. Incensed by what he considered as a blatant sell-out by his own countrymen to Poland's enemies, Mateusz expressed his intention of joining the Polish army.

'You can't go, Tata!' protested Ksawery, 'you'll be sixty next year!'

'I must!' replied the old warrior. 'This is to be my last great adventure!'

The army was commanded by Tadeusz Kościuszko, by this time a veteran of both the American War of Independence, and the French Revolution. The Polish forces came up against the Russians at Dubienka, near Lwów, on the border of Galicia and Poland. The Poles were defeated, with the loss of many lives. Mateusz Samojarski died on the battlefield with a raging anger in his heart. Father Józef's one and only excursion from Sarenki was to walk to Lwów, identify the body, wrap it and carry it back to Sarenki. He then personally dug the grave and buried the body with full Roman Catholic ceremonial. When he had finished, he shook his fist at the stormy sky and cried, 'Why, God, why? I thought you were on the side of Good!'

The following year Ksawery left fifteen-year-old Teofil at the Manor in his grand-mother Olga's care, and joined a rebel group operating from Kraków. Soon after Ksawery's arrival, Kościuszko resurfaced in the city, which was teeming with dispossessed peasants armed with scythes and baying for Russian blood: emigré mercenaries returning not only from Galicia and Prussia, but also from Paris, London, Milan and even as far as the United States of America. Kościuszko stood in the Great Square and proclaimed Insurrection, rousing the people to action. With a new, highly motivated army, which included Ksawery, he marched north. At Racławice, close to Kraków, Kościuszko again confronted the Russians. The battle was fierce, but the Poles won the day, and Kościuszko marched on in triumph to Warsaw. Ksawery rode in front of his cavalry unit, but did not share in his leader's final triumph. He was among the first casualties of that battle. His body was never found.

Losing both his father and grandfather within a two-year period had devastated the teenaged Teofil. He became morose and showed streaks of cruelty and he found him rebellious and difficult to cope with. His tutor resigned and returned to Kraków, after which Teofil sought the company of the more dubious young elements in the village.

*****

'You know you were the death of your grand-mother Olga,' growled Father Józef. 'You should be ashamed of yourself, Teofil!'

'It was a long time ago, Father,' said Teofil. 'A lot of sewage has flowed under the bridge. A lot of rage has been expiated from my heart over the past seventeen years. You were the only one who understood me, so understand me now!'

'You're wrong!' Father Józef slammed his fist down on the table. 'I only pretended to understand you because I was trying to get through to you! I only wanted to know why you were so uncaring towards your mother, and so abominably cruel to your Babcia Olga! God knows…' he shook his fist at the ceiling '… she had suffered enough! You weren't the only one deprived, you know. She did lose her husband and her only son within two years! She deserved better than being treated like some dogshit that had to be cleared up!'

Teofil sniffed. He remembered his Granny Olga as a tiny, wizened, broken old lady, looking much older than her seventy years at that time. She wore her stringy grey hair in a bun, and her blank, staring eyes set in a sallow face seemed to have a permanently uncomprehending expression. She hobbled about aimlessly with her stick, always dressed in black. Teofil recalled his hatred of her ugliness in grief and old age. He wanted to destroy this grief and old age, but ended up destroying her instead. He persecuted her without mercy, called her names, laughed at her grief and insulted the memory of his grandfather Mateusz; until one day, two years after the death of Ksawery, Granny Olga fell to her death down the stairs at the Manor. Teofil found her there, as ugly in death as in life: she had soiled herself as she fell. A surge of remorse flooded his whole being as he suddenly understood that his hatred was not for her, but for life's unfairness – old age, death, grief, politics and war. He cried bitterly over her body in a futile attempt at contrition. By the time his mother Świetlana and Father Józef appeared, Teofil had regained his sullen composure. At eighteen he had a great deal to prove to the world, and weeping over a despised old woman was a sign of weakness to his youth. His remorse was his best kept secret; for he had yet to discover that the strongest men wept, and the bravest quaked with fear.

'At least it was quick,' he had said with a forced smirk on his face, which belied the turmoil within.

Teofil never forgot the extremely violent thrashing he received from a very angry Father Józef. 'I never thought I'd ever raise a hand to anyone, Teofil,' said the priest, 'but on that occasion, by God you deserved it for the way you looked at your mother!'

'Anyway, it's all over now,' muttered Teofil, toying with his empty cup.

'No, it's not!' said Father Józef. 'And don't give me that stuff about sewage under the bridge and expiation of rage. I hear that crap every week in the confessional. As far as I'm concerned, you're still the same scum as you were when you left seventeen years ago, and you will be until you prove to me you're not.' He topped up Teofil's cup. 'And that will take a long time.' There was a pause before he continued. 'Confession would be a good start!'

'I don't believe any more, Father.'

There was a deafening silence, of the kind that comes suddenly after raised voices reach a point after which there is no more to be said. Maurice, who had not uttered a word during the heated reminiscences that alternated with gentle nostalgia, looked from one to the other. Like all titled persons, Teofil spoke good French, the language of Society, and the language they spoke amongst themselves. Polish was used for addressing the peasants. Father Józef only spoke Polish, and that with a heavy Lwów accent which he never lost. Maurice had picked up just enough Polish to join in most conversations, and he was able to follow what was said because he had heard it all before. No one can spend seventeen years going through hell with a comrade without being privy to his innermost secrets. Most of them, at any rate. After a long time, Father Józef rose with a sigh.

'It's late,' he said. 'I'll take you to the Manor. That old hag Marynia should have got it properly ready by now.'

III

Sleeping conditions at the Manor were improvisatory but cosy – at least in comparison with the sort of conditions that Teofil and Maurice had become accustomed to. *Pani* Marynia had managed to fetch enough kindling wood and logs to light a blazing fire in what used to be Teofil's bedroom. Then she had done a more than adequate job, considering the time available, of clearing the room of over twenty years of dirt and cobwebs, had thoroughly swept the floorboards, and cleaned up two cots. One of them had been Teofil's, and the other she had lugged in from the bedroom next door. Her husband, *Pan* Marek, had been more of a hindrance than a help, having been browbeaten into going by a combination of *Pani* Marynia's tongue and broom. Father Józef had been right in his assumption that old Marek was drunk. His contribution to the task in hand consisted largely of supervising, advising and opening the door when his wife arrived with the logs.

'Are all the inhabitants of Sarenki as awful as those two?' said Maurice when the old couple had left, cursing at each other in barely comprehensible grunts. 'I've met four so far.' He enumerated on his fingers. 'One, Father Józef, the crudest and most blasphemous priest I've ever met. Two, *Pani* Marynia, one of the most unpleasant and cantankerous old hags I've ever met. Three, *Pan* Marek, a lazy drunkard with all the charm of a sedated pig. And four…'

'Yes, I know,' interrupted Teofil. 'Me. A bitter and twisted loser. I'm thirty-four years old, and nothing to show for it!'

'Your words, not mine,' said Maurice. They sat down in front of the fire on a couple of rickety chairs, for neither was ready yet for sleep. 'This must have been a fine place once,' he continued, looking round. The room was lit only by the fire and one candle that flickered wildly on the mantel, for the whole house was draughty. It was a large room and the warmth was confined to the immediate vicinity of the fire. The light barely reached the walls and the ceiling, and only illuminated the two still figures with a burnt orange halo, while shadows danced darkly on their faces.

Maurice's eyes fell on a small wooden object in the corner behind the mantelpiece. It was swathed in shadow, so he could not make out what it was. Teofil followed his gaze.

'That's my old cradle!' he cried, a touch of excitement in his voice. He rose and went to fetch it, and placed it in front of the fire. It was a simple rectangular wooden box mounted on two rockers, one of which fell off as he lifted it. It had once been varnished, but only hints of the gloss remained. It was riddled with woodworm, but Teofil ran his fingers all over it lovingly, feeling it, taking pleasure from it. 'Old Staś the carpenter made it specially for me. It used to have a rounded hood at one end, only it must have fallen off. I'm surprised it has survived this long!'

Maurice looked intently at Teofil. It has been a long time since he had seen his friend smiling, taking pleasure from something. 'I see that in spite of that tough air that you like to present to the world there lies *une ame sentimentale, mon ami*?' he laughed. 'Perhaps you'd like to sleep in it tonight? Start all over again, *non*?'

Teofil looked at Maurice's laughing face, and his expression hardened instantly. 'It's just an old cradle,' he said, throwing it back into its corner. It fell apart. 'Now let's get some sleep.'

Without another word Teofil climbed onto his bed, fully clothed, pulled the straw palliasse over him, turned to the wall and lay still. Maurice gazed at the back of his friend's head, just visible under the shapeless sack. He wondered what it was he said that was wrong; but then put it down to one of Teofil's frequent abrupt changes of mood. He shrugged and pursed his lips before following his example and retired to his cot. But he did not sleep. He watched the fire fade in the hearth until the last embers gave way to total darkness, in which images of the last fifteen years – and more – returned to torment his wakefulness.

*****

Maurice Chavelet was exactly the same age as Teofil. He was born in a small village on the banks of the River Loire, near Tours, in 1778, the son of poverty-stricken peasants. He was brought up in the shadow of great wealth epitomised by the sumptuous Chateaux in what was considered as the Garden of France. The unbelievable wealth of the aristocrats who inhabited these magnificent palaces had awakened in the young Maurice a deep sense of the injustice of his own life of constant, gnawing hunger and deprivation. When he was eleven, he heard about the storming of the Bastille and the uprising of the starving masses in Paris, and immediately set off to join them.

After three years surviving on the streets of the French capital, observing at first hand the horrors of the people's revenge against oppression, Maurice left Paris. The idea of executions at the guillotine as an enjoyable spectacle had sickened him and killed off what was left of his hopes for a better life. He had not come to the city to see one injustice replaced with another, so he set off on the southern post road on the toss of a coin. After a year of wandering the countryside around Auxerre and working in the wine regions of Chablis, Maurice eventually reached Dijon, the capital of Burgundy. He found employment with a kind and hearty wine merchant by the name of Grandier, who took him in, gave him a home and a fresh start in life.

Maurice enjoyed his first and only taste of a stable home life. Mme Grandier mothered him as if he were her own, and he found a willing companion-in-pranks in their vivacious twelve-year-old daughter Marie-Claire. He loved his work, and came to regard the Grandiers as his family. This idyll continued for the next two years, until he was seventeen, when M. Grandier found him one morning in bed with Marie-Claire. Maurice spent the next twenty-four hours, dressed only in a blanket, just one jump ahead of the enraged wine merchant, who pursued him relentlessly through the streets of Dijon with a pistol.

His plight was recognised by a burly, red-faced farmer who was just leaving a tavern, where a morning's drinking had put him in a jovial mood. He was swaying gently as Maurice entered at a run. The collision was violent, and Maurice fell, dazed and naked, on the flagstone floor, his blanket beside him.

'Not so fast, my young friend!' laughed the farmer, grabbing the boy by the arm and hoisting him up. 'You look as if you're being chased by a father whose daughter you've just f- screwed!'

'*Monsieur*,' gasped Maurice, wrapping himself again in the blanket, 'as a matter of fact I am being chased by the father …!'

The farmer immediately pushed Maurice roughly into the crowded tavern. 'Take care of this one, Jacques!' he bellowed across the room at the innkeeper. 'He's being chased by a father whose daughter he's just screwed!' With that he left. Jacques beckoned to Maurice, who ran up to him, panting.

'In there,' cried Jacques, indicating a large barrel in a corner. Maurice, momentarily perplexed, thought this was some kind of a joke, but then he saw that the barrel had no lid. Without further hesitation, he jumped inside. Not one of the customers paid the slightest notice.

A few moments later M. Grandier burst into the tavern. 'Which way did he go?' he cried, waving his pistol in the air. Half a dozen thumbs casually indicated the back door leading into the courtyard. M. Grandier pushed past the tables and chairs, muttering *'pardon'* through his teeth, and left by the back door. The sound of bottles and barrels being knocked over outside did not elicit the slightest interest from the customers, who continued with their drinking and huddled conversations as if nothing had happened.

*****

Maurice smiled into the cold darkness as he recalled the incident, such a long time ago. Marie-Claire was the first in a long line of easy conquests. He knew he was good-looking from a very early age. As a little boy in Touraine he had been doted over by the village mothers, and in Paris he was looked after, at least nominally, by a carter's wife, who already had eight children of her own. As he grew older his shoulder-length black hair, dark, smooth complexion, handsome features and twinkling, brown eyes made up for his lack of stature. His easy, affable manner, as well as a predilection for getting into all kinds of scrapes, attracted girls like moths to a candle, especially those to whom romance meant adventure in which a fleeting moment of excitement in a hayloft was often the only escape from a drab life of drudgery. After a few years of awkward flirtations and stolen kisses with various young girls, he finally took the plunge, and graduated to the full-scale seduction of his employer's willing daughter.

*****

Recollections of further affairs dispelled some of the more recent horrors of Europe's battlefields, and Maurice eventually fell into a deep, dreamless sleep. He slept right across the grey dawn, and woke to find that Teofil had already risen and had rekindled the fire. He was sitting on the floor in front of it, trying to repair the broken cradle.

'What time is it?' groaned Maurice, closing his eyes again.

'Time you were up!' cried Teofil. 'There's a great deal to be done!'

'*Par exemple?*' said Maurice, not stirring.

'There's wood to be chopped, a house to be put in order, some fields to be ploughed, money to be earned and a home to be built. Then there are foreign powers to be expelled…'

'*Assez!* Enough!' cried Maurice. 'Just because you are of a mind to grab the day by the throat and beat it into submission does not necessarily mean with my help!' Suddenly he grinned, without opening his eyes, as the memory of his amorous recollections in the night returned. 'Only a pair of young silken thighs hidden beneath a milkmaid's dress will get me up. I'm going back to sleep.'

'You don't understand, Maurice,' said Teofil. 'What do you think I am doing?'

Maurice opened an eye and looked at Teofil. 'You are repairing your old cradle.'

'But why?'

'I don't know,' muttered Maurice impatiently. 'You threw it into the corner and it broke.'

'Ah, but while you were asleep, I mended it.'

'What was the point? It's only an old cradle.'

'It is MY old cradle. I accidentally broke it, so I repaired it. Then I sat in it.'

Maurice sat up. 'You sat in your old cradle?'

'A symbolic gesture, Maurice. It was your idea.'

Maurice recalled how Teofil seemed angry at the stupid idea of him, Teofil, sleeping in the cradle. 'You mean…?'

'A new start, Maurice,' said Teofil. 'I have just outgrown this cradle. It broke under my weight.' He grabbed the cradle and threw it onto the fire. It was tinder dry and crumbling from splinters and woodworm, and flared up almost immediately.

'*Monsieur le Comte* Teofil Samojarski,' he inclined his head graciously to Maurice, 'comes into his rightful inheritance!'

They watched as the expiring embers reignited and slowly consumed the cradle.

'*Mon Dieu!*' murmured Maurice, settling down once more, 'Napoleon was right when he wondered whether you Poles were capable of governing yourselves! You are all just a bunch of crazy, romantic dreamers!'

'Perhaps. Dreams sometimes come true. We shall see.'

Over the next few days Teofil and Maurice set about clearing the Manor and making it as habitable as possible. There was a great deal to be done, as the house had stood empty and neglected for thirteen years.

IV

By 1796 the Polish-Lithuanian Commonwealth had been finally wiped off the map of Europe, with the exception of the Grand Duchy of Warsaw, which Napoleon created in 1809 out of Poland's rump, as well as the tiny Republic of Kraków. Teofil, then an angry eighteen-year-old, proclaimed Poland truly dead and its people pathetic nonentities. 'I don't want to live in this land anymore,' he said to his tearful mother. 'I hate Sarenki. You can all stay here and rot for all I care. I hate Poles, and I'm ashamed of being one!'

'What are you going to do?' sobbed his mother.

'I'm leaving. For good!' cried Teofil. 'My life here doesn't mean a damned thing any more. I'm going to some civilised country that's got some prospects. Like the Austro-Hungarian Empire!'

Teofil knew that this would hurt his mother, as the Austrians had seized her family estate at Czarne Lasy. Her father, Prince Leonid Sczasny, had opposed the Austrian take-over in the Third Partition in 1794, with the result that his estate near Kraków had been confiscated. As their opposition consisted largely of dumb insolence and non-co-operation, and not, as in many other similar cases, armed resistance, the Sczasnys were left with the Lodge and six acres of orchards. The Manor itself was later taken over as a country residence for officers of the Austrian army, who used it for diplomatic receptions. Now the very thought of her only son decamping to the Enemy was hurtful in the extreme.

On a dry and sunny May morning in 1796 Teofil packed a small bag of provisions and belongings, and set off on foot from the village along the track going north. Not two kilometres past the last cottage of Sarenki, he was surprised by a large, awkward figure dressed in a black soutane who emerged from the wood, leading a horse.

'So, you're abandoning a sinking ship, like the rat that you are!'

'Father Józef!' cried Teofil, stopping in his tracks. 'If you've come to try to stop me, you're wasting your time. I'm going and I'm never coming back!'

'All right, I believe you,' replied the priest with a dose of impatience in his voice; after all, it was exactly what he had done when he, himself, was that age. 'And I wouldn't dream of stopping you. I think you should go. We'll all be better off without you and your tantrums. Now perhaps we might see a smile on your mother's face sometimes. But I just wanted to say goodbye, and hope that life will give you a good kick up the arse and make a man of you.'

'Thank you, Father. Goodbye.'

'And to give you Magda,' continued Father Józef, leading the frisky young mare forward. 'You're going to need her, as she seems to be the only friend you've got.'

'But...' Teofil was taken aback, 'Magda? Surely – she's your own – your very own...'

'She's just a horse,' growled Father Józef. 'She's named after Mary Magdalen, a common whore who eventually saw the error of her ways and repented. Perhaps she will do the same for you. Take her.'

Father Józef's manner was uncompromising. Teofil took Magda's bridle automatically, too overwhelmed to say anything. They looked at one another for a long time, until Father Józef broke the deadlock. 'A thank you might be in order, if you can bring yourself to utter it,' growled the priest.

'T-thank you...' stammered Teofil.

'Now go!' cried Father Józef. 'And don't dare to come back until you are a real man, or, so help me Almighty and Eternal God…' he shook his fist at the clear blue sky '…I'll flay your hide down to the raw meat and throw what remains to the wolves!'

With that Father Józef turned on his heel and strode back towards the village with his ungainly gait, swaying and stumbling on the hard, rutted track, for it had been a dry spring so far. Teofil watched him stagger round a bend and disappear behind the trees. A tear found its way to the corner of his mouth. He wiped it with a quick brush of his finger, and turned to Magda.

'So, it's just you and me, old girl!' he said. Magda knew Teofil well, for he had often ridden her. Father Józef used to make Teofil exercise her, hopeful of 'your redemption through love of God's creatures, who are superior to you!' He recalled his long rides in the forest and along the riverbanks with pleasure. Boy and horse had developed a truly loving relationship. Now he stroked her nose affectionately. 'Looks like the old villain is right, you are the only friend I've got,' continued Teofil, climbing into the saddle and patting her glossy neck. 'Come on, then. Let's see what's over the next hill.' A gentle spur and a tug of the reins, and Magda set off at a brisk canter towards the north, the direction of the track.

*****

Now, seventeen years later, Teofil had returned home along the same track. Only instead of Magda, he rode Mazurek. Whether or not his absence had made a real man of him remained to be seen, by himself as well as by Father Józef. He knew that the priest would be monitoring his every move, and, having formally and ceremonially 'outgrown' his old cradle, he was determined to make a good job of it.

The task of restoring and re-equipping the Manor was

daunting, and soon the house was surrounded by curious villagers, come to salvage what they could from the rubbish, as well as to pay their cautious respects to the returning prodigal. Most of them remembered him as a moody and sullen wastrel, and the older folk had been glad to see the back of him when he left. The villagers were pleasantly surprised to find he had changed into a perfectly agreeable man.

'In Sarenki nothing is wasted,' growled Father Józef. Having dispensed divine terror into the souls of his faithful, he had presented himself at the Manor armed with a basket of rye bread, cheesecake and a jar of stewed prunes. He blessed the hallway, shook his fist at the window at the head of the staircase and invoked God's mercy, understanding and absolution to visit the graceless villain and his foreign sidekick, who were about to take up residence once more in this once godly house. He then rolled up his sleeves, strode into what had been the kitchen and turned his attention to the fireplace. A chimney fall had dislodged some stonework, and the stone-mantled fireplace was a heap of rubble, bits of wood and old, damp soot.

Pani Marynia had been enlisted, with vague promises of money, to help with the cleaning. Father Józef added more metaphysical promises of Indulgences and remission in Purgatory, 'even though you don't deserve them, you crabby old *baba-yaga!*' Old *Pan* Marek was coerced to dump unusable furniture, broken flagstones and fallen beams in the courtyard for the benefit of those who might have some use for them. Since the promise of neither money nor remission from torment in Purgatory had had the slightest effect on him, Father Józef used the very real threat of 'bashing the hell out of your drunken, unwashed carcase,' perhaps the only argument that the old man understood.

Then there was the matter of the estate to consider. 'Who's been managing the farms?' said Teofil. They had cleared the hearth in the kitchen, and Father Józef had even managed to repair the chimney. The day was fine and crisp, with an intensely blue sky exacerbating the whiteness of the snow. It had been a long and hard morning, and the food that Father Józef had brought was very welcome.

'You need to see Kazio Gruszka,' said Father Józef. 'Only don't expect too much co-operation from him as he's been fiddling the accounts for the past twelve years. As long as there was some income from the estate your mother couldn't have cared less about what happened to it. She has never been back once since you left. So, our Mr Gruszka has turned his mind to some what you might call creative speculation. Your return has been quite a shock for him.'

*****

In the Autumn after Teofil left Sarenki, Świetlana, his mother, unhappy and very lonely, returned to Kraków to live with her parents at what was left of the family estate of Czarne Lasy. She appointed the Gruszka brothers, Kazio and Tadek as joint estate managers and caretakers of the Manor, respectively. At first, they did their job well and conscientiously and the peasants worked hard in the fields to produce the required quotas. There was regular correspondence between Swiatlena and the Gruszkas. But as time went on, the correspondence gradually dried up, and Swiatlena seemed content with the bi-annual statements of profits from her Kraków bank, which enabled her to pay her way at Czarne Lasy. The absence of the landowners from Sarenki encouraged some private enterprise on the wrong side of legality, and many of the peasants exploited the land for their own profit, and without the knowledge of the Imperial Taxman in Vienna.

At the turn of the century Tadek Gruszka died, aged just over fifty, having let the Manor decline into a serious state of dilapidation. *Pani hrabina* was totally disinterested in Sarenki, so his brother Kazio, instead of spending money on maintenance and repairs, managed to siphon off profits meant for the Manor into his own pocket.

Thirteen further years of total neglect had taken an even greater toll on the Manor. Now Teofil had returned, much to the consternation of the population, who saw their comfortable little bubble about to burst.

'Why didn't anyone stop Gruszka?' cried Teofil.

Father Józef moved his stool closer to Teofil. 'The village has done very well out of his deals,' he said conspiratorially. 'The only loser was the Emperor. And if you don't tell him, neither will we!'

Teofil grinned at the priest's brazen hypocrisy. Stealing and cheating were perfectly all right only if they were perpetrated in the name of Good, or against the Austrians! 'Where can I find Kazio Gruszka?' he said.

'His house is the same one as ever, up by the forest edge. It's got an orchard, and he keeps pigs, geese and hens. You can't miss it.'

'I remember it.'

'It's the best-kept house in the village.'

'From what you say, I imagine it would be!'

'Don't be too hard on him, Teofil!'

Teofil grinned and rose. Leaving Maurice to supervise the clearing of the entrance hall and the staircase, Teofil went out into the courtyard and made for the stable. Mazurek, his elderly horse, was pleased to see him and whinnied, his nostrils expelling steam into the cold, crisp air. Mazurek was not alone. Sitting casually on a wooden strut of the straw-filled manger, within striking distance of the horse's nose, was a scruffy young boy of about twelve. Seeing Teofil appear in the doorway, he jumped down and rushed past him into the courtyard as fast as his unshod feet would carry him.

'Wait!' cried Teofil, looking after the disappearing figure, but before he could say any more the boy was gone. A moment later the boy reappeared, creeping guiltily round the wall. 'Hello,' said Teofil, going to him slowly, afraid of frightening him again. 'What's your name?'

'Henryk,' said the boy.

'Who's your father?'

'Jan Staruch.'

'So, Henryk Staruch, what were you doing in the stable?' The boy looked as though he was about to take off again. Teofil laughed. 'I don't mind, you know, as long as you're not pinching my riding gear!'

Henryk's face hardened. 'I'm not a thief, *Panie hrabio,* sir!' he said adamantly. 'I didn't mean no harm! I – I just like horses, see…'

Teofil ruffled Henryk's hair. 'In that case you can have the job of looking after them for me!'

The boy's grubby face lit up. 'Thank you, sir! Thank you!' he cried excitedly. 'Wait till I tell my father!'

With that he ran off in the direction of the village. Teofil went into the stable and saddled Mazurek. A few minutes later he was riding up the winding track past the Church and towards the edge of the forest. The little spring was still bubbling gently out of the ground, creating a frozen miniature glacier that spread down the hillside towards the river. He followed the forest's edge past Staś the carpenter's cottage – Staś' father was a woodman, like his fathers before him. The creation of the village had turned the n'th generation woodman into a carpenter, who had learned and honed his considerable skills with wood through heredity, along with trial and error.

He momentarily thought about the old cradle, and was of a mind to call on Staś and tell him about how he had found it in the corner of his old bedroom. The cottage was quiet and deserted. Obviously Staś was out, so he decided against calling, and pressed on till he came to a well-kept stone-built house surrounded by an orchard of skeletal plum, apple and pear trees. He smiled wryly at the thought that 'Gruszka' was 'pear' in Polish. Smoke rose from the chimneystack. At a safe distance from the house, separated by a wooden fence, was a pigsty set in a field on the edge of a copse. There were coops among the fruit trees, and hens and geese wandered freely in the orchard. An acrid aroma that pervaded the cold, still air suggested that the sty was in use.

The house was surrounded by a dry-stone wall. The gate consisted of an opening with a pair of wooden posts on either side. Traditional peasant motifs were carved on them – no doubt Staś's handiwork. A short, wide path led to the front door. Teofil vaguely recalled the house, which definitely did not have a pseudo-Doric colonnade decorating the front door seventeen years ago. He raised an eyebrow, and a low whistle escaped his lips.

'So, this is what the old crook has been up to!' he thought, dismounting. 'I'll bet his son doesn't go around barefoot!'

Tethering Mazurek to a wooden rail at the gate, Teofil walked up and hammered on the door. That caused a cacophony of barking from somewhere behind the house. After a while, the barking subsided, and the door was opened by a plump red-faced woman in her mid-forties. '*Panie hrabio!*' she cried, crossing herself in a panic. 'What a surprise! We didn't expect –'

'I'm sure you didn't,' said Teofil. 'Good day, *Pani* Gruszka. May I come in?'

'*Pan* Gruszka is out, sir,' said the woman apologetically. 'Perhaps you will call tomorrow…?'

'I shall wait,' said Teofil with a smile, walking past her into the flagstone kitchen. He sat down, unbidden, at the wooden table, and noticed a pot boiling on the fire. The aroma was that of poultry and dill. For a few moments *Pani* Gruszka hovered, embarrassed, wringing her hands and wiping them nervously on her pinafore. It was evident that she had been feeding her poultry, as the pouch was bulging with feed. Beneath the pinafore she was wearing a long, pleated black skirt covering black boots, a white blouse with billowing sleeves and a heavily embroidered black bodice, in the manner of the peasants of the Kraków region. On her head she wore a red scarf, knotted at the back.

'P-perhaps,' she stammered, 'I should go and see if I can find *Pan* Gruszka…?'

'Perhaps you should.' No harm in intimidating the woman a little, thought Teofil.

Pani Gruszka hovered a little while longer before leaving the kitchen by the back door. A few moments later Kazio Gruszka entered. Teofil only vaguely recalled him, but now he noticed with wry amusement that he even looked like a pear – evidence of a life of plentiful food washed down with good ale and liquor. He was perhaps in his fifties, but might have looked that way even as a small child. He had a large, round head, a flat nose, bad skin and an enormous mouth seemingly set into a wide, permanent grin, which displayed a very incomplete set of teeth to grotesque disadvantage. His considerable paunch was clad in colourless and shapeless trousers tucked into muddy black boots, while his puny chest was draped in an equally colourless and shapeless tunic shirt. An old torn frock coat was meant to keep the cold at bay and he smelt of pigs. He was accompanied by four totally unmatched and very lively dogs, who greeted Teofil with enthusiasm. *Pani* Gruszka followed gingerly, and hovered in the doorway, still wringing her hands.

'*Panie hrabio!*' beamed Kazio Gruszka, spreading his arms as if about to embrace Teofil. The gesture was not reciprocated. 'Such an honour to see you again! After all these years! Please forgive my appearance – if I had known – the swine, you know – a peasant's work is never done – but if you had given us notice of your coming – *Pani* Gruszka would have prepared a feast in *Pan hrabia's* honour – a goose, perhaps – but as it is you find us feeding the animals, so we are both unprepared for such an honour – so please forgive – forgive – and how is your dear mother, may God bless her goodness?'

Teofil stood – or rather – sat his ground. *Pan* Gruszka was evidently extremely flustered, and was definitely on the defensive. He had formulated no plan as to how to confront him, and had settled for improvisation. He sat firmly in the chair, his legs crossed with more than a hint of insolence, and watched expressionlessly as the peasant poured out his nervous diatribe. When he had finished, Teofil slowly rose and looked out of the window at the pigsty.

'As far as I know,' he said, 'my mother is alive, as I have not heard to the contrary. I have not seen her, or heard from her for seventeen years. But you should know, *Panie* Gruszka.' He turned to the peasant and stared him in the eye. 'You are her estate manager. No doubt you keep in touch, to keep her informed as to how the estate is doing. So how is the estate doing? And how is my dear mother?'

The remnants of Kazio Gruszka's composure collapsed in a verbal morass of apologetic gibbering and vague excuses, all of which gave Teofil a complete panorama of the peasant's activities. Again, Teofil let him go on, and paid very close attention to what was in effect a veiled confession of theft and cheating on a grand scale, its effects stretching as far afield as Kraków and Lwów. Animal husbandry, timber, quarrying and crops, and even transport all featured in *Pan* Gruszka's schemes. Teofil listened impassively, staring out of the window, in his heart thoroughly enjoying this simple man's total humiliation and defeat.

Finally, his words turned to sobs. Teofil turned to him. 'You have done me no harm personally, *Panie* Gruszka, but for nearly fifteen years you have been cheating my mother out of thousands of *thalers* with your enterprises.'

'Yes, sir.'

'You realise I shall have to take action!'

'Yes, sir.'

'My mother shall be fully informed, and you shall have to make reparations. Naturally you will lose this house.' *Pani* Gruszka howled in anguish and rushed up to her husband. He held her tightly, still sobbing uncontrollably. 'I shall have to send for the Imperial Adjudicator in Lwów to assess the total value of your many enterprises. There will be a great deal of tax outstanding. You will be unable to meet the debt. You will be arrested, tried and sent to prison.' Both the Gruszkas burst into hysterics. 'You will be hearing more of this matter shortly, when I have made further enquiries.'

With that Teofil rose, spun on his heel, picked up a still edible apple from a bowl on the table, glanced callously at the sobbing couple, took a bite out of it, and walked out of the front door. His heart was beating and he was short of breath. He was seething with carefully controlled rage. A light grey twilight had descended when he climbed onto Mazurek and made his way back the way he had come. He bit further into the apple. It was already gnarled and wrinkled, but it steadied his nerve and his resolve. 'I'll let them sweat for a few days,' he thought through set teeth. 'After that they'll eat pigswill from my hand!'

V

'When are you going to go and see your mother? You've been back for over two weeks, and you haven't even mentioned her! She deserves better. Go and see her and say sorry.'

Father Józef's words of admonition had been gnawing at Teofil's psyche ever since he got up. He had spent most of that day on the roof of the Manor, replacing some sheets of roofing tin that had been removed during the past fifteen years. News of his visit to the Gruszka house had spread quickly, and all of a sudden, reparations were being volunteered, some anonymously, most accompanied with servile forelock-touching. The very morning after the confrontation with Kazio Gruszka the missing sheets of tin roofing had mysteriously reappeared behind the stable, much to Teofil's wry satisfaction.

That same evening a young girl appeared at the Manor with a goose, plucked and ready for roasting. Maurice met her at the door, and eyed her up and down with unconcealed pleasure, for she was singularly pretty.

'I have a gift for *Pan hrabia*,' said the girl shyly, her eyes fixed flirtingly on Maurice's face. 'A goose from *Pan* Gruszka, with his respects.'

'A goose?' echoed Maurice absently, returning the stare.

'For *Pan hrabia*.'

'From *Pan* Gruszka?'

'With his respects.'

With that the conversation seized up. Maurice and the girl

stared at each other, neither knowing what to say next. She was perhaps eighteen years of age, and her typical regional dress of full, long skirt, white blouse and embroidered bodice was colourful and freshly laundered. She had long, straw-blonde hair tied in bunches behind her ears, and on her head she wore a bright red headscarf tied at the nape of her neck. She had a delicately translucent skin, full, red lips, a pert nose and very blue eyes. It was obvious that she had been primed up to the nines to impress. The priming bore fruit, at least as far as Maurice was concerned. He stared at her as if entranced.

The deadlock was broken a moment later when Teofil emerged from the crumbling storehouse in the courtyard, which he had been clearing out. 'Who is it?' he cried, approaching. Having thus clumped roughshod over the spell that was just beginning to develop, Teofil accepted the goose graciously, found out that the girl's name was Lenka Sieńkowska, and that she was the grand-daughter of Staś Sieńkowski, the carpenter. Having thanked her, he then dismissed her peremptorily.

'A fine entrance, *mon ami*!' griped Maurice later, staring at the goose, roasting in its own fat on the fire in the kitchen. 'If you hadn't come along just then, I might have had her there and then!'

'In which case I saved an innocent young Polish virgin from the attentions of a lewd and lascivious French *roué*!' laughed Teofil.

*****

Over the next few days, a lot of 'respects' were paid, mostly backed up with sausage, stewed fruit, bread, soured cabbage, beetroots and *makownik*, the poppyseed cake. There were offers of help in restoring the Manor from Staś Sieńkowski, who volunteered his skills as a carpenter, and Genek Sroka the stonemason. Old Pankracy lugged a small barrel of his vodka to the Manor all by himself. At journey's end he insisted on helping Teofil taste the brew, in case the jolting had spoiled its flavour.

Out of all the villagers only Staś had no more than Teofil's friendship to gain. His family had lived off the forest for generations, and old Mateusz had bestowed on his family the freedom of the forests in perpetuity. If Staś had exploited this advantage it was all perfectly legal and above board. The rest, to judge by their demeanour, obviously had something to hide, and were taking every opportunity to get into Teofil's good books. Even Old Pankracy, whom Teofil remembered as the perennial innocent (as well as perpetually Old), seemed to have a guilty look on his face, which was exacerbated with each tot of vodka that he 'tested'.

In the meantime, Maurice found himself thinking fondly about Lenka. He strolled up towards Staś' cottage, hoping he might see her. Just as he reached the edge of the forest, Lenka emerged from it, clutching a faggot of firewood.

'Hello again,' he said nervously. He had not expected to see her so quickly, if at all, and her sudden presence flummoxed him.

'*Pan* Maurice!' she smiled in recognition, although the flirtatious twinkle she had worn when she had come to the Manor with the goose was not there. Nor was she dressed up to her nines. Beneath an enormous, shapeless shawl she wore a plain brown dress made of some heavy material, and an old pair of boots that had long lost their colour and lustre. A black scarf covered her hair completely, and her face was flushed and rosy from the cold.

'May I help you?'

'Thank you.' Maurice took the faggot from her. Their faces almost met, but both recoiled, slightly embarrassed, like strangers afraid to touch. They made their way in silence towards Staś' cottage. They both broke the silence at the same time: Lenka said, 'If you…?' while Maurice said, 'Do you…?'

'I'm sorry,' continued Lenka. 'You were about to say...?'

'No, p-please, after you,' stammered Maurice.

'I was only going to say that if you are looking for my grandfather, he is not here. He is in the forest setting traps for a wolf that has been causing some trouble.'

Maurice wanted to say, 'Actually, it's you that I have come to see,' but he was finding this situation difficult. His nervous indecision worried him, as he had always been confident in the company of girls. There was something about Lenka that made him uneasy. It was almost as if he were afraid of saying the wrong thing – of losing her even before he started. Finally, 'Perhaps some other time,' he said.

'Was it something important?'

'It can wait.'

They reached the cottage, and Lenka led the way into the small woodshed in the courtyard. It was stacked high with dry, weathered logs. Maurice added the firewood to a pile of dead twigs and branches in the corner.

'Thank you,' said Lenka.

'It has been my pleasure,' said Maurice. He stood looking at her, wondering whether she would invite him into the cottage. But no such invitation was forthcoming.

'I shall tell grandfather that you called,' she said.

'If you would,' replied Maurice with a polite bow. What kind of conversation is this, *parbleu*, to have with a beautiful girl? he thought to himself.

'Thank you again for your kindness.'

'It was my pleasure.' Maurice made as if to turn. With a superhuman effort of will, he summoned up hidden reserves of courage. 'Perhaps I shall s-see you again?' he said, his heart beating uncontrollably.

'No doubt. Sarenki's a small place.'

'Goodbye.'

'Goodbye.'

Maurice set off down the hill, wondering what had happened to his powers of seduction. He had not called into play any of the usual techniques that he had always used when setting his sights on a girl. There was none of the laughing banter, the carefully contrived rugged smile, the flattery and the barely perceptible double meanings that he always let drop at the appropriate moment with impeccable timing. Twenty years of extensive experience in the art of love had come to nothing when it really mattered. He had burbled his way awkwardly through a conversation with all the aplomb of a spotty youth trying to communicate amorously with a young girl for the very first time. It was a deeply disgruntled and dissatisfied Maurice who returned to the Manor with his tail between his legs.

'So, her maidenhood is still intact?' smirked Teofil after Maurice had told him everything about his meeting, including his dithering. 'You didn't kindle the firewood with your passion?'

Maurice sniffed. 'Perhaps I lose the touch, *mon ami*,' he said despondently. 'Perhaps the magic does not work anymore. I blame the climate in this tundra of a land! It is not conducive to the physical expression of love.

*****

The following days Maurice moped round the Manor being more of a hindrance than a help. A walk into the village – and beyond, half way up the hill towards the forest's edge – yielded no sign of Lenka. He did not want to call on Staś again with pretence of some excuse. When, after his first visit, the carpenter had called at the Manor to enquire why he had called, Maurice had found himself caught out. He had forgotten to think of an excuse. Staś then went away with a twinkle in his eye and a grin on his lips.

'I swear he suspects – ' muttered Maurice to himself.

Despite his high profile in the village, Maurice saw no sign of Lenka anywhere. Sunday came, and the church bell rang out its weekly summons, which was invariably answered by all, under pain of Father Józef's threat of eternal damnation. Teofil decided to go to Mass, but Maurice stayed in his bed. The business with Lenka made him feel that he had reached some kind of a crossroads in his life. The frightening thing was that it had occurred to him that Lenka was very young. He had never before considered that eighteen was particularly young. Girls were girls. As he lay in his bed, his hands behind his head, staring at the cracked ceiling, he analysed his predicament. He broke into a hot and cold sweat when he arrived at the inescapable conclusion that he was maturing. No, he was growing old.

He came abruptly back down to earth when Teofil returned from church. 'You should have come,' he said, warming his hands by the fire in the bedroom. It was blazing merrily, for Maurice had been feeding it.

'You know I don't believe in God,' replied Maurice. 'Neither do you. Why did you go?'

'Father Józef would never have forgiven me if I'd stayed away.'

'You need his forgiveness?'

'I need his approval, Maurice,' said Teofil thoughtfully. 'He's been very good to me, and I don't want to let him down. Besides, I suppose I've got responsibilities now.'

'He is rude to you, and shows you no mercy! *Mon Dieu*, you will be going to Confession next!'

'I already have. No, not in the sacramental way. We just talk. He's a good listener.'

'And you return the complement by going to Mass?'

'Lenka was there. I told you that you should have come. Everyone in Sarenki goes to Mass, or they'll never hear the end of it from Father Józef. His descriptions of Hell and the nature of damnation are Rabelaisian!'

Maurice looked thoughtful as his mind dashed from the monstrous writings of Rabelais to Lenka's pretty face framed in straw-blonde hair tied in bunches with colourful kerchiefs. 'I shall reconvert!' he cried. 'I've been trying to find her for days!'

The following Sunday Maurice presented himself, to Father Józef's astonishment, at Mass. Staś was there, but not Lenka.

After Mass Maurice greeted the carpenter warmly.

'Lenka is indisposed,' said Staś, even though Maurice did not enquire as to why she was not there. 'She has a cold and a slight fever.'

'How unfortunate,' said Maurice. The old villain knows, *parbleu*, why else would he, Maurice, have come to Mass? 'Please convey my best regards to her.'

'Perhaps you might convey them yourself?' said Staś. The old man bowed politely and left, leaving Maurice with the word 'When?' etched, but unspoken, on his lips.

'Do you feel spiritually edified?' enquired Teofil, coming up to him. Maurice closed his mouth, looked angrily at Teofil and walked away. All in all, he reflected, things were not going well on the Lenka front.

The congregation, most dressed in their best clothes, made a point of approaching Teofil, reminding him who they were, updating him on deaths and family news, and introducing newcomers and children born since his departure. They shook hands and bowed deferentially, and trusted that *Pan hrabia* Teofil was settling in well at the Manor, and if there was anything they could do, they needed just to ask. Teofil accepted all these expressions of respect with cool detachment and correct gratitude. Father Józef thought him uncaring and heartless. 'You could at least show pleasure,' he growled after everyone had returned to their homes for a frugal Sunday dinner. 'Do you intend to rub the faces of these people – your own people – in the mire,' he enquired, 'or will you leave it to the Austrians?'

'They've all been up to something while I've been away,' said Teofil. 'They can sweat a bit. I intend to show them who is in charge now.'

'In charge is your mother, in case you'd forgotten, and she's in Kraków,' said Father Józef. 'Anyway, when are you going to go and see your mother? You've been back for over two weeks, and you haven't even mentioned her! She deserves better. Go and see her and say sorry.'

The priest's words were still echoing in Teofil's mind, the following week, when he climbed down from the Manor's roof, glad that the job of replacing the tin sheets was finished. He stamped his feet and blew into his hands which were so cold that he could hardly feel them. Maurice, who had been helping Staś to replace a broken timber in the attic, emerged into the courtyard. He went up to Teofil excitedly.

'Staś Sieńkowski has asked me to supper,' he said. 'Lenka's recovered, and will be there too! What do you think of that?'

'I am horrified. I think you have intentions on the flower of Polish maidenhood that are not at all honourable!' said Teofil with mock reproach. 'I shall have to warn Staś!'

'You wouldn't!'

At that moment Staś appeared carrying some broken timber out of the house into the courtyard for chopping into firewood.

'Wouldn't I?' grinned Teofil. He turned to the carpenter and called, '*Panie* Stasiu!'

'*Panie hrabio*?' said Staś, approaching.

'Don't! Please!' hissed Maurice. 'I shall never forgive you!'

'I've decided to go to Kraków tomorrow,' said Teofil, ignoring Maurice. 'I should go and see my mother. I don't know how long I shall be. I'll leave Maurice in charge.'

'As you wish, sir,' replied the carpenter. 'Your mother will be overjoyed to see you again, after all these years!'

'I'm not too sure about that!' replied Teofil. 'We didn't part on the most cordial terms.'

'So, you'll be mending bridges, will you, sir?'

'I think you could say that.'

'Well, I wish you well, and please convey to her my best respects!'

'I will.' The two men turned from each other. It was obviously the end of the conversation, and a look of relief crossed Maurice's face. Staś was about to return to his work when Teofil called, as an afterthought, 'Oh, *Panie* Stasiu!' Staś turned. 'If you're asking Maurice round for supper, watch out for Lenka. Maurice is a lewd and lascivious *roué* with a penchant for eighteen-year-old Polish girls with blonde hair and blue eyes!' He turned to Maurice, whose jaw had dropped in horror. 'But I love him like a brother, despite his many faults and numerous flaws of character!' With that Teofil grabbed Maurice by the shoulders, and kissed him affectionately and noisily on both cheeks before going into the house.

VI

The next morning Teofil wrapped up warmly in his French greatcoat and set off well before dawn. He noted with satisfaction that there was a crescent moon in a cloudless sky, so the snow-covered track was well lit. *Pani* Marynia had prepared a bag of rye bread and a *kiełbasa* sausage that she had hung for several weeks to harden. A water bottle was filled to the top with Old Pankracy's vodka – an excellent and heartening antidote to both the cold and depression, for the old housekeeper gleefully promised a long and arduous journey across some very unpleasant, wolf-infested terrain, her toothless grin adding to the bleak picture.

The track followed the little river Skarbek for the greater part of the way, and by daybreak Mazurek had carried Teofil clear of the Beskid uplands that were the foothills of the Carpathians, and to the confluence with the River Poprąd flowing slowly northwards from the Carpathians to its rendezvous with the Dunajec just above the town of Nowy Sandec. The high banks, covered in virgin snow, overhung the river, but Mazurek found a fault where he could stumble his way down to the water's edge to drink, for the little used track was indistinct here. Teofil took advantage of the halt to chew a chunk of extremely matured but nourishing *kiełbasa*, washing it down with a long draught of Old Pankracy, which complemented the sausage perfectly. The morning was overcast, dark and bitterly cold, and even Mazurek seemed anxious to keep going. This was a sparsely populated region, with only occasional peasant hovels and the huts of woodmen and river folk in evidence. Turning right, Teofil followed the whimsical course of the pretty, youthful river until he saw the older and more mature Dunajec joining on the other side. It was a striking, almost sexual union, set in gently undulating, wooded countryside. Noon was already nigh when Teofil rode slowly into Nowy Sandec.

On one side of the track were low houses, their enormous roofs covered in thick layers of snow, while on the other there was a long, low white-washed wall enclosing a small manor surrounded by trees. Two bullock carts, both laden with winter beetroots, blundered their way, side by side, along the narrow track, their gnarled and toothless drivers, dressed in perhaps all the clothing they possessed, engaged in monosyllabic conversation. A few old women, shapeless and bent under endless layers of clothing and headscarves, shuffled along like creatures from another world. In the near distance there appeared what looked like a small palace. The windows glowed red, suggesting a blazing fire within. Before it there was a large square, with tethering posts and a horse trough. In this square there was a noisy gathering. Horses, sledges and dogs mingled with men, warmly clad and sporting a wide array of weapons. Men and beasts were milling about, shouting and gesticulating, barking and whinnying. Teofil rode up to a fur-clad rider armed with a rifle slung across his back.

'What is happening?' he asked.

'A hunt,' replied the other.

'Wolf?'

The fur-clad rider laughed aloud, taking a long draught from his drinking bottle. 'Not this time!' he cried.

Teofil idly wondered how the contents of his bottle might compare with his Old Pankracy. He bent down and proffered his bottle to the man. 'Try this,' he invited. 'You won't find a better firewater anywhere!' The other smiled his thanks through his thick moustache, took Teofil's bottle and drank deeply.

'Ah! That's good!' he said. 'Thank you! This is not local! You're not from hereabouts?'

'I am from Sarenki, in the hills to the south,' said Teofil. 'But I've been to Russia with Napoleon. I haven't been home long.'

The other looked at Teofil intently. 'Is that so?' he said. Teofil detected a hint of menace in his voice. The man turned his horse to the assembly. 'Hey, *Panie* Grocholski!' he called. 'I think you should come and talk to this one here!'

A group of riders detached themselves from the crowd and rode over. One of them, a heavily whiskered man in a grey greatcoat and a tall, red four-cornered cap as favoured by the Polish military, rode up to Teofil. He had a pistol tucked into his belt and his gloved hand rested on the hilt of his sword. He was mounted, Teofil noted, on a superb white horse – probably a *Lipizaner*. He was obviously in charge. The others, similarly dressed and armed with short lances strapped to their backs, surrounded Teofil.

'One of Napoleon's, Chief,' said the fur-hatted man.

'Your name!' barked the man called Grocholski.

Teofil did not like the tone of the man's voice. 'King Stanisław August!' he said sarcastically. 'Hey, what is this?'

'What are you doing in Nowy Sandec?'

Teofil's hackles rose. 'What business is it of yours?'

'Just answer the question!'

'I'm on my way to Kraków to start a revolution,' sneered Teofil. 'I've just come from Sarenki.'

'That place down south? You'd better come with me!'

'Why?'

'Because I'm arresting you on suspicion of the murder of *Graf* Leopold von Loebl, Imperial Inspector of Agriculture in the Beskid region of Galicia!'

'What are you talking about?' cried Teofil. He was cold, tired and hungry, and was in no mood to be confronted with idiotic charges from some petty official. 'I don't know any imperial inspectors. I've only been home a few weeks!'

'Filipowicz!' barked Grocholski.

The fur-hatted man rode up. 'Chief?' he said.

'Take him!' cried Grocholski. The one called Filipowicz spurred his horse and advanced. A surge of anger swept through Teofil. With a cry of rage, he spurred Mazurek into action, and turned the horse's head with a yank of the reins. Mazurek reared up with a whinny, and set off at a gallop back the way they had come.

'After him!' bellowed Grocholski. With that the whole posse of perhaps a dozen men, accompanied by barking dogs, set off in pursuit. As he passed the bullock carts making their way slowly towards him, Teofil rode Mazurek straight at one of them. At the very last moment he swerved with a blood-curdling yell, causing the astonished bullock to stagger with fright, sideways, into the path of his brother. Teofil rode hard past the two carts, missing them narrowly, and continued along the rutted track. The collision was not serious, but the front wheel of one cart became entangled with the rear wheel of the other, which must have been very weak, since it broke. The cart lurched on its side and shed its load of beetroots into the path of the oncoming posse, while the other cart slewed sideways on, with its bullock, lowing in terror, up against the low wall. The track was blocked.

'Get this stuff out of our way!' yelled Grocholski, reining in his mount. 'Come on! Move it, you stupid peasants!'

The two dazed drivers, one still in his seat, the other picking himself up off the ground, dithered indecisively, and tried without success to pull the two carts apart, muttering curses under their breaths. The two bullocks, in a panic, added their weight to the struggle, but only created more entanglement and confusion. By the time a gap was cleared in the *melée*, Teofil had gained valuable time, and had reached the outlying fields and woodlands which stretched to the confluence of the two rivers a few kilometres upstream.

From a small hill overlooking the river, he had a good view of the town and its environs. He could see signs of his pursuers in the distance, but they were well spread out and some were straggling, while others were fanning out in all directions. Teofil grunted with satisfaction. The immediate danger was over, but he could not afford to take any chances: Mazurek's tracks were there for all to see and follow, so at the end of the day there could be no escape. After a few minutes of canter through the stark woodland, Teofil spurred Mazurek once again into a gallop diagonally down the other side of the hill and across a smooth plain to rejoin the river to his right.

All of a sudden Teofil was aware of a rider bearing down on him from his left. Surely it cannot be one of his pursuers, he thought. They would need to have overtaken him by quite a long way to come at him from that angle. He decided to keep going, at least as far as the river before deciding if the mystery rider was a friend or a foe. He was almost there when he noticed that the rider had reached the river at a small wood half a kilometre upstream, and that he was waving and gesticulating wildly that he should stay put. The rider then rode into the river, and slowly made his way up to where Teofil sat, nervously looking up and down the river, expecting his pursuing party to appear at any moment over the hill. As he came closer, Teofil could see that the horseman was dressed in a long, black riding cloak.

'May lightning strike you, you son-of-a-bitch, and the Devil take your blackened soul to roast in Hell for evermore!' came a strangled cry from beneath the hood. 'Wait right there!'

'Father Józef! What in God's name…?' cried Teofil.

'Don't you dare take the Lord's name in vain, you blasphemous hound!' cried Father Józef, his piggy eyes only just visible under the hood of his cloak. 'Only I'm allowed to do that! You're in great danger!'

'I know!' said Teofil. 'There's an official of some kind in Nowy Sandec that thinks I've killed some imperial inspector, or something! There's a whole army after me!'

'I know!' said Father Józef. 'That's why I'm here. I heard about it earlier from the sons-of-bitches that did it. They're a gang of Napoleon's displaced veterans who are roaming the countryside pretending to be patriots by killing Austrian and Russian officials. They're arresting everyone who looks as though they might have been connected with Napoleon.'

'Who are they?'

'A hellhound name of Grocholski. Chief of Security at Nowy Sandec.'

'He's the one that's after me!'

'Well, you don't mess with him. Your coat's a dead give-away. The bastard's giving veterans a very hard time. This lot have ended up in Sarenki. I've put them in the Manor.'

'You what?!'

'God will pay the rent. We'll talk about it and negotiate terms later!' said the priest. 'The most important thing is to get you away from here.'

'How?'

'There's a chance this plan will work. Listen carefully, or you'll end up shot at dawn. Ride along the river into that wood, back the way I came. When you get there, hide Mazurek and yourself. That should not be too difficult. There's quite a lot of cover. Then lie low.'

'For how long?'

'As long as it takes!' growled the priest impatiently. 'How should I know? Meanwhile, I'll cross the river and continue on the other side. The bastards will follow my trail, not yours. I'll lead them a merry *krakowiak* towards the west while you go north. Skirt Nowy Sandec, and I'll meet you in Bochnia tomorrow evening. Stay at the White Eagle. Did you tell them your name?'

'King Stanisław August.'

'That would have cheered them up no end! Don't use that name again. Use your own. Put your coat on inside out, and don't mention Napoleon! Do you understand?' Teofil nodded. 'Now bugger off!'

With that Father Józef spurred his horse, splashed across the river, climbed the western bank and made off at a gallop. Teofil did not stop to watch him go, but turned and gingerly made his way upstream towards the thick wood. It was heavy going, for although the stream was shallow, it was very rocky. He reached the wood just as two riders appeared over the hill. Stopping for just one moment to ascertain the direction of Teofil's tracks, they broke into a gallop and came to the river.

Teofil dismounted and tethered Mazurek to a fallen tree lying at an angle against another. He crouched down and held his breath as he watched the two riders inspect the riverbank. One of them was Grocholski; he could tell by the high, four-cornered hat and the white stallion, almost invisible against the snow. The other was Filipowicz, who was obviously his deputy. The son-of-a-bitch has still got my Old Pankracy, thought Teofil bitterly. What was it he had said? They were going hunting, but not wolf?

'A manhunt!' thought Teofil. 'Just what I need!' He was cold, and would have given anything for a drink of vodka!

The two men seemed to be marking time suspiciously, glancing up and down the river, as well as back up the hill. 'What the Hell are they waiting for!' hissed Teofil through his teeth. 'Go! Get a move on!' He wondered what had happened to the others. There were at least a dozen gathered in the square. He remembered how he had seen them from the top of the hill. There were certainly less than a dozen then. Some had straggled, perhaps because their horses were not up to a cross-country manhunt.

'There were some pretty tired-looking nags among them,' he recalled.

Also, they had been fanning out. Teofil smiled. Not a good idea when you're trying to follow tracks, he mused. 'The rest are probably all following one another round and round in circles!'

Grocholski rode to the other bank, dismounted and inspected Father Józef's tracks. His comrade seemed impatient, judging by the restlessness of his horse. After what seemed like a heated discussion, the two horsemen finally set off in pursuit of Father Józef. 'Yes!' Teofil whisper-shouted, waving his fist in the air. He watched them ride out of sight, among the hilly woodlands and fields on the west side of the river. He gave them a good half-hour before emerging from his hiding place, stiff with cold, for the day was drawing slowly to a grey close.

'May the good Lord bless you, you blasphemous old villain!' grunted Teofil, turning to the south west. He hoisted himself up onto Mazurek, crossed the river and headed off towards the north west.

VII

The White Eagle at Bochnia was bustling with life, not surprisingly as it was on the main post route between technically independent Kraków, in the Duchy of Warsaw, and Lemberg, or Lwów, the most important city in Galicia. The downstairs room was full of merchants, refugees and soldiers wearing a great variety of unmatched uniforms. A year after Napoleon's ignominious retreat from Moscow many uniforms had ceased to have any relevance beyond a means of keeping warm. Large numbers of Poles who had strained at Napoleon's leash to get at the Russians had now lost confidence in him, along with all hope of a restored state. Teofil was among many who had deserted from the French Grande Armée. The Prussians had also sided with the Russians, and many French deserters had stayed on in Poland, not knowing what sort of a France they would come home to.

The babble of conversation was multi-lingual, with the local Polish and Ruthenian blending with German and French. Napoleonic greatcoats were worn with Russian furs, and Polish hats went together with the Prussian jackets of Polish speaking deserters from the forces of the turncoat King Friederich Wilhelm III, putting distance between themselves and Poznań. Ex-army units from all over Europe remixed as partisan groups, guerrillas or plain simple bandits. It was all a matter of how thousands of ex-combatants saw themselves. A freedom fighter in one camp was a bandit in another. Loyalties could be bought for a jug of beer and a square meal. Life was cheap, and the future uncertain, and there was talk of a congress to be held in Vienna which would decide how the new boundaries of Europe would be re-drawn. Nationalities would be revised, and no one knew which country they would be citizens of in the months, and years to come. The White Eagle was a bustling melting pot where a stranger could be killed in a drunken brawl, or be assassinated as a foreign agent by a highly motivated partisan unit from any one of the numerous organisations operating in this area alone. It may well have been at this time when the saying originated that when three Poles meet, four political parties would follow.

Poland as a concept was in a quandary. The Poles had offered Napoleon their allegiance in exchange for the promise of their nationhood restored. Napoleon had rewarded them for their loyalty by setting up the Duchy of Warsaw, a small but significant puppet state which included the ancient Polish capital of Kraków. Napoleon demanded proof that the Poles were capable of governing themselves before committing them to full independence. Some hopes, reckoned the rest of Europe.

Teofil looked about him as he supped off a bowl of hunter's stew, potatoes, rye bread and beer. It was very good. But then, Tadek Bawół, the proprietor of the White Eagle, had established good contacts with local bandits and peasants fiddling their masters, as well as landowners and merchants, some of whose wares had inexplicably fallen off the backs of carts. His hospitality, his kitchen, his liquors and his services were renowned as being among the best on the Kraków-Lwów highway, and even the Austrian authorities turned a blind eye to some of his less than legal activities, as long as they kept some basic standards of living alive.

Teofil remembered both Tadek Bawół and the White Eagle. He had stayed here in the spring of 1796, when he had first left Sarenki on his angry odyssey to nowhere. Tadek had hardly changed since then. A little more fat, a few more lines on his face and deeper creases separating his chins and jowls were all to be expected, for he was a large man, powerfully built but hearty, well-fed, well-oiled and good-natured as befits an innkeeper. The inn had been quieter then, and the sparse clientèle had worn the resigned look of a defeated people. Then, as now, he had supped off hunter's stew.

*****

No one smarted from Poland's final partition more than the angry eighteen-year-old Teofil Samojarski. The seething rage within his heart had driven all sense of decency out of him. His behaviour, as anyone in Sarenki would testify, was brutal, and he would vent his anger not on the injustices of life, but on the people on whom these injustices lay.

It seemed like an age ago that he had gone on to Kraków, then under the Habsburg yoke, and put his ear to the ground in search of a war against the System. His efforts bore fruit, and he joined a band of irregulars under Colonel Denisko, who had assembled a small Polish force, sponsored by the French, in Moldavia, beyond the furthest reaches of the Carpathian Mountains.

That same year Teofil saw action against the Austrians, but the campaign came to nothing. His unit had disintegrated, and Teofil, an aimless wanderer of no admitted fixed abode, was press-ganged by the Austrian army and sent to defend Austrian possessions in Italy.

Life in the Army was not as bad as it had seemed at first. Like all the other Slavs in his unit, he was treated with utter contempt by the Viennese officers, but he was fed and clothed, and the barracks were adequate.

The following year Teofil went into battle under the Austrian commander General Beaulieu against Napoleon's forces at the Bridge of Lodi, in the defence of Milan, a battle that the

Austrians lost. Teofil and several hundred Polish speaking conscripts constituted cannon fodder for the Austrians, and charged straight at the French army with surrender flags aloft. Teofil himself ran straight into the arms of a chubby, dark-haired young corporal with a downy moustache and laughing eyes.

'All right, *mon brave*!' laughed the corporal. 'Take it easy! You're safe now.'

'I – I wish to render myself...' panted Teofil, in French.

'*Polonais, hein*?'

'Yes. Is my accent that bad?'

'It is the turn of phrase, *mon ami*. You Poles are all surrendering! What is your name?'

'Samojarski. Teofil Samojarski.'

'Corporal Maurice Chavelet, at your service!'

*****

'So, you made it, you son-of-a-bitch!' growled a familiar voice. 'Foiled the bastards again, you and I, eh?'

Teofil shook himself out of his reverie and returned to the present with a start. 'Father Józef!' he cried.

'Who else were you expecting, other than the good Lord come down to damn you in Hell for all time!'

'Why, what have I done?' said Teofil.

Father Józef pointed at the empty bowl. 'Stew, eh? Tell me you forgot it was Friday, and I might get Lord Jesus Christ to agree to Absolution! I can sway it.'

'I hadn't forgotten, Father,' grinned Teofil. 'The rules say you can eat meat on a Friday if you are on a journey. And make no mistake, I'm on a journey!'

'How was it?'

'Very cold. Your plan worked perfectly. There were only two pursuers left, Grocholski and his tame side-kick, Filipowicz.'

'I know!' cried Father Józef. 'They caught up with me at dusk.

Obviously, they couldn't see me clearly in the half-light, but I still led them a merry dance. I rode like a bat out of Hell! They were very angry when they realised they were chasing a priest. Hey! Landlord!' Father Józef raised both his voice and his head. His jaw, exposed, had an enormous, purple bruise on it. 'Give me some of that stew of yours and a large jug of beer!'

'What have you done to your chin?' said Teofil, peering at the underside of the priest's face.

Father Józef grimaced as he rubbed the bruise. 'That Filipowicz lost his temper and laid one on me. He should not have done that.'

'Why?'

'Because first I blessed him, then I beat the shit out of him,' replied Father Józef. 'Then I told them that if they even contemplate further violence against my person in thought, word or deed, they will bring the wrath of Almighty God in the guise of a bolt of lightning on themselves and the plague on their families, me being His priest. We reached an understanding, and the two of them buggered off back home.'

'Then?'

'I rode north till I came to a farm in the middle of nowhere. Very poor they were. They gave me some bread and cabbage and let me sleep on the hay in the barn. Folks are generous to priests on the move. I shall have to take up travelling, Teofil. I've always wanted to travel. Like you.'

'It's not all it's made out to be.'

'Not if you've got to stomp around the world in your boots killing your fellow man, I agree. Me, I'd take my chances and beat the love of Almighty God into my fellow man's black soul!'

Tadek Bawół brought the stew and the beer. *'Smacznego! A good appetite,'* he beamed.

'May the Lord repay!' Father Józef pointed at the stew with his thumb and forefinger, and traced a cross above it. 'Bless, Lord

God, this grub, for which I thank you, even though it's meat and it's Friday, and put the sin on my slate until I expiate it by seeing this miserable sinner safely to his mother, whom he has failed to honour as specified in the Fourth Commandment, the ungrateful son-of-a-bitch that he is. Amen.'

That night Teofil and Father Józef slept very soundly. The next morning, they breakfasted early and set off on the final leg of their journey.

*****

The road to Kraków was busy. Coaches with bored-looking Austrian officials, cursing their luck in being posted to remotest Galicia, trying to pass bullock carts with uneven wheels trundling along in the opposite direction and ending up in a ditch, miscellaneous riders, alone or in groups, the occasional horse and buggy carrying a local rich young blood to a rendezvous with some fair young countess in a minor manor, traders honest or otherwise, bandits afraid to try their luck on the busy road, Lvovians travelling to Kraków, and Krakovians travelling to Lwów. Ultimately everyone shapeless and anonymous, wrapped as warmly and bulkily as respective economies allowed.

An hour out of Bochnia Kraków came into view. There was a road block around a cluster of houses. Austrian, French and Polish militia were milling about in total disarray. Ox-carts, coaches and riders mingled with toothless babushkas and barefooted peasants weighed down with goods and foodstuffs in baskets or in enormous slings of blankets.

'The frontier,' said Teofil.

'*Halt!*' barked a Captain in German. 'Identifications!'

Father Józef, reined in his horse and stretched his face into a beaming smile. '*Jawohl! Jawohl!*' he laughed. '*Ein zwei drei! Ich bin ein Dumkopf mein Herr, du bist ein Dumkopf. Ich liebe dich mein Liebling…*' adding under his breath, in Ukrainian '…you

Austrian bastard!'

Father Józef became an instant centre of attention, as the largely Polish crowd surged forward, grinning unashamedly, to see an Austrian official being baited by a local priest. The Captain leaned forward and his hand went for his pistol. Teofil recognised an awkward situation about to fall on their heads, and rode forward to defuse it.

'Please excuse him, Captain,' he said gently in German. 'Father Józef Baraniuk doesn't speak German, except for some childish phrases learned when he was a boy. He is the parish priest of Sarenki. He has a tendency to clown, but he's on the side of Good. He goes down well with the peasants! He's from Lwów. Lemberg.'

'That will explain his extraordinary behaviour!' said the Captain resignedly. 'Your name!'

'Permit me to introduce myself. I am…' he inclined his head and rolled he eyes almost perceptibly, '…Count Teofil Samojarski. My estate is at Sarenki, in the Carpathians. Father Baraniuk and I are travelling to Kraków to see my mother, C-countess…'

'I beg your pardon, *Herr Graf*,' he replied, bowing perceptibly, 'we are looking for subversive elements that have been reported on this road.'

'Ah, in connection with the murder of *Herr Graf* von Loebl?' said Teofil.

'You have heard of it?'

'There was talk in Bochnia of bandits who are terrorising the area. A lawless road it seems, these days, Captain!'

'They execute raids in Galicia and escape into the Duchy. Proceed, *Herr Graf*.'

Teofil proceeded, throwing Father Józef a knowing grin. Next came the Poles. In their blue-grey greatcoats and tall, four-cornered caps they were trying to deal with everybody at the same time. There was total chaos. In overall charge were three French officers on horseback wearing Napoleonic hats. They had obviously decided to leave all frontier formalities to the Poles themselves, and merely looked on with resigned indifference.

'The one in the middle could be an understudy for Napoleon!' said Father Józef with a broad grin. 'Let's go to them, and we might get somewhere, else we'll be here all day!'

Teofil and Father Józef pushed their way through the crowd towards the three Frenchmen. The one who, according to Father Józef, resembled Napoleon removed his hand from under his jacket and rode to meet them.

'It is not permitted to pass without authorisation,' he said. 'Your passport…'

Teofil took a deep breath and put on a haughty look. 'I am Count Teofil Samojarski of Sarenki, and a loyal veteran of Emperor Napoleon's campaigns!' he announced, in French, taking out his documentation. 'I am travelling to Kraków with Father Józef Baraniuk, to see my mother in Czarne Lasy. It is just outside Kraków.'

'I know Czarne Lasy, sir,' said the officer, his face lightening up. Teofil noted that he did indeed resemble the young Napoleon. He was not yet thirty, with short, dark, glossy hair and brown eyes, finely sculpted chin and aquiline nose gave him a classical look. Teofil was not expecting this, and hesitated.

'We cannot wait for this…' Teofil waved his hand at the shouting crowd and his documents at the officer, '…rabble to sort themselves out! I insist the formalities be dealt with swiftly, and that you let us pass unimpeded.'

The Frenchman glanced at his colleagues, who were grinning broadly. He turned back to Teofil.

'Perhaps you are related to Countess Samojarska?' enquired the officer.

'Why yes,' replied Teofil, by this time totally subdued. 'She is my mother.'

'Then I should inform you that she is well. You see, I am billeted at Czarne Lasy, her ancestral home, which the French Military establishment is renting from the Family. She lives in the Lodge with her mother.'

Teofil was put out, and it showed. 'I have not seen her for seventeen years.'

'Then I suggest your visit is long overdue.'

'Father Baraniuk and I have business in Kraków first.'

'In that case I shall make a point of advising your mother forthwith of your impending arrival. Please proceed, Count – Father. Perhaps we shall meet again at Czarne Lasy?'

'Perhaps.'

'Lieutenant Marcel Terrassin, at your service!' The officer bowed gallantly and returned to his colleagues.

Teofil and Father Józef rode on, down the winding dirt road, towards the bridge over the River Vistula, the boundary of the Republic of Kraków. A solitary craft, its sails furled, was floating idly with the stream, perhaps laden with wool from the Tatras, and destined for the merchants of Warsaw, in the Grand Duchy. Skirting the far bank were the walls of the city of Kraków, spread out compactly in the valley. Behind the city, the hills, and the north beyond, were clearly visible. To the left the city was dominated, like a Slav acropolis, by the imposing Wawel, the royal palace and cathedral complex perched on top of its craggy hill that had been the residence of the ancient Kings of Poland. To the right, on the far side of the city, the two towers of the Church of St Mary stood out against the hills beyond.

'Welcome to Poland,' muttered Teofil wistfully as they crossed the bridge.

VIII

Father Józef had wanted to pay his respects to the Bishop of Kraków whom he had not got round to seeing in all the forty years he had been at Sarenki. The Bishop, as it happened, had been unable – or unwilling – to see some peasant priest from the Galician outback immediately, so he and Teofil had put up at the *Biała Róża* Inn, just beside the Barbican. Fortunately, the delay had not been entirely fruitless. Kraków was an historic city with a great deal to offer the questor. While Teofil revisited some old haunts and tracked down old acquaintances – mostly spent ex-revolutionaries now more inclined to talk than to action, Father Józef visited all the churches, and marvelled at the Gothic and Renaissance splendours of the Bernardines Monastery, the Corpus Christi and Holy Trinity Churches. Above all he was fascinated by St Mary's Church. On the evening of their first day Teofil and Father Józef met in the square outside the Church, with its unidentical twin towers.

The two men silently contemplated the two towers, utterly incongruous in their lack of logic. Like many unidentical twins, the towers were completely different, one taller than the other, the result of a legendary private feud between two architects, each sworn to build a taller monument to God than the other.

'According to the legend the loser threw himself off his own tower,' said Teofil.

'The son-of-a-bitch,' muttered Father Józef.

All of a sudden, the cold air was pierced by the sound of a trumpet from the evening sky. From the taller of the two towers a fanfare was being played by a trumpeter. This was done every hour on the hour, by tradition in commemoration of the boy bugler who, 600 years previously, had alerted the citizens of Kraków to the arrival of the invading Tartar hordes in the middle of the night. His warning, which he sounded to the four points of the compass, was cut short by a stray Tartar arrow. The warning did not save the city, but went on to serve as a memorial to the spirit of the people of Kraków in the defence of their city on that far distant occasion. The fanfare, or *hejnał*, aborted at the point where the boy ceased to play, had been played every hour, to the four points of the compass, ever since.

Meanwhile Father Józef persevered with his mission, and two days later his patience was rewarded with a short audience with the Bishop's secretary, during which he was complimented for building the Church at Sarenki with his bare hands. After which some polite inanities and blessings were exchanged.

'Two days wasted, just to have the honour of discussing the weather in the Carpathians with some boring old fart in a clerical frock!' growled Father Józef angrily, as they rode slowly northwards along the cobbled road to Czarne Lasy. It was already getting dark.

Czarne Lasy Manor was situated on the wooded hills just to the north of Kraków. The track from the city to the main gates was paved. When the Austrian Military Establishment first moved in, hundreds of peasants had been press-ganged to quarry, cut and lay the stones for the convenience of the Emperor's men, their horses and their cohorts. A high stone wall separated the track from the estate. Somewhere beyond the wall, hidden from view, stood the Manor.

The horses slowly made their way up the track, the slow, tired clip-clopping of their hooves the only sound in the wintry twilight. They came to the main entrance – a pair of large, wrought iron gates forged into two massive stone pillars. The red, green and gold emblem of the House of Sczasny was still built into each gate. Two soldiers stood guard, one at each pillar. The arrival of the two riders evinced a delayed, half-hearted response.

'*Halt!*'

Teofil had heard that word uttered with far greater conviction in Prussia. In any case, the two riders had already halted. The guards were young lads, probably local, and it had no doubt been a long, cold day, and was now promising to be a further long, cold night.

'I am Count Teofil Samojarski,' said Teofil. 'We wish to see my mother, Countess Samojarska, at the Lodge.'

A horseman rode down the driveway from the direction of the Manor at a gallop. He pulled up sharply at the gate.

'Count Samojarski!' he said. 'I have been expecting you and the Reverend for two days. I saw you coming up the hill.' Because of the half-light, it took Teofil and Father Józef a few moments to recognise Lieutenant Terrassin. He turned to the guards and ordered the gates to be opened. 'Permit me to escort you to the Lodge. I have informed the Countess your mother of your impending arrival, and she is expecting you.'

Lieutenant Terrassin turned his horse and led the way slowly along a dirt track that veered off from the main drive to the Manor, till they came to a small, two storey timber lodge, varnished a dark brown, nestling cosily among the encroaching trees. It had a high, carved gable and a veranda going all the way round, except where it was interrupted by the entrance. This was fronted by a pair of Doric-style columns supporting a triangular pediment. An orange glow testified to the warmth of a hearth within.

'*Voilà*, the Lodge. I shall leave you here, *Monsieur le Comte*, Father. I hope we shall meet again. Over dinner, perhaps?'

'*Merci*. Perhaps,' said Teofil.

Terrassin bowed graciously and rode off into the thickening

twilight.

Teofil's meeting with his mother was a strained affair, saved from being a total disaster only by the tactless tactics of Father Józef. Whether these were perpetrated by accident or design never became clear, but they did serve as a catalyst for diffusing what could have led to an even more unpleasant situation. After all, handling Father Józef's social graces, or rather, lack of them, was an acquired art, and a great deal of air tended to be cleared during the acquiring.

The visitors were ushered into the drawing room by *Pani* Wisia, the elderly housekeeper. No candles were lit, but the room was filled with the dancing glow of the bright fire burning in the hearth. The furniture was simple but still retained a certain faded elegance. Patterned rugs hung on the walls next to blackened family portraits, and carpets that smelled of dust were scattered on the bare floorboards.

'So, you have come at last. I suppose better late than never.' Countess Świetlana Samojarska was in her mid-fifties, though she looked older. An unhappy life had carved numerous lines on her face, each one with a sorry tale to tell; and despair had drained her eyes, once sapphire blue, of any lustre. She was dressed for warmth and comfort rather than for elegance, as social calls were evidently few and far between at the Lodge. The arrival of her prodigal son had not dispelled the air of apathy that pervaded her whole being. Her tortured face gave no hint of the beauty that had once so entranced Teofil's father, the ill-fated Xavier: in the dancing glow of the fire he actually found Świetlana ugly.

'Who are these people, Świetlana? Tell *Pani* Wisia to make them go away. We are not at home tonight.'

Teofil looked up. In the corner of the drawing room, wrapped in blankets, sat a wizened and toothless old woman with long, straggly grey hair and blankly staring eyes. A claw-like hand protruded from beneath the blankets, grasping the head of an old walking stick.

'Take no notice of your grandmother,' said Świetlana. '*Babcia* Elżbieta's senile.'

Teofil's eyes went towards the old woman, and their eyes met. They were as near lifeless as eyes could be. When her husband Prince Leonid Sczasny died at the turn of the century, his wife chose to remain at Czarne Lasy, where she lived alone until her daughter came to live with her, the generally accepted reason for the move being to get away from Sarenki, and everything that it had stood for. And that included Teofil.

'Then she'll be requiring a priest soon,' interpolated Father Józef after a pregnant pause, trying to make conversation. Świetlana turned to him. 'You've aged,' she said. 'You always looked old. Now you look older.'

'We all age. Senility is a dreadful thing,' said the priest. 'You remember old Wiesiek? He became senile and died very soon afterwards.'

There was a pause. Teofil closed his eyes tightly and gritted his teeth. 'I haven't been looking forward to this, *Mamusiu*,' he said finally. 'I don't know how to deal with it!'

'Ask your Father Józef!' barked Świetlana, nodding her head at him. 'He's the priest. He always claimed to understand you. He knows all the answers!'

'You're not helping, *Mamusiu*!'

'Why should I help? You're the one who went off seventeen years ago in a fury of hate for everything and everyone, especially me! You never did tell me what I did to deserve what you did to me!'

'I want to make amends.'

'It's too late for amends!'

'It's never too late, *Pani hrabino*!' said Father Józef.

'What do you know about it, Father?' sneered Świetlana. 'Your little world is cocooned in Sarenki where you enjoy yourself cursing everyone, listening to their confessions and scrounging food from your flock! What do you know of real human suffering in the world? Of oppression? Of the damned Habsburgs and their Emperor? Nor are the French any better! Nor my own son! What do you know of the real world?'

Father Józef's temper snapped. 'The real world?' he rose and advanced on Świetlana menacingly and leaned his hands on the arm of her chair. 'You dare to preach to me about the real world? The real world is the Kingdom of Heaven where…' Father Józef shook his fist vehemently at the ceiling '…Almighty and Eternal God is King!'

'Father Józef…' Teofil tried to restrain him, but was roughly rebuffed.

'In His eyes we are all His children, and He will judge us according to how we survive the tribulations that He sends to test us! You are not the only one to have been tested! I suggest you offer your troubles up to God as a penance, say a few Our Fathers and stop pitying yourself. And as for the Emperor, did not Christ say render unto God what is God's and unto Caesar what is Caesar's! And that, I should imagine, goes for emperors too! So please leave old Franz out of it, and let Almighty God deal with him as He sees fit. Remember the Emperor has no say in the Kingdom of Heaven, because that's the real world, and you would be wise to remember it!'

Father Józef stormed back to his armchair and sat in it heavily. There was a pause, broken only by the crackling of the fire, and the ascending scale of a rising wind playing the trees outside. Teofil took a deep breath and pursed his lips. Świetlana shook with suppressed emotion.

'Why is that man shouting so, Tereniu?' said *Babcia* Elżbieta. 'Tell *Pani* Wisia to get rid of him! He is so uncouth!'

'Shut up, you stupid old woman!' cried Świetlana. Then, with a look of resignation, she rose and went to her mother, knelt beside her, and put her hand on her mother's. 'It's all right, *Mamusiu*,' she said soothingly. 'It's all right.' She turned to Father Józef and burst into tears. 'God can be very cruel, Father.'

'What do you expect? An instant sainthood? His Kingdom's got to be earned in this vale of tears!'

Świetlana stumbled over to Father Józef and fell to her knees. 'Bless me, Father,' she sobbed.

Father Józef stood up again. He had never minced his words, and he was not prepared to start now. He described a cross over her head with his thumb and forefinger. 'Bless, Almighty and Eternal God, this bitter woman, and forgive her lack of faith in your goodness, and remind her that her son, prodigal like the one your son Jesus preached about, has returned to seek amends, and get her to kill the fatted calf, or whatever passes for one these days, for him. Amen.'

Then he sat down again.

IX

The guest rooms at the Lodge were cold, musty and had not been aired for months. Świetlana did not at first deem it necessary to actually kill a fatted calf, or to make any special preparations for her prodigal son's return, but *Pani* Wisia, who obviously managed to keep some semblance of spirit up despite being at the endless beck and call of a depressed widow and her demented mother, had done her best. At least the beds were clean and the linen fresh, and she ensured that warm fires crackled in the grates.

'It is good that you have come, *Panie hrabio*,' she said to Teofil conspiratorially, carrying a basket of logs into his room. 'But you must give your mother time. She has suffered much – my God! we have all suffered much – but she is so glad that you have returned. I know,' she nodded her head sagely; 'I can see the signs. Be kind, be gentle. She will come round.'

Pani Wisia was right. During the ensuing days Teofil noticed hints of sparkle returning to his mother's eyes. The apathy slowly gave way to the beginnings of a new interest in life. Teofil took *Pani* Wisia's advice, and did his best to be kind and solicitous. Seventeen years in the French army had not entirely dulled his sense of long-rejected breeding, such as it was, and he managed to dredge up almost-forgotten reserves of gracious behaviour.

Teofil's mother, on the other hand, wanted to know all about his adventures in the French army. His threadbare account of the past seventeen years did not impress her. 'Are you saying that you have spent all those years as a common soldier?' she said.

'Why did you not become an officer? You might have made a real career in the Army!'

'I don't really want to talk about it,' he replied. 'It's all history now. Napoleon's finished, and I'm thirty-four years old, and nothing to show for it.'

'What about this Maurice? He sounds to me like a very common type!'

Teofil got up, walked to the window and peered intently at the open park of Czarne Lasy just visible beyond the skeletal trees. The snows had melted, the Asiatic cold had begun its homeward migration, and there was a hint of seasonal change in the air. He and Maurice had seen many seasons change, some for the better, some for the worse. After the fall of Milan, they had stayed on to help occupy Northern Italy. They were good days. The sun shone, they were young and in charge, the wine was good and the wenches forthcoming. A few good battles helped to vent their innate blood-lust, in both their cases brutalised by humanity's almost perpetual state of war. A deep bond of friendship was forged between Teofil and Maurice, and they had never been apart since. They shared everything, from the dregs at the bottom of a water bottle in the African desert to a ravishing black-eyed beauty in a Syrian brothel as they adventured their way back from Napoleon's Egyptian fiasco.

At Napoleon's Coronation as Emperor, they drunk one another under the table, after which Teofil spent a fortnight nursing Maurice back to life with the help of countless remedies for alcoholic poisoning submitted by a variety of well-wishers.

The following year at Austerlitz Maurice repaid his debt by dragging a badly wounded Teofil off the battlefield and into an icy ditch, where he managed to save his friend's life by stemming the torrent of blood pouring from his side, and shielding him for three days from the bitter cold with the warmth of his own body.

'Maurice has seen me through hell and back,' said Teofil.

'Without him I would not have survived. I like to think I did the same for him. He is the best there is, mother.'

'The hell has been of your own making, Teofil. As a *szlachcic* of noble birth you should have been an officer.'

'What good is noble birth, without one's own country, *Mamusiu*? Only when Poland exists again as a real nation will I accept any kind of noble birth. Till then I prefer to eat, sleep and fight with ordinary men. Like Maurice. It's the only life I know.'

'You'll be thinking like a Republican next!'

'I already do, mother.'

This horrified Świetlana, and she withdrew into her depression once more. But despite frequent relapses she was becoming more open and friendly, and even tried to show some understanding for Teofil's radical views, which contrasted utterly with her sense of traditional values and upbringing.

'These modern ideas,' she sighed. 'I shall never come to terms with them. I am too old to change my views.'

Świetlana found Teofil altered beyond recognition from the morose youth of yesteryear to a singularly caring human being. He had obviously succeeded in expiating his early wrath during the course of the hell of his own making on the battlefields of Europe and the Levant. If any good had come from this hell, it had certainly made a man of him. Now he had come home, like St Luke's prodigal son, intent on repairing what he had so cruelly put asunder all those years ago.

His attitude might well have been different with regard to his grandmother Tatiana. In his youth a festering hatred for the ugliness of old age would have brought out the cruel tormentor within. His mother had made no mention of the treatment he had meted out to his other Granny Olga seventeen years ago. Now that seething hatred might well have returned at the sight of the senile old woman, now crippled, incontinent and beyond all hope of a dignified closing chapter to her earthly years. Teofil spent time looking after her, talking patiently to her and helping the long-suffering *Pani* Wisia with her nursing duties.

Marcel Terrassin called every day to see that all was well at the Lodge. He entertained a sneaking regret that his unit had taken over a noble Russian family's manor. Officially, the French Army 'rented' the house from the Sczasnys, but in reality, they took over the quarters after the Austrian military when the Duchy of Warsaw was proclaimed six years previously. It made a certain sense, as the Manor had been adapted to military needs. The Sczasnys had high hopes of regaining their ancestral home, but it was not to be. Świetlana's father had died at the turn of the century, a bitter old man. However, as a gesture to show that they were not an occupying army as such, the French paid Princess Świetlana compensation, conveniently called rent. The fact that Terrassin did not really approve of the idea was obvious. He was courteous and solicitous – almost apologetic – at all times, called both ladies by their correct titles and kissed their hands by way of greeting – unlike many of his peers, to whom titles and even good manners smacked of the old order that the French Revolution had gone so far to do away with.

'Admit it, Lieutenant,' cried Father Józef to a bemused Marcel Terrassin, as he climbed onto his horse, a week after his arrival with Teofil at Czarne Lasy, 'beneath that French Republican exterior there lurks an insufferable snob!'

'I admit to nothing of the sort, Father!' laughed Marcel, 'everyone knows that my snobbery is entirely sufferable! We shall miss you, Father.'

Father Józef turned to his horse. 'If I don't get back to my flock at Sarenki, they'll all become heathens or protestants, and I'll be out of a job! It's time I went home.'

'I'll ride with you as far as the River.'

'God bless you, Lieutenant!' Then he raised his voice. 'Goodbye, and may God bless you all. You too, Teofil. See you soon back at Sarenki! In the meantime, don't do anything I'd enjoy!'

With a final guffaw Father Józef spurred his horse and the two horsemen rode off at a canter towards the gate.

The following day Marcel Terrassin came to the Lodge. 'I was wondering, *Monsieur le Comte*,' he said to Teofil, 'if you would care to dine with us on Saturday. My sister, Eloise, is coming from Lyon, and will be staying in Kraków till the summer as my guest.'

'I would be delighted, Lieutenant,' said Teofil. 'Thank you.'

Dinner at the Manor was a comparatively informal affair, which suited Teofil well. The officers present, and their wives, came from all strata of society, and there was, in Teofil's opinion, a refreshing lack of formalities. Talk was largely of shop, with liberal lashings of culture, as would be expected among discerning French. Napoleon's fortunes, following the retreat from Russia, overhung with a fateful sword of Damacles, were the subject of speculation and subtly altering loyalties.

'The man should never have made himself Emperor,' said the elderly Captain Louis Laroche, who had been through the Terror and had survived. His intake of Burgundy wine, imported in preference to the *'vinaigre épouvantable'* of the surrounding wine regions of Hungary, Moravia and Moldavia, had been considerable, and he was becoming garrulous. 'He's betrayed the Republican ideal by what he did. Thought we'd got rid of kings and the like!' The others looked at him and remained silent. These thoughts were lurking in everyone's mind at this time, but it was not seemly for an officer of the French army to voice them. But then, reflected Terrassin, Laroche, who but for the Revolution would have been common cannon fodder, was himself not entirely seemly.

Conversation turned from Napoleon to Napoleon and the Arts. David's gigantic painting of the Coronation was vehemently compared to the famous portrait by Lefevre.

'He looks like someone playing Julius Caesar in a cheap opera by Grétry!' bellowed Laroche.

Major Claude Davantier, a career soldier who was happier playing the works of Rameau and Mozart on the flute with other musicians in a chamber music setting, had been among the first to hear the Symphony that Beethoven had written to celebrate Napoleon's achievements.

'He dedicated it to Napoleon, and called it *Eroica* – the Heroic,' said Davantier, 'but tore up the dedication after his coronation.'

'Can't say I blame him!' grunted Laroche. 'Would have done the same myself!'

Teofil himself was the subject of a certain curiosity as a Polish *szlachcic* who chose to fight for France as a common soldier. He was considered to be the result of the perfect Napoleonic ideal. Some of the officers had seen the same action as Teofil at Jena, which was cause for some nostalgic recollections. Others were in Warsaw in 1807 to see Napoleon establish the Grand Duchy, as was Teofil.

The presence of Teofil led to speculation about the future of the Polish nation.

'Personally, I think they will turn the Duchy or Warsaw into a Russian puppet state,' said Davantier. 'There's a rumour that the Tsar will be crowned King of Poland.'

'I understand from my brother, that you served in the Russian campaign, *Monsieur le Comte*,' said Eloise Terrassin. Teofil's mind had only been half on Napoleon and other military matters through the thick and thin of five courses and endless small-talk, for Eloise Terrassin, who had been placed next to him at the table, was certainly a distraction.

He had accepted Terrassin's invitation at face value, as an agreeable social event; and he had not even considered the possibility of Mademoiselle Terrassin being a stunningly beautiful woman in her mid-twenties. Her thick, auburn hair was gathered up to crown a face of perfectly classical proportions. Her eyes, alert and intelligent and of a green that suggested new springtime foliage, sparkled seductively in the light of the myriad candles flickering in the candelabra on the table, and matched her full dress of emerald Lyonnais silk edged with *guipure* lace. Her nose was straight, yet with a hint of pertness that betrayed a sense of fun, perhaps suppressed by the constrictions of a formal event. Her lips were full and red, and matched the Burgundy wine that she held poised momentarily at her lips. Her shoulders were bare, and the sculpted curve of her collarbones cast dancing shadows on her golden skin, suggesting life in a climate where the sun shines warmly.

'It was bitterly cold, Mademoiselle Terrassin, and memorable only inasmuch as that I would sooner forget it,' said Teofil his gaze penetrating the seductive green of her eyes. 'I would much rather speak of warm things!'

X

Teofil was very obviously smitten by Eloise Terrassin, a fact that did not escape anyone's notice at Czarne Lasy, both at the Manor and at the Lodge. Reactions were mixed. Świetlana suggested that, although Eloise was a very beautiful young woman, he should really set his sights on a nice Polish girl from a noble house. Old *Pani* Wisia found the whole thing terribly romantic, and her rejuvenation was plain to see as she tackled her daily chores with a twinkle in her eye and a song on her lips. It was almost as if she were herself in love, albeit by proxy, and she rejoiced in Teofil's evident happiness. As for Marcel, he was teased mercilessly by his peers at the Manor, and even the vehemently anti-royalist Captain Laroche regarded Teofil as a 'good aristocrat – every modern social circle should have one!'

Major Claude Davantier was the most creative tormentor. A week after the dinner, Teofil had arranged to go riding with Marcel and Eloise to Ojców Castle. It was a bright, dry morning, and although the weather was not yet warm, the bitter Siberian cold was gone for good. Teofil entered the spacious hall at the Manor just as Eloise and her brother were coming down the stairs, dressed in riding breeches. At the precise moment when Teofil's eyes met those of Eloise, the sound of Gluck's Dance of the Blessed Spirits filled the building. A moment later Claude appeared at the top of the stairs, playing the flute with exaggerated gestures of mock romance.

'Austrian music, sir?' hammed Marcel when Claude had finished. 'This will surely lead to rapiers at dawn, sir! What's wrong with Rameau or Gossec?'

Teofil and Eloise merely smiled, slightly embarrassed at this display of romantic Gallic banter. Neither was inclined to resent or deny that there was a mutual attraction between them that was bound to develop. Their body language, both towards each other and towards all the inhabitants of Czarne Lasy, suggested a devil-may-care recklessness which came naturally to Teofil. Eloise, he noted with pleasure, had more than a streak of the reckless about her, and often threw convention to the wind and spoke her mind more than was as yet accepted in a male-dominated post-Napoleonic European society.

Up till now, their assignations were simply walks in the grounds of the Estate, and two informal lunches. One was at the Lodge when Eloise was inspected and vetted with the traditional Polish attention to breeding and suitability by Świetlana. Eloise was later pronounced socially acceptable considering modern changing values, and French being preferable to any other foreign nationality.

The other lunch was at the Manor, hosted by Marcel himself, to which both Świetlana and her totally uncomprehending mother were invited. It was a disaster, as Granny Tatiana, first confused and then panic-stricken, began to howl hysterically during the meal that the Austrians were trying to poison her in her own house.

The ride to Ojców was good. The air was crisp and bracing as the three riders galloped off towards the north west. The undulating countryside was interspersed with woodlands draped across hilltops, or nestled cosily in the folds where the hems of hills met. For an hour the horses were tested to the full, and were not found wanting. Eloise had proved to be a formidable horsewoman with considerable skills, which she displayed to spectacular advantage during occasional forays into contests of speed, manoeuvre and jumping. Teofil, who had spent a large portion of his life in the saddle, was most impressed.

'Our family originates from the Camargue, where horsemanship is *de rigueur*,' said Marcel. 'Eloise has been riding almost as long as she has been walking.'

Now the horses, after a hard and testing gallop through a tangled obstacle course of a wood, were tired. Condensation issued like released steam from their flaring nostrils, as they picked their way slowly up a grassy slope. All three riders had shown off their respective equestrian skills, especially Teofil, who had been determined to impress Eloise in return.

There was now a lull in the competition for a pecking order in the saddle, and Marcel let up somewhat with regard to his function as chaperone to his sister, and rode on ahead. Teofil and Eloise read the signs and held back.

'Where did you learn to ride so, Monsieur?' said Eloise, her skin glowing from the freshness of the wind and her auburn hair now in some disarray and protruding from the constrictions of a voluminous scarf.

'I have ridden all my life,' replied Teofil. 'But it was Father Józef who taught me recklessness when I was a boy. He is the only man alive who has maintained faith in me, even though he always regarded me as a faithless heathen!'

'Surely not!'

'I was a thoroughly unpleasant youth, and the bane of everyone's life,' continued Teofil, adding with a teasing twinkle in his eye, 'though you would never have suspected it, *Mademoiselle*, seeing this finely sculpted and perfectly mannered specimen of young – all right, fairly young – Polish *szlachta* seated proudly on a horse before you!'

'*Monsieur*, you are teasing me!' laughed Eloise.

'Naturally, *Mademoiselle*!' said Teofil. 'It is my long-established technique to tease those women that I would wish to make love to!'

'Have you made love to many women during your travels, *Monsieur le Comte*?'

'I withhold my reply, *Mademoiselle*,' said Teofil with mock solemnity, 'lest I prejudice my chances of winning the hand of the woman I love!'

'May one know who that is?'

'One may not! Yet!' said Teofil conspiratorially. Then he called out to Marcel and pointed over his head. 'Marcel! Look! Ojców!' He and Eloise broke into a canter and caught up with Marcel.

Ojców Castle was a dramatic keep, built into – and blended with – a rocky hilltop overlooking the valley of the little River Prądnik. Its tall tower was visible from afar, a beacon stabbing the clear blue sky for the approaching trio of riders. The long, winding valley was narrow and flat, and enclosed on either side by monolithic limestone crags, singularly imposing inasmuch as they were not very high. The Prądnik was swollen, babbling merrily down towards the Vistula, bloated with the thawing snows of the valley.

Below the Castle sprawled the village, no more than a hamlet of small, timber cottages. A winding path led up to the arched gatehouse, built into, and almost hidden by, a vast protruding boulder.

'King Stanisław August has stayed here,' said Teofil as the three peered through the iron gates into the courtyard within. A heavily wrapped figure of indeterminable age or sex, bent almost double, emerged and made its way to the gates with the aid of a walking stick. Only a pair of lustreless eyes were visible under the hood and scarves that bound the lower part of the face.

'Good day,' said Teofil. 'I am *Hrabia* Teofil Samojarski.'

'Who?' came a muffled shout from beneath the layers of cloth.

'Samojarski. I have come to pay my respects to *Pan Hrabia* Teofil Załuski!'

'Who?'

'*Hrabia* Teofil Samojarski.'
'*Pan Hrabia* Teofil?'
'Samojarski.'
'*Pan Hrabia's* not here! Go away!'
'No, I am *Hrabia* Teofil Samojarski!'
'Don't say! I know *Pan Hrabia* Teofil Załuski, and he's not here! Go away!'
'Will you be so good as to inform *Pan Hrabia* Teofil Załuski that *Hrabia* Teofil Samojarski of Sarenki is a guest at Czarne Lasy, the estate of the Princes Sczasny, and has called to pay his respects and hopes to call on him again one day soon?' yelled Teofil through the wrought iron gate.

'No, he isn't!' came the reply, now almost hysterical. '*Pan Hrabia's* gone away! You can't come in! Go away!'

'Look, will you listen to me, you deaf old…' Teofil searched for a mildly derogatory name that might cover both sexes, failed, and looked to his companions for help. Marcel was looking out over the valley, specifically nonchalant and uninvolved. Eloise had turned away and bowed her head, and was trying to suppress snorts of laughter into her hand, which she had placed over her nose. Teofil saw there was no point in pursuing the matter. 'Oh, never mind!' he muttered, turning away.

The inn in the village was more hospitable, even though it was little more than a hovel. The cabbage soup, stewed in much re-cycled pork fat and reinforced with chunks of bread on the verge of staleness, made a nourishing if not entirely appetising lunch. Teofil had learned the hard way not to be too fussy about what he ate, and Eloise looked upon it as a gastronomic adventure, to be savoured and put down to the overall experience of palate-broadening travel. She dismissed Teofil's apology for the Polish rural cuisine, and ate with relish. Only Marcel found the fare disgusting, and transfixed his portion with a look of undisguised distaste, and poked it round the bowl a few times before abandoning it, no doubt to be scooped back into the cauldron after their departure. He reserved his appreciation for the very adequate local vodka.

Conversation revolved round the excellence of the ride, the dramatic beauty of the valley and the evident deafness of whoever it was that passed for a caretaker at Ojców Castle. The afternoon saw the three companions riding further into the valley, following the River Prądnik, till they came to a small timber chapel, painted a light brown, built on stilts and supports over the stream, like a bridge.

'Oh look!' cried Eloise excitedly. 'What a delightful chapel! It's like a church in miniature!'

The trio dismounted and looked round. The interior was covered in rough carvings and simplistic pictures – all on religious themes. Above the simple altar hung a bas-relief, made of beaten plates of roofing tin of the Virgin Mary cradling baby Jesus – obviously modelled on the famous Our Lady of Częstochowa. A brightly painted wooden statue of the Virgin Mary dominated a small side altar. Carved wall panels with pictures inside emulated the ornate panels found in most European churches and cathedrals, the only hints of Baroque influence in an otherwise folk-oriented church.

There were pews for maybe twenty-five worshippers. Marcel knelt, crossed himself and bowed his head in prayer. Teofil and Eloise walked round, admiring the crude but distinctive peasant art and craft. A small, framed painting by the door caught Teofil's attention, only because it showed a deer. An incongruous painting for a church, but which recalled Sarenki. A close inspection revealed the signature in the bottom right-hand corner: Mat. Samojarski.

'The devil…' grunted Teofil before stopping himself. Marcel and Eloise came up. 'It's one of my grandfather's!'

Teofil recounted the tale of how Grandfather Mateusz first

came to Sarenki, and painted the deer that gave the village its name. He told of his art, and how his paintings had become dispersed throughout eastern Europe, both legally and otherwise. He compared the little chapel to the church of St Francis of Assisi in Sarenki, built largely by Mateusz himself with the help of a younger, more idealistic Father Józef.

'But this picture may be one of the stolen ones!' cried Eloise. 'You should make enquiries!'

Teofil led the way out of the chapel. 'Can you think of a better place for it than a little chapel on a stream in the valley?' he said.

There was no immediate reply. Then, as the three companions mounted for the ride back to Czarne Lasy, Eloise said, 'Perhaps I shall have a chance to visit Sarenki, before I return to France, *Monsieur le Comte*?'

'Would your brother think it amiss, if you were to call me Teofil?'

Marcel, who had spent the day silently questioning his own role of being specifically superfluous to what was obviously developing into a romantic relationship, pretended not to hear.

'Even if he did, I would allow him no say in the matter!' came the reply. 'And you must call me Eloise.'

'In that case, Eloise, I shall ask Marcel's permission to invite you to Sarenki at the earliest opportunity!'

'Did you hear that, Marcel?' cried Eloise excitedly.

'What?' muttered Marcel absent-mindedly.

'You heard! Teofil – *Monsieur le Comte* Teofil – has invited me to Sarenki!'

Marcel dithered, and Teofil cast him a diplomatic lifeline. 'Both of you, naturally!'

'Yes, of course. How kind.'

Teofil noted the unlaundered look that Eloise cast him.

XI

It was a beautiful April morning, and the trees were a mottled orgy of different greens vying for attention with the whites and pinks of apple, plum and cherry blossom. *Pani* Wisia conceded that winter was over, and served a breakfast of scrambled eggs on the veranda.

'I think I'll go into Kraków,' said Świetlana. Teofil looked at her in surprise. It was not like his mother to take such initiatives. She had spent the past few years in virtual seclusion, shunning society and only venturing beyond the confines of the estate on occasional long walks in the surrounding countryside.

'But you haven't gone to Kraków for years, *Mamusiu*!' he said.

'Then it's about time I did,' came the reply. '*Pani* Wisiu!' *Pani* Wisia's step was lighter than ever and she almost bounded out onto the veranda. 'Go up to the house and arrange for a carriage. I wish to go into Kraków!'

Pani Wisia's face fell in astonishment. 'But, *Pani hrabino*! Is this wise? You haven't gone to Kraków for years! The carriage has not been used since Napoleon came to Warsaw. It must be in a state of serious disrepair!'

'Then go and have it inspected by the French!' ordered Świetlana with an uncharacteristic air of authority. 'And if it's no good, then try and borrow one.'

'But who will drive?'

'Ask the French to lend me a soldier or hire a peasant! Or I'll drive it myself! Anything! I just want to go into Kraków!'

An hour later an open two-seater carriage drew up outside the

Lodge. Marcel Terrassin jumped down and entered. He was met under the portico by Świetlana, dressed for an outing.

'I understand the Countess wishes to go into Kraków?' said Marcel, kissing her hand. 'I would consider it an honour if she would allow me to drive her. I, too, have a mind to visit Kraków – it is such a beautiful morning, *n'est-ce pas?*'

'You are very kind, Lieutenant,' said Świetlana, 'but I could not possibly impose on your goodness! A common soldier perhaps – '

'Nonsense, *Madame la Comtesse*, I have business in Kraków anyway, and I rejoice that the weather will make my duty all the more agreeable, as indeed, will be the pleasure of your company!'

'You are so persuasive, Lieutenant,' smiled Świetlana, climbing into the carriage, assisted by Marcel at his most gallant. 'I accept!'

Pani Wisia had installed Granny Tatiana in an armchair that Teofil had lugged out of the house and placed on the lawn so as to afford her a lovely view of the blossom-laden trees lining the track. Teofil smiled with satisfaction as he watched the buggy disappear down the tree-lined track. It was good that his mother had begun to live again.

'Is Świetlana going to the ball in Kraków?' said Granny Tatiana, waving at the buggy.

'She will be the belle of the ball, *Babciu!*' smiled Teofil.

'That is good,' came the reply. 'She should not mope about the house so. It is good for her to get out and about in society. Will the King be there?'

'He will be the first to ask her to dance the Polonaise, *Babciu.*' Teofil had learned to humour the old lady, and give a living dimension to her fantasies, unearthed from a better, finer past such a long age ago. He smiled at her, drinking in the adoration that glowed faintly in her tired old eyes, patted her shrivelled, freckled hand affectionately, turned and went indoors.

He thought it was time to write to Maurice. It was now almost a month since he had left Sarenki, and in all that time he had not got round even to letting his friend know that he was still alive. He settled down at the table in the drawing room, prepared pen, ink and paper. 'Czarne Lasy – April 1st 1814,' he wrote. '*Mon cher* Maurice…'

He placed the pen against his teeth and stared at the wall. There was so much to write, so many thoughts to express, he did not know where to begin. The episode at Nowy Sandec, the appearance of Father Józef, Czarne Lasy, his mother and grandmother, Marcel Terrassin – Eloise Terrassin. Once again Teofil found the thought of Eloise distracting, and he was unable to formulate his opening sentence. He also found added distraction in the sounds of *Pani* Wisia cleaning and sweeping winter's legacies from the verandas, and his mind began wandering. Having acknowledged to himself that his concentration was in tatters, he put down the pen, rose and went out into the welcoming sunshine. A stroll round the grounds might help to focus the mind. A hundred yards down the track he met Eloise coming in the opposite direction. She stopped abruptly, and then continued indecisively, almost as if she were caught trespassing in a place forbidden to her.

'Such a beautiful day,' she stammered, 'I thought perhaps a stroll; I was trying to write a letter to my parents. I could not think what to write…'

'What a coincidence!' laughed Teofil. 'I, too, have been having trouble with a letter to Maurice!'

'What a coincidence!' echoed Eloise.

'Perhaps we might walk together awhile?' said Teofil.

'Marcel has gone to Kraków.'

'With my mother.'

'A beautiful day to go to Kraków.'

They walked on in silence towards the Lodge. Granny Tatiana had dozed off and did not see them approach. *Pani* Wisia did, however. A ghost of a smile fleeted across her cracked lips.

'May I offer you a cup of coffee?' said Teofil. 'I usually have one at about this time.'

'Thank you,' said Eloise. 'I would like that.'

'Bring us some coffee, please, *Pani* Wisiu,' said Teofil. 'We'll take it on the garden table by the summerhouse.'

Pani Wisia brought a tray of freshly ground coffee and *babka* cake to the wooden garden table at the back of the Lodge. She positively radiated goodwill as she poured out two cups.

'I'm afraid I shall have to leave you now, *Panie hrabio*,' she said, with a twinkle in her eye that she failed to conceal. 'Today is laundry day. But I shall be back by 2 o'clock to serve dinner. Will *Panna* Eloise be staying to dinner?'

Eloise opened her mouth to speak, but was pre-empted by Teofil. '*Panna* Eloise will be dining with me.'

Pani Wisia's eyes glazed momentarily before departing. They watched as the housekeeper hoisted the linen basket onto a small two-wheeled cart, and disappeared pulling it round to the front of the Lodge. For a good while they nibbled at the *babka* and sipped the coffee in silence, listening to the birds setting themselves up excitedly for the season's nesting and breeding.

'It is so peaceful here,' said Eloise, listening to a pair of early bees exploring for flowers. 'I shall be very sad to leave Poland when the time comes.'

'Perhaps there will be no need for you to go,' said Teofil.

'What do you mean?'

Teofil bit his lip thoughtfully. 'I would very much like you to see Sarenki.'

'I thought that was already agreed.'

'I would very much hope that you will like Sarenki, Eloise.'

'I'm sure I will,' laughed Eloise, rising. She strolled over to a solitary cherry tree and broke off a small sprig of blossom, which she put to her nose.

Teofil followed her. She was wearing the same emerald dress that she had worn the very first time that they had met, up at the Manor. Again, Teofil noticed how the dress harmonised perfectly, this time with the pink blossom. He took the sprig from her hand and wove it carefully into her hair. Eloise allowed him to do it. She had lowered her green eyes demurely, and was trying not to breathe heavily, although her heart was beating with an excitement that she had not known before. Apart from Teofil's fingers in her hair, there was no physical contact between them – and yet they were so close that it needed only a touch, a look, even a breath – to unleash the pent-up passions of the past two weeks, for too long thwarted by the impositions of etiquette. Marcel had performed his duty as chaperon to his sister, and it was obvious that he did so unwillingly. Now, by chance, he was not here. Nor was Teofil's mother, who made no secret of taking her own chaperoning duties very seriously. Her eagle eye was omnipresent, like a lurking conscience, to frustrate any attempt to so much as take Eloise by the hand in any way that was not entirely correct. Granny Tatiana was an unknown quantity. She might be senile, and unaware of what was going on around her, but could still let drop an unfortunate remark within the wrong earshot.

Only the wildly romantic *Pani* Wisia could be trusted to engineer a favourable situation. In her eyes Fate had decreed that Teofil and Eloise should become romantically entwined, but it seemed to her that Fate was being foiled at every turn, and needed a good prod. Consequently, she had bided her time patiently, and had deemed the time ripe to strike. Teofil knew perfectly well that laundry day was tomorrow, and yet she had gone to the trouble of staging some singularly capricious theatre so that the lovers would be in a position to effect Fate's decree.

Teofil's fingers flitted from Eloise's hair down her smooth cheek to her chin, and lifted her face to his. Slowly she raised her eyes and looked deeply into his.

'Your eyes are like the richest emeralds from the New World,' he whispered. 'You are so beautiful, Eloise!'

Slowly their lips met. The kiss, at first tender and tentative, quickly became hard and fierce, as the passion pent up in their hearts gushed furiously between them. Teofil held her tightly, his feelings wildly and exquisitely out of control, his mouth hungrily seeking out every part of her beautiful face. He kissed her forehead, her eyes, her cheeks, and returned to her moist lips for more.

Je t'aime! he gasped. 'Eloise, I love you so much!'

Je sais.

Teofil's hand sought and found hers. He held it tightly, while at the same time he slid down onto his knee, put his cheek against her belly, and kissed her hand passionately. His heart was beating uncontrollably.

'Eloise,' he whispered, gasping for breath. 'Will you – would you…?'

'Yes?'

'Would you – marry me?'

Eloise disentangled herself and laughed.

'Dearest Teofil!' she cried at the sky. 'You know I will!'

'And you will come to Sarenki with me?'

'Yes, yes!'

'We'll get Father Józef to marry us!'

'That should be fun!'

Teofil grabbed Eloise to him, lifted her up and swung her round and round, laughing with sheer abandon. This turned into the stately walking step of a polonaise, with Teofil bellowing out one that was popular at the time. Eloise recognised it and joined in, imitating the open-throat shout-singing that was a feature of some Polish folk songs. She rested her hand on Teofil's proffered elbow, while they promenaded with mock majesty round and round the garden table. All convention was cast to the warm springtime breeze, and they became like uninhibited children without a care in the world.

The idyll was suddenly interrupted by a figure coming round the Lodge. Teofil and Eloise aborted their wild polonaise like children caught doing something naughty.

'Maurice!' cried Teofil in amazement when he saw who it was. 'What in heaven's name…?'

Maurice looked as though he had been in a battle. His riding outfit was torn and dirty, his hair was dishevelled, and he had several days' growth of beard, giving him a villainous appearance that startled Eloise. He wore a hunted look, and it was obvious that the prank that he had interrupted held no meaning for him whatever.

'Teofil!' he cried, desperation in his voice. 'I'm glad I've found you! I haven't heard anything from you since you left.'

'I started writing this morning…'

'Never mind that now. You've got to get back to Sarenki!'

'Why? What's happened?' Teofil walked up to him, held him by the shoulders and looked him over in horror. 'Maurice, you look terrible!'

Maurice looked round. His eyes rolled manically until they finally rested on a very startled Eloise. 'I'm sorry,' he said. 'I seem to have interrupted – a celebration, perhaps?'

'Eloise, I would like you to meet Maurice Chavelet, my very good friend and companion-in-arms. Maurice, this is Mademoiselle Eloise Terrassin.'

Maurice's hunted look left him as he took Eloise's hand and kissed it. '*Enchanté, Mademoiselle*,' he said. 'And what is a beautiful French girl doing here in Kraków?'

'My brother is stationed here at Czarne Lasy,' replied Eloise. 'He is an officer of the French army of protection.'

'Then I shall look forward to making his acquaintance.'

Maurice turned back to Teofil. 'We need to talk, Teofil. *Excusez-nous, Mademoiselle.*'

'Before we do,' interrupted Teofil, 'I think you should know something. May I tell him, Eloise?'

'Of course.'

'A few moments ago,' said Teofil, 'Mademoiselle Terrassin agreed to be my wife. I'm afraid our celebration had become a little – uninhibited. I'm sorry.'

There was a stunned silence. Maurice's hunted look returned. He strode nervously back and forth, looking this way and that, as if he were in a turmoil of indecision.

Then he stopped and turned to Eloise. 'Forgive me, *Mademoiselle*,' he said. 'You must think me unforgivably rude.' He took her by both hands, and kissed them. 'Please accept my most heartfelt congratulations! I am so happy for both of you, and I only hope I shall be in a position to observe your happiness myself in the years to come.'

'What do you mean?' said Teofil.

'We need to talk, Teofil, you and I. And, of course, Mademoiselle Terrassin. What I have to recount now concerns you as well.'

Part Two

I

On the morning of the day that Teofil left for Czarne Lasy along the northern track, three men rode into Sarenki from the east. The day, only just broken, was overcast and bitterly cold, and they were dressed – rather, wrapped up – for maximum warmth. All three wore the long greatcoats of Napoleon's Grande Armée. Their faces, what could be seen of them under swathes of cloth, were unshaven and raw from the biting wind that blew across the Beskid. They had evidently been riding all night. They made straight for the Church, where they were met by Father Józef who was sweeping the floor.

'Welcome!' he leered. 'We don't see many visitors passing through. Can I help you?'

'Are you the priest?' said the first.

'I'm Father Józef, the parish priest. This is my church, the Church of St Francis of Assisi.'

'What is this place?' replied the man, who was evidently the spokesman. The other two merely kept their distance and said nothing.

'Sarenki. Where are you bound for?'

'Hungary. We just need somewhere to hole up for a while.'

'Merciful Jesus!' growled Father Józef conspiratorially, 'are you on the run from the law?' The three looked at one another nervously. Father Józef read the signs, and became suspicious. 'What have you done?' he growled.

'You don't need to know that, priest.'

Father Józef did not like this mode of address. He drew himself up to his full size and transfixed the spokesman with a hard stare. 'You'd better play your cards right, my lad, and tell me exactly what's going on,' he snarled, 'or I'll beat the shit out of the three of you before feeding your balls to the wolves with you still attached to them. And if you so much as raise a finger against my person, me being a servant of…' he waved his fist at the ceiling '…the almighty and everlasting God, the whole village will tell on you! And you don't call me priest, you call me Father! Understand?'

The other two remained still, but the spokesman was taken aback by this outburst. Again, he looked nervously at his companions, but no expression was discernible under their wraps. Finally, the spokesman spoke. 'There's been an assassination. The Imperial Inspector of Agriculture. Count Leopold von Loebl.'

'Jesus! Did you do it?'

The spokesman hesitated before answering. 'No.'

'You're lying!' cried Father Józef.

'There were witnesses who say they saw three Napoleon veterans. They're looking for French uniforms and arresting anyone connected with the Grande Armée.'

'Jesus Christ! Teofil!' hissed Father Józef under his breath. Then, to the three, 'Wait outside!' He went to fetch his horse, and led the three riders to the Manor. Maurice was there, tousle-haired, unshaven and bleary-eyed, pumping water into a bucket from the well in the courtyard.

'Maurice,' said Father Józef. 'I want you to look after these three. The Austrians are after them, and they need somewhere to hole up for a while.'

'Why, what have they done?' yawned Maurice. It was obvious that he had only just got up, and was not yet ready to face the day.

'Nothing. That's the point.'

'Then what are they supposed to have done?'

The spokesman said, 'They think we killed the Inspector of Agriculture.'

Maurice looked up, and noted the greatcoats. 'I'd have done it myself if I knew he was in town. Grande Armée?'

The other nodded.

Maurice sniffed. 'How long?'

'Till they get tired of looking.'

'That could take weeks!'

'Please, can you help?'

Maurice rubbed his neck and winced. 'You'll need to get rid of those,' he said, pointing to the coats. 'All right. Follow me.'

'I'll leave them in your hands. God will repay!' said Father Józef excitedly.

'I hope so!' called Maurice after him as he turned his horse and galloped off. 'The roof's leaking again!'

Maurice installed the three men in an annexe that had not yet been cleared out. He showed them the stables, gave them each a straw palliasse, told them where to find wood for a fire, a broom, and left them to their own devices. The spokesman nodded his gratitude, and the three of them moved in. Soon smoke was seen issuing from the chimney, suggesting that the three men had made themselves as comfortable as circumstances would allow.

In the meantime, Father Józef returned to his cottage only to gather together some extra clothing, a chunk of bread, a sausage and a water bottle filled with Old Pankracy, called to *Pani* Marynia not to expect him back too soon, and galloped off in Teofil's wake. In cases of treason, it was local policy to round up hundreds of suspects who might conceivably be guilty, imprison some and execute others. It was hardly justice, but it was effective in keeping down the political crime rate. Most acts of treason were counterproductive, and unpopular; insurrection and revolution were one thing, but assassinating the Inspector of Agriculture – a totally innocent official with no political significance – seemed a pointless act that only made matters worse.

Teofil was in mortal danger. He still had his Napoleonic greatcoat, and he made no secret of his days in the Grande Armée. If he were taken for questioning, he would definitely be suspected, especially if he should fall into the hands of Captain Jerzy Grocholski, the sadistic Polish psychopath who had sold himself body and soul to the Austrians. As Chief of Security at Nowy Sandec he enjoyed – literally – the privileges of absolute power within his limited sphere of jurisdiction. By merely letting him be, the authorities could count on order in the area. Grocholski was a big shark in a small pond.

Father Józef found himself in two minds about the three strangers. Firstly, he harboured a sneaking regard for anyone who struck a blow against those that 'ground the faces of the innocent into the mire', even if it meant killing. He was almost certain that they were guilty, despite their spokesman's rather unconvincing denial. On the other hand, he cursed the trio for what they almost certainly did, because he knew that many people would die needlessly as a result, including possibly Teofil.

Teofil's tracks were not hard to follow, and at midday he saw Nowy Sandec from the top of a hill. Pausing awhile, he caught a glimpse of a horseman making for the river below at a gallop, pursued by two riders from the direction of the town.

'*Z kurwy syn!* Son-of-a-bitch!' growled Father Józef, spurring his horse once more into action. 'They don't waste much time!'

Meanwhile, back at Sarenki, the three fugitives weren't seen again till the following morning, having presumably caught up with a great deal of lost sleep. Maurice was at the well as usual, pumping water, when the spokesman emerged from the annexe, looking even more scruffy without the greatcoat. He was dark, slim and of medium height, and his luxuriant stubble almost qualified as a beard. In a different set of circumstances, he might have been strikingly handsome, but his unkempt appearance combined with a frightened, hungry demeanour gave him an air of menace. He was followed at a nervous distance by the other two.

'Sorry about all this, squire,' the spokesman said, scratching under his arm. 'We've all had a hard time!'

Maurice was unwilling to allow himself to get too involved. Like Father Józef, he knew perfectly well that they had done it. He had met a lot of freedom fighters in his time, and could spot them within range of the whites of their eyes. And now he was after a quiet life. He rinsed his head under the icy water spurting from the spout. 'Think nothing of it,' he muttered.

'You French?'

'Depends who wants to know.'

'I do.'

'Who are you?'

'Boris.'

'Boris who?'

'Just Boris.'

'Russian?'

'Russian Jew. From Minsk.'

Maurice rubbed himself down with a towel. 'Then yes, I'm French.' He made for the door without looking at them.

'Louis's French.' One of the others stepped forward and barred his way at the door. He was a big man, with close cropped black hair, piggy eyes and a sallow face covered in stubble. 'Don't cross him or he'll break your legs.'

'Thanks for the warning.' He turned to his countryman, pushed him gently out of the way with the back of his hand and went into the house. 'Ça va?'

'*Ouay*,' said Louis expressionlessly.

The others followed him into the kitchen. The warmth was exquisitely welcome, and there was a pot of coffee in the grate. The third member of the trio shuffled up. He was a small, wiry man with beady eyes that darted from one person to another with almost manic precision.

'This is Jacek. He's Polish. He can read too,' said Boris.

'How do you do,' said Jacek nervously, shaking Maurice by the hand. 'Jacek Skopyta. I'm from Białystok. Delighted to make your acquaintance, *Monsieur...*' He looked questioning, but Maurice was not giving anything away. Jacek turned to the fire. 'Coffee! What a beautiful aroma! Reminds me of when I served in Bosnia!'

'Any chance of a cup?' said Boris. Maurice waved his hand at the pot indicating that they should help themselves. There were four cups on the table. The three wasted no time in accepting the invitation.

'Have you got any money?' said Maurice.

'We can pay.'

Maurice put another log on the fire, then turned to the larder and brought out a loaf of bread, which he placed on the table beside the cups.

'Then I'll get you some *kasha* and a pot of *smalec*.'

'No *smalec*,' said Boris. 'Pork fat. Not kosher.'

'Suit yourself.'

'I prefer to.'

Maurice began to positively dislike Boris. His manner seemed designed to annoy. But then, he did not want to become involved. 'You can have some bread and coffee now. But let's get one thing clear. If you're on the run I don't want anyone in the village asking questions. You're here because Father Józef says so, and what Father Józef says goes in this village. But I want you out of this house at the earliest opportunity.' He turned to Louis menacingly. '*Compris?*'

'Ouay.'

The visitors breakfasted hungrily.

'Did anyone see you arrive?' said Maurice.

Boris shrugged, but Jacek said, 'Someone is bound to have seen us! And if they have, they'll certainly ask questions!'

Jacek was right. Word quickly spread that three strangers were holed up at the Manor, and soon questions were indeed being asked, especially as the three kept themselves to themselves and never ventured out into the village. Maurice had agreed to buy their food for them from the village, and was asked endless questions in the process, to which he could not find any answers that would satisfy the curiosity of the villagers.

'They're Russians on the run,' he explained to Lenka when they met in the village. 'They say they're freedom fighters from Lithuania. I don't really know. I don't want to get involved.'

'I hope they go soon,' she said. 'It makes me nervous – having strangers like them around!'

Then there was the question of Father Józef's sudden departure. Speculation was rife that it was connected with the three strangers. Sunday came and went, and the villagers became concerned. Father Józef had never once let them down. Sunday Mass had always been the one immovable feature of Sarenki.

*****

A week after the trio's arrival Kazio Gruszka set off for Nowy Sandec. He usually rode there once a month on estate – or rather – his own private business, and stayed overnight with his cousin Antek. This time he wore a worried expression; he knew he would have to rein in his enterprises in the wake of Teofil's return. What was more, Teofil had gone off to see his mother, and would doubtless explain the discrepancies of the past thirteen years to her. Kazio was already in serious trouble, with the sword of Damacles hanging precariously over his head, and Teofil teasing the thread with his knife. He would definitely have to play his cards right over the next few months if he was to survive a scrutiny of his activities.

When Kazio Gruszka returned the following day, he was the bearer of news that he thought might just be the trump card he needed to claw his way out of his predicament.

'There's a warrant out for a gang who assassinated Count von Loeb, the Inspector of Agriculture!' he confided to his wife, Frania.

'Mother of God!' cried Frania. 'What happened?'

'He was going to Bochnia in his carriage. Apart from the Polish driver, he had his young Hungarian assistant with him. Half way there the carriage was ambushed by three armed men, who opened fire with pistols. They killed the Inspector with a bullet through his head, but the other two were only wounded, and left for dead after the men escaped.'

'But why?' said Frania, 'the Inspector is just a minor official. What did they hope to gain?'

'I don't know. It seems like a pointless murder.'

'There'll be trouble!' said his wife. 'They'll think it's political.'

'You can count on it,' said Kazio conspiratorially.

'Did the driver and the Hungarian have a description of the assassins?' said Frania.

'Their faces were covered,' continued Kazio, 'but they wore Grande Armée greatcoats.'

'Those three at the Manor wore French greatcoats!' said Frania nervously. 'Do you think it could be them?'

'I would count on it!' replied Kazio. Then he added, after a pause. 'Of course, it could be most unfortunate for *Pan hrabia* to be harbouring wanted criminals in his house.'

'But *Pan hrabia's* not here,' said Frania. 'He doesn't know about them.'

'Has that ever stopped the Austrians?' said Kazio.

That night, after supper, Kazio Gruszka sprawled in front of the blazing fire in the kitchen grate, lit a pipe and reflected long and hard.

'Tomorrow I shall go to Nowy Sandec,' he said at last.

Frania looked up from her knitting. 'But you've only just been, dear,' she said.

'There's a small matter that I forgot to attend to. I shall only be gone two days.'

'As you wish, dear.'

II

A second Sunday passed without Father Józef there to celebrate Mass, and some of the villagers of Sarenki, victims of years of indiscriminate indoctrination, were in mortal fear of losing their souls to the Devil. Old Staś the carpenter, who acted as self-appointed sacristan at the Church, called the village to prayer, in an attempt to stem the fury of God. He enlisted the help of Father Józef's regular altar boy, Little Irek, son of Big Irek, the pig farmer. With the conspicuous exception of the three strangers holed up at the Manor, as well as Maurice, the whole village turned out – if only to gossip and speculate on developments, to which was added the unexplained second departure of Kazio Gruszka to Nowy Sandec the day after his return from his first visit.

At noon on the Monday a posse of maybe a dozen horsemen rode into the village along the northern track, and made their way straight to the Manor. Most of the villagers saw their noisy and high-profiled arrival. They stopped whatever they were doing, and followed them nervously towards the Manor. As more and more joined their ranks, they found confidence in numbers.

The posse stopped in the courtyard of the Manor, and positioned themselves in a semi-circle around the entrance, rifles at the ready. Two of the riders then dismounted and made their way towards the door. The first was a heavily whiskered man in a grey greatcoat and a tall, red, four-cornered cap of the kind sported by the Polish military. His deputy who walked two paces behind him, held a rifle across his chest. He was clad in furs, and had a scarf across the lower part of his face.

'Great God!' muttered Old Pankracy, 'it's Grocholski and his deputy Filipowicz! There's trouble!'

Grocholski cupped his hands over his mouth, and shouted at the Manor. 'Count Samojarski!'

Almost immediately the door opened, and Maurice emerged, looking dirty and dishevelled, for he had been re-plastering the walls. He looked in astonishment at the riders. 'Count Samojarski's not here,' he said. 'What is this?'

'I'm Captain Jerzy Grocholski, Chief of Security at Nowy Sandec. I have reason to believe that Count Samojarski is harbouring traitors to the State in this house.'

'Count Samojarski left three weeks ago,' replied Maurice. The implications of this deputation clarified itself instantly in Maurice's mind, and he tried hard to think fast. 'There's no one here except me.'

'And who are you?' said Grocholski.

'I'm Maurice Chavelet. I'm responsible for restoring the Manor for *Pan hrabia*. As you can see, I'm covered in mud and dung!'

'So, you're in charge in Count Samojarski's absence?'

Maurice had no choice but to commit himself. 'I suppose you could say that.'

'Then I am saying it!'

'So, what do you want?'

'I wish to ascertain whether or not a gang of three murderers is sheltering in this house.'

'As I said, there's only me here.'

'Then you would have no objection if we conducted a search?'

'I have no authority to permit it, Captain,' said Maurice. He was beginning to curse Father Józef for having set up this situation, which he could see no way of circumventing. I would have to clear it with *Pan hrabia* Samojarski.'

'In the absence of *Pan hrabia*,' said Captain Grocholski with a leer, 'I am authorised as an officer appointed by his Majesty Emperor Franz II to instigate a search of these premises!'

Before Maurice could answer, Grocholski signalled to his men, who promptly dismounted, formed into groups and made their way into the house, the stables and the outhouses. At a safe distance stood groups of curious villagers, milling around in a seething hive of indecision. Snippets of conversation hinted at a crowd divided between loyalty to innocent men being relentlessly pursued by the powers of oppression, to a need for security by volunteering information. The deciding factor was that no one knew who these strangers were. Were they, or were they not murderers? If they were indeed murderers, as the Captain had said, then whom did they murder? Besides, the Captain was well-known as a ruthless interrogator, and ingratiating oneself with him by telling him what he wanted to know might prove to be the wisest course to take.

The search did not take long. The arrival of the posse had taken the fugitives totally unawares, and they were dragged out into the courtyard, fighting to escape. Boris, seeing the futility of struggling, soon gave himself up to the fur-clad deputy Filipowicz, who promptly hit him across the mouth with his rifle butt. As Boris lay, stunned, on the ground, he received a series of hard kicks in the kidneys, in which several of the others gave a helping foot.

The fiercest fight was put up by Louis, whose powerful body galvanised itself monstrously into action. The three men who had chosen him as their quarry wished that they hadn't. Louis lashed out with deadly accuracy and awesome power, and his muscular arms, with hard hams for fists, packed a punch so ferocious that his opponents would not have thought possible. He kicked one assailant in the groin with such force that the man fell to the ground, where he remained, doubled up in agony and effectively out of the immediate fight. The burly peasant who had been holding him from the back was hurled over Louis' head. His skull struck the edge of the well noisily as he fell. He lay there, unconscious, while the third was virtually beaten and kicked to a pulp. A rifle lay where it had fallen, by Louis' feet. He picked it up and singled out Captain Grocholski, who had mounted his horse once more, and was supervising the raid from a position of advantage. But the Captain's interest lay at that moment in Jacek, and he did not see the weapon pointing directly at him from a distance of some six metres.

Jacek, who was obviously by far the least virile of the three, had broken free from his captor, and had set off at a sprint across the courtyard towards the two-metre-high stone wall, beyond which a small expanse of open ground led to an arm of the forest. Were he to reach the forest, he would stand a good chance of escape. His captor had been momentarily taken aback, before setting off in pursuit. Jacek, however, had proved fast on his feet, and had reached the wall well before his pursuer. With an agility that he probably was not even aware of himself, he had leapt onto the wall. Grocholski reached into his belt and drew his pistol. Jacek's arms reached over the top, with his legs flaying wildly as he tried to find a purchase to hoist himself over. He had managed to get one leg onto the top of the wall, as in a riding position, when a pistol shot rang out. Jacek's body lurched forward and stopped its frantic thrashing. He lay along the top of the wall, absolutely still. A trickle of blood made its way down the grey stonework. After a few moments, Jacek's body moved perceptibly, but his feeble attempt at crawling cost him his balance. He fell back onto the ground just as several shots rang out. Captain Grocholski, startled, turned just in time to see Louis' powerful body slowly crumpling to the ground, blood spurting from his face and chest. Beyond stood Filipowicz and two others. They had ceased their assault on the hapless Boris to see their chief in danger of his life. They had probably fired with less than a second to spare.

Grocholski acknowledged the debt with a barely perceptible nod, then turned his horse to the stone wall. Jacek was lying on his back, helpless and in pain, under it. He had fallen onto a jagged stone, and his spine was damaged. He was unable to move. Grocholski slowly rode up to Jacek and stared down at him. Jacek stared back, panting with terror.

Grocholski turned his horse again. It was a magnificent white Lipizaner, obviously a gift from a grateful Imperial source in Vienna. It was Grocholski's pride and joy, as well as being a symbol, in the eyes of the people, of the Chief's allegiance to the foreign oppressor. Grocholski knew this, and used the fact for psychological advantage. He now made the beautiful animal perform a series of tricks, such as walking on his hind legs, walking backwards, dancing and turning in a small circle. His control over his mount was, to an impartial observer, a splendid sight. All the while he was watching Jacek with a hint of a smile on his whiskered face. After a few minutes Jacek began to wonder what the reason was for this equestrian posturing. His answer came in the grand finale to Grocholski's act. The horse, confused and panic-stricken by a series of conflicting orders, shouts and jabs from his master's spurs, apparently lost control over his actions, and became seemingly unaware of the human being on the ground.

While alternating very quickly between standing on hind legs and kicking with them, the horse was guided onto the prostrate body beneath the stone wall. Jacek screamed in agony as he was repeatedly trampled by the horse's panicking hooves. When the horse finally realised what was happening and laid off with a terrified whinny, Grocholski looked again at the body. From their vantage point beyond the gates the villagers stood in deathly silence, gazing with awe and horror at what they had seen.

'What kind of a man is it who can get a horse to trample a human to death?' said someone.

But Jacek was still alive, although only able to whimper, as he had lost the strength to scream. Grocholski drew his pistol and aimed at Jacek's head. 'Frenchman!' he called, without looking up.

'That means you,' muttered Filipowicz to Maurice.

Maurice had also watched the scene with a mixture of horror and abject terror. Was he next on the hit list of this callous monster? He went up to Grocholski.

'Some trick,' he said.

'I know more.'

'What do you want?'

'Just to tell you that harbouring traitors is a serious offence, and that you are going to learn the hard way just how serious.'

'The C-count...' stammered Maurice, his mind unable to seek a way out without incriminating his friend.

'...is not here to save your greasy French skin!' cried Grocholski. 'I called you over because I want this murderous scumbag to apologise to you before I kill him for having landed you in the shit by foisting himself in your house!'

'This is not my house!'

'Tell that to the Emperor!' laughed Grocholski, his pistol still pointing at Jacek's head. He turned to his victim. 'Say sorry to the greasy Frenchman.' Jacek began gibbering incoherently. Through his mumblings a few words of apology were just discernible. 'Good. The Frenchman accepts,' said Grocholski. He then took careful aim, and broke into a smile before shooting a still gibbering Jacek through the forehead.

In the meantime, Boris had regained consciousness and was writhing helplessly on the ground. He had witnessed the final moments of the Lipizaner's star turn, but his own agony had erased it largely from his mind. Grocholski rode over to him, and bade Maurice follow. Boris managed to get up into a kneeling position.

Grocholski stared at him long and hard. '*Shalom!*' he said finally, with a leer.

'Fuck off,' gasped Boris, clutching his sides.

'Only after I kill you. A nice Jewish virgin, I think. But before I do, you're to apologise to the greasy Jew-loving kosher Frenchman for having landed him in the shit.'

'Go to hell.'

Grocholski untied two loops of rope attached to his saddle, and threw them both to Filipowicz. The latter felled Boris again with his rifle butt, and as he writhed on the ground, he attached the two ropes to his ankles. Then Grocholski and Filipowicz attached the other ends to their respective saddles, and rode off side by side, at a gallop, dragging Boris behind them. As they rode out of the main gates, they scattered the horrified villagers. They rode through the fields beyond, side by side, describing a big arc, until they arrived back at the gates again. Maurice was there to meet them.

'Well, Jew?' cried Grocholski to Boris, who was moaning in agony. He was covered in blood and mud. 'Are you ready to apologise to the Frenchman?'

'Go screw a sow, if she'll have you.' The words were just discernible.

'Shame.' He turned to Maurice. 'You might have to forgo his Hebraic apology, Frenchman. He may not survive this one!'

The two horsemen set off once more round the field. This time they parted slowly as they rode side by side round the field until they were about two metres apart. Then they came together once more before arriving back at the gates.

'Oh dear,' said Grocholski, glancing casually at the heap of mangled meat at the ends of the ropes. Boris' body had been torn into two from the groin. 'The Jew didn't apologise to you before he died. That's Jewish manners for you.'

Grocholski looked around and smiled with satisfaction. Some of the villagers turned away and were sick. Others were surreptitiously making their way homewards. Most were milling about in a daze, not knowing how to deal with a situation such as this. If only Father Józef were here.

Filipowicz released the ropes from Boris' ankles. The crowds watched in silence as he then tied Maurice's wrists together behind his back, then tied a noose around his neck. The other end of the noose was attached to his saddle. 'The walk to Nowy Sandec will do you good. Fall, and you'll strangle yourself,' he whispered to Maurice.

When they were ready Grocholski turned to the crowd, like an opera star drinking in the accolade of his public. 'I should remind you,' he announced, 'that his Majesty Emperor Franz II expects law and order to prevail in all parts of his Empire! Lawbreakers, especially traitors, will be very severely punished. These three…' he glanced around at the human remains scattered in the courtyard '…were guilty of the murder of Count Leopold von Loebl, the Emperor's Inspector of Agriculture, whose strictly humanitarian brief was to instigate more efficient ways of producing food for all! For that he paid with his life. Added to their crimes was resisting arrest. They have paid the price. I thank those of you who helped in the arrest and execution of these traitors. They will be well rewarded for their loyalty to the Empire. Long live the Emperor!'

With that, the posse, with Maurice trotting along at the end of his tether, set off back in the direction of Nowy Sandec. The villagers, their faces blank with disbelief, watched them go.

'I wonder who it was that helped in the arrest and execution?' said someone.

'I think I've got a pretty shrewd idea,' came a reply.

III

'They took Maurice?' howled Lenka. 'Where did they take him?'

'Nowy Sandec,' said her grandfather.

Lenka had spent the morning baking bread and *babka* cake, and had missed the events at the Manor. Staś, who had witnessed the whole affair, hurried back to his cottage on the edge of the wood as soon as Grocholski's men had gone. He was shaking with shock at what he had seen, and was now trying to fathom out how he was going to break the news to Lenka. The brutal killings of three total strangers would be bad enough to describe, but for his grand-daughter the arrest of Maurice would be more directly distressing.

Ever since the evening when Maurice had come to supper for the first time Staś knew that Lenka was fond of him, possibly even in love. And Maurice, in turn, had made no secret of his fondness for Lenka. Staś had added a pinch of salt to Teofil's jokey remark that Maurice was 'a lewd and lascivious *roué* with a penchant for eighteen-year-old Polish girls with blonde hair and blue eyes.' He knew it was just Teofil's way of saying that Maurice was deeply struck by Lenka. His behaviour since then had certainly not been that of a lewd and lascivious *roué*, but of a decent, honourable man. He always asked Staś if he might walk with Lenka in the fields or in the forest, and Lenka often came to the Manor to help with light work, such as cleaning. When she returned Staś could tell by the glazed look in her eye and a certain swaying motion in her step that there was more to these assignations than cleaning. Besides, he had often seen them walking hand in hand, and exchanging kisses when they thought no one was looking.

Staś was in no doubt that his grand-daughter was indeed deeply in love.

He had listened often enough to Teofil's tales of their – particularly Maurice's – amorous adventures all over Europe and the eastern Mediterranean. At no time did Maurice treat Lenka as just another adventure. Staś liked Maurice, and Maurice, who had long ago lost all touch with his family, looked upon the old carpenter almost as a father, which was very important to Lenka. She was brought up by Staś ever since she was five, when both her parents – Staś' son and his wife – died within weeks of each other during a cholera epidemic that had swept Galicia at the turn of the century. Staś had doted hopelessly on his pretty and vivacious little grand-daughter, who had so delightfully compensated for the tragic loss of his only son.

And now, perhaps this rootless Frenchman will further compensate him as his surrogate heir. For if their relationship should lead to marriage, the three of them would without doubt find mutual support. Staś was a fiercely independent character, as were all his fathers before him, who had relied on the bounties of the forest for their livelihood right up to death. It would be against his make-up to impose himself on family in his declining years, but deep down he knew that Maurice and Lenka would always look after him, and that willingly.

But his primary concern was not for his own security but for Lenka's happiness; and that was about to be cruelly shattered. When her father broke the news to her, she was devastated, and could not stop crying.

'What has he done, *dziadziu*?' she wailed, tears dropping all over her unbaked bread, 'he had nothing to do with any of these murders! Why have they taken him away?'

'Don't cry, my little kitten,' soothed Staś, pressing her to him. 'Perhaps it will all come right in the end, when they discover he was innocent of the whole business.'

'When has that had any bearing on anything?' cried Lenka, suddenly very angry. 'Those villains can do what they like, with no one to stop them! Well, *dziadziu*, I'm telling you! I'm going to do something about it!'

With that she rushed out of the cottage.

'Wait, Lenka!' called Staś after her. 'For God's sake don't do anything…' but Lenka was gone '…silly.' He muttered this last word under his breath. There was no point in chasing after her. She could run like a deer, and he could only walk slowly. He sat down and contemplated the mess of dough and tears on the kitchen table. Best let her be, he thought, before considering the implications of the events of the past fortnight. The Beskid region of the Carpathians was mercifully remote enough to escape some of the worst upheavals in the Polish lands. Nowy Sandec, Bochnia, Jasło all have had their share of troubles, but Sarenki has been relatively trouble-free since the days of Mateusz and Ksawery.

That a gang of murderers chose Sarenki to hide in was unfortunate. That is, if they were indeed the murderers in question. That fact will probably never be verified. Did Maurice know? Was he knowingly harbouring wanted traitors? Or was he an innocent dupe who got caught up in a conspiracy? The mystery, he reflected ruefully, will most probably go into some shallow grave with him.

Whoever the fugitives were, one thing was certain. They were betrayed by someone in the village. Grocholski had publicly thanked those – how many were there? – who had helped. It was obviously calculated to sow suspicion in Sarenki, and to divide the populace. And whose side were these betrayers on? The answers will show a village divided. Already there were mixed feelings with regard to the return of *Pan hrabia* Teofil. Several baskets of illicit nest-eggs have gone bad, and some, like those of the Gruszkas, faced total ruin and possibly imprisonment. Some will look upon the fugitives as guilty of murder, and deserving of just punishment; others will see them as freedom fighters, and choose to seek out whoever betrayed them with revenge in mind.

Whichever way he looked at these questions, Staś's thoughts always turned to his neighbour. Did Kazio Gruszka go to Nowy Sandec just to tell Grocholski that there were three suspicious fugitives in Sarenki? Did he know who they were? Had he learned something from his previous visit to Nowy Sandec? News never reached Sarenki unless someone, usually Kazio Gruszka, actually brought it. Besides, ingratiating himself with Grocholski might stand him in good stead when dealing with the Count. He looked out of the window, from which he could see the Gruszka house. Frania Gruszka was quietly feeding the geese, unaware of the traumas of the day. Kazio had not yet returned from Nowy Sandec, and he wondered whether he should pay her a visit, and confront her with his suspicions; then he decided against it. He would bide his time.

The other villagers were less patient in their outlook. They congregated outside the Church to vent their anger, and the name of Kazio Gruszka was on everyone's lips.

'Where is the bastard?' someone asked.

'You don't know it was him!'

'And anyway, perhaps they were guilty of murder!'

'He was just a minister of agriculture, for God's sake!'

'That still didn't give Grocholski the right to make such a theatre out of the executions!'

'There was no trial!'

'When is there?'

The majority consensus was that Kazio Gruszka had learned about the murder of Count von Loebl on his first visit to Nowy

Sandec. He had gone back to report that three fugitives were in hiding at the Manor, an act of revenge, perhaps, against Teofil for having exposed his fraudulent activities. As such it had been a futile gesture, as Teofil had been absent. It was the innocent Maurice who had borne the brunt of the plot. He was well liked, and his arrest deeply shocked the community. His relationship with Lenka, which everyone knew about, was generally approved of, with the exception of the hopelessly love-struck Władek Górski, a tall, gangling youth who lived with his parents in a cottage adjacent to Big Irek's smallholding. Sarenki was a young village, and many of the inhabitants had arrived as displaced persons since the partitions. There was not the suspicion of incomers that prevailed in most long-established communities.

'There's nothing we should do until Kazio returns and answers a few questions.'

Kazio Gruszka returned late the following afternoon, but he was in no fit state to answer any questions. He was tired, slumped forward into the saddle of his horse, which ambled unhurriedly into the village as dusk began to fall. Big Irek was driving home to his farm in his ox-cart, accompanied by Little Irek, and was the first to see him approaching along the north track. He stopped his cart, jumped down and grabbed hold of the reins of Kazio's horse. Kazio himself was barely conscious. He was a mass of bruises and his face, hands and clothes were covered in blood, most of it clotted.

'Merciful Lord!' gasped Big Irek. He turned to his twelve-year-old son, who was still in his seat. 'Irek, drive home and tell mama what's happened! I must see *Pan* Kazio home!'

Little Irek, whose face was contorted with horror, delayed a good while before obeying. Still transfixed by the sight of the barely recognisable Kazio, he prodded the ox, and the cart creaked off once more and wobbled its way along the track. His father led Kazio's horse back into the village and up the slope towards the Gruszka house. Staś saw him coming and emerged from his cottage.

'Mother of God!' he said. 'What have they done to him?'

Staś and Big Irek helped a hysterical Frania undress and bathe Kazio before putting him to bed. He was in a terrible state. His whole body testified to systematic torture and beatings. Spasmodic yelps of pain in certain positions suggested broken bones, and Big Irek, used to the butchery of livestock, managed to diagnose a broken collarbone and several ribs.

No amount of coaxing would evince any explanation from Kazio, whose only utterances were incoherent moans issuing from a heavily swollen mouth. Night had already fallen by the time he drifted into a fitful sleep. His wheezy breathing became steady, and his nervous shudders ceased.

'I'll leave you now, *Pani* Franiu,' said Big Irek, 'but I'll be back in the morning. I'll borrow *Pan* Kazio's horse, if that's all right.'

'Yes, of course. Thank you, *Panie* Irku,' sobbed Frania. 'You've been such a help!'

Staś stayed on. All his thoughts of confrontation had been erased. This was beyond betrayal and the apportionment of blame. Kazio Gruszka, even if guilty, had won the right to Christian charity. No one deserved the kind of treatment that had been meted out to him, no matter what he did. Staś chose instead to sit with Frania, watching Kazio by the flickering light of a solitary candle. Then Lenka arrived, looking tired and flustered. She had gone off for a long walk to be alone with her thoughts, and it was already dark by the time she returned to the village once more.

'I saw *Pan* Irek,' she cried. 'He told me what happened! My God, *dziadziu*! What is happening to us?'

Staś looked at his grand-daughter and a tear liquefied in his eye and made its way slowly down a crease on his parchment cheek. He saw the portents; the future – Lenka's future – looked bleak.

Was it all starting again? Why did God put innocent people into this terrible land, and why did He give them the capacity to love it so? And why does he keep testing them beyond their capacity to endure? He gazed long and hard at Lenka, trying to think of something soothing to say, but a terrible weariness had descended upon him, and no words came.

*****

Late the following day Father Józef rode into Sarenki to find the whole place in a state of shock. Everyone had stopped work, and villagers were drifting about in a nervous daze.

'*Pani* Maryniu!' he cried, storming into his cottage. 'What in God's name has been going on around here?'

'You went away without telling us where you were going,' moaned *Pani* Marynia accusingly. 'Three weeks you left us without a priest, and the Devil came! That's what!'

'What Devil? What are you babbling about, woman?'

Father Józef found it difficult to follow *Pani* Marynia's account of events, interspersed as it was with curses and apocalyptic visions of Hell, as sent to the village by God. Father Józef's arrival, however, was observed by a number of villagers, and deputations began arriving at his cottage.

'Thank heavens you're back, Father!' said Old Pankracy, who had spent the past two days wandering round the village, talking to anyone who might listen. He had been loath to stay at home, because of the horrific images that kept visiting him.

'I'm glad you're home, Tata,' said Little Irek. 'I've missed serving at Mass.'

'Where the Devil have you been?' cried Big Irek. 'You've got some explaining to do, Father! All Hell's broken loose since you went away!'

Reactions to Father Józef's return were mixed. Some, like Old Pankracy, were merely glad to have him back, while others, like

Pani Marynia, were convinced that his absence left a void into which the Devil slid effortlessly to visit tribulation on the village. Others still, like Big Irek, questioned Father Józef's actions, and blamed him, at least partly, for what had happened. Everyone hoped, however, that Father Józef would soon sort everything out, as he had always done. The whole matter was thrashed out as thoroughly as the known facts allowed, including speculation that Kazio Gruszka was behind it all.

Father Józef, horrified at what had happened, was unable to find any answers. His usual bombastic manner had been completely blunted, as if he were not quite sure how to deal with this situation. 'I'd better go and see Kazio Gruszka,' he muttered.

'I'll take you,' said Big Irek.

As he walked with a very angry Big Irek up to Kazio Gruszka's house, he tried to explain that the reason for his departure was to warn Teofil of the possible danger which, as it turned out, happened to be very real.

'All right,' said Irek, 'so you saved Count Teofil from Grocholski. But why didn't you come back? You knew who those three were, and you installed them at the Manor! There's many around here don't think it was very clever, especially with *Pan* Maurice taken away.'

They had arrived at the Gruszka house, and a frantic *Pani* Frania came rushing out to meet them. Father Józef was relieved, as he had no answer to Irek's accusation either.

'Please, Father!' sobbed Frania, 'give him the Sacrament! He is dying!'

Father Józef stood over Kazio, and the two men stared at one another for a long time. Kazio looked dreadful, but he had regained consciousness, and was able to speak through his bruised mouth.

'Father…'

'Who did this to you?'

'Grocholski. And some others. Filipowicz...'

A seething rage enveloped Father Józef, and he fell prey to conflicting emotions.

'You bastard!' he cried. 'You rode to Nowy Sandec just to betray us all to Grocholski! You deserved everything you got!'

With that Father Józef stormed out of the house and back to his cottage.

IV

Father Józef's uncompromising attitude stunned the village. The consensus was that Kazio Gruszka had been guilty of going out of his way to betray three strangers who had asked for sanctuary, an act which led to some extremely distressing scenes. But now the betrayer was himself betrayed. Kazio's horrific injuries had turned accusation to pity, but not in Father Józef's book. Kazio Gruszka had been guilty of betrayal, and deserved punishment.

That's the side of Good.

At the same time, Father Józef felt guilty for having placed the fugitives in Maurice's care at the Manor, although he was loath to admit it, even to himself. He felt, in retrospect, that he did not have the right to demand this of Maurice. Their leader had spoken to him in confidence, and had admitted to – perhaps even boasted of – the crime. In his simplistic revolutionary thinking Father Józef had been impressed by their supposed act, yet at the same time his admiration was at odds with his religious thinking. Thou shalt not kill meant just that, even if it is done in the name of Good.

The following day Father Józef buried the three bodies in the graveyard behind the church. Just a few villagers attended the funeral, among them *Pani* Marynia, and her husband who had mercifully remained sober, Staś and Lenka. Big Irek had expressed his intention to attend, but farming matters were too pressing, so he sent his son with instructions to say a prayer for the repose of their souls.

Staś spent the next couple of days constructing a wooden cross to place at the head of the grave.

'What words shall I carve on it?' he asked Father Józef. Apart from Maurice, no one had any idea of the fugitives' names – and one of them, it was suspected, was Jewish anyway, to judge by Grocholski's anti-Semitic taunts.

Father Józef thought hard for a few moments. Then he said, writing it down for Staś, who could not read or write, 'Just write THE UNKNOWN PATRIOTS.'

Over the next few days Father Józef prowled around the village like a hungry wolf, and most of the villagers nervously gave him a wide berth. Two exceptions were *Pani* Marynia, who constantly demanded of him the immediate expulsion of the Devil and the re-instatement of God in the village, and Big Irek, who grabbed every opportunity to berate him.

'What about Count Teofil?' said the farmer, confronting him on the track. 'He is now well and truly compromised. Grocholski will not rest till he's got him. The least you can do is let him know what's happened. It must be you, you're the only one who can write.'

'All right, I'll write to him,' muttered Father Józef unconvincingly.

'When you've done that, I'll get Jan Staruch to ride to Bochnia and catch the post.'

But Father Józef did not write the letter. He always put it off till tomorrow. It was almost as if he hoped that the whole problem would just go away. His prevarications upset the villagers. They had always been used to his uncompromising guidance, and even accepted his present condemnation of Kazio Gruszka's actions. Kazio had committed a serious sin, and was guilty in the eyes of God. Earthly retribution had been made, and it was up to God whether there would be further spiritual retribution. Everyone lived by God's commandments as interpreted – often liberally – by Father Józef. He always had an answer to people's problems, even if they were wildly illogical, but at least they knew where they stood. Whatever his advice, it was accepted without question. Sarenki was a simple, sheltered world, where births, marriages and deaths were the highlights of a simple, sheltered existence. Life revolved around the soil, the forest and survival. Needs were basic, love came and went, and laughter alternated with tears.

That Sunday Staś rang the church bell as usual while Father Józef prepared for Mass. Little Irek, back in his role as altar boy, viewed Father Józef with some trepidation, having listened for three days to his father's disapproval of the priest. As usual, the whole village turned out but there was not the habitual air of jolly fraternising, as those who had not seen each other all week came together. Most people came early to gossip in front of the church, and afterwards generally visited friends to share a drink, or even a meal. This time it was different. There was a nervous, strained atmosphere. Everyone was anxious about the sermon. Kazio Gruszka was expected to be at the epicentre of an angry diatribe, even in his absence, for he was still laid low.

In the event, Father Józef's sermon concerned love for God's creatures, and leaned heavily on St Francis of Assisi. Quoting Genesis, he spoke of the beasts that had been placed on Earth for Man to have dominion over, and of Man's consequent responsibility towards them. He even dispensed detailed advice on the least distressing way of slaughtering livestock.

It was not a good sermon. Father Józef delivered it without his usual bombastic rantings. The villagers had become used to these, and expected them, even if they were laced with gruesome metaphors and colourful imagery. Instead, he droned on in a disjointed monotone, often repeating himself. Never once did he shake his fist at the roof and invoke the wrath of God in the guise of anything from a thunderbolt to a plague of frogs on evildoers, an act that generally amused and uplifted the righteous among his congregation. Furthermore, his advice on slaughtering pigs smacked of the sensational, and caused considerable unease, especially in the wake of the massacre at the Manor.

After Mass Father Józef stayed in his sacristy instead of meeting his flock, as was his custom. The villagers, sensitive to the atmosphere, just drifted back to their homes.

*****

The next day, exactly a week after the killings, Lenka disappeared. She went to bed early on the Sunday evening, but when Staś went to her room to wake her the following morning, she was gone. Staś shrugged his shoulders. Perhaps, he thought, she had risen very early to go into the forest, or maybe she could not sleep and had gone for a long walk. She missed Maurice dreadfully, and had spent the past week seeking solace in her own company. Staś had decided to let her be, reckoning that she would eventually get over the fact that Maurice would not be coming back. Grocholski was not in the habit of arresting people only to release them again.

At noon there was no sign of Lenka, and Staś ate dinner alone, still adhering to his idea that she just wanted to be left alone. However, as dusk descended and there was still no sign of his grand-daughter, he began to worry. It was already dark when he made his way down to Father Józef's cottage. *Pani* Marynia opened the door, with a candlestick in her hand. The candle cast a flickering shadow over her aged face, giving stark relief to the deep, rutted lines and making her toothless jowls look menacing and ugly.

Father Józef could shed no light on the matter of Lenka's disappearance, and what was more, he did not seem very concerned. Staś made his way back despondently to his cottage. There was a light flickering in the Gruszka house. Staś was tempted to call on the Gruszkas, but decided against it.

The killings had turned all village relationships upside down, and no one knew whose side anyone else was on. Even the sides themselves were indistinct. Staś had to force himself to enter his cottage, now so cold and empty, and a feeling of dread hanging over it. He went into his kitchen and sat down in the rocking chair that he had built himself fifty years ago, and stared into the glowing embers of the fire in the grate. How clever was Grocholski, he reflected, to have punished a whole village by sowing seeds of mistrust and enmity in a community which had lived – and cheated – together in perfect harmony.

And now his only reason for living, Lenka, had disappeared, and he was too tired, emotionally and physically, to speculate what might have happened to her. He had accepted that Maurice was gone, and now he was well on the way to accepting that, for some reason, he would never see his grand-daughter again. As he rocked gently forwards and backwards in his beloved rocking chair his thoughts went back to better days. He recalled Teofil's cradle, which also rocked. He was particularly good at building things that rocked. He wondered whatever had happened to Teofil's cradle.

That night, old Staś Sieńkowski died peacefully in his sleep. He was found the following day by Frania Gruszka, who had come to express concern, especially as Lenka was nowhere to be seen. She had heard that Lenka had disappeared. Staś was buried the day after by Father Józef, who knew exactly where to find the coffin and the wooden cross that Staś had built for himself many years ago.

The main question on everyone's lips was where was Lenka. On the Thursday two clues to the mystery presented themselves. Firstly, her distinctive woolly pixie hat was found just outside the gates of the Manor. Secondly, Maurice's stallion, Robespierre, had been missing from the stables at the Manor since the Monday. After the killings four horses remained there, Robespierre and the three belonging to the fugitives. If he had thought of it, Grocholski would probably have 'confiscated' all four horses. No one knew what to do with them, so Father Józef decreed that they should stay put for the time being, and placed them in the care of Henryk, the twelve-year-old son of Jan Staruch, a slow witted but very willing peasant who did odd jobs in the village and the outlying farmlands.

Equally slow-witted Henryk, who was mad about horses, had spent most of his time hanging about the stables ever since Teofil and Maurice had arrived, just to be with the horses – and also because it was warm. Henryk had never worn shoes. Being nervous and shy, however, he always ran away whenever their owners appeared. He was overjoyed on being given the job of feeding the horses, mucking out the stables and exercising them, which he did brilliantly riding bare-back.

'He was gone come Monday morning!' wailed Henryk under Father Józef's interrogation. 'It wasn't my fault, Father, honest! I looked after them and minded them just like you said! I was going to tell you, except I forgot.'

Father Józef would normally have teased Henryk and accused him of selling the horse to buy vodka, for which he would have threatened a plague of locusts on the lad's head. Instead, he looked thoughtful and walked away, leaving the boy thinking he had done something wrong.

'Looks like she's run away,' muttered Father Józef.

*****

Lenka had made up her mind to go in search of Maurice on the day he was arrested. When she stormed out of the cottage telling her grandfather that she was going to do something about it, it was just an angry threat with no substance. But having walked off her initial rage, she decided that she was indeed going to do something about it, and began to formulate her plan. All she knew was that Maurice had been taken to Nowy Sandec, so that is where she would go. The problems were that her grandfather would stop her from going, and would certainly enlist the help of Father Józef, whose opposition would be final, or at best very difficult to overcome.

She would have to go in secret, which meant preparing her ground carefully. The first thing would be to find a horse, and she knew that Maurice's horse, Robespierre, was still in the stables at the Manor. But young Henryk was there most of the time, and she did not want to involve him in her plans. He would only be blamed and get into trouble. So, she bided her time, spying out the land under the pretext of a walk in the countryside. When Henryk was exercising one of the other horses, she surreptitiously went to the stables and checked out Robespierre as well as the bridle and the saddle.

Then she walked the northern track until she was satisfied that she would not take any tracks leading to the forest or some other cottages. She hoarded provisions and collected up extra warm clothing. On the Sunday she packed everything in two cloths, which she tied up at the four corners in such a way that they could be hung onto the saddle.

That night she went to bed very early and managed, despite a heart throbbing with excitement, to snatch six hours of sleep. She had no idea how advanced the night was when she woke. Fortunately, the sky was clear and a wan crescent moon hung in the black sky. She got up quietly, dressed warmly, put on her woolly pixie hat, and crept into the kitchen. Her grandfather was fast asleep, snoring heavily. By the light of the moon, she crept through the village and on to the Manor. The horses, startled, snorted. Working by feel and memory, Lenka found the saddle and put it on Robespierre. The stallion seemed aware of an impending adventure, and stamped excitedly at the prospect of a night ride.

Lenka knew very little about horses, but over the past week she had studied the way horses were saddled and bridled, memorising what she saw, so preparing Robespierre was not as hard as she had at first imagined. She led him out of the stable, through the courtyard and out of the gate. She then climbed into the saddle, making very heavy weather of it. After several attempts, during which she must have exasperated the beast with her ineptitude, she finally managed to sit in the saddle. She placed her feet in the stirrups, grabbed the reins, and clicked her tongue. Robespierre set off at a canter, and Lenka almost fell out of the saddle with fright. In the event her distinctive woolly pixie hat fell off. She was in two minds whether to dismount and pick it up, but decided against it. It would be too difficult to find in the dark, and besides, Robespierre was already on the move, and she didn't know how to stop him.

Moonlight certainly helped Lenka, and soon she was finding herself in control of Robespierre. She suspected that the horse was aware of her lack of equestrian skills, and was being singularly co-operative.

Dusk was falling when Robespierre finally reached the top of the hill overlooking Nowy Sandec. Lenka was more relieved than she could say. Her back was in agony.

V

Maurice was only half alive by the time he was thrown into a freezing cold, damp dungeon in Nowy Sandec.

After his arrest he was forced to walk for the first part of the journey, a noose around his neck attached to the saddle of Grocholski's horse, and his wrists tied behind his back. The posse ambled along, apparently in no hurry, till they reached the River Dunajec, when Grocholski came into his own once more. At this point the river was rocky and fast flowing from the thawing snows. It was deep in the middle, although at the edges the water was no more than a foot or two deep.

'Time for your bath, Frenchman!' leered Grocholski. 'Wash that filthy Napoleonic grease off your body, eh?'

With that he rode into the icy water, and made his way downstream. His Lipizaner picked his way skilfully among the rocks on the riverbed, and Maurice had no alternative but to follow. For a short while he trotted along on the bank, not daring to allow himself to be pulled into the freezing current. Grocholski allowed him the illusion for a while, then pulled the Lipizaner further into the middle of the stream, where the water was deeper, and came up to the horse's flanks. Grocholski saw that Maurice was still able to hug the bank, so he spurred his horse onward. The magnificent beast broke into a series of jumps in the water, as if he were romping about, splashing and playing. Maurice could not handle the increase in speed, slipped and fell. The tether pulled him into the shallows near the bank. Grocholski, having achieved his purpose, emerged from the deep and continued downstream in the shallows, dragging Maurice by the neck along the rocky riverbed.

Every few minutes he stopped, while Filipowicz, who was following with the rest of the mob along the riverbank, hauled him out of the water and laid him out on the bank to check that he was alive, and to revive him for the next round.

Maurice managed to stop himself from drowning, although every time he was laid out, he coughed water. Apart from a few bruises and an aching neck, he was relatively unhurt. His greatest discomfort was the gnawing cold.

Finally, Grocholski deemed that time was running short, and bade Filipowicz to remove the tether and tie it under his arms.

'You have spent too much time on your bath, Frenchman,' said Grocholski. 'Now we must hurry to get to Nowy Sandec before dark. I fear you will have to run. But,' he added with a laugh, 'if you get too tired, you can always lie down and have a rest. But don't worry, we won't leave you behind!'

The rest of the journey was taken at a canter, with stretches of gallop over the wide, grassy fields. Maurice tripped within the first minute, and spent the rest of the time being dragged along behind Grocholski's Lipizaner. Fortunately, the ground was soft and grassy. Grocholski knew what he was doing, thought Maurice on one of the very few occasions when he permitted himself to think – a respite from the nauseating discomfort of being dragged, hour after hour, along the ground.

Somewhere along the line Maurice lost consciousness. When he regained it in very slow stages, he was aware of being wet and bitterly cold, lying in the dark on a stone slab. After a while he tentatively moved a muscle, and a nauseating ache instantly pervaded his whole being. He tried to lift his head, but the pain was too much, and he relaxed once more, panting from the effort. He licked his lips, and found them parched and cracked, despite the overall feeling of freezing wetness. He began to shake uncontrollably. Gradually, the whole Grocholski incident came back to him, and the more he thought about it, the clearer the reasons for his abduction were becoming. He was obviously wanted alive but softened up. The process had been achieved with remarkable skill. A careful examination of his aches and pains suggested that no bones were broken, although his bruising was considerable, and his wrists chafed from the effects of having being tied.

He came to the conclusion that Grocholski wanted to milk every drop of capital out of the affair. His credibility will already be considerable. Acting on information, he had in his own mind successfully tracked down and apprehended the murderers of the Inspector of Works. As they violently resisted arrest – irrefutable proof of their guilt – they had to be overpowered and executed on the spot. He, Grocholski, will be commended by the Imperial authorities for his dogged pursuance of duty. Maurice was afraid that by arresting him as the traitorous Frenchman who had been harbouring the criminals, and bringing him back to Nowy Sandec, Grocholski will be in a strong position to unearth a whole cell of dissidents led by Count Teofil Samojarski, no less, and his peasant henchmen. It could, reflected Maurice, be the end of Sarenki. It would not be the first time that a whole Polish village is razed to the ground and its inhabitants butchered.

With these disturbing speculations troubling his tormented mind, Maurice fell once more into a deep sleep.

Over the next week Maurice was allowed to recover gradually. An exploration of his cell, which was in perpetual darkness, only revealed that it was large and empty, and had four corners. He selected one corner in which to defecate, and hoped he would maintain enough sense of direction in the disorientating darkness to identify it on subsequent occasions. He was brought a bowl of cabbage soup and a lump of bread at certain times, which he had no way of identifying.

After what seemed like an age Maurice was hauled out by two burly peasants, dragged along a stone corridor and out into a large courtyard swathed in blinding white light. He was shoved violently onto the ground, where he knelt, cowering as he was surrounded by figures. He could not make them out, as his eyes, not accustomed to light, tried to cope with the brilliant blue sky of a sunny spring noon.

'Welcome to Nowy Sandec, Frenchman,' said the familiar voice of Grocholski. 'I trust you slept well. You are at the Palace.'

'How long…' croaked Maurice.

'A week.'

'What do you want from me?'

'I want Count Teofil Samojarski.'

'Why?'

'He made a fool of me.'

Maurice had no way of knowing that Teofil had given Grocholski the slip, with Father Józef's help, only a fortnight previously, and that Grocholski usually takes these things very much to heart. 'I don't know where he is,' he muttered casually.

'You were looking after his house. He is responsible for whoever stays there. He will answer for his crime in allowing his house to be used as a shelter for traitors who have committed crimes against the Emperor.'

'He knew nothing about it. He's gone away.'

'In that case, I hold you responsible for sheltering criminals at the Manor.'

'I didn't know who they were,' said Maurice. 'They said they were on their way from Lithuania to Hungary, they were tired, and wanted to stay for a few days before moving on.'

'And you believed them?'

'I had no reason not to.'

'Did you not know about the murder of Count von Loebl?'

'How could I?' said Maurice. 'News never reaches Sarenki,

unless someone brings it.'

There was a pause. Maurice risked looking up. The light was still very strong, but his eyes were beginning to get accustomed, and his gaze wandered all around. He was in the middle of a courtyard surrounded on four sides by what looked like an official building. Three sides constituted what might have been a palatial residence, four-square but nevertheless elegant, while the fourth, from which he had been dragged, was a conglomeration of outhouses, stables – and dungeons. Apart from Grocholski there were half a dozen men hanging around, looking half involved, including Filipowicz. A few carriages were scattered in the corners, mostly dilapidated, but one gleaming and of a smart design – obviously Grocholski's. There was an elevated wooden platform, about a metre and a half high. Maurice momentarily wondered what it was for. A few horses were tethered nearby, their restless hooves echoing in the courtyard. A tall archway, with an enormous pair of heavy oak doors, studded with iron and locked, led to the outside world.

Grocholski followed his gaze. 'Don't even consider it, Frenchman,' he said, 'there is no way out. I want that bastard Samojarski, and you are going to tell me where I can find him, or you will go back to your cell until you do.'

Maurice was silent. He considered telling Grocholski that Teofil was in Kraków, where the Austrians had no jurisdiction, but then thought better of it. A villain like Grocholski would not let something as tame as frontier formalities interfere with his schemes. Besides, Grocholski could just bide his time until Teofil returned, but by then the whole affair would be old and stale. Grocholski had already gambled a week softening Maurice up, and he now needed a further result to consolidate his triumph. He did not for one moment believe that Maurice did not know where Teofil was. He knew perfectly well that the two were lifelong friends, and Teofil would certainly have told Maurice where he was going before leaving him in charge of his Manor. Unfortunately, Maurice was not giving anything away.

Grocholski's face darkened as he snapped his fingers at the men in the courtyard. They immediately set to and beat and kicked Maurice about his face and body. When they had finished, leaving him, moaning weakly and lying face down on the cobbles, Grocholski came up to him, turned him over with his boot, and smiled. 'Next time,' he said, 'we'll kick your balls in, so you won't even have the pleasure of masturbating in the dark, Frenchman!'

The burly peasants dragged Maurice back into his cell, and threw him in. A further week went by, during which Grocholski kept his promise. Maurice was dragged out into the courtyard and beaten senseless at regular intervals.

*****

One night, after three weeks of captivity and systematic torture, Maurice was awakened by the door being carefully unlocked. His heart sank, for he had gone through a particularly severe beating only a few hours before, and had only recently regained consciousness. He found the prospect of further torture unbearable. He had not been fed for several days, although he was given water to drink. The door creaked slowly open, and he was aware of silent footfalls on the stone floor coming towards him. This gave him a fright, and he wondered what new techniques Grocholski had devised for him. Usually, he was dragged out of his dungeon amid noise and shouting. Then he heard a voice whisper.

'Maurice…'

'Who's that?' he cried, panic stricken.

'Sh!' came a hiss. 'It's me, Lenka.'

Maurice tried to swallow, failed, and coughed. 'What…'

'I've come to get you out of here!' whispered Lenka. 'Do as I say, and I'll explain later.'

With an effort Maurice managed to grab hold of this situation. It was totally unexpected, and he found it impossible to conceive that Lenka was in the dungeon. He put out his hand and came into contact with Lenka's face, so familiar, at the same time so unreal in this terrible cold darkness. 'Lenka…' he croaked, running his icy fingers along her chin.

'I've got the keys to the courtyard doors. I've left them unlocked. Can you move?'

Maurice felt himself all over. 'I feel terrible…'

'I don't care how you feel,' interrupted Lenka's voice. 'You've got to escape. The doors are open, and the whole palace is asleep. Your horse is in the stable, saddled and ready to go.'

The prospect of escape gave Maurice extra strength. He wanted to talk, to know more, but knew there was no point. He got up gingerly, and felt himself all over. There were agonising aches in his ribcage and in his groin, but he was able to stand. Walking was painful and difficult, but he reckoned he could surmount this problem once he started moving. He took Lenka in his arms, and kissed her tenderly. She accepted his love for only a few seconds, before pushing him away.

'There is no time, Maurice,' she sighed. 'Go to Czarne Lasy. It's not yet midnight, and you could make a good start. Turn right when you get out, and right again at the church. That road leads to Bochnia.'

'What about you?'

'I have things to do.'

'You're not coming with me?'

'As I say, I have things to do. Go, and we'll meet soon back in Sarenki.'

Without a further word, Maurice kissed Lenka briefly on the lips, and staggered out into the courtyard, putting all ideas of reasoning out of his mind. Leaving the darkness of the dungeon, he emerged into the cold night. There was no moon, and the clouds were broken enough to allow starlight to twinkle on the glistening cobbles, for it had rained that day. The stable was only a few feet away. Robespierre was delighted to see him, and paced restlessly about, his eyes fixed with sheer happiness on his master. Within a couple of minutes, Maurice was out of the courtyard. He turned right, and rode slowly till he reached the church. He turned right again. The Bochnia road was rutted, and the puddles reflected the sparse starlight. Maurice spurred his horse into a gallop, his exhilaration at being free overcoming the excruciating pains all over his body.

Lenka saw him go. She had locked the dungeon, and then the heavy courtyard doors. She then returned to Grocholski's apartment in the Palace, crept into his office and carefully replaced the keys on the peg in a cupboard. She then returned to Grocholski's bedroom, removed her gown, and climbed very gently, naked, back into bed.

Grocholski woke, turned, and placed his hand on Lenka's flat stomach.

'You're cold,' he murmured, half asleep.

'It's a cold night,' she replied.

'Then let me warm you.'

Grocholski was by now fully awake. Lenka lay back, clenched her teeth and opened her thighs. Grocholski thrust himself into her, and, grunting rhythmically, pounded her body relentlessly with his lust until, satisfied, he turned away and immediately went back to sleep again. For the next hour she cried silently alone, before falling into a fitful sleep.

VI

Teofil bade Maurice sit at the wooden garden table. Eloise excused herself on the pretext of fetching another cup from the Lodge. The two men watched her disappear inside.

'She is very beautiful,' said Maurice.

'Yes.'

'I have come at the wrong time, perhaps?'

'Nonsense, Maurice!' said Teofil. 'It is good to see you at any time. You know that. I would want you to be the first to know about Eloise anyway!'

'Your mother…'

'…has gone to Kraków for the day,' interrupted Teofil. 'There's no one here except your grandmother Elżbieta. You probably saw her on the front lawn. She's senile, poor thing.' Maurice grunted and looked about him casually. The Lodge and the garden looked very pretty in the warm spring sunshine. He rose awkwardly when Eloise returned with a cup and saucer and a plate. Although he knew the rules of etiquette, he had had little opportunity to put them into practice. The two men watched in embarrassed silence as Eloise poured out three fresh cups of coffee and cut three slices of *babka*. The childish polonaise, rudely interrupted, and Maurice's totally unexpected appearance, looking despicable, at the very moment of an engagement threw all three off-balance, and conversation was obviously going to be difficult. Maurice studied the coffee service attentively. It was delicate bone china, rimmed with gold plate, and obviously of French design, replete with cherubs and roses. Maurice was not accustomed to such finesse, which added to his air of indecision.

They nibbled at the *babka* and sipped their coffee in silence. Teofil studied his friend intently over the rim of his cup, and for the first time noticed with alarm the truly appalling condition he was in. 'But Maurice!' he cried, 'what has happened to you? You look terrible!'

'You notice, *hein*?' said the other, with a touch of malice in his tone. 'Perhaps it is because I have just escaped from prison in Nowy Sandec.'

Teofil and Eloise stared at Maurice in shocked disbelief. 'Merciful heavens!' spluttered Teofil. 'What were you doing in prison?'

'Being beaten senseless every day by a villain by the name of Jerzy Grocholski, chief of security at Nowy Sandec, for apparently allowing three political assassins to shelter in your house!' said Maurice. He looked at Eloise. 'While you have been away some interesting things have been going on in your village.'

'What are you talking about?' cried Teofil.

Maurice recounted everything that he knew, from the day the three fugitives arrived, through their massacre by Grocholski's mob, to his, Maurice's, arrest, torture and eventual rescue by Lenka.

'Lenka?' said Eloise.

'A girl from the village,' said Maurice. 'We have discussed marriage.'

'I see.'

'I do not think you do, *Mademoiselle*,' said Maurice.

'What in heaven's name was Lenka doing in Nowy Sandec?' interrupted Teofil.

'That is *précisement* the question I have been asking myself since my escape,' said Maurice. 'What in heaven's name was she doing in Nowy Sandec. And how in heaven's name she knew where I was, and how in heaven's name she'd secured the keys to the prison.'

The implications manifest themselves very suddenly to Teofil, whose speculation remained unuttered on his wide-open mouth. Eloise came to the rescue. 'You mean, she may have – befriended – this Grocholski? Could she have done such a thing?'

Maurice pursed his lips and looked away. Teofil stood up and began to pace furiously up and down the garden. 'Yes, she would!' he raged. 'Poles are conditioned from birth to betray! They are forced into it by whichever bastards rule us! What choice do we have? What choice did Lenka have? To let Maurice rot in Grocholski's jail, or to let herself be fucked senseless by that bastard to save him!'

Eloise suppressed the need to look shocked at the language. 'You don't know that,' she said quietly.

'Don't be naive, Eloise,' cried Teofil. 'If you're to be the wife of a Pole you'd better get used to the price of just staying alive. Just being!'

There was a long silence. 'What am I going to do, Teofil?' said Maurice after a while, a helpless pathos in his tone that Teofil found totally uncharacteristic. Was he a beaten man?

Before he could answer *Pani* Wisia appeared in the doorway. '*Panie hrabio!*' she called, approaching. 'I heard voices, and I wondered…'

Teofil looked impatient. 'It's nothing, *Pani* Wisiu,' he said dismissively. 'This is Monsieur Maurice Chavelet, a friend of mine who has arrived unexpectedly.'

Pani Wisia surveyed Maurice with ill-concealed disgust, then turned back to Teofil. 'Will he be here for lunch?'

'Yes.'

'Will he be staying?'

Maurice opened his mouth. 'Yes,' said Teofil.

Pani Wisia sniffed. 'Then I suppose I'd better get a room ready,' she said with bad grace.

'If you please.'

'As you wish, *Panie hrabio*.' She turned to go.

'By the way,' said Teofil. *Pani* Wisia half turned. 'You might like to know that *Panna* Eloise and I are going to be married.'

'Good,' said the housekeeper non-committally. 'I hope you will be very happy.' She turned and disappeared into the house. Teofil looked at Eloise in bewilderment, but elicited no response.

'Look, Teofil,' said Maurice, getting up, 'I am come at a bad time. Perhaps I shall go. This is my war, and I must fight it in my own way.'

'Sit down, Maurice,' ordered Teofil impatiently. 'We've been through a lot together. Your war is my war. It's always been so. We'll get that bastard Grocholski, you and I, just like we used to. I know you'd do the same for me. We'll get Lenka back. I promise.'

For the time being there was no more to be said. Lunch was served by a very surly *Pani* Wisia. Teofil, Maurice and Eloise ate in silence, none giving anything away by the expression on their faces. Each was trying to formulate his or her thoughts, and arrange them into some sort of order. Even old Countess Zofia, after the initial introductions, decided that she did not know anyone, and kept herself to herself.

At the end of the meal Eloise stood up. 'I think,' she said tentatively, 'I will return to the Manor. I have some letters to write.'

Teofil stood. 'I will walk with you.'

'Thank you.'

'*Pani* Wisiu!' he called. The housekeeper shuffled in. He continued in a tone of controlled rage, '*Pani* Wisiu, Monsieur Chavelet has just escaped from a prison where he was tortured by traitors in the pay of the Austrians for merely sheltering some travellers in my house at Sarenki. What is more, his jailers are making use of his fiancée even as we speak. Monsieur Chavelet is not a villain, as your expression suggests, but my very good friend and long-time companion-at-arms. I would be grateful if you would show him the respect due to a man of honour. He is in great pain, and in need of a bath and a physician. Please see to it.'

Teofil did not wait to read either Maurice's or *Pani* Wisia's expressions. He turned to Eloise and escorted her from the room.

*****

As soon as they had emerged through the front door, Eloise spoke. 'What about us?' she said, trying to control a tremor in her voice. It was her turn to seethe. She had suppressed her feelings admirably during lunch, as befitted her upbringing, but now that she was alone with Teofil, these feelings were swelling to the fore like a tide.

'I must do this for Maurice,' said Teofil.

'Do what?'

'I don't know yet. I must help him get Lenka away from Grocholski.'

'Grocholski's after you! He wants your head! Why?'

'Probably because I tricked him on my way here. Which is all the more reason for me to get him first.'

'But he's working for the Austrians, Teofil! You can't touch him! They'll get you the moment you step onto Austrian soil.'

'So, what do you expect me to do?' cried Teofil.

By the time they arrived at the Manor they had reached no conclusion. Teofil found himself in a no-win situation. He could not return to Sarenki, and exacting revenge on Grocholski would only bring the Austrians down on him. The parting was cool, and the kiss functional. The silly polonaise round the garden table had sunk without trace.

By the evening Maurice was looking – and feeling – considerably better. *Pani* Wisia, chastened by Teofil's reprimand, had done everything she could for Maurice. A badly needed sleep was followed by a hot bath. *Pani* Wisia prepared various compresses and bandages heavily imbued with herbs and spices, of varying efficacy, from recipes passed down from her forebears. Maurice luxuriated in their scents, and even the burning mustard seed felt like a dose of pure goodness.

A physician was summoned, and diagnosed several broken ribs. He swathed Maurice's chest tightly in linen, and advised at least a fortnight of rest. Maurice kept the excruciating ache in his genitals to himself – preferring in his shame to believe that they would eventually heal themselves in their own time.

Pani Wisia had prepared a room for Maurice, and filled it with every amenity that a sick man would wish. The bed linen was freshly aired, and spring flowers by the window filled the room with scent. Jugs of fresh hot water were brought hourly to the marble-topped table, so that Maurice's brow could be soothed.

A plate of *babka* and poppy-seed cake, bottles of vodka and ale were there in case he felt peckish, thirsty or depressed; there were books, candles and even a bell for him to ring if there was anything he needed.

At sundown Teofil brought Maurice's supper on a tray. 'I had to wrench it from *Pani* Wisia,' he said. 'and force her to allow me to bring it up to you.'

'You really put the wind up her,' said Maurice, trying to grin. He had spent so long being almost anaesthetised by pain that now, having been largely patched up, he began to be more aware of individual aches. 'She's been fussing over me like a demented bee! I'm very grateful to her.'

After supper a council took place round Maurice's sick bed. Światlena was brought into the equation, as was Marcel Terrassin, who had been fully briefed by Eloise. He had returned from Kraków with Światlena just before sundown, and they had walked straight into the new situation. Marcel immediately went to Eloise, who briefed him thoroughly about the state of play. He returned to the Lodge straight after supper.

Two points dominated the discussion. Firstly, there was the betrothal of Teofil and Eloise. Marcel was delighted, despite the cloud of doubt that now hung over his sister's future. He congratulated Teofil warmly, and kissed him on both cheeks. And Światlena, to everyone's astonishment, was overjoyed.

'You should have done it long ago, Teofil,' she said. 'But then you always were a ditherer!'

Pani Wisia entered to change Maurice's compress during this discussion, and added her congratulations. She knew perfectly well that she was largely responsible for the engagement. Now that it had happened, she made a show of unmitigated surprise.

'*Panie hrabio!*' she wailed, tears welling up in her eyes. 'Who would have thought –? I – I never suspected for a moment that you and *Panna* Eloise –'

Teofil mentally compared this performance with her previous perfunctory acceptance of the situation. He restrained himself from telling her that it was all her doing, but decided that one reprimand was enough for the day.

Only Maurice was showing signs of despondency. Their age of camaraderie had been coming to an end with the defeat of Napoleon, and of Polish dreams of nationhood. The new era betrayed few clues as to the future. Only love rode above the politics of the world. It had looked as if the transition from the male comradeship of the battlefield to the rewards of romance and love – long overdue in both their cases – would be smooth. Maurice had Lenka, and learned that he had lost her the very day that Teofil had won his Eloise. It was not that he resented Teofil's happiness – he resented the cruelty of fate.

The second point was the Grocholski problem. Marcel was quite adamant. 'It must be a duel,' he said. '*Monsieur* Chavelet must challenge this Grocholski to a duel.'

'Lieutenant Terrassin,' said Maurice, 'it may have escaped your notice that I am in no fit state to fight a duel! And Lenka is still in Grocholski's hands. How long before he finds out that it was Lenka who helped me escape? I will not be fit to fight for a good while yet. Time is not on my side.'

Teofil suggested a raid on the Palace at Nowy Sandec. 'Perhaps some of your soldiers might help, as paid mercenaries?'

Maurice's laugh turned into an agonised coughing fit. 'A raid!' he spluttered. 'When will you Poles learn that life is not just a story-book of heroics?'

'Not practicable, Teofil,' said Marcel quietly. 'I could get shot for committing troops to a private Polish adventure.'

Everyone retired, mentally exhausted, without having arrived at any conclusions. Światlena was the first to go, pleading tiredness after her day in Kraków. Eloise had been suppressing yawns, which did not go undetected by Marcel. They left soon after. Teofil watched Maurice fall prey to utter exhaustion, and fall into a deep sleep.

VII

Teofil slept very fitfully. He tossed and turned, tormented by one of those endless dreams that go round and round, torturing the consciousness remorselessly with one theme – in this case the predicament of Maurice and Lenka. It completely overshadowed his own betrothal, and banished Eloise firmly from his mind. Finally, he clawed his way out of the mire of his subconscious, and sat up. He opened his eyes wide and stared at the darkness. There was a hint of moonlight ensconced in the crevices of his surroundings, and soon his eyes became accustomed to the dim and oblique light, and he was able to make out most of the objects in his room. He had no wish to go back to sleep and get further entangled in the web of fears waiting to envelop his brain once more. Instead, he confronted the problem that was torturing his mind in the cold darkness. It only took him a few minutes to come to a decision. He knew what he had to do – destroy Grocholski himself. He was not going to wait for Maurice to recover. There was no time for that. Every hour was now an eternity for Lenka. With only a moment's hesitation he rose and dressed himself. As quietly as he could he made his way to the front door, and emerged into the night. He noted with satisfaction that the moon, though by no means full, was high and bright enough for his requirements.

He walked briskly to the Manor. A cursory glance at the building told him that the Company were all asleep. Marcel's and Eloise's windows were dark, and the only sound was the snort of a horse in the stables at the back.

The Company had no real reason to fear intrusion, so there was only one sentry on nominal duty. Deep, rhythmic breathing from below the stone stairs leading to the front door suggested that the sentry was fast asleep. The front door was kept locked at night nevertheless, but Teofil knew the layout well, and made for the grain store at the back. Sure enough, the door opened at the press of the latch. A scuffle within suggested that some rats may have been disturbed by his arrival. The grain store led directly into the kitchens. Negotiating these was hazardous, despite the moonlight flooding directly in through the windows. There was always a chance of knocking over some stacked pans.

The kitchens led directly into a corridor, equally replete with obstacles, this time in the shape of urns, vases and French furniture, all now invisible as there were no windows to admit the moonlight. Teofil made his way very carefully, feeling the air before him with outstretched hands, trying to remember from previous visits where everything was. After a time, his hands made contact with the door that led into the Hall. Running his hand down to the door handle, his elbow nudged the edge of a small occasional table positioned next to the door. The movement caused something on the table – probably a vase – to topple. It fell onto the parquet floor with a clatter, but did not break. Teofil froze. It was only a small clatter, but in the deep, dark silence it sounded deafening. He listened to the night, but silence had returned. He pressed the handle and emerged into the Hall, relieved to see moonlight once more seeping through the skylight far above.

The room directly opposite was used as the armoury. Teofil crossed the open Hall towards it. He turned the handle, but the door was locked. He cursed under his breath. He looked about him, irritated. Beside the door was a writing desk with drawers in it. He fumbled with the drawers, feeling inside each one, until he found a small bunch of keys. His relief was thwarted when he found that none of the keys fitted the door to the armoury. He cursed again, and continued to search the drawers, but to no avail. He looked about him in desperation, and made out, on the opposite side of the Hall, what looked like a matching writing desk. He replaced the keys and crossed over to it, and tried all the drawers. They were largely full of papers, coins, medallions and assorted bric-a-brac. Only one of the drawers was locked.

Exasperated, Teofil sat in a tall chair beside the desk and sighed. A door at the top of the stairs opened, and a figure emerged and immediately made its way down the stairs. Teofil froze again. There was nothing he could do but stay put and hope that there was not enough light by which to see someone sitting in a chair. He watched as the figure shuffled past him not two metres away.

Somewhere nearby a door opened. Then there was the sound of water running into water, punctuated by the noise of wind being copiously broken. The wind and water stopped, the door was closed, and the figure retraced its steps, shuffling past Teofil, up the stairs and back into its room. The deafening silence returned to the night.

Teofil waited a while before moving. Then he went back to the first desk, retrieved the bunch of keys, and tried them on the locked drawer. He hissed with satisfaction when one of them opened it. Groping inside, he found yet another bunch of keys. He took them over to the armoury door. To his enormous relief, one of them fitted.

The armoury was a large room with big windows. The moonlight streamed in, showing it to be full of muskets, pistols, barrels of powder and ammunition, as well as swords. To Teofil it was all very familiar, with the possible exception of some of the latest guns, manufactured in France since the assault on Russia. Teofil knew exactly what he wanted, ignored all the latest weaponry and settled for a small, powerful, short range musket that he deemed would be more than adequate for the task in hand. His needs were completed with some powder and ammunition, which he placed in a leather pouch.

Teofil locked everything behind him carefully. The weapon's absence is bound to be noticed eventually, but he hoped that it would be later rather than sooner. He went back the way he had come. In the corridor he accidentally kicked the object that he had previously dislodged, but elected to let it be, rather than risk further upsets by trying to find and replace it in the dark.

Once outside, he made for the stable, where he found Mazurek – or rather, Mazurek recognised him with a snort and a neigh. His riding tackle was in its place, and very soon his horse was saddled and ready. The gun and the pouch were fixed firmly onto the saddle. Teofil mounted and clicked his tongue almost inaudibly. Mazurek heard and understood the order, and made his way slowly towards the trees behind the Manor. The main gates would be locked, as usual, so the only way out of the Grounds would be through the woods and into the valley of the Vistula.

By the time Teofil had stealthily crossed into Austrian Galicia, having circumnavigated the sleeping guards on both sides of the border without any difficulty, the moon had set, and the first light of dawn was spilling onto the hills ahead. There was now no point in wasting time. Teofil spurred Mazurek, who galloped straight into the oncoming, spring day.

By mid-morning they had reached Bochnia, where Teofil stopped at the White Eagle for breakfast and a drink, and a nosebag for Mazurek. After that they turned south. The sun was beginning its approaches onto the horizon on his right when Nowy Sandec came into view. Teofil, who had been riding on a crest of rage and retribution, reined in Mazurek. While the horse shifted restlessly, snorting at the joy of the trek and the open road, a sudden fear descended on Teofil. The heady romance of revenge was about to become fact, and the realisation hit him like a thunderbolt. His mission was to kill Grocholski and the consequences had not entered the equation until now. He had not even considered them. Would he go through with it? Or has he been the victim of Polish wishful romanticism?

He cursed as he wavered between proceeding with his plan or going back to Czarne Lasy to lick his wounded polishness. It was, after all, Maurice's war. Perhaps Maurice was right, and he should not become involved. Besides, there was Eloise to consider. She was not very taken by the idea of Teofil embarking on a wild escapade to avenge someone else's problem. Maybe he should go with her into self-imposed exile and leave Sarenki to its fate. Poland is, after all, just a never-ending headache, and opportunities were opening up in countries like France, and even in America.

America! Yes, he thought. Tadeusz Kościuszko had fought in the American War of Independence. Then he returned to Poland to repeat his triumph, and ended up languishing in a Russian prison. Somewhere at the back of his mind he recalled Cyprian Samojarski, his grandfather's older brother. At eighteen, disillusioned with his chaotic homeland, he had, by all contemporary accounts, gone to America on a whim, and has never been heard of since. Teofil, to whom his great-uncle's sudden departure seemed quite familiar, occasionally wondered whatever had happened to him.

He finally also decided that there was no hope for Poland, turned Mazurek round and rode slowly back towards Bochnia. With some effort he pretended to wear a light heart and assured himself that he was doing the right thing, despite a nagging feeling lurking behind his consciousness that he was opting out of something much more important.

He had been riding for a good half-hour when he caught up with a trio of old women carrying fagots of wood on their backs. Around a bend just ahead a carriage came careering round at breakneck speed, its wheels only just negotiating the curve. It was pulled by four horses, and contained four young men dressed in the foppery of the idle Austrian set. They were laughing uncontrollably. The horses, unable to swerve in time, ploughed into the babushkas head-on. All three were trampled under the horses' hooves, after which they were caught up in the wheels, one of them dragged along by the axle for fifty metres before the driver could control the horses enough to stop them.

The four men, suddenly sober, jumped down to inspect the damage. They turned the limp bodies over with their feet. Two of the women were dead, the third, moaning pitifully, lay by the side of the road, her face and hands covered in blood. One man crouched beside her, obviously trying to do something helpful. It was equally obvious that he had no idea what to do.

'Come on, Hans,' said another one of the men. 'Leave her, and let's get out of here!'

The men looked at one another and nodded. The one they called Hans seemed to make up his mind. He got up and followed the others as they made their way back to their carriage. Teofil rode up nervously.

'Oi, you! *Polski!*' said another, 'they were just rubbish, they were nothing. You saw nothing, understand?'

The four gave Teofil a menacing look as they passed him, trusting that intimidation would be sufficient to ensure their safety. It usually was. Teofil watched them set off again, at a more leisurely pace towards Nowy Sandec. He then rode up to the wounded woman, dismounted, removed his coat and placed it over her. Then he gave her to drink from his water bottle, and bathed her wounds.

'Can you travel, *babciu*?' he said.

The babushka licked her lips and pointed to a small cluster of cottages on the hillside just above the bend in the road. 'I live there,' she croaked. 'Please –'

Teofil looked up. The hamlet was only half a kilometre away. 'Wait here, *babciu*,' he said, 'I'll get help.'

With that Teofil jumped into the saddle once more and galloped off towards the cottages. An old peasant was sharpening his scythe on a stone.

'You must come quickly!' cried Teofil. 'Three babushkas have just been knocked down by a carriage, and one of them is still alive!'

The old peasant's comprehension and movements were very slow. He gradually stopped sharpening his scythe, then got up and slowly looked about him. After a lot of deliberation, he seemed to make up his mind. Behind the cottage there was an ox cart. He pulled it round to the front with an effort, stopping every couple of metres. Then he picked up a stick and set off at a leisurely pace across the adjoining field. Teofil watched in astonishment.

'Where the devil are you going?' he asked.

The old peasant chewed and spat, revealing two teeth. 'Get yon ox,' he grunted, pointing to a beast at the other end of the field.

Teofil grabbed the peasant's stick and galloped across the field. The ox started in terror. Teofil got behind it, and poked it till it began to bound, lowing with fear, in the direction of the cottages. While the old peasant, so soundly outdone in speed and initiative, hovered helplessly, Teofil attached the ox to the cart. When he had finished, he noticed that the old peasant was in place in the front of the cart, stick in hand.

'I'll take over now, young'un,' he grunted. Teofil noticed a hint of embarrassment in the old man's eyes and left him to it, while he galloped back to where the old woman was still lying in the road, breathing heavily.

'Someone's coming to help, *babciu*,' he said. 'Everything will be all right.'

'Th-thank you,' muttered the old woman. 'What's your name?'

'Samojarski.'

'Count Teofil Samojarski?'

'Yes.'

The old woman chomped her toothless gums. 'He's after you. He's going to get you,' she said.

'Who?'

'Who!' the babushka showed disdain. Her eyes looked towards Nowy Sandec. 'Grocholski. That's who.'

Teofil followed her gaze, and held her bloodstained hand tightly. All his indecisions returned with a vengeance. Whichever way he looked at things, all his roads seemed to lead to Nowy Sandec – and Grocholski. Was this babushka a messenger from God, telling him which path to take? Of course not. There's no God. On the other hand – . 'You won't tell, will you?' The old woman shook her head slowly. 'It'll be all right. Here comes help.'

The babushka turned her head. The ox cart was trundling along the road towards them. 'You did well, to get old Igon to come, the lazy old sod.'

Teofil grinned at the old woman's irreverence. He squeezed her hand. She squeezed it back. The cart drew up. Teofil and Igon loaded the two corpses and the babushka onto the cart.

'Be all right now,' grunted Igon. 'Best be on your way, young'un.' He turned to the babushka. 'Nothing but trouble you give me, Janina, you silly old bag-o'wind!'

Janina looked at Teofil. 'You watch out for Grocholski, *Panie hrabio*!' she cried, touching her nose with her gnarled finger. Teofil watched the ox cart trundling back to the hamlet. He half wanted to follow it, to make sure old Janina reached home and care safely.

Then he made up his mind. He turned south again and galloped off towards Nowy Sandec.

VIII

Teofil reined in Mazurek and rode into Nowy Sandec slowly, partly from nervousness, and partly in order not to draw attention to himself. The road was busy with peasants, babushkas, geese and ox carts mingling with the smartly dressed landowners, merchants and officials. Teofil exchanged appreciative smiles with a beautiful, elegantly attired young woman being driven in a two-seater chaise by a gnarled, toothless and weather-beaten peasant ill-disguised as a coachman simply by being clad in a frock coat, leggings and a frilly cravat. A solitary Jewish merchant, bearded, dread-locked and wrapped in a long, black cloak and hat was walking ahead, stooped and furtive eyed. An Austrian official rode past him, his riding boot brushing the Jew although there was plenty of room. '*Raus, Jude!*' cried the official disdainfully. The Jew bowed several times and stepped aside deferentially.

Teofil came to the Church and turned left down a wide track flanked by the handsome stone mansions of the merchant classes. He turned left again into a narrow, twisting track leading up to the Palace, the official residence of the Austrian governor responsible for Nowy Sandec and the surrounding countryside. That is, when he chose to be present, instead of living at his palace in the far more exciting city of Lwów, or Lemberg as the Austrians called it. In front of the Palace was the large square, beyond which the road continued south, narrow and enclosed on both sides by walls, to the river Dunajec and on to Sarenki. The track, along which he had come from the opposite direction only a few weeks previously, reminded Teofil of the last time that he had had dealings with Grocholski, and a cold shiver jogged down his spine, despite the exceptionally warm spring afternoon.

Teofil rode into the Square, dismounted and tethered Mazurek to a post beside a trough. The horse drank gratefully while Teofil casually sat on the edge of the trough and surveyed the scene.

The Square was a hive of activity, and many people were coming and going through the two entrances to the Palace. The first was the front door, decorated, like many Polish palaces, with a pair of small Doric columns and a triangular pediment on top. The other entrance was the archway that led, through a pair of enormous oak doors, into the courtyard within. Teofil studied the faces, hoping to catch a glimpse of Lenka, Grocholski or Filipowicz. The thought of asking Filipowicz for the return of his Old Pankracy made him smile wryly, giving him some respite from his shaking nerves. But none of the faces in the milling crowd was familiar. Most people were wearing despondent expressions. Visiting the Palace usually meant paying taxes, having property confiscated, or going to jail.

Teofil looked first to the right, down the narrow track that led south to Sarenki, then to the left, down the twisting hill the way he had come, then at the Palace in front of him. He had been imagining himself bursting into Grocholski's office, gun at the ready, and threatening to shoot him unless he produced Lenka immediately. Grocholski, the coward that he was, would grovel pathetically, surrender Lenka without question and beg for mercy. Teofil would show him none, as Grocholski had shown no mercy when he killed the fugitives, and would shoot him anyway. Then he would take a sobbing and terrified Lenka away, back to a grateful Maurice in whose arms she rightly belonged.

There was no sign of Grocholski anywhere, and he did not bargain on storming into his office, wherever it was, amid such a throng of people. He turned his rage back upon himself, cursed his indecision, and was again contemplating giving up and returning to Czarne Lasy.

But then his attention was drawn, as was everyone else's, by a commotion caused by a noisy posse riding up the twisting track from the direction of the Church. People and geese scattered, and ox carts hove to against the walls to get out of the way. In the lead was Grocholski, two captives with ropes round their necks tied to the saddle of his white Lipizaner. Their hands were tied behind their backs and they were running and stumbling, trying desperately not to trip. Less than a metre behind them rode Filipowicz, lashing at them with a whip. Several other riders, armed with sticks and clubs brought up the rear, shouting obscenities and laughing as they went. Several people, babushkas and barefoot children among them, were knocked down by the riders, who appeared totally unconcerned at the distress they were causing. The posse swung under the archway and into the Palace courtyard.

Teofil thought quickly. This might be his only chance to get Grocholski, and he made up his mind to take it. He jumped to his feet and followed the posse, along with one or two brave but curious men, into the courtyard. The posse, still mounted, formed a circle round the terrified and panting captives. They then proceeded to lash at them with their clubs, sticks and, in Filipowicz's case, whip, while Grocholski tugged at their nooses as if he were manipulating puppets.

No one took any notice of Teofil. Everyone, including bystanders, were all engrossed in the torture of the captives. Teofil, a raging calm having descended on him, quietly took up a position behind what looked like an elevated loading platform, which came up to his shoulders. He took the gun from under his cloak and loaded two barrels carefully. No one paid him the slightest attention. He then positioned himself behind the platform, rested the gun across a wooden strut and pointed it at

Grocholski. The security chief had presented himself as a sitting target in profile. His horse was still, and the only movement from him was the dance of his hands and arms as he tormented the hapless men at the other ends of the ropes.

Teofil found that his hand was rock steady and his mind crystal clear. Nothing mattered except the impending kill. The past and the future had no meaning, only the present, the moment of retribution, of cold revenge. He took aim at the still, grinning head, and his finger coiled slowly round the trigger.

Suddenly Teofil relaxed. No, it was not enough to just to kill him. He had to know what was happening to him. Otherwise, revenge has no meaning. Still pointing his gun, Teofil raised his head. 'Hey! Grocholski!' he shouted above the din of the tormentors.

Only Grocholski heard, as one hears the sound of one's own name penetrating through noise. He turned, and their eyes met. The grin instantly left his face to be replaced by a look of triumph alternating with fear. 'Samojarski!' he cried. 'What are you doing here?'

'To kill you, you bastard!' Teofil returned to his aim. Grocholski was still a sitting target, even though he was poised for instant action. At the very moment that Teofil fired, Filipowicz noticed the sideshow, and turned his horse in the direction of his chief's gaze. At the same time Grocholski, his reflexes suddenly sensing the immediate danger, moved. Teofil's aim was not very accurate – perhaps because his raging calm had left him, and his hand was shaking with trepidation. The shot missed Grocholski, but Filipowicz clutched suddenly at his collarbone. A crimson stream trickled down his black tunic.

'Shit,' muttered Teofil. He panicked, and immediately loosed the second barrel at Grocholski without taking careful aim. The shot went wide.

Within moments Teofil was seized and his useless gun

wrenched from his grasp. By now he was shaking with terror, as the full realisation of his failure hit him. The next few minutes were a morass of screaming faces, raised arms, horses, kicks and punches being thrown, while he was being dragged, screaming in pain, over the cobbles and across a threshold. Suddenly it all stopped, and he was only aware of aches all over his body. He opened his eyes tentatively. They were sticky and covered in blood and his vision was blurred, but he could make out that he was on the floor in a room. Towering over him was the out-of-focus figure of Grocholski, whom Teofil recognised by his clothes rather than by his features.

'So, you came back,' said the security chief. Teofil said nothing. Grocholski paced over to Teofil and looked straight down at him. 'You realise that for the attempted murder of a government official the penalty is death.' Again, Teofil said nothing. His mind was a total blank. 'And as you know, I never show clemency.' Grocholski looked questioningly at Teofil, as if inviting comment. None came. 'You will die, Samojarski. You will come to terms with that fact.' Still no reply. 'You made a bit of a mess of Filipowicz. He's not very happy about it, but he'll live. Wounding a deputy is punishable by beating. No doubt Chavelet's told you about our beatings.' Grocholski strode over to the window and looked out. The late afternoon sunshine was flooding into the room. 'The girl will die too. I have no further use for her. I have fucked her enough. I have others to fuck. There's no point in returning her to Chavelet, is there. Not after she'd been thoroughly fucked by Grocholski, eh?'

Teofil's temper snapped. He had so far successfully stonewalled Grocholski's taunts and threats. The old babushka, Janina, had warned him not to give in to his threats, but his graphic insinuations with regard to Lenka was more than he could stand. Like a cornered wolf he sprang at Grocholski as he stood by the window, grabbed him by the neck from behind and squeezed with all his might. Grocholski was initially surprised by Teofil's action, the result of the madness of distilled rage. He had underestimated this rage. But a security chief is essentially a man of action, and after the shock of having been literally taken aback, Grocholski brought his elbows into play. Their impact found Teofil's sensitive lumbar regions, and Teofil relaxed his hold enough for Grocholski to take the initiative. He was a powerful man, and had a considerable weight advantage over the slim Teofil, that even the superhuman power of his rage could not overcome. The fight was soon over, and Teofil, even more battered and bruised, found himself on his bloodstained patch of bare floor once more. He tried to lift himself out of a pool of his own blood, but a strong kick in the face made him lose consciousness in a shower of black diamonds.

When he awoke, he was lying on a stone floor in total darkness. He had no idea how long he had lain there. He felt himself all over. He was a mass of aches, but no bones seemed to be broken. He raised himself into a sitting position and tried to clear his fuzzy and throbbing head by taking deep breaths. The ploy only made him aware of the foul stench of human excrement, itself an agent for renewed conscious thought. He surmised that Maurice might have occupied this dungeon only two days ago, and the excrement may well have been his.

His speculations were interrupted by the door opening. Two figures were dimly visible in the doorway. Some daylight obviously seeped into this dungeon from somewhere.

'Chief wants you,' barked a voice.

'How long have I been here?' said Teofil, getting up gingerly.

'Just the one night. Let's go.'

Teofil was led along a corridor and out into the courtyard. What Teofil had mistaken the previous day for a loading platform had become, by the erection of a gallows, into a place of execution. A motley crowd, ranging from peasants in rags to upright guards in military garb, was milling about some sitting on the platform, chatting, others leaning idly against the walls. Two barefooted children were swinging merrily from the noose.

'For *Pan hrabia's* benefit,' muttered Teofil's escort sarcastically. A cold chill ran down Teofil's spine, as he realised that he was going to die. He was ushered into Grocholski's office once more. Grocholski was seated behind his desk studying a number of documents spread out before him. But his attention was drawn to Lenka. She was standing in a corner of the room by the window, her face pallid and totally without expression. Her blue eyes were steely and motionless, and showed no recognition of Teofil. It was as if she were not entirely there, but in some far away land beyond her dreams. Teofil opened his mouth to speak, but could not.

'She will witness your execution, Samojarski...' said Grocholski, not looking up, but sensing Teofil's surprise at seeing her; then, looking up, he continued, '...so that she will know what to expect when her time comes.'

'You bastard –'

'Unless – ' Grocholski put his fingers together and leaned back.

'Unless what?'

'You're a gambling man, Samojarski.'

'What are you saying?'

'Answer the question.'

'All right,' said Teofil. 'I have played cards in my time.'

'Good, good.' Grocholski cast the two escorts a dismissive glance, and they left, closing the door behind them. 'Because I propose a little game of chance, just you and me.' Teofil sensed some delaying tactic. He said nothing, but stared at his captor expressionlessly. 'All – or nothing. Life and death. For you, that is.'

Teofil looked at Lenka. 'Is she in on this?'

'She knows nothing beyond that she is to watch you die.'

'Go on.'

'A cut of the cards. You win, you are free to go. An impartial enquiry instigated by myself will find that the three fugitives from Imperial justice will have duped you and Chavelet into believing that they were *bona fide* travellers on their way to Hungary. The matter will be closed.'

'Maurice Chavelet?'

'Will be free.'

'What about Lenka?'

'She will go with you,' said Grocholski. 'We were lovers, you see, but the affair – came to an end. These things happen, don't they?'

Teofil gritted his teeth. 'And if I lose?' he whispered, 'I am executed by your clowns out there.'

'No, no, no!' said Grocholski, rising, and going over to Lenka, who recoiled from his casually outstretched hand. 'You and the girl will only be executed if you decline to play. Accept my proposition, and you will both live.'

'Then what –'

'If you lose?' Grocholski returned to his desk and picked up a large, official-looking document. 'These are the deeds to your estate at Sarenki. I found them by chance in some legal stuff here at the Palace. It confirms the ownership of the whole estate as having passed into the hands of...' he squinted at the document, '...one Count Cyprian Samojarski on May 16 1773.

'So?'

'If you lose, you will sign Sarenki, and the title, over to me, having sold it to me for one thaler. Which, naturally, I shall honour.' Teofil was speechless with amazement. He looked at Lenka, but was unable to fathom any reaction from her whatever. 'Before going free, both of you, that is,' added Grocholski with a smile.

'I – I refuse!' cried Teofil. 'How can I gamble away my inheritance, my title? I've fought all my life for this!'

'Is that your decision?' said Grocholski quietly.

'Yes! No. Wait –'

Grocholski waited. Teofil went to Lenka, held her gently by the shoulders and looked intently into her eyes. She looked at him pleadingly, trying to make sense of what was happening.

'How do I know you'll keep your word?' said Teofil.

'You don't. Neither do you have the choice. Unless, of course, you want to die like a true Pole, for some unattainable ideal. And take the girl with you.'

'You're leaving me with a triple chance: gaining my freedom, losing my inheritance and trusting your word. Some choice!'

'If it's any re-assurance to you,' said Grocholski, his tone quiet and reasonable, 'I do not intend to be a murderous bastard for the rest of my life. It's got me to where I am today, but now I've had enough. I would like to sample a more elegant, refined way of life. I would like to be what our Russian brethren call *kulturny*. I would like to surround myself with beautiful paintings, more of your grandfather's perhaps. I have one here at this Palace. I would like to lead a fashionable assembly in the Polonaise on a cold winter's evening in an elegantly furnished manor warmed by blazing log fires, while wolves howl in the forests outside. I've always wanted to have a title, with a stately manor, lands, serfs, and riches. I have a good head for business, you see, and I could make an estate work. The Habsburgs have been good to me – largely by ignoring me, except when I am seen to have done something patriotic, when I am rewarded. I am already a rich man, Samojarski, and lined up for a title. I have money stashed away in Vienna, Berlin, even in St Petersburg. And most importantly, I am in a position to buy your title.'

'You'll never –' began Teofil.

'You'd be surprised. No, indeed; the days of Ferdinand and

Maria Theresia are long gone, and today we live in a totally different climate, and I intend to spend the rest of my days in the sun. Necessary precautions in these uncertain times, for who knows what the Congress in Vienna will decide about the Empire's future.'

'You'll never pull it off!' said Teofil. 'Once a peasant always a peasant. You haven't got the breeding, and that's something money can't buy!'

'But have you?' smirked Grocholski. 'Whatever you may have had, seventeen years as jobbing cannon fodder for the French? That's breeding?'

'We go back to the battle of Grunwald!'

'And I go back to my illiterate father who never knew where he came from, and took it out on me!' said Grocholski. 'But I'm sitting here, a rich man with power at my fingertips and friends in high places, and you are facing death at the end of a rope and pathetic career as a nonentity!'

Teofil said nothing, because he knew it was true. 'All right,' he said finally. 'Cut the cards.'

Grocholski smiled barely perceptibly. He opened a drawer and took out a pack of cards. They were brand new. Lenka, who had been following every word, turned to the window and stared sightlessly at the world outside.

'Highest number wins. Best of three,' said Grocholski.

'Agreed.'

They both shuffled and cut the cards, then Grocholski placed the pack, face down on the desk.

'Highest number goes first?' said Teofil.

'As you wish.'

Teofil picked up a 6 of spades. Grocholski's was a 2 of diamonds. Both were discarded. Teofil picked a Jack of diamonds, to which Grocholski answered with an 8 of clubs.

Teofil felt he was more alive than he had ever been before in his life. His King of Spades that followed made his heart beat unbearably. But it sank when Grocholski picked up an Ace of Diamonds. His relief was plain to see.

Teofil's destiny hung on the last card. He closed his eyes and picked. When he opened them, he was devastated to see that it was a 2 of Hearts. Grocholski was not foolish enough to gloat. His 3 of Clubs, however, clinched his entry into Polish landed gentry. Teofil sank into a chair, his devastation total, and buried his face in his hands. At that moment he would gladly have marched to the scaffold. At least he would have died like a Pole – for nothing. Instead, he had gambled away his inheritance like the lifelong loser that he was. It will be hard to face his mother, Eloise, Marcel. Even *Pani* Wisia. Worst of all would be to show his face at Sarenki. Father Józef would kick his backside and beat him till he was black and blue. And that from the only man who ever had any faith in him.

His only consolation was that he had saved Lenka's life. Always assuming that Lenka wanted her life saved. She remained, still and uncomprehending, staring out of the window. There was no way of telling what torments went through her young mind.

'Sign here,' said Grocholski, dipping a quill into a phial of ink, and handing it to Teofil. Teofil took it and signed mindlessly where Grocholski indicated that he should do so. Then Grocholski delved into his pocket and took out a thaler coin, which he casually dropped onto the desk. Teofil ignored it.

The two escorts entered the room, no doubt in answer to an unheard summons. 'Please see *Pan*...' he stressed this mode of address '...Samojarski and *Panna* Sieńkowska off the premises,' he said. 'And cancel whatever's going on outside.'

Late that same afternoon, Teofil and Lenka rode in silence into the glorious sunset along the road back to Kraków – and exile.

Part Three - 1818

I

The night was foul by any standards. The heavily wrapped coachman, soaked to the skin and half frozen from the cold, did his best in turn to coax and threaten the four unwilling horses to negotiate their way through the water filled potholes that blighted the Kraków to Warsaw post road. The cold November rain had not let up for three days, making the potholes slippery, and the muddy banks dangerous. The coach should have been in Warsaw at sundown the previous day, but the appalling weather conditions had delayed the journey. Now it had been dark for over five hours, and the prospect of yet another night spent trying to sleep in the endlessly jolting carriage was looming high.

In the coach, cheek by jowl, were a man and his wife, with their little daughter of toddler age. The woman was very pregnant with a further child, which was evident despite countless layers of clothing. The jolting of the slow-moving and uncomfortable carriage was causing her considerable distress, which her solicitous husband was doing his best to dissipate.

'Not far now,' he said kindly. 'We should be approaching Raszyń soon, and that's the last town before Warsaw.'

Also in the carriage were a Jewish merchant, a Russian official and his wife, and a studious-looking young man in spectacles, who spent most of his time reading, light permitting. The motley passengers had not sought one another's company during the four-day trip. The Jew was virtually ignored, the young man evidently preferred the company of books to people, although he did make a token gesture of childish communication with the little girl. The Russian official made no secret, when talking loudly to his wife, of his utter disdain for all things Polish.

The passengers became aware of houses lining the road, some with the light of candles or fires flickering within.

'Raszyń,' said the Russian. 'The last of these endless settlements they call towns in this benighted province!'

The description was apt. Poland was, in effect, a province of Russia. It was now three years since the Congress of Vienna had redrawn the map of Europe in the wake of the final defeat and exile of Napoleon. The Duchy of Warsaw, Poland's germinal hope of a restored nation, had had its frontiers contracted, and had been designated as the Kingdom of Poland, with Tsar Alexander I of Russia as King.

The decree had met with a mixed reception. The notion of nationhood restored had been dashed, although the Tsar was known to be an enlightened and intelligent man who was well disposed to Poles, and had even hinted at granting eventual total independence. He was on very friendly terms with some of Poland's leading families. In the meantime, he had installed his brother, Grand Duke Constantine, as Commander-in-Chief of the Russian Garrison in Warsaw. The Grand Duke lacked the intelligence and vision of his brother, and was known for his violent temper tantrums. That, combined with his ferociously ugly looks which had earned him the nickname of the Wolf, did little to reassure the Poles, who craved independence and nationhood without delay. Small revolutionary cells were being nuisances everywhere, minor but irritating thorns in the side of the Russian Imperial occupation machine.

The coach lurched to a halt at a small cluster of houses. The Russian official unbuttoned the leather curtain that covered the glassless window and looked out.

'It's a road block,' he said. 'They're stopping all carriages and checking the travellers. Must be some trouble from the Poles up ahead.'

The man and his pregnant wife looked at one another in dismay and frustration. The studious young man pretended that nothing had happened, but the Jewish merchant's breathing became nervous and audibly bronchial. Outside the sounds of people shouting and horses neighing could be heard above the rattle of rain on the roof of the coach. Suddenly the door of the coach was flung open and a Russian officer with a flaming torch, flanked by two guards, looked inside.

'Papers!' he barked in Russian.

The Russian official spoke to him in his native tongue. 'What is the trouble, officer?' he enquired politely, handing over a sheaf of papers.

One glance at these told the officer all he needed to know. 'Mikhail Petrovitch Mossolovsky,' he read, with a bow. 'Travelling from Kraków to Warsaw on Imperial business. Your papers are in order, Mikhail Petrovitch. Apologies for the delay, but there has been trouble in Warsaw with dissidents. We shall not delay you longer than necessary.'

Mossolovsky looked with disdain at his travelling companions and visibly gritted his teeth. 'Bloody Poles,' he muttered to his wife under his breath, but just audibly enough for his fellow travellers to hear.

The Jewish merchant's papers were apparently in order, although the officer dropped them onto the floor as he returned them. Despite this act of humiliation, the merchant was visibly relieved.

'Teofil Samojarski,' intoned the official, reading the next offering of documents, which he allowed to get wet in the pouring rain. 'And Eloise Samojarska.' He pronounced it *Ello-eesseh*. *Making a meal out of it.* Russian bloody-mindedness, thought

Teofil.

He answered with as much dignity as he could muster. 'That is correct,' he said.

The officer turned to the pregnant woman. 'That is not a Polish name.'

'I am French.'

'Napoleon is shit.'

'My thoughts precisely!'

'The – the French are shit.' Eloise remained silent. The officer cleared his throat and nodded to the little girl. 'Your daughter?'

'Franciszka. She's nearly four.'

The officer studied the soggy papers intently by the flickering light of the torches. Teofil noted his distinctive Slav features, although his two guards were evidently from further afield, judging by their Asiatic appearance. The Russians used Asiatic soldiers because to them Europeans all looked the same. If their Russian overlords said 'kill', they would do so without being aware of any ethnic differences.

'These papers do not entitle you to enter Warsaw,' said the officer. 'You will get off.'

'But we must get to Warsaw for my next connection!' protested Teofil. 'We've been delayed enough! Can't you see my wife's pregnant and my little girl is exhausted?'

The officer relented. 'Where are you heading for?'

'Lithuania.'

'What is your business in Lithuania?'

'We are going to live there.'

'It states in your papers that you live at Czarne Lasy, between Kraków and Lwów.'

'The estate belonged to my mother's family.'

'All right. You may proceed. There is a carriage at sun-up from the Market Square in Warsaw for Königsberg in Prussia. The route through Grodno is closed to Poles.' He took a pen and a phial of ink from his pouch, and scribbled a message in Cyrillic script onto the now soaking document. The ink and the rainwater ran, and Teofil reckoned it might as well have been Chinese. 'Make sure you are on it, or it will be the worse for you.' He turned to the studious young man. 'Your papers!' The young man obeyed.

'Krzysztof Żywiecki,' read the officer. 'A student at the Jagiełło University in Kraków, eh.'

'Yes, sir.'

'A clever bastard, are you?' The young man shrugged. 'Going to Warsaw?'

'Yes, sir.'

'To join the other troublemakers, I suppose.'

'What troublemakers, sir?'

'Don't give me that innocent shit! All you so-called students are nothing but a bunch of fucking troublemakers! Get him out of there!'

The two Asiatic guards hoisted the terrified young man out of the carriage and dragged him off to a nearby hut where they interrogated him. The process was heard by everyone at the roadblock. The officer picked up the book that the young man had left on his seat. He ripped it up and threw the remains onto the sodden earth, before signalling to the coachman to proceed.

The coach lurched off slowly, overtaking several other ones that were still being checked out. There were militia everywhere, marching detainees off for interrogation, and eventual arrest or release.

It was already midnight when the coach finally rumbled past the palaces of Wilanów and Belweder, through the southern suburbs of the Duchy's capital. The Jewish merchant got off in the Krakowskie Przedmieście, to be accosted by a group of Russian soldiers. The coach moved on and Teofil never knew what befell him. The Russian couple alighted when the coach stopped beneath Zygmunt's column beside the Royal Castle. They were met by another group of soldiers who emerged from the Castle, saluted, and escorted them smartly in.

Only the Samojarskis were left as the coach continued along St Jan's Road and into the spacious and deserted Market Square. All was dark and quiet, and there was no hint of the trouble that the officer had spoken of. There was evidently a curfew in operation, as there was not a soul in sight in the streets of Warsaw, apart from the soldiers. Teofil saw his exhausted family off the coach, for the coachman had refused them permission to sleep inside it. He and the postilion, both soaked to the skin, exercised their right to the interior. The post hotel was, according to a sleepy night watchman, full, even though it looked derelict and deserted. There was no arguing with him, even over a purse, so Teofil returned to where his family were sitting despondently on their three trunks, Franciszka fast asleep in her mother's arms. Fortunately, the rain had finally stopped, and occasional shafts of moonlight appeared among the darting clouds that rushed across the night sky.

Lugging the trunks under an archway and onto a covered walkway, the family settled down on the damp pavement to try and snatch a few hours' sleep before the Königsberg coach arrived. Teofil just hoped that no soldiers would appear. If there were a curfew in operation they might well be in trouble.

An earthquake would not have woken Franciszka, curled up into a fitful sleep, propped up against a trunk.

It was going to be a long night.

II

Teofil tried to sleep but could not. His mind was unsettled, and the past four years floated uneasily past his fevered consciousness. On a cold and snowy morning in January 1814 he and Eloise were married in the little church on the river at Ojców, in an attempt to salvage whatever romance could be salvaged from the Grocholski fiasco, for the aborted polonaise under the pink blossoms was now only a distant memory from another world. Marcel Terrassin gave his sister away, and Maurice acted as best man. It was a simple ceremony, tinged with sadness rather than anger. Teofil and Eloise continued to live at the Lodge at Czarne Lasy.

Two days later Maurice married his Lenka in a little church in downtown Kraków, the name of which no one was able to recall in later years. It was a cold match. The spectre of Grocholski loomed over them every moment of the day and night, and no amount of counselling from Teofil, Eloise, Marcel and – especially – *Pani* Wisia, could dispel the hideous presence of the new Lord of Sarenki. Maurice and Lenka accepted the job of manager and housekeeper at the Manor, which entitled them to a married couple's apartment at the top of the house. Maurice and Teofil had begun to get on each other's nerves, and both agreed that this was a wise move. Maurice, furthermore, had grown weary of the Polish experience. The wars had come to an end, and he was thinking seriously about returning to France in a last-ditch attempt to salvage something of his life, which had now become virtually meaningless, despite their still strong love for one another. Lenka approved, thinking that a new life in a new land might dispel some of the evil spectres that had dominated their lives in Poland.

As the white winter gave way to spring, Teofil retreated into a deep depression that seemed endless and hopeless. He was constantly tormented by images of his mother, which would not let go, and he missed her terribly. Światlena, devastated at the loss of Sarenki, had suffered a stroke on Christmas Day 1813, two weeks before Teofil's wedding, from which she never really recovered. He began to neglect Eloise and took to spending a great deal of time in Kraków, seeking out the company of old cronies and revolutionaries. His drinking became heavy and often got seriously out of hand.

During the opening months of 1814, the French began to leave in anticipation of the rulings of the impending Congress in Vienna, and Maurice became increasingly lonely for French company among whom he found some respite from Grocholski's ghost. He took to visiting Eloise at the Lodge, just to talk. Eloise, herself lonely because of Teofil's neglect, welcomed the warm friendship that Maurice was able to offer. Lenka, in anticipation of her new life in France, seemed not to mind this arrangement, which she put down to Maurice's keeping up his 'frenchness'. In turn, Teofil was actually grateful to Maurice for cheering Eloise up. He trusted his friend absolutely – perhaps not entirely wisely. It was almost as if Fate had some further decrees up its mysterious sleeve.

Pani Wisia, who on a previous occasion had managed to manipulate Fate, decided that the time had come to do so again; except that this time her task was to thwart any attempt by Fate to put asunder what God (with, she would unashamedly claim, a little help from herself) had joined together. Consequently, she was always at hand, eagle eye ever alert, and even laundry day ceased to be an immovable feast.

However, by the middle of May Teofil's spirits inexplicably revived, and everyone entertained high hopes that he had overcome the depression which had been devouring him since the Grocholski affair, especially Eloise. After what seemed like an eternity of neglect and moodiness, he became loving and solicitous once more. He even gave up drinking, much to everyone's relief. However, this state of affairs was not to continue. On June 19 a second stroke killed Światlena. Teofil was devastated, and his mood swung right back to where it was before. He proved to be worse than useless at making any kind of funeral arrangements, which Marcel had agreed to undertake on his behalf. He spared no effort or expense on the event, which was embellished with a guard of honour consisting of the half a dozen French soldiers still on duty, and she was laid to rest with full honours at Kraków's Rakowicki Cemetery.

On the evening of the funeral, Teofil rode to Kraków and embarked on a bender that lasted a full week. Eloise spent the evening all alone howling her eyes out. It was past midnight when, in a fit of despair, she fled in her nightgown from the Lodge, and ran barefoot across the moonlit grounds to the Manor, if only to escape the dreadful sense of loneliness and isolation. As she approached, she saw a light still emanating from Maurice and Lenka's apartment at the top of the house. She picked up a stone and threw it at the window, not really knowing why she did it, or what she expected would happen. She was therefore quite surprised when a ground floor window opened.

'*Qui est là?*' cried a man's voice.

'*C'est moi*! Eloise! *Est-ce que* Maurice – Marcel – Maurice *est là?*' she replied, not realising that she was sounding vague and indecisive.

'*Madame*, it is the middle of the night' said the voice, 'Lieutenant Terrassin is in bed; is this really important?'

'It's all right, Corporal,' Maurice's voice came from the upper window. 'I shall deal with this.'

'As you wish, *Monsieur* Maurice.' The ground floor window closed.

'Wait there, Eloise.'

Eloise opened her mouth but no words came. She paced forwards and backwards until the main door opened and Maurice appeared, silhouetted against a glow of light coming from the hallway.

'Maurice, I –'

'Come in, Eloise.'

Eloise made her way up the steps and allowed herself to be gently ushered into the building. Maurice led her into one of the reception rooms coming off the hallway and lit a candle, which instantly competed with the moonlight flooding into the room.

'No candle, Maurice. Put it out.'

Maurice's raised eyebrow was not visible in the moonlight. 'As you wish. Now, Eloise, what's the matter?'

The tears that Eloise had been just able to control during her flight across the grounds now burst through her eyes like a dam, and she threw her arms around Maurice and held him tightly. Maurice's reciprocal hug was warm and loving, but tentative. 'Hold me,' she whimpered. They stood holding one another for a whole minute before Eloise's mouth sought out and found Maurice's.

'Eloise…' began Maurice in a tone of consternation. Then, 'Eloise…' the tone changed to a sigh of passion, which grew in intensity as they hungrily sought out each other's pent-up frustrations as the moonlight flooded the ornately furnished room.

When Eloise returned to the Lodge the moon had disappeared behind gathering clouds. A serene quietness had replaced the sense of panic of only an hour previously, as she reflected on the dangerous threshold that she had crossed. She climbed into her bed and lay awake for a long time before falling into a fitful sleep.

Pani Wisia, off duty, had slept soundly throughout the whole episode.

Later that summer news came that Światlena had left not only the estate (for what it was worth at the time) but also a large sum of money to Teofil. It consisted primarily of the Sczasny fortune, which her father had invested in enterprises in Paris and London in his wife's name before his death. This was done in secret, as speculation was not the done thing among the Polish aristocracy. Added to this were fifteen years' worth of profits from Sarenki – less what had been skimmed off by Kazio Gruszka. Teofil, therefore, was a very wealthy man. When Poland swung bodily into the Russian orbit, he transferred all his money to St Petersburg.

On February 21 1815 Eloise gave birth to Franciszka Amélie – one Polish name and one French. At first the presence of a child brought such joy to the Lodge as had been long missing, and the sun seemed to shine every day at Czarne Lasy.

Summer came, and so did the Russians. A small company, led by Prince Modeste Ivanovitch Chernoyelsky moved into the Manor. The Prince was a dilettante soldier, more interested in his social life than in warfare. He was charming, handsome and elegant, and chose to spend most of his time in Kraków, where he had taken a house in Floriańska Street. His troops were something else. Mostly Ukrainian peasants from the steppes, few had seen more of life than a hovel shared with pigs and fowl. Also, they mostly remembered, through their parents and grandparents, that it was the Poles who had rubbed their faces in the mire a couple of generations ago, and had no love of things Polish. They treated the Manor as they would a byre, and within a year they had reduced it and its surrounds to a semblance of a barnyard. They urinated and defecated wherever they felt like it, and chopped up the furniture for firewood.

Maurice and Lenka fled from this barbarism back to the

Lodge, where the men no longer ventured. The Prince, himself a cultured man with a modicum of respect for Polish sensibilities, had made it clear that the Lodge was strictly out of bounds under pain of a flogging. On one occasion two drunken men had imposed themselves on Eloise as she walked with Franciszka in the grounds, but were beaten up by Maurice and Teofil and dumped on the steps of the Manor. A mass revenge attack was planned, but fortunately the Prince returned unexpectedly and intervened. The two men, as well as every fifth man at the Manor, were flogged. The Prince invited Eloise, Teofil, Maurice and Lenka, to watch the punishment, which was carried out by a large, bald Mongolian with a leather thong. Refusing the invitation would have been seen as a snub. The scenario was indelibly etched on each of their minds, further lessons in the Nature of Oppression.

Christmas 1816 was a happy one. Franciszka, was now old enough to enjoy the *Gwiazdka,* or Little Star, and the birthday of Jesus, even though she did not yet understand its significance. Teofil's depression had largely gone, and he had managed to pull himself together again. Over *Wigilia*, the traditional Christmas Eve feast, at which *Pani* Wisia had baked a fresh carp from the Vistula in dill, Maurice finally announced that he and Lenka would go to France in the New Year.

He also announced that Lenka was pregnant, and that the baby was due in July. The news brought a joyful reaction from everybody. Teofil, especially, understood and thoroughly approved. It was evident that Maurice and Lenka had managed somehow to overcome the Grocholski affair, and put it behind them. A new start in a new land was the best possible option for them. Both couples knew that only radical changes in both their situations would save them from grinding stagnation. Now at least Maurice had taken the bull by the horns and come up with a concrete decision.

Maurice spent the next few weeks in preparation. He wrote to Marcel Terrassin, and by mid-February he had accumulated a number of letters of introduction to various people who might be able to offer him work in the new France. The wine-growing region of Bordeaux was high on the list of possibilities; a friend of Marcel owned a vineyard in the St Emilion area, and was looking for a manager who might, given the right circumstances, eventually become a partner. It put him in mind of his youth in Dijon, and M. Grandier, the wine merchant who had taken him in. And, of course, Marie-Claire…

Teofil decided to make Maurice a gift of money to see him and Lenka through the next few months. He went to Kraków to see his banker for the money. By a strange co-incidence it was also laundry day and *Pani* Wisia, who had come to terms with Fate's quirks, observed it as usual, and even took Lenka with her.

Spring was well advanced and the time of Maurice and Lenka's departure arrived. Maurice came to say goodbye to Eloise – the kind of goodbye that he did not want to say in front of Teofil or Lenka. They had all been through so much, and their lives had intertwined in so many ways. And now their deep friendship, built on so much suffering and so many moments of joy and understanding, was coming to an end. France is so far away. Suddenly, with total spontaneity, Maurice and Eloise clung to each other, not wanting to let go. Tears came to Eloise's eyes. '*Adieu,*' she whispered, '*ne m'oublie pas, mon cher.*'

'*Jamais,*' replied Maurice.

'*Tu m'aimes un peu?*'

'*Un peu.*' Their lips met, gently and without passion, as if it were the most natural thing in the world. He then turned to Franciszka, who had toddled into the room. Maurice bent down, picked her up and gave her a big hug. '*Do widzenia, kochanie,*' he cried. 'Be a good girl always for *Mamusia* and *Tatuś.*'

Tears came to his eyes as he put her down gently.

Eloise noted this. 'She has brown eyes,' she said quietly, not allowing her voice to crack. 'You understand?'

Maurice nodded barely perceptibly. The subject had never been broached until now. 'I know,' he said. 'Teofil reckons it's a throwback to his great-grandmother, who was Armenian.'

'Leave it at that.'

'Of course.'

The next day Maurice and Lenka were outside the Cloth Hall in the Market Square in Kraków. The bugler in the taller tower of St Mary's Church just above them sounded the hour to the four corners of the compass. With a final glance at the tiny, familiar figure with his trumpet gleaming in the sun, they climbed into the coach that would take them south into Austria, across the High Tatra Mountains into the rolling hills of Moravia and on to the Bohemian capital of Prague. Lenka was relieved to find a couple of well-armed Góral mountain men sprawled, grinning villainously, on the roof of the coach, almost inviting an assault by the Zbójnicy, those mountain brigands whose romantic but ruthless exploits instilled terror into the hearts of all but the most intrepid travellers.

*****

Now, four unsettled years later, in the Polish capital of Warsaw, Teofil looked up at the sky. A cold dawn was breaking, and the first people, wrapped against the wet chill, were already going about their business. Somewhere in the distance gunfire was heard, in series of short bursts at regular intervals. Teofil was under no illusions about dawn executions. He closed his eyes and gritted his teeth while he waited for the next series of shots to pierce the cold air. His gaze fell to the sleeping Eloise, still clutching Franciszka to her breast. He looked through the child at Eloise's enormity, and remembered that day when Maurice and Lenka left. That night marked the end of an era, and he was feeling very emotional. Whenever he had made love to Eloise during those days, he noted a distant coldness in her reciprocation. He had put it down to her disapproval of his socialising habits.

Then he had thought no more about it.

*****

Teofil's reveries were interrupted by the arrival of the connection, a good hour earlier than anticipated. Teofil rose, left his family to their continuing slumber, and approached the driver. Unlike the driver of yesterday's coach, this one was smartly dressed in formal livery. The coach itself was immaculate and brightly painted with the coat-of-arms of the House of Hohenzollern discreetly emblazoned on the doors. Four well-fed and fresh horses looked fit to take on the challenge of the northern road. It was a Prussian coach.

'Königsberg?' said Teofil.

'*Jawohl*,' replied the driver merrily, giving a friendly salute. 'We leave early, because the roads in the marshlands are bad after the rain.'

Teofil sniffed. Why can't the Poles be as friendly and efficient as the Prussians. The driver had obviously risen early, cleaned his coach, selected four horses from the stables of the Prussian transport company in nearby Miodowa Street, and had turned up for an early start. But then, had anybody notified the prospective passengers?

Within a quarter of an hour the family were loaded and comfortably seated, the driver paid. Apart from a solemn priest who had anticipated the early start, they were the only passengers. The coach set off towards the Vistula, and Warsaw's only bridge. The coach rumbled through the suburb of Praga and continued in a north-westerly direction, never completely leaving sight of the river. At Nowy Dwór several rivers flowed into the Vistula, their function to drain the lakes and marshes to the north. Here the post road swung away from the Vistula and headed northwards, over pontoon bridges of boats and ferries. A foretaste, Teofil pointed out to Eloise, of the Mazovian lakes and the wild, desolate frontier regions with Prussia, home to a myriad marsh birds and boat people.

The driver was right. The landscape took on an increasingly bleak and marshy aspect, and the road was largely waterlogged. At first the fresh horses, collected at Nowy Dwór, coped admirably, but the strain soon began to tell, and progress flagged until fresh horses at Ciechanów started the whole cycle again.

By evening they had reached the frontier town of Mława, which boasted an inn, although the driver, despite the fact that it had started raining again, elected to go on to Nibork, over the border, where reputedly the inn was better.

Frontier formalities were straightforward. The guards on both sides had no mind to go out in the wet night for longer than was absolutely necessary. Teofil gazed at the wet blackness outside, but there was nothing to see of the Kingdom of Prussia.

III

The *Goldener Hirsch* in Nibork was only better than its counterpart in Poland by comparison. It was a fairly clean and comfortable little house owned by a skinny, hen-pecked Pomeranian by the name of Zaletnik. His large, sweltering wife, who looked as though she bustled even when standing still, dominated the building with her presence. Seeing Eloise's condition, she galvanised herself into action and turfed her uncomplaining husband out of the marital bed in order that the mother-to-be should have the best that her house had to offer.

She then fed the company with steamed carp from the River Nida and dill potatoes, a veritable feast and a welcome change from the largely inedible survival rations on which they had been living since their departure from Kraków. *Pani* Zaletnikowa could not do enough for the company.

'Maybe I should take more pregnant women on my run,' whispered the coach driver to Teofil. 'I don't usually get to eat as well as this!'

After supper came poppy-seed cake and strong black tea, topped up at regular intervals with boiling water from a smouldering samovar in the corner of the room, while *Pani* Zaletnikowa did everything she could to spoil Eloise and Franciszka. She sat the little girl on her knee, told her stories which alternated with ecstatic prattling about the joys of parenthood, and her regret that the Good Lord had not seen fit to equip *Pan* Zaletnik with the ability to impregnate her undoubted fecundity. *Pan* Zaletnik spent the evening bolt upright, immobile and silent, in his wooden chair, staring into the fire.

'And now to bed!' intoned *Pani* Zaletnikowa finally, rising to her enormous feet. She turned to the driver and the postilion. 'Franz and Gerhard, the stables, as usual.'

'Always the stables!' grunted Franz with mock outrage. 'Twelve years I do this run, and I still don't get to have a room!'

'You get rich, you get a room,' laughed *Pani* Zaletnikowa. 'Till then, you sleep with your horses!'

The priest had excused himself after supper, blessed the house and muttered 'May God repay,' and went to seek free lodgings with the local priest.

'I hope God can pay in *thalers*,' muttered *Pani* Zaletnikowa ruefully. 'The taxman will not take blessings!'

Eloise was put, with Franciszka, in the Zaletniks' own bed. Teofil and *Pan* Zaletnik were happy with a straw mattress each in front of the fire. *Pani* Zaletnikowa then turned to her husband. 'Henryk, I'm putting you in charge,' she said. 'If there's any problem, I'll be next door with *Pani* Ania.'

'Yes dear,' whispered *Pan* Zaletnik. With that, the exhausted company retired for the night.

A distant clock was chiming midnight when Teofil was awakened by the gentle touch of a hand on his shoulder.

'What? Who's that?' he cried; his speech blurred with sleep.

'Daddy, come quickly. It's mummy.'

Teofil sat up abruptly at the sound of Franciszka's voice. The little girl was shivering in her nightdress, and her face, by the light of the smouldering embers in the fire, wore a frightened look. He leapt up and put on his greatcoat – still the same Grande Armée one, and ran upstairs, followed by his daughter. There was a fire in the bedroom, still playing merrily. Eloise was writhing in the bed, uttering moans which rose every so often to cries of agony.

'Eloise!' cried Teofil.

'The waters – it's coming!' wailed Eloise. 'The baby. Get help.'

'Franciszka,' said Teofil, 'go downstairs and tell *Pan* Zaletnik to fetch *Pani* Zaletnikowa. And hurry!'

'Yes, daddy,' said the child, and disappeared from the room. He sat on the bed and grabbed Eloise's hand. 'It's all right, Eloise, my love. Everything will be all right!'

'The baby…'

'…will be fine. *Pani* Zaletnikowa is on her way. She will know what to do!'

A few short moments later *Pani* Zaletnikowa appeared, a vast, Valkyrian apparition in flowing white, with an oil lamp which she placed on the marble-topped table by the window. Behind her, hovering nervously in the doorway, was *Pan* Zaletnik.

'Right!' she intoned, taking immediate and unconditional charge, 'you and you…' she pointed to Teofil and Franciszka, '…out! You…' she pointed to her very bemused husband, '…hot water and towels – lots of them! Do you understand?'

Pan Zaletnik at first looked as though he did not, but after a delayed reaction he turned and went downstairs, followed, unwillingly, by Teofil and Franciszka.

'Out!' *Pani* Zaletnikowa encouraged a quickening exit.

'What's the matter with mummy, daddy?' said Franciszka, taking her father's hand.

'Your mother's about to have a baby, darling,' said Teofil.

Once downstairs, *Pan* Zaletnik came to life.

'My wife is very good in these situations,' he said, adding another couple of logs onto the fire. He emptied the samovar of its hot water into a jug and took it upstairs. Then he came down and filled the cauldron that hung over the fire with water, and topped up the samovar. 'Your wife is in good hands.' Teofil smiled nervously. After a long pause *Pan* Zaletnik continued, 'She has done this before, you know.'

'Good, good.' Teofil wrung his hands.

Pan Zaletnik, satisfied that the fire was burning well, paused in the act of sitting down in his chair. 'P-perhaps...' he stammered in an awkwardly crouching posture, '...a fortifying glass – of something – perhaps?'

Teofil paced to and fro like a caged tiger. 'Thank you, no,' he said absently, before realising that he was being offered a drink. 'On the other hand, perhaps, yes. How kind.'

Pan Zaletnik straightened himself, opened a cupboard and got out a bottle of clear liquid and three glasses. He poured out two, and one of milk, which he gave to Franciszka. The men drank theirs straight down.

'Another.'

'Thank you.'

There followed a long silence, as the three watchers sat and watched the fire resuscitating itself.

'Why is mummy having a baby?' said Franciszka.

'Because –' having babies was not something that Teofil had ever discussed with Franciszka, and suddenly he found himself floundering out of his depth. 'Because mummy and I wanted you to have a brother or sister to play with.'

'Who's going to bring it?'

'Bring what?'

'The baby.'

'No one's going to bring it, Franciszka. Your mummy's going to have it.'

'But they've got to bring it if it's not there yet.'

'Another vodka?'

'Yes, yes. Thank you.' Teofil gulped it down gratefully. The moans and cries upstairs were becoming louder and more frequent. He looked at Franciszka, who was still looking at him with a question mark on her face. 'It's – well, it's already there,' he garbled.

'Where?'

'In – in her tummy.'

Franciszka giggled. 'You are funny, daddy!' she laughed. 'I suppose that's why she's so fat!'

'Yes, that's right.'

Franciszka's face fell, as she realised this was no joke. 'In her tummy?' she said incredulously.

Teofil leaned forward and took the little girl's hand. 'When I say your mummy is going to have the baby, that means it's going to come out of her tummy.'

Franciszka looked at her father in disbelief. 'You mean, she will burst?'

Teofil smiled and winced at the same time. 'No darling. The baby will come out – between her legs.'

'Out of her bottom!' cried Franciszka gleefully. 'Like poo!'

Out of the corner of his eye, Teofil saw *Pan* Zaletnik blanch in embarrassment, obviously wishing desperately that he were somewhere else.

'Yes – I suppose you could say that.'

The noises upstairs were reaching a crescendo.

'Does it hurt?' said the child.

'Yes, darling. I'm afraid it does.'

Franciszka looked serious. 'Did I come out of mummy's bottom too?' she said.

'Well – ye-es.'

'Ugh!' Franciszka took another sip of milk before handing the glass over to her father with a yawn. 'I don't want any more, daddy. I'm going to sleep.' With that she curled up in the chair and within seconds was out for the count.

'Brilliantly handled,' said *Pan* Zaletnik after a while.

'An unexpected duty.'

'One that I shall never be called upon to execute.'

'You have no children, I understand.'

'My wife, alas, is barren.'

'Quite so.'
'Another?'
'Thank you.'

Copious quantities of vodka helped the long vigil to pass. Every so often *Pani* Zaletnikowa shouted down for more hot water. At daybreak Franz and Gerhard appeared, their coach ready for the road, only to be told that there would need to be a delay, as *Pani* Samojarska was in the process of giving birth.

'If it's not the weather,' said Franz philosophically, 'it's a birth! Never know what the post roads will turn up next!'

The priest arrived at the very moment when a loud screech rent the cold, wet morning. Teofil rushed upstairs, followed by the incredulous priest, who had just been informed that a baby was about to come out of her mummy's bottom. After a while the door opened and *Pani* Zaletnikowa emerged, flushed with the glow of pure joy.

'*Panie* Samojarski,' she intoned, 'you have a son! As handsome and dashing a fellow as you could hope to meet! It has not been a difficult birth, for he is small. Mother and son are both well. Congratulations!'

'May I see –?' Teofil began, swaying gently.

'Not just yet, *Panie* Samojarski,' she said. 'Your wife and son are well but exhausted and need a little rest…' at which moment Teofil fainted and collapsed onto the floor '…and so do you, *Panie* Samojarski! Ah, Father, help me get *Pan* Samojarski onto this couch.' And she proceeded to do it single-handedly.

An hour later Teofil came to and apologised for his faint, which he put down to a combination of exhaustion, excitement and *Pan* Zaletnik's vodka. *Pani* Zaletnikowa forgave him, blamed her husband for his excessive hospitality with a withering look, and pronounced Teofil fit to take Franciszka by the hand and go in to meet her new baby brother.

For a good while, father and daughter stood, transfixed by

the sight of the little baby, cradled in his mother's arms. His eyes were closed, and he was asleep. A radiant joy shone through Eloise's gaunt appearance, as she smiled with love at her Polish family.

'He's beautiful!' sighed Franciszka, entranced by the sight of her brother. 'Can I play with him now?'

'Not yet, darling,' said Teofil. 'He's still very tired. Being born is very tiring, you see.' Franciszka accepted this unconditionally. 'Who does he take after, I wonder,' continued Teofil, gently uncovering the shawl to reveal more of his head. There was more than a hint of Eloise about him. He was very slight – *Pani* Zaletnikowa estimated that he was below average in weight, his face was round, his skin smooth and dark, and he had a rich mop of black hair. After a contemplative pause, he said, 'he doesn't look anything like me! He must take after you. A Terrassin, eh? Still, that's more than good enough for me!' He kissed the baby gently on the forehead, then kissed Eloise on the lips. 'Thank you, my love,' he said tenderly. 'A million times, thank you.'

Eloise pronounced herself willing, if not entirely fit, to travel onwards the following day at daybreak. Franz was quite happy to comply; after all, a delay of one day was nothing very special, and he usually took such emergencies in his stride. The priest did not seem to mind, either. He was travelling to Königsberg to visit a cousin, and the time of his arrival was open ended.

'Will you baptise him, Father?' asked Eloise, for she knew that Teofil, now that Father Józef was no longer around to beat the love of God into his wicked soul, would not.

'I would be honoured,' replied the priest.

That evening, before supper, the whole company, augmented by *Pani* Ania from next door and several other friends and neighbours, crowded into the Zaletniks' bedroom. Eloise and the baby lay in bed, where *Pani* Zaletnikowa had provided fresh linen and her best coverlet. Franz and Gerhard were there, wearing slightly embarrassed expressions, as if not really understanding why they had been invited. *Pani* Zaletnikowa had prepared the marble-topped table with a crucifix, a picture of the Virgin Mary, two candles, a large earthenware bowl, a napkin and a small jug of water, which the priest blessed. The Zaletniks were pronounced godparents to the child, a duty that they joyfully embraced.

'It means you will come to visit us!' said *Pani* Zaletnikowa.

When all were assembled, the priest proceeded with the full ceremony of baptism.

'What is the boy's name?' he said.

'Julian,' said Eloise. 'Julek.'

'Henryk – Franz – Gerhard –' added Teofil on the spur of the moment, glancing in turn at *Pan* Zaletnik and the two coachmen. Their surprised delight was plain to see.

'Julian Henryk –' began the priest.

'What is your name, Father?' interrupted Teofil.

The priest looked amazed. 'Why, Józef,' he said. 'Józef Siekiera.'

'Father Józef! Excellent!' said Teofil, tears of joy welling up in his eyes at the happy co-incidence. 'Józef!'

The priest looked quizzically around for more interruptions. Finding none, he sprinkled water onto the boy's forehead, and intoned, 'Julian Henryk Franz Gerhard Józef, I baptise you in the name of the Father, the Son, and the Holy Spirit.'

'Amen!' came the response.

'Cost you an extra fare now,' muttered Franz to Teofil. 'But on account of the little beggar being called Franz, I'll leave it to your Excellency's discretion.'

'You and Gerhard'll not be out of pocket, Franz, I promise,' grinned Teofil. Then he raised his head above the assembly and called out, '*Panie* Zaletnik! Bring out your vodka! The House of Samojarski has a son and heir, and I'm paying!'

IV

The most impressive view of Spytkowiec Manor was from the back. The long driveway from the Main Gates at the Lodge soon joined the banks of the River Sesupe, which bisected the great Estate before meandering on downstream to the town of Mariampol and on to the Baltic Sea. The first glimpse that Teofil would have had of the Manor was where the river widened into a small, reed-lined lake in the course of a right-angle turn. This lake, smooth as a millpond, mirrored the Manor, seen from the back, and its landscaped arboretum, so perfectly, that on this bright, sunny day Teofil could have been forgiven for wondering which way up the panoramic view should be. The driveway skirted the lake, and where the river narrowed again at the bend it crossed an ornamental bridge, built by a French architect before French architects became anathema to the Russian psyche, and went on to describe a semi-circular avenue of English chestnuts planted when the Estate was first built over a century previously, to end at the colonnaded portal of the front entrance.

The rains had finally stopped and an unseasonal luminosity pervaded the cold, northern air on the day when Count Jan-Chrysostom Barnicki and his wife Tatiana drove to Mariampol to meet the Samojarski family off the Königsberg to Vilnius coach. The day had dawned fine and cold, and the still-wet countryside sparkled with a million diamonds in the bright sunlight, which the silver birch trees and the never-ending carpets of still golden leaves reflected with almost blinding clarity.

Everyone fondly called Count Jan-Chrysostom Barnicki Chrys, pronounced the English way. He was born in 1770, forty-eight years previously at the Barnicki family estate of Spytkowiec. His mother was Natasza Samojarska, the older sister of Mateusz Samojarski, who had left Lithuania over seventy years previously to take up his inheritance at Sarenki. Natasza constituted the last of the Samojarskis in Lithuania, whose estate, Maliny, was adjacent to Spytkowiec.

She had married her neighbour, the handsome and dashing Count Kacper Barnicki, known before his death as Old Kaz. The two estates were merged and repartitioned, so that Maliny ended up with just the small Manor and a few acres. The new, shrunken Maliny had been passed on to Natasza's grandson, also called Kacper, or Young Kaz, whose career as Russian Imperial ambassador to the Kingdom of Sardinia kept him away from Lithuania for years at a time. He was happy merely to have a *pied*-à-*terre* in his family lands for those rare occasions when he chose to come home. The Barnickis kept an eye on Maliny in his absence.

Spytkowiec, on the other hand, was a hive of fine living and culture. Since the death of Old Kaz in the opening year of the century, it had been ruled with a rod of iron by the formidable Natasza, known affectionately as Maminka. A true familial matriarch, no decision was ever taken, however insignificant, without her expressed approval. Her opinion was valued almost as if she were a Delphic oracle, and not just by the family. Strong men and strangers have quaked in her presence while she dispensed orders disguised as advice on any topic from love through the arts to politics. She loved nothing better than to be at the centre of a family council, or lecturing children sitting, entranced, at her feet. The whole family loved her as much as she loved them.

At the time of Poland's Second Partition, the same year in which Maminka's brother Mateusz fell in battle against the

Russians, Chrys had married Princess Tatiana von Rautenberg, herself a Russian of German descent. The event was viewed with mixed feelings, not least by Maminka herself, who only saw in her a plain nonentity with very little conversation but a good sense of style and taste, who went on to bear him two daughters. Poland's three partitions were partly the result of the collaboration of some Polish landed families, who reckoned that allegiance to either the Prussian, Russian or Austrian thrones would have social and political advantages over nationalism. The concept of Polish nationhood was a grey area. Old Kaz had been an ardent Russophile, and had spent much time in the Imperial, social, and artistic circles of St Petersburg. Maminka had supported her husband in a wifely way, although she was devastated at the death of her brother Mateusz at Dubienka at the hands of the Russians.

It was mid-afternoon when the coach clattered over the ornamental bridge over the River Sesupe and drew up at the front portal of Spytkowiec. Apart from a row of servants, and stable staff come to put away the coach, Chris introduced his wife Tatiana, followed by his two daughters. 'Teofil, this is your cousin Jadwiga. She is twenty.'

Jadwiga was a sturdy lass built in the heavy, Russian mould. She had a not unattractive, slightly horsey but good-natured face, and a warm, wicked expression which suggested a willingness to join in any pranks that may be going. To a man looking for feminine beauty she had nothing to offer. Her ill-fitting and casual clothes and not coiffured, colourless hair suggested a total and unselfconscious lack of pride in her appearance. 'I am delighted, Cousin Jadwiga.'

'Call me Inka, Cousin Teofil,' she chortled, squeezing Teofil's hand with all her might. 'Everybody does! I'm sure we'll have lots of fun! Do you ride?'

'Indeed, I do,' said Teofil. 'I have ridden a lot in my time.'

'Oh, jolly good!' laughed Inka. 'I'll bet you're one hell of a horseman, eh?' She nudged Teofil with her elbow. She turned to Eloise. 'You must be Cousin Eloise. *Bon jour*, Eloise, *je suis absolument enchantée de faire ta connaissance, quoi!*' She kissed Eloise affectionately. She turned to the baby, cradled in Eloise's arms. 'I say, I didn't realise you had two nippers!'

'I didn't,' smiled Eloise, 'until two days ago!'

'Julek was born in an inn in Nibork,' said Chrys. 'An amazing thing, don't you think?'

'How incredible!' laughed Inka. 'My heartiest congratulations! To you both!'

'And,' Chrys announced in a deferential whisper, which hinted strongly of the best yet to come, 'this is Jolanta.'

Teofil was stunned. Jolanta was the antithesis of her sister. He immediately saw her as the ultimate ice queen, cold and as ravishingly beautiful as an Italian sculpture. She had black hair that flowed free down to her shoulder blades and a pale, translucent skin that was as smooth and perfect as marble. Her eyes were blue – or perhaps green – at any rate a bluer shade of turquoise. Where Inka radiated hearty camaraderie, Jolanta was not giving anything away. It was evident that, in Chrys' eyes, she was the most perfect creature in the world.

Jolanta's expression was cold and reserved. 'How are you, Cousin Teofil,' – she gave each in turn a formal peck on the cheek – 'Cousin Eloise, Aunt Tatiana. And you,' she crouched down and let drop a hint of a smile, 'must be Franciszka!'

'How do you do, Aunt Jolanta,' said the little girl. 'I hope you are well.'

'And I hope you are even better!' said Jolanta. 'I'm sure we shall be great friends.'

Straightening herself again, she inspected Julek and let out a sigh of admiration – almost of orgasmic pleasure. 'Cousin Eloise! He is beautiful! My congratulations to you both!'

The introductions complete, Chrys led the way indoors. 'Maminka is resting,' he said, 'but will be down presently. But first things first!' He insisted that Eloise and baby Julek should be put to bed immediately, a suggestion that Eloise made no attempt to decline. Chrys had enlisted Dr Kaldiskis, the finest physician in Mariampol, to come and attend to Eloise. Her exhaustion was near total, and she was barely able to stand when she reached the bedroom of the wing that had been allocated to the Samojarskis.

'Thank you,' she smiled to the maid, 'please inform the Count that we are delighted!'

Teofil was tired, but the excitement of the past few days made the adrenalin run, and he was in the mood to talk.

Chrys ushered Teofil into the spacious drawing room. A blazing fire roared in the grate of an ornate, marble mantelpiece, on which an exquisite Louis XVI clock caught Teofil's eye. One corner was dominated by a pianoforte. Teofil looked it over. He picked out the first two bars of a popular Beethoven Minuet with one finger – a dubious skill shared by most tavern patrons at the time. 'It's a new Viennese Graf,' said Chrys. 'Beautiful beast, eh? Unbelievable touch. Do you play?'

'No. But I love music. Unfortunately, I haven't been able to indulge myself. There are not too many pianofortes on battlefields!'

'All that will now change,' said Chrys, giving the bell-pull by the mantel a tug. 'Jolanta plays. She studies at the Conservatory of St Petersburg. I bought the Graf because of its soft touch, which suits Jolanta perfectly. She may be persuaded to play for you. You will not hear a more delicate Mozart on this side of the Vistula, I promise you.'

'I'm a Beethoven man, myself,' said Teofil.

Chrys winced. 'I'm afraid I don't go for these modern chaps too much.' A liveried butler entered. 'Champagne, Igor,' said

Chrys. 'The '94. And make sure it's cold.' Igor bowed and left. Chrys and Teofil sat on a Lelarge *canapé* sofa. 'The year of the last partition. Must keep these Russkies in good humour, eh?'

Teofil remained silent. Twenty years ago, he would have happily strangled the Chryses of this world as collaborators who have sold their heritage to foreign powers. But then, the Barnickis have not done badly out of the deal. He knew that Spytkowiec controlled an enormous area containing about ten villages and a thrall of some three thousand serfs working several thousand acres. Even though over half of the profits ended up in the coffers of St Petersburg, what was left was about four times greater than before the final partition, when the region was annexed by Russia.

Igor returned with a bottle of chilled Champagne and two Bohemian crystal glasses on an ornate tray of Russian silver. The tree motif of the Barnicki House was engraved in the centre. Chrys dismissed Igor, opened the bottle without making a sound, and poured. He handed one glass to Teofil and sat down.

'*Na zdrowie*,' he said, raising his glass.

'*Na zdrowie*,' replied Teofil. The two men sipped appreciatively in silence for a while.

Chrys broke the silence. 'So, Teofil, how do you see your role in the development of Spytkowiec?'

'I'm not entirely certain. I have money, but no longer any land.'

'You gambled away your Estate, man! You've only yourself to blame!'

'It was that or certain death. I had no choice.'

'There is always choice!' said Chrys.

'I could have gone over to the Austrians,' said Teofil.

'Why didn't you?'

'It was my country, my inheritance, my people.'

'You are a romantic patriot,' Chrys sipped his Champagne.

'How unfashionable!'

'So I see,' Teofil pointedly cast about at the magnificently furnished room. He was having difficulty keeping his temper.

They drank in silence.

'I didn't think was it a good idea to have you here, Teofil,' said Chrys, getting up to refill the glasses. 'It was Maminka's idea. Blood is thicker than water, and all that. But then, she's a Samojarska. Remember that I'm not. My family have worked Spytkowiec successfully for nearly two hundred years. I hope we shall continue in the same vein. I don't want to have to clear up any disasters.'

'You won't have to,' replied Teofil. 'Just take my money, and accept me for what I am.'

'Which is?'

'A rich man who's been beyond the Vistula, knows a thing or two, and could come up with some good ideas given an environment in which he can function.'

'That's not enough.'

'It's all I've got.'

The ornately panelled double door was opened by two servants. Standing in the doorway, dead centre, was a tall, stately woman with grey hair carefully and exquisitely coiffured. She wore a simple, shimmering gown of black silk edged with the finest Flemish lace. She paused for effect, pointedly looking for and finding Teofil with her piercing blue eyes before entering.

'Teofil! Darling! Welcome to Spytkowiec!' she cried, her arms outstretched towards Teofil, who had leapt to his feet. 'I hope my son has not been feeding you all that rubbish about not wanting you here! He seems to forget that this is MY house, and I want you here. Don't take any notice of Chrys. He's a Russian spy, you know! I wouldn't mind, but that he's proud of the fact!' She caught sight of the Champagne and wrinkled her nose. 'Great God, Chrys! The '94! This is your rich cousin Teofil, come to bail you out of your financial problems! You might have opened a decent '95 for God's sake!'

'Teofil,' said Chrys, only slightly bemused. 'Meet Maminka. Your Great-Aunt Natasza.'

'Great-Aunt Natasza sounds frightfully Russian,' came the haughty reply. 'You will call me Maminka, Teofil. Now kiss me!'

Teofil obeyed. He had the distinct feeling that he would grow very fond of his Great-Aunt Natasza. Maminka.

V

The first year of the Samojarskis' tenancy of the West Wing of Spytkowiec passed with only limited acrimony between Teofil and Chrys. The brunt of ill-feeling passed rather between Chrys and Maminka, for, as became apparent with the passing months, she was not supposed to have let drop hints of Chrys' financial difficulties. The good years – for some – since the partitions were slowly but surely declining into recession, and the Barnickis' profligate spending in St Petersburg, Paris, London and Vienna in the heady days of Catherine the Great was generating come-backs.

All that came to an end with the final partitions of Poland followed immediately by Catherine's death two decades previously. Post-Napoleonic Europe and the reign, however benign, of Tsar Alexander I constituted a new era, with new values and radical thinking. Teofil gladly invested money in Spytkowiec, and even paid off some of Chrys' outstanding debts. He was merely glad to have a family home, even if only a nominal one.

'Chrys can't bawl you out any more, Teofil,' said Maminka as they strolled along the river bank the following spring. 'He needs you more than you need him, and he knows it. But now you must consider the future. Bail him out here and there, if it makes you feel better, but hold on to the bulk of your money. I'm an old woman now, and I shan't be around much longer, even though I've still got my wits about me and can still call my constitution that of an ox. I doubt you could cope with Chrys without me around. Be warned.'

Teofil had made his mind up to take Maminka's warnings seriously. She was, after all fending off eighty. He was well aware that he could not just live at Spytkowiec, supporting Chrys, for the rest of his life. He had his own future, and that of his family to consider. He himself had now reached forty, not the ideal age at which to start a new career – indeed, just a career, for he now considered his years in the French army as wasted. He had come to working terms with the fact that Poland could not be won back, even though, deep down, his patriotism still smouldered like an ember that refused to die, as if waiting for just that tuft of tinder-dry grass and a faggot to make it flare again.

That tuft and faggot materialised during the golden autumn of 1820. Chrys, in a moment of supreme benevolence, had offered to take his wife Tatiana, Teofil and Eloise to Vilnius for the day to celebrate their wedding anniversary, and would not be back till late. Inka disappeared somewhere into the countryside – which was nothing unusual. She often took off at a moment's whim, sometimes not returning till the following day. No one minded, since they all knew she was forest-wise, knew everything there was to know about the wildlife, was a superb horsewoman and was very unlikely to be attacked. Jolanta was in St Petersburg, pursuing her musical studies at the Conservatory: there was also a rumour of a dashing cavalry officer somewhere in the equation, which she dismissed as totally unfounded. Maminka had requested time with Julek, now of a toddling age heavily laced with reckless adventurism.

'I wish to teach Julek to channel his death wish into something that will eventually hold him in good stead to get the better of his rivals in later life!' she announced.

The following day Teofil took Eloise and Franciszka, now seven and an irrepressible tomboy, for a ride to Maliny. Teofil had bought her a champagne filly with an ancestry that zig-zagged back to Arabia, picking up various Asiatic genes on the way. The result was a horse of some considerable character and whimsy. Franciszka was devoted to her, and called her Bronia. Like her parents, she had a natural seat on a horse, and in a remarkably short time, child and filly had developed a sound relationship, based loosely on the principle of mutual scratching of backs. The day that Franciszka neglected to groom Bronia was the day that she returned home, bruised and battered after a fall. Franciszka's lessons in animal care were painful, but ultimately effective.

Maliny Manor was an hour's ride away from Spytkowiec, through birch forests like a giant's silver needles sticking into a golden pincushion. Franciszka loved these rides, which invariably ended in a picnic of *pierogi* stuffed with mushrooms and dill, honey cakes and fruit juice. Besides, the forests were full of animals to delight her, from the vicious but beautiful little mink to the possibility of the odd bear foraging for a beehive, or even a herd of bison.

The Manor was set in a landscaped lawn dotted with shrubs and trees. It was small and of simple design, four-square, two-storied sandstone with a small Doric pediment supported by two columns above the front door. They had ridden here several times before, partly to check that all was well, and partly to enjoy the picnic beside the lake, for Franciszka enjoyed watching the fish jumping in the sunlight. In the absence of Young Kaz the lake was only fished by the occasional peasant who braved the law – harsh enough to demand the death penalty in certain circumstances, to catch something for his family to eat for many days. But poachers, even if seen, were generally ignored; Chrys considered it churlish to prosecute a hungry peasant merely because of the odd carp taken in secret.

'Stolen apples taste the best, don't you think?' he used to joke.

On this occasion Teofil, Eloise and Franciszka rode from the forest into the clearing to find that there were people in the Manor. Several horses were tethered underneath the trees beside the house. Teofil signalled Eloise and Franciszka back into the wood, before following them.

'Poachers?' said Eloise. 'Can't be! There are too many.'

'Wait here, and don't show yourselves,' he said, dismounting and tethering his horse to a branch. 'I'm going see what's happening. I don't like the look of it one bit.'

Teofil crept round the edge of the wood till he was in line with the side of the house, where there were no windows, and he was not likely to be seen. Then, darting from tree to tree, he reached the wall of the house. The sound of voices talking softly could be heard. Teofil crept round to the corner of the house and chanced to look round it. The voices grew louder. Crouching down, he crept along till he came to the first ground floor window. It was open, and he could now hear the voices quite clearly. There was a mixture of men and women. One voice in particular was utterly familiar, which made Teofil reckon that everything was completely above board, and he was about to stand up and show himself.

However, mingled with the voices was the metallic clatter of some kind of equipment being handled, which made Teofil suspicious. He was tempted to lift his head over the sill and look surreptitiously inside. As he dithered with indecision, the drift of the talk reached his ears, and he froze. He stayed in place for only long enough to verify his immediate suspicions. Then he crept back the way he had come, and made the dash across the lawn to the edge of the forest, where he found Eloise and Franciszka waiting anxiously.

'Let's get out of here,' said Teofil.

'But Daddy, what about the picnic?' moaned Franciszka.

'It's not safe, darling,' said Teofil. 'We've got to go.'

'What is it, Teofil?' said Eloise anxiously, 'who's there?'

'I'll explain later,' replied Teofil. 'Let's go, quickly. We'll stop and have the picnic at the Entrenchment.' He was referring to a clearing on a small hill with a winding ditch under it, a favourite play area for Franciszka.

'But I'm starving!' she wailed. But to no avail. For once Teofil showed no concern whatsoever for Franciszka's well-being.

The picnic at the Entrenchment was really for Franciszka's benefit. When the little girl was out of earshot looking for rabbits in the surrounding woods, Teofil told Eloise that the people in the house were discussing armed rebellion. 'But the worst of it was that Inka was among them!' he said. 'What was more, they were handling arms, which were being collected and hidden somewhere on the estate.'

'But where?' asked Eloise.

'They just talked about a cache,' said Teofil. 'Probably somewhere in the forest where no one would look. They certainly wouldn't dare to keep it in the House. I didn't want to wait in case they found me.'

'So, knowing that the House is unoccupied, they use it for their meetings, and use the forest to hide their guns!' said Eloise.

'It looks like it.'

'This is an extremely dangerous situation, and could have very serious repercussions!' said Maminka on their return and after Teofil had explained about the conspiracy. Franciszka had been despatched to play on the lawn, while Teofil and Eloise joined Maminka in her drawing room upstairs, where she had been resting. 'You must tell no one about what you saw!'

'Could it be just a bunch of hotheads, or is it a serious revolutionary cell?' said Teofil.

'I have always suspected that there was a working cell in the region,' said Maminka. 'Especially as arms are involved.'

'And Inka –' began Eloise.

'Inka's involvement doesn't surprise me one little bit,' said Maminka. 'That girl is a volcano of turbulent feelings just waiting to explode.'

'You surprise me, Maminko,' said Teofil. 'I took her to be a decent, hearty and good-natured lass.'

'It's the image that she hides behind,' replied Maminka. 'Surely you must have noticed how the poor girl suffers from the shadow of her sister!'

Teofil shrugged. 'Well, perhaps –'

'It's obvious,' interpolated Eloise. 'If I were dumpy, jolly and horsey and had a stunningly beautiful and talented sister like Jolanta, whom their father dotes on shamelessly, I would be hiding behind some façade too.'

'But a revolutionary – a fighter?' cried Teofil mockingly. 'Can you see Inka with a rifle, shooting at a Russian battalion?'

'Yes.' There was an adamant look in Eloise's eye.

'But she's a woman – a girl, for heaven's sake!'

'So was Marianne!' There was a pause as Eloise out-stared an incredulous Teofil. Defeated, he sighed and looked out of the window. The image of Marianne, the symbol of the French Revolution, leading the masses, bare-breasted, to glorious victory over the oppressor, gave way to an image of Inka with a rifle held across her vast, exposed breasts, leading a mixed bag of unkempt Poles, White Russians and Lithuanians against the Tsar's forces. It made him smile and wince simultaneously, which resulted in an inane leer.

'The age of the woman of action is coming, Teofil,' said Maminka. 'You would do well to remember that. The woman who takes control of her own destiny may be rare, but she is germinating in today's Europe. She will be a force to reckon with during the course of this century. You will mark my words, Teofil, when you come across her in the years to come. She will be harder than any man, and more ruthless, for she will have the Teofils of this world to contend with.'

Teofil looked blank. He was trying to imagine Inka as a ruthless fighter. 'What are we going to do about her?' he said finally.

'Chrys must be told.'

'Chrys is an idiot,' snorted Maminka. 'He will bungle it. You must do nothing. Let Inka be mistress of her own destiny.'

Teofil was aghast at the idea. 'But she'll get caught! You're condemning her to death!'

'No, Teofil! I am bequeathing her life! What has she got if she should lose the only thing that is important to her? Without her conspiracy she is just a dumpy, jolly and horsey lass condemned never to be desired by a man! By belonging to a revolutionary group, she has passion, she belongs, she is alive. Think about it.'

'You're being a patriot by proxy!' cried Teofil accusingly. 'And you're prepared to see your grand-daughter killed in the process! Maminko, you will never cease to amaze me!'

'I hope not!'

The following day Inka returned and continued as if nothing had happened. Neither Maminka nor Teofil nor Eloise gave the slightest hint that they knew what was going on at Maliny. Franciszka was not told, in case she should let the secret slip by accident. No further mention whatsoever was made of the matter.

VI

In December Jolanta came home from St Petersburg, and Teofil made a point of studying both girls intently for signs of jealousy, resentment or any other factor that might trigger off some kind of emotional backlash. But neither sister was giving anything away. Inka continued to be her usual, jolly self, and absent herself without explanation, but only for the occasional day, weather permitting. The snows had come, and the bitter Baltic cold discouraged adventures too far from a blazing hearth and a cellar of wine and vodka.

It was Eloise who noted a barely perceptible thaw in Jolanta's demeanour.

'You may well be right,' said Teofil, removing his snow-clad boots, with difficulty, in readiness for bed. He had gone out into the night with a flaming torch to shoot – or at least to frighten away – a wolf that had been prowling dangerously close. 'Do you think there's a man?'

Eloise, already in her nightshirt, pulled back the duck down quilt, and climbed into bed. 'I should think without a doubt.'

'A dashing young cavalry officer, maybe?' Eloise slid sensuously down the bed and pulled the quilt up to her chin.

'She denies it.'

'But not very vehemently, I've noticed.'

'No harm in dashing young cavalry officers. A girl like Jolanta should have at least one in tow!' Teofil was having difficulty with his breeches. 'A curse on Russian tailors!'

'I know!' giggled Eloise, sitting up straight. 'She's fallen head over heels in love with a wild brute of a peasant, and they're having a mad, passionate affair, with secret assignations involving violent, unbridled sexual practices in some hayloft!'

'In this weather?'

With a grunt of relieved pleasure, Teofil released himself of the breeches at the expense of two buttons, which flew across the room like two missiles. 'Jolanta? That'll be the day!' he laughed. 'My wager is still on the cavalry officer.'

Confirmation of everyone's suspicions – and Teofil's wager – came two weeks before Christmas when a letter arrived for Jolanta from St Petersburg.

'Good news?' enquired Eloise casually over breakfast of *bliny* and strong black tea.

Jolanta read the letter very carefully before replying. 'No. It's nothing, mother. Just a friend from the Conservatory.' She ate in silence for a while, before continuing nervously. 'Actually, it's a very good friend. He would like to come and spend Christmas with us, father, if you will permit it.'

The reaction was immediate. The clatter of forks being placed on plates merged with Inka's choking guffaw of pleasure. 'By Jove, Jola! Not your legendary dashing young officer, eh?'

Jolanta smiled wanly. 'Yes, I'm afraid so,' she almost whispered.

'But darling, how marvellous!' said Tatiana, 'of course we'd be delighted to see him, wouldn't we, Chrys?'

'So, it's true, all this rumour of a mythical beast lurking at the back of your life,' said her father.

'Yes.'

'You no longer deny it?'

'No.'

There followed a hubbub of congratulations and expressions of pleasure, which Jolanta drank in with ill-concealed delight. Eloise got up and went over to her and kissed her, while Inka, who was sitting beside her, gave her a friendly nudge which almost pushed her out of her chair.

'Who is this man?'

The noise ceased abruptly, as everyone turned to the other end of the dining room table. Maminka, having placed her fork carefully on her plate and wiped her lips with her napkin, had spoken, the napkin still crumpled in her hand. The question was repeated. 'Well, Jolanta, who is this man?'

Jolanta turned to the old lady and smiled. 'His name is Arkady Petrovitch Osvetlensky, Maminko.'

'I do not know the family. What does he do?'

'He is a Captain in the Russian Cavalry, Maminko.'

'And he is young, dashing and handsome?'

'As a matter of fact, he is.' Jolanta suppressed a ghost of a giggle.

'I shall reserve both judgment and approval until I meet him,' said Maminka, placing her crumpled napkin on the table and rising. 'You may invite him for Christmas, Jolanta.'

Maminka left the dining room in a stunned silence.

In Russia Christmas is celebrated, in the Orthodox faith, on the Feast of the Epiphany, on January 6, but Arkady arrived on the first afternoon of 1821, in his own carriage, which he drove himself.

'A strenuous journey, I should imagine, Arkady Petrovitch,' said Chrys, over a welcoming glass of vodka beside the blazing fire in the drawing room. 'How are the roads from St Petersburg?'

'Not entirely uninteresting, *Panie hrabio*,' came the reply. 'The land is somewhat monotonous to the south of the capital, but Lithuania has its attractions. Travel is one of my passions. I am a devotee of the open road, whenever I have the opportunity.'

'And life in the army affords you this passion?' said Tatiana, who entered the room at that moment, went up to her husband and held his arm.

'Indeed.'

'Ooh! I'll bet you've been to lots of exciting places!' chortled Inka. Arkady smiled and bowed in assent.

'You travel alone, Captain?' said Eloise.

'When on leave, invariably. I thus enjoy total freedom to observe how things are in foreign lands.'

And no doubt how the women are too, thought Teofil wryly. Arkady had come up to everyone's expectations. He was, indeed, dashing and handsome, with a capacity to charm the most austere critic. He was tall, slim and fair, with a straight, Roman nose, high cheekbones and intelligent blue eyes. His moustache, trimmed to perfection, was only slightly darker than his hair, and gave him an air of rakish recklessness. His immaculately tailored and pressed dress uniform, unblemished boots and ceremonial sword in place testified to the services of a good valet at the *White Hussar* in Mariampol, where he had spent the previous night in preparation for meeting Jolanta's family. 'I, too, have travelled extensively, Captain,' said Teofil. 'France, Austria, and the Levant.'

'Moscow?' said Arkady pointedly.

'Y-yes. Moscow,' mumbled Teofil awkwardly.

'Alas, my travels have taken me east rather than west,' replied Arkady. 'Persia, the Caucasian region, as well as Siberia and the Turkic lands beyond the Caspian Sea.'

'You shall tell us of your adventures, Arkady Petrovitch, after dinner!'

Everyone turned to the straight-backed chair in which Maminka had been sitting in silence, listening for hints of breeding and intelligence during the small talk. Her tone, though characteristically uncompromising, was not unfriendly. Jolanta knew her grandmother well enough to glean that, so far, she approved of her young cavalry officer. What she made perfectly clear, however, was that tales of adventures in far-off lands were not the stuff of the essential small-talk that etiquette required for an occasion such as this. Inka's face fell visibly as she realised she was being deprived of lurid tales, at first hand, of Asiatic horsemanship, macho posturing and exotically clad, black eyed temptresses seducing tribal chiefs in enormous tents, as described in the kind of books she enjoyed reading.

Maminka successfully engineered the rest of the day. Further small-talk revealed that Arkady's family were respected landowners with an estate, to the east of Moscow, large enough for Maminka's approval. Likewise, his army career, which began with some distinguished action in the closing stages of Napoleon's expulsion from Russia, had blossomed, and Tsar Alexander was known to have spoken well of him. He was now stationed at the garrison in St Petersburg, where his duties were largely social and ceremonial.

'I'll bet you go to lots of fantastic balls, where all the girls fancy you terribly, eh?' chuckled Inka, her eyes glowing with unashamed admiration.

By late afternoon, when Arkady was shown to his rooms and the house retired to prepare for dinner, Maminka had decided that Jolanta had made an excellent choice, with the one inescapable reservation that he was not a Pole. However, taking all things into consideration, she decided that tales of adventures later that evening would be perfectly in order.

Over the next few days, Arkady enhanced the approaches to Christmas with his presence. Always charming and witty, he made a perfect complement to Jolanta. Teofil, whose ingrained cynicism often sought out a darker side to all things fine, had to admit that Arkady and Jolanta were a beautiful couple, gilded by fate and blessed by the good fairy. But because of this same cynicism, he could not help but to wonder where the catch was.

'You think there's a catch?' said Maminka.

'I don't believe in perfection,' replied Teofil, cracking his whip. It was a cold, crisp day with an icy blue sky, and Maminka had expressed a wish to be taken for a sleigh ride along the road to Mariampol.

'You are wise,' said Maminka. 'There is no doubting their beauty. But beauty is skin deep. What is important is that they are both very intelligent and talented people. I believe they are very well suited for a good match.'

'They're too good to be true, Maminko,' said Teofil. 'There must be a flaw somewhere.'

'Well, he is Russian!'

Maminka sniffed, and they rode on in silence. Both of them had largely come to terms with Poland's partitions although deep down both harboured a rueful resentment of all things Russian. At their level, life under the Russians had not been bad. Russian peasants and Polish peasants got on well enough, and among the nobility national frontiers hardly existed. Despite the war, French was still the language of the ruling classes of all nationalities. But Russia was still seen as a foreign power of occupation, and essentially anathema to the patriotic soul. The Samojarskis were Poles at heart, rather than Russians, Slavs or pan-Europeans. Teofil, especially, had a sneaking regard for the conspirators of Maliny. Had he been younger, and more reckless, he might even have joined them.

Age, coupled with a weariness of fighting a seemingly undefinable patriotic war had mellowed him into cutting his losses and counting his blessings. These were, after all, quite considerable, and as long as he had money, Spytkowiec would give security to Eloise, and be a good place to bring up Franciszka and Julek. The fact that they would probably grow up to be good Russians preyed a little on Teofil's mind, but at the end of the day the future belonged to them, and given the right upbringing and a start in life they will be in a position to take charge of their own destinies in the new Europe.

As indeed will Arkady and Jolanta. It was obvious that

they were deeply in love, and that an engagement would be announced sooner rather than later. Both craved, even planned, for a world where justice, prosperity and freedom would be everyone's heritage, where frontiers would be crossed in peace rather than in anger. Their generation will forge a new, more enlightened Europe, and if the forging smiths are people of the quality of Arkady and Jolanta, then the New Order should lead to a new enlightenment across their war-ravaged continent.

'Our day is gone, Teofil,' said Maminka thoughtfully as Teofil guided the sleigh through the gates of the estate. 'It belongs to our children now.'

The Roman Christmas came, along with all the family joys that go with it. Arkady presented Jolanta with a diamond necklace. Jolanta presented Arkady with her piano composition, entitled *The Legend of the Golden Pumpkin*. It was beautifully hand-scripted by Jolanta herself on finest quality paper, and bound in leather and embossed in gold by the finest craftsman in St Petersburg. On the inside of the front cover was a small window containing a slip of paper with the words 'To Arkady, with all my love, Jolanta. Christmas 1821.'

'How did you come up with such a funny title?' said Inka, screwing up her nose. 'Sounds like a book! Why don't you just call it a Sonata or something?'

'It's based on a children's fairy story that used to make us laugh,' said Jolanta. 'It's in the new, romantic style. All the titles are like that these days.'

After everyone had admired the craftwork and the fineness of Jolanta's script, they insisted on hearing the composition, and turned their chairs round to face the pianoforte. It was already open, and a candelabra reflected itself on the polished walnut and rosewood surface, since they had been singing carols round it before dinner. Jolanta sat down and placed her long, slender fingers on the keyboard. Arkady's heart skipped a beat at the perfection of the scene. The candles spilt such light and shade onto Jolanta's beautiful face and bare shoulders as would have made the finest painter reach for his brushes and canvas. Before beginning, Jolanta cast her cavalry officer a look of love and a ghost of a smile.

Then she played. A rippling, harp-like accompaniment with the left hand set a peaceful scene of tranquillity, from which, after a few bars, her right hand painted a soaring, romantic melody line. This eventually gave way to more whimsical sections, some lightweight, some bouncy with a weightier feel about them. A certain flurry of notes made Arkady laugh – all of which suggested that the music held a specific meaning for the lovers, which was lost on the other listeners.

After about three or four minutes, the music reverted to the original *arpeggio* accompaniment, and the soaring melody line returned and resolved itself into a quiet and peaceful cadence. The applause and congratulations were noisy, none louder than Arkady's.

'Really, to understand the music you should know the story first,' said Jolanta, who had noticed Maminka's baffled expression.

'I am too old to understand this new thinking,' said Maminka. 'To me music is music, and stories are stories, and they should not mix. But whatever it was, my dear, it was very interesting and beautifully composed and perfectly executed. Now you may kiss me.'

'I say,' said Inka, 'you should get it published, you know, it's much better than a lot of the stuff that's around nowadays!'

'No chance!' said Jolanta. 'No publisher will touch a woman's work.'

'It's not fair!' said Inka. 'You're just as good as any man! I mean, take Maria Szymanowska, or even Amelia Ogińska for inst –'

Maminka stopped that argument before it could germinate.

She had disapproved of the emancipation of women, which some progressive circles had been advocating. She believed very strongly in women's only two possible roles in society: 'in the home, subservient to their men folk, or directing them ruthlessly from behind. In addition to bearing children, that is.'

A week after Christmas Arkady's leave came to an end, and he returned to St Petersburg for the Orthodox Christmas, and to resume his duties after his conquest of Spytkowiec. He was followed at the beginning of February by Jolanta, to resume her studies at the Conservatory. Winter gave way to spring, and the delicate forests came to pea-green and silver life in the new warmth of the sun. Inka's forays, under the pretext of studying the wildlife, became longer and more frequent. Only Teofil and Eloise muttered comments to each other under their breaths.

Maminka, on the other hand, took no notice whatsoever, and devoted her energies to teaching Julek how to outwit his elders.

VII

Arkady's sleigh had bells that were in tune with the chord of 'A' – for Arkady – a harmless affectation that gained him considerable credibility with his many friends and fellow officers. It was seen as an essential *accoutrement* to his musically talented fiancée. After Jolanta's return to St Petersburg Arkady had formally requested Chrys' permission to propose to Jolanta. Maminka's permission to give permission had been readily granted. Jolanta herself, at first dubious about involving sleigh bells in music theory, succumbed to the new Romantic tide, in which many radical and fantastic ideas were gaining ground, both in style and social attitudes as well as in the arts.

It was the end of February, and the snow still lay crisp and hard on the pavements of St Petersburg, making the northern evening glow wanly by the light of the oil lamps seeping yellowly from the windows. Jolanta was putting the finishing touches to her hair and face, with the help of her room-mate, friend and fellow music student, Ida Koniewska, when they heard a chord of 'A' approaching in the road below.

'He's here!' panicked Ida. She was the same age as Jolanta, but her attractive face was full of character rather than beauty. Endowed with a singularly powerful soprano voice, she was studying to be an opera singer. Highly volatile and temperamental, as befitting any budding opera diva, she panicked spectacularly at the slightest excuse, and usually accompanied these turns with a coloratura cadenza which ended with a screech on high C.

A few moments later Arkady entered, resplendent in his

ceremonial uniform. He was accompanied, correctly, by *Pani* Ivanova, the landlady of the two bedroomed, second floor apartment that she rented to the two girls. *Pani* Ivanova would never allow a man into the apartment unescorted, so she waited with him in the drawing room, pretending to dust the fitments. The apartment was furnished in good taste with decent furniture, and the rugs hanging on the walls gave the room a cosy air of warmth. In a corner stood a piano, a testament to *Pani* Ivanova's preference for music students.

Arkady put *Pani* Ivanova at her ease with some idle small talk.

'Where are you taking her tonight, Captain?' enquired *Pani* Ivanova, having exhausted all weather possibilities.

'To Prince Yevgeni Komarovsky's,' said Arkady. 'He is giving a ball tonight in honour of his English cousin, who is visiting Russia. Jolanta has been asked to play.'

At that moment Ida preceded Jolanta into the drawing room, and ushered in her flat-mate theatrically while warbling a scale ending in top A. 'Beho-o-old Jolah-ah-ah-anta the Fair!'

'Trouble with you, Ida,' laughed Arkady, 'is that your whole world is an operatic stage!'

'How else can I attract the attention of the man I love to distraction to my wares?' cried Ida, ham-acting for all her worth. 'I cannot accept that your heart belongs to another, Arkady!'

'You youngsters never take life seriously!' muttered *Pani* Ivanova, shuffling out of the room. The mood they were in was unlikely to lead to any hanky panky, she thought to herself. 'I'll leave you all to your mad devices!'

'You do so at your own risk, *Pani* Ivanova!' laughed Arkady after her. Then he turned to Jolanta. 'You look stunning!' he said admiringly.

'You don't look too bad yourself,' replied Jolanta, sliding up to Arkady, and running her hands sensuously down his lapels.

'Beware…' Arkady dramatically turned his head away '…lest

you awaken in Ida's heart a frenzied attack of uncontrollable jealous rage, and cause her to…' he clutched at his chest and fell to his knees, '…run her sword through my heart of stone!'

'They would forgive me, for it would be a crime of passion!' said Ida. Suddenly she was serious. 'Anyway, have a great time at the Prince's. Play divinely, Jolanta, and…' she cast a final, flirtatious glance at Arkady '…don't do anything I'd enjoy!'

The ball at Prince Komarovsky's was a splendid affair. A small orchestra playing formal dances alternated with a Jewish band that purveyed a variety of popular music, from Hungarian gipsy csardas, through Polish mazurkas to wild Ukrainian gopaks, in which the more fit and athletic officers were egged on by the cream of St Petersburg's womanhood to show off how many straight-kneed leaps they could achieve from a crouching position. As the evening wore on and the Champagne and vodka began to talk, the repertoire increased to some very wild Georgian dances picked up in the Caucasus during the course of tours of duty in that spectacular region.

Jolanta's short recital took place early in the evening, before the party got out of hand. The admiring and respectful company had assembled in the drawing room to listen to some Mozart, as well as more modern pieces by Beethoven, Schubert and the young Swedish composer, Franz Berwald. When she had finished, there was very warm applause. She rose from the piano chair and was immediately surrounded by admirers, mostly men, all anxious to express their enjoyment of her performance. Jolanta drank in the adulation with every sign of enjoyment.

'What possessed you to play Berwald?'

The remark stood out in the general hubbub of congratulations only because it was uttered with a foreign accent. English, perhaps? Jolanta turned to the source of the question and found herself looking at a not very well-dressed man, perhaps in his mid-twenties, with a smooth, swarthy complexion slightly darker around the chin, very long, black curly hair and the most devastating pair of dark eyes she had ever seen. Jolanta was immediately put off her guard, for the eyes seemed to be laughing.

'I beg your pardon, *Panie* –'

'Meadows,' came the answer, at the same time as a hand took her gently by the elbow and ushered her away from the crowd. 'Daniel Meadows,' he took her hand and kissed it gallantly, 'at your service, Countess. My compliments on your performance. A most perspicacious reading of the Schubert.'

'Thank you.' Jolanta looked round, flustered at being so gently and unobtrusively hijacked. Arkady was now centre stage, drinking in Jolanta's reflected triumph. She turned back to her abductor. 'Thank you. An English name, *Panie* Meadows, if I am not mistaken?'

'I am Irish, *Pani hrabino*. An understandable misapprehension.'

'And what have you against Berwald, *Panie* Meadows?'

Daniel Meadows collected a Champagne bottle and two glasses from a passing tray, and poured. 'A composer of *petits riens*, *Pani hrabino*,' he said. 'I speak of his pianoforte compositions, of course.'

'You play yourself?'

'I vamp a little.'

'But not Berwald?'

'I'm generally a Mozart/Haydn man, myself, and Bach on Sundays.'

Daniel Meadows' easy and affable manner dispelled Jolanta's initial apprehensions. 'I too,' she smiled.

'Perhaps we might exchange interpretations some time?'

Before Jolanta could answer, Arkady, freed of the shackles of secondary adulation, approached.

'There you are Jolanta!' he cried.

'Arkady, may I present to you *Pan* Daniel Meadows, from

Ireland,' said Jolanta. 'My fiancé, Captain Arkady Petrovitch Osvetlensky.'

'Your servant, sir!' Arkady bowed.

'How do you do, Captain.'

'Are you in St Petersburg long, sir?'

'Not a week. I have been staying in Moscow.'

'A fine city. A splendid party, sir. Please excuse us.'

Arkady whisked Jolanta away to where a group of young bloods and their womenfolk were lining up for a Polonaise. That was the last Jolanta saw of the enigmatic *Pan* Daniel Meadows until two months later, when Jolanta chanced to see a poster at the Conservatory advertising a concert at which one Daniel Meadows (from Ireland) would be premièring his Piano Concerto with the Student Orchestra of the St Petersburg Conservatory.

'Who is Daniel Meadows?' enquired Ida, in reply to Jolanta's amazed look as she studied the poster.

'He's an Irish adventurer who apparently vamps a bit on the piano,' said Jolanta, barely able to disguise a tremor in her voice. 'I met him briefly at Prince Komarovsky's ball. He didn't like Berwald.'

'My dear Jolanta,' said Ida, 'no one likes Berwald! He's Swedish, you know.'

'He's quite devastating, actually!'

'I find him boring.'

'Who?'

'Berwald.'

'I'm talking about Daniel Meadows!'

'Oh.'

That Ida had not heard of Daniel Meadows was perhaps understandable, as the pianoforte and the operatic faculties cross-disciplined but seldom. Jolanta, however, felt she should have heard about this forthcoming concert.

'That's because your head is in the clouds!' said Ida. 'You should take part in Conservatory life a bit more, like you used to. Now it's just your tutorials and Arkady.'

Arkady was unable to take Jolanta to the concert, as his unit was due for a month of manoeuvres on the Karelian side of Lake Ladoga, so she asked Ida to accompany her.

'Not on your life!' she growled. 'I hate pianists, especially those who write piano concertos. It's all just meaningless posturing by thumping a pianoforte keyboard faster and louder than anybody else!'

'That's a fine thing for a temperamental opera singer to say!'

'My dear, opera posturing is meaningful. We've got words to back it up. That's the difference!'

In the event Jolanta went on her own, although she managed to lose herself in a crowd of students who all knew each other, so she did not need to feel guilty at going unchaperoned to a public function.

The concert turned out to be the most important turning point in Jolanta's life. Most of the works were student pieces being given an airing, and in the case of most of them, it would be the only airing that they would ever get.

But the highlight was undoubtedly the Meadows Piano Concerto in E flat, where he improvised the orchestral *tuttis*. The first movement owed a debt to late Mozart. It was a swiftly flowing, lightweight sound painting which conjured up in Jolanta's mind all the joys of the countryside, with subtle, but immediately attractive tunes that tripped from pianoforte to orchestra and back with the effortless ease of magpies sparring. The second movement, billed as a Nocturne, was a lyrical meditation on night thoughts, in which Jolanta could almost hear the silvery tones of moonlight and cascading stardust.

Daniel Meadows' touch was as delicate as lace, and some of the softest passages, backed by barely audible shimmering strings, played *tremolando,* sounded distant, like far-off elves at play. The third and final movement was the only one which hinted, yet only vaguely, at what Ida called posturing. It was a breathlessly sparkling rondo, which filled the hall with exploding diamonds of sound, and built up into a complex and spectacular fugal finale. The finger work was impeccable, the effect dazzling.

The Concerto sprinted to its natural conclusion, and the hall burst into a mixed applause, as the young, who embraced the new Romanticism, superseded the measured, polite but ultimately faint-hearted clapping of the older, more classical-minded establishment. But Jolanta heard nothing of this. She sat absolutely still, immobilised by the heaven that was whirling in her head, while at the same time mesmerised by the dark archangel, the sacred bearer of this beauty from some other, less tangible world. The audience noisily left the auditorium, with words like 'divine', 'magnificent' and 'brilliant' mingling with 'interesting', 'modern' and 'incomprehensible' buzzing all around.

There were no words in Jolanta's mind, only sensations. She walked among the seats in a daze, seeing nothing, aware of no one. She bumped into one or two people, who apologised to her, but she took no notice. In the outer hall there were still a number of people, mostly friends and relatives of performers, waiting to go home with them. Jolanta made her way absently towards the doors into the street, only because it seemed like the obvious thing to do. She reached the doors at the same time as a small, hurrying figure dressed in a thick, black overcoat several sizes too big, and an enormous fur hat that almost obliterated his face. His swift flight stopped abruptly at the door, to allow Jolanta to pass first. Jolanta, not aware of this politeness, walked through. The figure having half turned in her direction, grunted in recognition.

'Aha! She who plays Berwald!'

Jolanta half came down to an earthly plane. She paused and

looked at the overdressed figure. The eyes were almost completely hidden, but there was no mistaking the swarthy chin.

'*Pan* Meadows!' she heard herself say.

'*Pani hrabina* Jolanta Barnicka,' came the excited reply. 'You attended the concert?'

'Yes.'

Daniel Meadows removed his hat and looked intently at Jolanta, as if waiting for her to continue. But Jolanta merely continued to stare.

'Did you enjoy it?' he said finally.

'Yes.'

There was another pause. 'My concerto?'

'Yes.'

'Perhaps we should move out of the doorway. There are people waiting to pass.'

'Yes.' But it was only a moment later that Jolanta realised that there was a small crush trying to get past that she moved back into the inner hall. The movement broke Jolanta's trance, and she managed to focus on the situation.

'Your fiancé is not with you?' said Daniel.

'Alas, no. That is, no. He is on manoeuvres in Karelia.'

There was a slight pause before Daniel continued: his Russian was fluent but heavily accented with Irish brogue. 'I am taking coffee and cakes with some friends at Igor's Coffee House. I wonder if you would do me the honour of joining me.'

'Thank you. I would like that.'

Together they went out into the chilly springtime night.

VIII

Coffee and cakes were a euphemism to disguise a night of unbridled debauchery in one of St Petersburg's most popular nocturnal dens. Igor, a wild and unprincipled Cossack with an enormous beard, served more vodka than coffee, and more *bliny* – to soak up the alcohol – than cakes. It was primarily the haunt of radical intellectuals, writers and artists, and students who constituted the bulk of his trade. Jolanta's sheltered and correct life caused her to eschew such places. Arkady may well have patronised Igor's in the company of other young bloods, but he would never have taken Jolanta there. The speluncar and smoky atmosphere hit her hard, especially as she was already reeling from a turbulence of emotions. It was almost as if the Romantic movement had hit her physically as well as emotionally. This was a world that she had inadvertently fallen into, and could not find the will to climb out of.

Daniel Meadows was met with wild cheers and endless rounds of applause. An exquisitely dressed young dandy detached himself from a raucous crowd and ushered him and Jolanta into the bosom of his company.

'Daniel! You were superb!' he cried. 'Ah! *Pani hrabina Barnicka*! Such a pleasure!' He took Jolanta's hand and kissed it.

'You know Prince Freddie Komarovsky-Wellingborough,' said Daniel.

'Of course,' Prince Freddie interrupted with a bow, 'we met, albeit briefly, at my cousin Yevgeny's ball, which he threw in my honour. Your Schubert will be etched on my soul for all time,

Countess.'

'You are a music lover, your highness?' said Jolanta.

'Music is my life, my soul. But please, call me Freddie. Everybody does. Titles are such a bore in a free-thinking society, don't you think?'

'Only if you will call me Jolanta.'

'That is agreed.'

Jolanta recognised many of Prince Freddie's crowd. They were all at Prince Yevgeni's ball. Jolanta recalled the elegant formality – at least of the first part of the evening – and immaculate dress, the stately polonaise and the trays of Champagne being taken round by gloved servants, and wondered how the same company could congregate in a smoky den such as this, raucously drinking vodka, dressed in outrageous clothes seemingly designed to irritate the very establishment to which they all belonged.

'Your cousin is not here?' said Jolanta.

This was met with a bellow of laughter. 'Yevgeni? Here at Igor's? Never!'

'Yevgeni is the archetypal English lord!' said Daniel. 'In England Russians have a reputation for being wild and barbaric. It is a view much reinforced by Freddie, who, as you know, is English, but behaves like a Russian.'

'The English still consider me a Russian despite two generations and most of my relatives being English!'

Prince Freddie's grandmother had married into English nobility in the mid-eighteenth century, but had retained her title and name by a curious arrangement not in general usage at the time. Prince Freddie was an extrovert and a dilettante, foppish and affected, as were many high-bred young Englishmen of his generation. Despite his superficial and often debauched lifestyle, he was an ardent music lover, a passable violinist and collector of folk music. About five years previously he had visited Ireland to scour the land for Celtic airs that he intended to publish.

There he heard Daniel Meadows playing his own compositions at a manor in the Wicklow hills. Both were guests of a dissipated, titled Anglo-Irish wastrel whose only interests were music and wenching, as he liked to call it under certain conditions. Prince Freddie had never heard such playing in his life, and had decided to shelve his plans for the publication of a collection of Celtic Airs, and become an Impresario with the initial self-imposed brief of making Daniel – and himself – rich and famous throughout Europe.

After Moscow's recovery from the attentions of Napoleon, Prince Freddie brought Daniel to study in the land of his forebears, specifically to Moscow, with the idea of turning him into a Russian pianist and composer. The ploy had largely worked, as Daniel, having first studied under Russian teachers, went on to conquer Moscow with his superb musicianship coupled with a singular mastery of light and shade. He was now engaged in a concert tour of the Russian Empire, and had already made a name for himself in Kiev and Warsaw. The highlight of his tour was St Petersburg, which Prince Freddie deemed a fitting venue for the first performance of his Piano Concerto, written during the previous autumn in Prince Yevgeni's dacha east of Moscow.

Daniel had quickly adapted to Russian ways, had mastered the language and the alphabet, and was a devotee of Russian culture, read the literature and even converted to the Orthodox Catholic faith. On the other hand, he had a wild, barbaric temperament, and enjoyed living life to the full. His swarthy complexion and dark eyes won him an enormous pool of female admirers, from which he drank copiously and with total abandon. He also drank more literal liquors, often to excess. His exquisite performances were invariably followed by the seduction of the most beautiful women alternating with bouts of very heavy drinking, as Jolanta discovered at Igor's that night. By midnight he was kissing her passionately in a corner, and by two o'clock he was drunk out of his mind. Jolanta allowed the heady atmosphere to envelop her very being, and, despite a token attempt to keep her own drinking moderate, could not help but be caught up in the atmosphere.

It should have been a night to remember, but it was not. When she woke the following day, it was already well past noon. She opened her eyes with great difficulty, and was visited by a spasm of nausea and a state of total amnesia as far as the previous night was concerned.

'Welcome back from the Underworld!' said a voice. Jolanta turned to find Ida standing over her bed, looking concerned.

'Where –?' mumbled Jolanta.

'In your bed.'

'Why –?'

'You were drunk.'

'When –?'

'At five o'clock this morning.'

'What –?'

'A disgrace, that's what!' said Ida. 'How could you, Jolanta? You of all people! *Pani* Ivanova is shocked! When they brought you home–

'Who?'

'Prince Freddie and some others, actually! It's just as well it was him, otherwise *Pani* Ivanova would have hit the roof! But because he's a Prince she was only shocked, which is lucky for you, otherwise you might have been out on your ear, then where would you have been? I'm really amazed at you, Jolanta, and have you thought what will happen when Arkady finds out you've been going on the town during his absence? No, I'll bet you hadn't thought of that! I'm beginning to think I should have gone to that concert with you, then all of this would never have happened.

Ida went on in this vein for a good while longer, but Jolanta was no longer listening. The word Arkady had caused a shiver of apprehension to run down her spine. She felt herself under her bedclothes. She was wearing a nightdress. Someone, most probably Ida, possibly with some help from *Pani* Ivanova, must have put her nightdress on for her, as she certainly had no recollection of doing so herself. The other, greater problem, was who had undressed her, why and when. Indeed, where? She felt herself gingerly for signs of violation, but found none. The only aches and pains were in her head and stomach. She heaved a sigh of relief as she realised that her virginity was still intact. But there was no doubt that she had been playing with fire.

'I'm in no doubt that you were playing with fire! My God, Jolanta! You might have been raped by the whole of that lot!'

Jolanta spent the rest of the day trying to come down to earth, but found it very difficult. She had tasted a forbidden fruit, and had found it tangily sweet. The image of Daniel Meadows as the Dark Angel of Music kept presenting itself, and she came to the inescapable conclusion that she was totally and irrevocably in love with him. She loved his laughing eyes as much as his slender hands; his swarthy complexion, wild black hair and permanent look of being unshaven as much as his delicacy of touch with which he could conjure up elves and streams out of sound. She loved not a man, but a totality, a being that existed on another plane. Arkady, dear, nice, only human Arkady was as nothing compared to the god that was Daniel Meadows.

That evening a note came, addressed to Jolanta, and was taken up by a very stern-faced *Pani* Ivanova. When she had gone without having said a word, Jolanta opened the envelope with trembling fingers. It was from Daniel. It was short and to the point. 'Would you have supper with me tomorrow evening? Will call at seven. D.'

Jolanta paced the room like a dervish, turning round and round, saturated with a mixture of panic, lust, excitement and thoughts of elves, streams and fugues; but most of all a desperate anxiety about how to inform *Pani* Ivanova that she will not be in for supper tomorrow. Will she suspect? Does she already know? Will she be angry? My God! She might evict me!

That night Jolanta could not sleep, and the following day, she could not settle to anything. She missed her composition class, instead spending the whole day in restless idleness pacing about the apartment, staring out of the window and sitting at the pianoforte wondering which note to start with. Ida was not there, for she had classes and an opera society rehearsal that would not free her till late evening.

By five o'clock she was ready, her hair allowed to hang down in carefully cultivated disarray over a simple dress of a peasant design.

At seven o'clock Daniel arrived, almost an anti-climax following the day's nervous fluster. After the fantastic night of the concert a fairy godmother had caused midnight to strike and turn everything back to normal. The elves had vanished, the streams had dried up, and the Dark Angel had turned into an ordinary, good-looking young foreigner who was taking her out to supper.

Over a pleasant, unassuming meal at the 'Siberian Wolf', an agreeable hostelry patronised mostly by merchants, travellers and students, Daniel told Jolanta of his humble origins among the Mountains of Mourne in the north of Ireland. He told of his father, a gardener in a stately home where the squire had a pianoforte on which little Daniel was allowed to play. At five he was picking out Irish pentatonic tunes, which he found very easy as he could play them using the black notes only. The squire was a fair pianist himself, and his wife sang, and together they constituted what was in effect Daniel's early musical education.

At thirteen he left home to become a jobbing musician, playing jigs and airs in alehouses throughout Ireland.

'It was there they taught me how to drink!' he said with a laugh. 'And I've never looked back!'

When he was fifteen, he heard Mozart for the first time. He was passing a music shop in Dublin at the time. He entered the shop to find a scruffy middle-aged man trying out different pianofortes. Daniel surreptitiously listened, for the man was very good, but was unable to make up his mind which instrument to buy, at which point Daniel stepped forward. Excuse me, sir, he had said, it's the little one sounds the best to me, sir, from where I was listening, sir.

The scruffy man looked in amazement at the equally scruffy urchin with the laughing eyes, and, probably recognising a kindred spirit, burst out laughing. Why, you young rascal, he had said, if it's good enough for your ear, then it's good enough for mine! And he bought the delicate toned Pleyel in preference to the harder Erard.

The scruffy man was, in fact, a music teacher. When he heard Daniel play, he took him on without a fee, and taught him to read music and the rudiments of theory. One day, when you're rich and famous, he had said, you can call on me and buy me a beer.

'And did you?' said Jolanta.

'I've not been back,' replied Daniel. 'I'm not rich and famous yet, but I'm working on it.' He looked intently into Jolanta's eyes. 'But when I do, I would like to have you by my side.'

Over Turkish coffee Daniel placed his hand over Jolanta's. He had never known her as the ice queen, she had changed so much after the concert. By the light of the oil lamps her skin was smooth as silk, and the colour of warm oranges. Her eyes glowed with the passion of a young girl in love for the first time, twin windows of a raging fire burning, out of control, within her heart.

'May I play to you, Jolanta?' he whispered.

'Where?'

'I have a piano in my lodgings.'

No further words were necessary. Daniel paid the bill and they went out into the cold, clear night.

IX

Daniel's lodgings were a simple attic room with a skylight through which a blaze of stars twinkled from a black sky. In an iron stove a fire burned, radiating heat in the room. Some cheap icons hung above the mantel, and the walls were draped, like all walls in Russia, with rugs. A table, a sideboard, some chairs, a large bed and a piano were the only furniture. The floorboards were bare, but partially covered with a Turkish carpet, now a little moth-eaten in parts.

Daniel lit an oil lamp, and brought out a bottle of vodka and two glasses. They drank two tots each, straight off.

'May I play you some of my Nocturnes?' said Daniel.

Jolanta nodded, and Daniel sat at the pianoforte and unravelled a sound nightscape of such tender peacefulness that Jolanta was, again, transported onto a higher plane. She closed her eyes and rode moonbeams with silver manes to the stars. Like a magician, Daniel cast such spells as Jolanta did not know could even exist. She danced with elves, sailed paper ships to magic lands, did battle with hunchbacked Karelian ogres and was abducted by Arabian princes with curved scimitars. The tender kiss on her neck in the ensuing silence was just an extension of heaven. She reached out, took his hand and caressed those fingers, sculpted wands that had conjured up such delicious sensations in her soul. Daniel kissed the palm of her hand, and baby angels ran down her spine.

The volcano in her heart erupted, and Jolanta spun round to face the man she knew had to be her lover, hungry for his mouth, his body, his whole being. She needed to be taken, ravaged and ravished a thousand times over and thus to be impregnated with the very essence of her Dark Angel, to be at one with him. Their lips met with a hot thirst that refused to be quenched, no matter how hard and how long the kiss lasted. Panting with desire, Jolanta allowed Daniel to undress her, but he was too slow. Far too slow. Why can't he go faster? In the end she took over. After an eternity of seconds they stood, naked, facing one another in the burnt orange glow of the little attic room. Jolanta tensed her body to go to him, but Daniel pre-empted her.

'Please, don't move!' he said. Jolanta untensed and looked at Daniel quizzically, her head slightly inclined to one side. 'I need to look at you, to see you as you really are. I want my desire for you to be full. You are so beautiful, I want the sight of you to be enough to – to –' Jolanta's gaze dropped from his face to his erection, hard, glowing crimson, criss-crossing veins throbbing with anticipation. They continued, absolutely still, gazing at one another, yet delaying the act for as long as possible. It was Daniel who could wait no longer. He reached out, and took Jolanta in his arms, and squeezed her with all his might. Jolanta felt his hardness pressing against her flat stomach. She tensed her stomach muscles as hard as they would go, and pressed them against him with a slight wriggling movement. Daniel's breath stopped suddenly, then his whole body convulsed violently with a long-drawn-out grunt of ecstasy. A softening of muscle and a warm trickle down her stomach gave her a sensation more intense than she could have previously imagined. She held him tightly, and her mouth broke into a smile of pleasure. He had shown her heaven, and she had been able to reciprocate.

Daniel released himself from her grip and collapsed onto the bed. Jolanta sat beside him. He took her hand, and held it tightly. 'I love you,' he muttered. 'I've never loved anyone as I love you.'

Jolanta leaned over him and kissed him tenderly on his lips. Daniel pulled her over onto him, and they began to wrestle playfully, kissing and enjoying every nook and cranny of each other's bodies. The feel of her hot flesh, its passion still unresolved, roused him again. Her eyes were glazed, and her fine, smooth breasts, delicately embroidered with tiny veins, heaved in time to her breathing, and he read her hunger. He also knew that she was a virgin, and that he would have to be gentle. He lay on top of her, and felt her thighs parting, slowly and tentatively. Gently he prepared the way and slowly he worked himself into her, using her moisture to ease his passage. Her body was tense, treading fearfully in unknown territory, yet trusting her beloved guide implicitly.

A little cry from her signalled the irrevocable penetration. Daniel withdrew, anxious not to cause more pain than necessary, his passion temporarily shelved. Jolanta did not stop him, but lay back, still and quiet. A tear trickled down her cheek. He kissed her tenderly on the forehead, and got up. The fire was getting low, so he put another log into the stove.

'Play to me,' he heard her whisper. 'A song of love.'

Daniel went to the pianoforte, sat down and started to play. What fell from his fingers was rhapsodic, with alternating moods of tender romance and wild passion. Jolanta lay still, listening.

'What is it?' she said.

'A song of love,' came the reply.

'Who for?'

'You.'

'But it can't be – you've only just – we've – when did you write it?'

'Right now. This is my song of love to you, Jolanta. I'm composing it now!'

Jolanta got up and went over to the pianoforte. 'You mean, you're improvising it as you go along?'

Daniel executed a flurry of notes while he laughed aloud. The music and the laughter matched perfectly. Jolanta was impressed. A wide grin suddenly spread on her face. 'In that case,' she said, 'I shall give you something to write about! Just don't stop playing!' She crouched down beside him and insinuated herself under his hands and between his knees. She then took him in both hands and began kissing and massaging him. The music took a distinct turn for the worse, and the time signature changed from bar to bar, until it nearly ground to a halt. 'Don't stop!' warned Jolanta. 'Nor you!' gasped Daniel.

After a while Jolanta stood up between his knees, facing Daniel, and climbed onto his lap. 'Keep playing!' she said as she manoeuvred herself into position astride him. She then slowly insinuated himself inside her. By this time the music was chaotic and had lost all meaning and tonality. Jolanta, with a final wriggle, accommodated his total penetration. She held him tightly, while keeping absolutely still, waiting for his music to regain rhythm and direction. Daniel, taken up by this act, which he had certainly never come across before, had got into the spirit of it, and read Jolanta's mind. She had given him enough respite to allow him to take a grip on the music, and within a few moments the song of love had regained something of its original timbre. This time a distinct melody had appeared, which Daniel began to develop and improvise around.

Jolanta then began to rock to the rhythm of the music, and Daniel matched the action accordingly. Eventually passion took over again, and Jolanta, who set the pace of the lovemaking, lost control in a frenzy both came to a glorious orgasm, which Daniel acknowledged with a passage of tempestuous chords, even going so far as to modulate to the key of her final moans. He himself followed soon after, but his musical exhaustion by now was such that he could only manage a sustained discord, followed by a very ordinary cadence.

'That didn't sound very good,' said Jolanta, frowning.

'Never judge an orgasm by its music!' gasped Daniel.

Ten minutes later Jolanta was lying in Daniel's bed, awake and in a daze of happiness. She was trapped in an eternal Now, from which she wished never to emerge. Daniel had put on a gown, and was seated at the table, pen poised over manuscript paper. He was trying to write down the rhapsody that was part of the total act of love that he and Jolanta had just experienced. It was not easy, for although the melody that had eventually emerged was a beautiful one, and easy enough to recall, it was the overall shape, the design of the whole that was creating problems, and would have to be honed and moulded into the shape and form of a piece of composed music. He had been brought up in the classical traditions, where strict rules of symmetry applied; yet this was the New Music, Romantic, in both senses of the word, free and uninhibited by the constraints of the old ways.

By four o'clock Jolanta was fast asleep, still as a statue, and even her breathing was imperceptible. The oil lamp was burning low when Daniel wrote in the finishing cadence, small and pathetic, yet absolutely accurate. Finally satisfied, he put down his pen and extinguished the oil lamp. There was a chill in the pre-dawn air, so Daniel filled up the stove with logs, and climbed into bed.

Jolanta woke. She reached out and took her Dark Angel in his arms. Half an hour later, in a somnolent daze they made love once again, gently, almost automatically, both falling into deep sleep immediately afterwards.

Pani Ivanova was shocked. 'What am I going to tell the *Pan hrabia* your father?' she howled, 'when he finds out that you did not come home last night? You are a wicked, irresponsible girl, and if you were mine, I would flay your hide till it bled!'

Jolanta tried to explain that she had spent the evening with Daniel at Prince Yevgeni's house, had drunk too much (for which she invented a profuse and humble apology) and had spent the night there as a guest of Princess Ileana Komarovska. She knew that *Pani* Ivanova would not dare to check this story with Prince Yevgeni, and hoped she could get away with it. But there was no pulling the wool over *Pani* Ivanova's eyes. As a professional landlady to students, she had seen and heard it all before. 'You spent the night with that pianist, and now God will punish you for it, you mark my words!'

Jolanta spent the next three weeks living on a cloud. She and Daniel made love whenever they could find the opportunity, even though she always returned to her apartment, for fear of further censure from *Pani* Ivanova. Only Ida was party to the full facts, which she enjoyed with a relish that no operatic plot in existence could surpass. She even undertook to practise her singing at the pianoforte during the day, while the lovers retired to the bedroom to make love to the strains of arias by Mozart, Gluck and Cimarosa – confident that *Pani* Ivanova, believing that a musical daytime soirée was in progress, would not dare to interrupt.

Daniel, in the meantime, was much in demand to play at real soirées in the noble houses of St Petersburg. As an Irish-Russian, he was a fashionable artist to have around, and all the most cultured houses vied ferociously for his talents. His repertoire consisted primarily of Mozart and his own compositions, as well as those of Haydn, Beethoven and Schubert. Included in his programme was a new composition, entitled *Romance in D*, which elicited a mixed response from his listeners. Some considered it Romanticism gone haywire, others found it unusually exciting, and pointing the way to the future, while the classicists found it undisciplined, atonal and lacking in symmetry and order.

Everyone was agreed on the weakness of the ending.

A number of titles had been jokingly tossed about by Daniel

and Jolanta, among them *Cascade of Love of the Elves, Chanson d'une Nuit d'Amour, Sous les Etoiles, Ode Fantastique à Venus*, and, almost taken seriously, *A Song of Love*. Both Daniel and Jolanta considered all these as too obvious, especially as the whole of St Petersburg now knew of Society's newest affair, and both drew the line at a public exposé of their act of love executed from the keyboard. *Romance in D* was accurate, anonymous and utterly conventional. Not even Ida suspected the truth behind Daniel's latest, enigmatic composition.

In the meantime, the gossipmongers were out in force, and very soon friends and acquaintances of Arkady were put in the picture.

'Arkady's going to find out about you and Daniel the moment he gets back from Karelia!' said Ida. 'You can't just go on like this, Jolanta! You can't ignore tomorrow and just hope it will go away! You've got to make up your mind how you're going to play this! Please!'

Jolanta knew that Ida was right, yet her euphoria would not go away, and she could not hoist herself out of her dreamlike state.

The catalyst for action came two days before Arkady's return from his stint in Karelia. It was the first warm day of Spring. Daniel and Jolanta met on the Nevsky Prospekt after Jolanta's classes.

'I'm leaving St Petersburg,' said Daniel without preamble. 'Prince Freddie has finalised arrangements for my tour of Germany and Austria.'

'But when are you going?' asked Jolanta, taken aback.

'I'm leaving for Königsberg the day after tomorrow.'

Jolanta panicked. 'But Daniel! I shall not see you again?'

'I thought perhaps you would come with me?'

'Come with you? To Prussia?'

'And Austria. I don't want to go without you, Jolanta. I want to stay with you for ever!'

'And I want to be with you for always, too!'

'Come with me.'

Jolanta placed her hands on the parapet and looked out over the river. It was flowing fast, fed with the thawing snows. The time of reckoning had come, and she suddenly knew that if she didn't do something positive, however painful, she would lose out on every count, and be left with nothing but a tarnished reputation that would weigh her down for the rest of her life. To up and go meant throwing in her lot with Daniel to the exclusion of all else. She would be cast out by her family, including her father, and Arkady would certainly drop her without further ado. He, too, could not afford a wild slut of a wife – for that is how she would appear. Also, Daniel was a womaniser and heavy drinker, and it is possible that she was destined to be just his latest adventure.

She could let Daniel go, and return to Arkady. She could either keep the secret from him, not an easy option as he would be bound to find out one way or the other; a man like Arkady cannot be cuckolded indefinitely, if at all. Or she could confess and beg forgiveness, and hope his love and understanding would stretch to ending up second best to a quite remarkable affair.

The third alternative would be to forget them both, and return to the bosom of her family at Spytkowiec to nurse her psyche and try to get over it all, perhaps with Maminka's help. As a last resort, she could join a nunnery.

'Join a nunnery,' she muttered.

'What?' said Daniel.

Jolanta came back to earth. 'Oh, nothing,' she said vaguely. 'I was just thinking.' Suddenly she became intense and held Daniel's hands tightly. 'Oh, Daniel!' she sobbed, 'you know I want to go with you! You know I love you more than anything in the world! But you must give me time!'

'You've had three weeks already!'

'I need more!'

'You haven't got more! The day after tomorrow I'm leaving for Könisgberg; and the day after tomorrow Arkady returns! Unless you know what you're doing, all hell will break loose!'

'Give me till noon tomorrow!'

'Noon tomorrow, then.'

Jolanta watched as he walked briskly away. She wanted to call after him, but realised it would be futile. She now had twenty-four hours in which to make up her mind and choose between heaven and hell.

The trouble was that she could not tell which was which.

X

By mid-morning the following day Jolanta had decided to cast her fate to the winds and go with Daniel. She would write to her father – and Maminka – from Königsberg, explaining all and begging for their understanding and forgiveness. She was writing a tearful and passionate farewell note to Arkady, which she had asked Ida to deliver after she had gone, when she heard the sound of a horseman arriving in the street below. She rushed to the window, but the horseman had already dismounted. He had not even tethered his horse. A few moments later the door to the apartment burst open, and there was Arkady, with a bewildered *Pani* Ivanova coming up behind, standing in the frame. His face was a mask of blind fury.

'Is it true?' he cried. 'Tell me it isn't true!'

Jolanta wrung her hands in panic. 'Arkady,' her voice warbled nervously. 'You're back. I thought tomorrow…'

'You thought wrong.' Arkady stormed into the apartment. 'I'm back, and the first thing I hear is that my fiancée is a slut and a foreign piano player's whore. Again, I'm asking you, is it true?'

'If you will let me explain…'

Arkady's eyes fell on the table, where a pen, ink, paper and an envelope caught his eye. He picked up the paper, while Jolanta tried to stop him. 'I'm sure this contains all the explanation that's needed!' He read. 'My dearest Arkady. What I have to say is very difficult for me. Let me start by saying that I have loved you deeply, and I still respect you as a person – ha! that's a fine thing, Jolanta. That's just what I need from my fiancée, her respect! – but by the time you get this letter I shall be gone. Well, Jolanta, I've now got the letter, you're still here!'

'Don't make it difficult for me, Arkady,' sobbed Jolanta. 'It's not the way I wanted it!'

'Really? Then how did you want it?' said Arkady, throwing down the letter. 'I want the truth, told plainly and simply, without excuses or sentimental apologies in operatic-style letters! Where are you going?'

'To Prussia.'

'When?'

'Tomorrow.'

'With whom?' Jolanta burst into a fit of uncontrolled sobbing. 'With whom?' He repeated, shouting.

'With Daniel!' she wailed.

'The piano player? Your Irish lover?'

Jolanta could only nod through her tears. Arkady turned briskly, bowed to a very perplexed *Pani* Ivanova, and stormed down the stairs, leaving Jolanta howling. *Pani* Ivanova approached. 'You've been a wicked girl, and God is now punishing you for your sin! Don't think I don't know what you've been up to, my girl! No good ever comes of these things! I told you at the time, but you didn't listen! You've only yourself to blame.'

But Jolanta wasn't listening. She had picked up the letter, and had screwed it up. She held it like a handkerchief, and absent-mindedly dabbed her eyes with it. She collapsed into an armchair and continued to howl uncontrollably. *Pani* Ivanova dithered, torn between righteous indignation and kindly understanding of a confused young girl whose emotions had careered wildly out of control. But she was only the landlady, with a good reputation for keeping an orderly house. She clicked her tongue impatiently and left.

An hour later Ida came back to find Jolanta in a state of total hysterics. She had skipped her afternoon choral class because word of Arkady's return had spread. Ida went straight to Prince Yevgeni's, as being the most likely source of information about latest developments. Prince Yevgeni, evidently deeply embarrassed by developments, was 'not in', but Prince Freddie was. He was extremely distraught.

'Arkady's company returned early this morning,' said Freddie in answer to Ida's enquiry. 'He learned about Jolanta and Daniel within ten minutes.'

'Who told him?' said Ida.

'Heavens!' said Freddie, 'does it matter? Everyone knew, and it was just a matter of time.'

'Jolanta's having hysterics.'

'I'm not surprised. But there's more.'

Ida blanched. 'He's been to see Daniel!' she gasped. Freddie nodded and turned away. 'You don't mean –?'

'I'm afraid so,' muttered Freddie. 'Pistols at dawn.'

'Mother of God!' Ida fell onto a *chaise-longue* and looked thoughtful. 'Can he shoot?' she asked.

'No.'

'He'll get killed, for God's sake!'

'He'll be lucky not to!' There was a deep bitterness in Freddie's voice. 'I'm his second.'

'It's criminal!' said Ida. 'The finest pianist of our generation! Possibly in the whole of Europe! It's not fair. Freddie,' she rose, 'you must speak to Arkady! There's got to be another way!'

'I have, and there isn't.' Freddie paced about in fury. 'How do you think I feel? Daniel's mine! I found him, nurtured him, made him what he is today. Now that idiot is going to kill him! My friend and protégé! Christ! What a waste!'

After only a moment's hesitation Ida rose and left. She went straight to Arkady's house – the company were given a month's leave after their stint in Karelia. She begged, cried, cajoled, and even threatened Arkady to call off the duel, but the young

Captain was not to be detracted from the duty that he knew he had to do.

Seeing that her entreaties were falling on seriously impinged dishonour, she then rushed over to Daniel's lodgings. The pianist was there, perched on the edge of a chair by the stove, quaking with terror. Ida tried to persuade him to flee for his life there and then.

'Get yourself onto a ship to England!' she begged. 'There must be one leaving any time now!'

'There isn't!' whimpered Daniel, his voice shaking uncontrollably. 'Don't you think I haven't enquired?'

'What about a coach? There must be a coach leaving for Poland or Königsberg! What about Helsinki?'

'There is, except that his friends are watching the post halts! There's no escape, Ida! I'm doomed, as good as dead!'

Ida spent the rest of the day seeking out any officers or officials who might be in a position to stop the duel, but was stonewalled all along the way. It was evident that a Russian officer's honour took precedence over the life of a drunken, foreign piano player every time. The rules of the game were crystal clear. In desperation she returned to Prince Yevgeni's house.

'Can't you mount a raid?' she asked Prince Freddie. 'An armed group, or something? We can always find a gang of villains who'll do anything if we paid them enough! They could charge in shooting, and rescue Daniel!'

'They'd have to kill Arkady first! No chance!' wailed Prince Freddie. 'Arkady is a Captain in the Tsar's guard. We'd never get away with it!'

It was late that night when Ida returned, utterly exhausted to the apartment, and told Jolanta about the impending duel. Jolanta, her tears long dried up, was sitting on the edge of a chair, her eyes exhausted and her face an empty parchment. She had not the strength to cry any more. Her reaction was a glazed expression as she gazed into a non-existent distance.

The night seemed endless as the two girls kept vigil. Despite their exhaustion, neither was able to sleep, although Ida managed to doze fitfully in short bursts. Dawn came, grey and cold, casting a sombre shade of colourlessness onto the surface of the River Neva. Ida and Jolanta were both wide awake, and sat, immobile, only occasionally catching each other's eyes.

The sun was already up, and its wan light promised a hazy but pleasant spring day. A horseman rode up and dismounted on the cobbles below. Jolanta and Ida looked at one another, but neither moved. After an eternity, footsteps were heard on the stairs. The door opened and *Pani* Ivanova, looking distraught, ushered in Prince Freddie. The look on his face was not revealing anything, but the two girls knew exactly what he had come to say.

'He's dead?' whispered Jolanta.

Freddie nodded. 'A bullet straight through the forehead.'

Jolanta's volcano of emotions, smoking but dormant, erupted as never before. She rushed around the room, screaming and howling hysterically, and could not be restrained. Ida tried to put her arms round her, but was violently rebuffed. *Pani* Ivanova, to whom the whole affair was beyond her capacity to deal with, staggered in a daze, and sat down heavily in a chair. Prince Freddie, also not used to any drama heavier than an operatic plot, did not know where to put himself. He dithered about the apartment, as if looking for something with which to ease the situation, but finding nothing. Finally, Ida put her hand on his arm. 'Go, Freddie,' she said. 'There's nothing you can do.'

'But –'

'Just go, man!' she cried. 'You'll just make matters worse if you stay!'

Freddie looked from Jolanta to Ida and back again, his mouth open, like that of a fish. It was only when he looked at *Pani* Ivanova, who nodded and indicated the door with her eyes, that he left, pausing and turning only momentarily, before disappearing down the stairs.

During the rest of the morning Jolanta had howled herself into total exhaustion. Ida, with *Pani* Ivanova's help, put her to bed, where she slept fitfully. *Pani* Ivanova, whose righteous attitude had melted into a true sense of compassion, was as helpful as she could be. Ida, despite her predilection for ham-acting her real life, was a tower of strength, both to the bewildered landlady, and to Jolanta. She waited till her room-mate was asleep, before leaving her in *Pani* Ivanova's care.

'There are some things I need to do, *Pani* Ivanova,' she said. 'Please look after her, and if she should wake and I'm not here, please re-assure her I shall be back presently.'

She returned later that evening, armed with a leather bag for Jolanta, which she did not want *Pani* Ivanova to know about. Jolanta, however, slept right through the evening, and all night. Ida stayed in the apartment the whole time, even getting up in the night to make sure Jolanta was all right.

The following morning Jolanta woke. 'What time is it?' she said, seeing Ida in the room with her.

'Just after ten,' said Ida. 'You've been asleep for over twenty hours.'

'Great heavens,' she muttered. 'I'd better get up.'

Ida looked quizzically at Jolanta. She was acting as though nothing had happened, as though the past three weeks had been a temporary madness, a visit to a fantasy world of operatic dimensions. Now the final curtain has fallen, and it was time to return to reality.

'How – how are you feeling?' she asked.

'Fine.'

'I'm glad.' Ida picked up the leather bag. 'This is for you.'

Jolanta yawned and focused her eyes. 'What is it?'

'See for yourself.'

Jolanta took the bag and opened it. Inside was a collection of Daniel's compositions, with the Piano Concerto on top. She put it all straight back, closed the bag and placed it on the floor beside her bed. 'You went to fetch these?'

'I thought you should have them. Not Freddie. Especially,' Ida almost smiled, 'the *Romance in D*.'

This elicited no response from Jolanta. 'Thank you,' she merely said. 'Is there any tea?'

There was. Ida watched Jolanta drink in silence. The transformation was beyond her understanding. Jolanta had reverted to being an ice queen, cold and inscrutable, beautiful as the pale moonlight, even though dishevelled before her morning toilet.

Fortified with the strong black tea, Jolanta rose, got washed and dressed, did her hair, and looked fit to face the world. She spent the rest of the afternoon at the pianoforte practising. Beethoven. His latest Sonata to reach the music publishers of St Petersburg.

That evening Ida had a previous supper engagement with two basses who were vying for her favours, so she left *Pani* Ivanova in charge, and went out. Jolanta ate the supper on a tray that *Pani* Ivanova had prepared for her with considerable relish. She then went back into the bedroom and opened the leather bag. She rummaged through the sheaves of hand-written music, till she found the *Romance in D*. Her fingers trembled as she took it to the pianoforte, put it on the music stand, and placed her fingers on the keys. Then she stared long and hard at the music, before removing her hands from the keys. She picked up the music, returned to her bed, and sat there, propped up on her pillows. She then opened the music and read the score – in her head. Slowly, as the story unfolded, her ice melted, and tears like liquid diamonds came to her eyes and trickled down her marbled cheeks. After the silly little cadence, she closed the score and wept, silently and bitterly, alone.

Part Four - 1822

I

That same summer Maminka died seemingly of a broken heart. Her hopes of an idyllic union between Jolanta and her handsome young cavalier utterly dashed. Jolanta gave up her studies at the Conservatory and returned to Spytkowiec, where she embraced apathy and indolence. Her father was devastated. He found it difficult to come to terms with the fact that Jolanta was a lesser being than a perfect goddess, flawed and in many instances ostracised as a whore. He ended up storming round the estate in a depressive sulk. Inka tried hard to be supportive, but to no avail. A different sister in the same circumstances might have harboured a secret delight at the downfall of such a paragon of talent and beauty, but not Inka. Her concern was absolutely genuine. Maminka had rued the escape of such an eligible young cavalier as Arkady, for her sense of social standing was strong and she shared with the whole family the delightful prospect of a fairy-tale wedding. Teofil and Eloise were circumspect about the matter: Teofil, especially, took the view that this was all part of life's rich but tragic pageant, and left her alone, judging that that was what she wanted.

Whatever the truth of Jolanta's wants and needs, she sought solitude. She never once played on the pianoforte, despite entreaties by all the family, who believed in music as the Great Healer. She had reverted to her original ice queen image, cold and inscrutable, and only those closest to her knew the torment without end that was raging in her heart. To the world at large she was just the same as ever before, beautiful and aloof, polite and correct in every way; but she had lost all interest in life, and only emerged from her room to go on long walks on the estate, and that only in bad weather. Hot, sunny days were spent in her room in brooding melancholy. She never once mentioned Arkady or Daniel, and always changed the subject if ever anyone else made any mention of them. The only legacy of the affair was the case of Daniel's works, the only constant in her room, which she always kept beside her bed. Very often she would take out the music and read it, in her head, like a book. Her favourites were the Piano Concerto, and, of course, the Romance in D.

The death of Jolanta's soul had been too much for Maminka. She tried everything from coaxing to threats in an attempt to get her beautiful grand-daughter to pull herself together and make some attempt at rebuilding her life, but Jolanta had erected a wall of resistance that even Maminka's iron will could not penetrate. Defeated, Maminka also seemed to have lost the will to continue, the evidence being that she ceased to take any active interest in family matters, and declined to give advice. In early June she fell badly on the stairs, and dislocated her hip. As a result, she took to her bed, from which she was not able to direct the everyday life of Spytkowiec. What was more, she did not seem to want to. She became increasingly weak until the morning of Midsummer's Day, when her maid found that she had died peacefully in the night.

Maminka was buried, at her request, at the cemetery of the Catholic Church of the Holy Cross at Mariampol, where she had married Old Kaz, such a long time ago. She had harboured a deep love of that church ever since.

The funeral was marred by an incident that was to turn the fortunes of the Samojarski and Barnicki families. During the singing of a favourite Polish funeral hymn, two Russian officials, who had been sitting at the back of the church, strode up to the altar and peremptorily stopped the service.

'What is the meaning of this?' said Chrys, annoyed. 'Why are you interrupting my mother's funeral?'

'You are singing a prohibited hymn,' was the answer.

'What do you mean, a prohibited hymn?' cried Chrys, 'what right have you to prohibit hymns?'

'The words contravene new directives from St Petersburg. The words tell of interment in the soil of the Fatherland.'

'Yes, well?'

'Fatherland is a Polish expression that negates the authority of Mother Russia. Your mother will be buried in Russian soil, and the words must express this.'

'The Tsar has decreed this?'

'Correct. Otherwise, you may proceed with the service.'

Despite feelings of angry frustration no one wanted to make an issue of it over Maminka's coffin, so the funeral service continued as from the end of the offending hymn. The Russians had returned to their places at the back of the church, where they slouched disdainfully, pointedly looking bored. Teofil glanced at Inka, and noted that she was quaking with a seething rage that he had not imagined her capable of.

After the funeral everyone returned to Spytkowiec in silence. Only then did Teofil make a point of seeking out Inka, who had immediately repaired to the stables.

'Going for a ride?' he asked. Inka nodded. 'May I ride with you?' Inka waved her hand at the stable, indicating that he was free to do just as he wished. Both saddled their horses in silence for a few moments. 'You're angry,' protested Teofil.

Inka's response was immediate and voluminous. 'Well, aren't you?' she cried. 'Those fucking Russians are treating us like shit! Banning a hymn, for God's sake! I could have murdered those bastards on the spot!'

Teofil pursed his lips. Inka had never used such strong language before. 'Why didn't you?'

'What a stupid question!' said Inka, leading her horse out into the yard.

'Not at all. You should have killed them.' Outside, Inka hoisted herself ungracefully into the saddle, and rode off. 'You've got the weapons!' Teofil shouted after her.

Inka drew up suddenly and turned her horse. 'What do you mean?' she said, looking menacingly at Teofil. The latter climbed neatly into the saddle and rode up to her. 'What do you mean by that?' she repeated.

'I know what you're up to, you and all that lot up at Maliny.'

Inka blanched. 'You know?'

'Let's ride.' Teofil put his horse into a gallop. Inka followed. When they were out of sight of the Manor Teofil slowed down to a canter, and Inka followed suit. Teofil then recounted the day, the previous autumn, when he, Eloise and Franciszka almost interrupted the meeting of the cell. Inka listened gravely.

'Where do you hope it will all get you?' concluded Teofil.

'Free!' cried Inka.

'How many of you are there?'

'About five hundred. We call ourselves the Unborn Future.'

'Poles?'

'Some Lithuanians too.'

'Where do you get your guns from?'

'England. France. Even America. They arrive by sea at Königsberg, then they're smuggled in from Prussia, mostly across the marshes of the Mazury.'

'Who's in charge?'

There was a pause. 'I am.'

Teofil laughed long, but mirthlessly. 'So, you hope to lead five hundred assorted Polish and Lithuanian hotheads calling themselves, romantically, the Unborn Future against the Tsar's highly trained forces to glorious victory and freedom!'

'You're laughing at us! At me!' There was a genuine anger in Inka's tone.

Teofil stopped. 'No, I'm not!' he said. 'I do not laugh at love of the Fatherland.'

'Then what –?'

'Look, Inka, I don't know what your plans are for your cell, but I wonder if you know what is at stake? Do you realise that five hundred untrained locals taking on the Russian army is a suicide mission?'

'We're prepared to die for our country!'

'All right. So, you all die for your country, and we will all say thank you over your graves and out of Russia's hearing! All that will achieve is five hundred less hotheads for the Russians to have to cope with.' Inka looked for, but found, no answer. 'Then, as a warning, the Russians will round up five hundred more and shoot them in a forest clearing.'

'Whose side are you on, Cousin Teofil?' she blurted finally.

'The side of reason. I found it reasonable to fight with Napoleon because I believed he held the key to a free Poland.'

'He lost!'

'But I'm still alive to fight another day. So, what chance have your Unborn Future? One good riot, and you all become the Well Dead Past!'

Inka mellowed. 'What do you suggest?' she said.

Teofil thought for a while. 'Leave me to think about it.'

'You'll join us?'

'I didn't say that.'

'But you'll help us!' Inka broke into a smile and poked his shoulder with her hand. 'Oh, Cousin Teofil! You are a dark horse! Who'd have thought! Oh, gosh!'

When they got back from their ride, Teofil told Eloise about his talk with Inka.

'You crazy idiot!' she cried, 'you're not getting yourself involved with that lot! The Unborn Future! I wonder how many councils of war it took to dream up that name? And you're going to go along with them?'

'I'm just going to try to get them to stay alive longer, that's all!'

'Can't you stop them?'

Teofil shrugged. 'No. They've got a sense of Destiny. They will not be deflected.'

*****

In the event, nothing further happened politically for two years. Chrys, opting for a safe and quiet life, had made the executive decision to play along with Russian policy as far as church worship was concerned. It was, he fully realised, designed to erode, slowly but surely, Polish culture. Polish songs, hymns, poetry and literature which referred to Poles being oppressed on their own soil were ruthlessly stamped out. Anxious not to inflame the authorities, Chrys insisted on church services being politically correct and above board, thus preventing a repetition of the unpleasantness at Maminka's funeral. Teofil and Inka, though seething inside, were forced to acquiesce.

The University of Vilnius, a hotbed of nationalist intrigues and patriotic fervour, was endlessly targeted with sanctions, with whole departments closed down. No one understood why the Tsar, who had initially promised that Polish culture would be allowed, even encouraged, to flourish, had now changed policy. The Unborn Future's ranks swelled, and membership had risen to over a thousand disgruntled patriots from all walks of life. Ex-students, writers and poets joined, along with peasants and artisans. Teofil kept aloof from them all, although Inka kept him posted about latest developments. His advice was sparse and non-committal, usually suggesting that the whole thing was a waste of time, and could only end in a bloodbath.

The crunch came in the autumn of 1823. Inka returned from a meeting at Maliny at a gallop, and immediately went to find Teofil to tell him the bad news. A meeting of the Polish-Lithuanian Friendship Society in Vilnius had been raided by an armed Russian force. The raid was ferocious by any standards. All those present were arrested, but not before they first put up a fierce fight in which at least a dozen writers and artists were killed, and many more hurt, some badly. The Russians then laid the house waste, smashing up whatever they could, and making a bonfire in the courtyard of paintings and every piece of material that was not written in the Cyrillic script. Several arrested members of the Society belonged to, supported or merely knew about the Unborn Future – as well as other revolutionary cells in the region.

'They might talk!' wailed Inka.

'I thought they were prepared to die for the Fatherland!'

'Not if they're tortured!'

'You should have thought about that before you started!'

'What am I to do, Cousin Teofil?' Inka was desperate. 'They'll tell the Russians everything, and we'll all be rounded up and shot!'

'Then I suggest you all get a priest to your next meeting, and make preparations to meet the Creator!' he cried angrily, before storming off in a fury. He knew that an impasse had been reached, and that a decision had to be made one way or the other. The discovery of the existence of the Unborn Future would have consequences reaching beyond the Maliny set-up. Inka was the daughter of Count Jan-Chrysostom Barnicki of Spytkowiec, which would make the whole House guilty by association. Chrys would certainly be arrested and interrogated. Teofil, a known veteran of the Napoleonic wars, would have his French connection dredged up and thrown violently in his face.

He sighed deeply and clenched his teeth. Again, his life, his home and his security had fallen into jeopardy. 'Is there nowhere in this benighted land that I can rest my head and call home for my family?' he thought, cursing himself for his involvement, however peripheral, in Inka's death wish.

The following day Inka rode to Maliny and back again.

'We're in trouble,' she said. 'They're beginning to round up members from Vilnius, mostly those connected with the University.'

'And?'

Inka's face contorted with pleading. 'Cousin Teofil, I want you to lead us!' she wailed.

'No chance!'

'Please, Teofil! You're a soldier! You're a patriot! You've got to help us, before it's too late! You can do it! We've thrashed the Russians before, and we can do it again! This time we'll keep the offensive going until we win. That's what's been wrong with our successes in the past – we've never carried them through! There are revolutionary cells everywhere, at least three in the Grodno region. If Lithuania goes up, so will the rest of Poland. We can make it different this time! But we need leadership, we need you! Now!'

'I don't know,' muttered Teofil indecisively.

'You know that if the Russians get me, they'll get you too! Think of Eloise and the children, Cousin Teofil! Where will it put them?'

Teofil listened to the words that he had hoped, deep down, that he would never hear spoken. Inka was right, curse her. There was no way out.

'All right,' he said. 'We go to war.'

'I say, Cousin Teofil!' chortled Inka, 'you are a brick!'

II

Teofil realised that there was no way out of the situation. It was only a matter of time before the Russian machine of oppression would descend on Spytkowiec. Divide and rule was the order of the day, and anyone could be automatically guilty of treason even by the most casual association. The fact that Inka was not only a member, but a leader, of a revolutionary movement meant the end of Spytkowiec, should the truth ever come out. Even Young Kaz would be recalled from Turin to be irrevocably cast out into the cold, his diplomatic career over. Teofil cursed Inka for having placed the whole family's future in jeopardy, but there was nothing to be done except to take the initiative to find ways of minimising the inevitable showdown. The one advantage was time. It had not yet come to a co-ordinated series of dawn raids by security forces. That will surely come later, when the psychological war begins. In the meantime, he had to pack Eloise and the children off to safety immediately.

'Has Chrys any idea of what's happening?' said Eloise, seething with fury and heartily blaming Inka for wrecking all hope of a secure future.

'No, but I'm not concerned for Chrys,' said Teofil. 'He can sort out his own problems when the time comes. I've sorted enough of his in the past couple of years. It's you and the children I'm concerned about. I want you to take them to Nibork, ostensibly to visit the Zaletniks. They are Julek's godparents, and have said they would like us to visit.'

'What about you?' said Eloise.

'I'm going to see what I can do to save the situation when the time comes. I certainly won't want you here.'

'You'll get killed, Teofil!'

'No. I'm not going to get involved in the fight, and if I try to mediate, I might just be able to get Spytkowiec off the hook.'

'You'll talk to the Russians?'

'I don't see any other way. Do you?'

Eloise looked thoughtful, but did not answer. 'It must look as though you and the children are going to have a short holiday with godparents in Prussia,' continued Teofil. 'I'll just say I'll join you later. That should keep suspicions at bay.'

Inka was made party to the plot, and after discussion the day after tomorrow was deemed the best time. Teofil hurriedly wrote to the Zaletniks to warn them of his family's impending arrival, and Inka rode with the letter to Mariampol to catch the post coach.

'You should have a very pleasant time,' was Chrys' comment on the proposed trip. 'The weather promises to be fine, and the marshes are very dramatic at this time of the year.'

Eloise and the children left not a day too soon. The morning after their departure a small platoon arrived at Spytkowiec. Their arrival, in the wake of the Vilnius troubles, caused some consternation. Everyone congregated in the Hall.

Captain Valery Semienko was in charge. He introduced himself formally. 'We have reason to believe that a cell of rebels is operating in this area, *Panie hrabio*,' he said politely, but with a hint of menace.

'Nonsense!' said Chrys. 'Mariampol is a peaceful region. I am not aware of any dissident activity hereabouts. I am in constant touch with the serf leaders, and I have my ear firmly to the ground. I would have heard about anything untoward. I know about the troubles in Vilnius, of course –'

'Mariampol lies within the sphere of influence of Vilnius,

even though Vilnius is in the Russian Empire,' said Captain Semienko. 'Some of the troublemakers apprehended in Vilnius are Lithuanians from this region.' He turned to Teofil. 'Count Teofil Samojarski, I believe?'

'*Pan* Samojarski, Captain.'

'Of course. How – modern.' Semienko inclined his head with a hint of a smirk. 'You have not lived here long, I understand.'

'I arrived five years ago.'

'From Austria.'

'Galicia,' said Teofil pointedly.

'In Austria,' replied Semienko equally pointedly. 'You had some – trouble – with your inheritance?'

Teofil's temper began to fray. How dare this upstart meddle in his past. 'I gambled away my estate to a vicious bastard who held my life in his hand! Look, what has all this got to do with the Vilnius business?'

'Before that you were in the Grande Armeé?' Captain Semienko continued unabated.

'So?'

'You took part in an attack on the Russian Empire.' The menace in Semienko's tone was now clear-cut. 'Why?'

'My past career is of no concern of yours, Captain!'

'I suggest,' Semienko pointed a finger accusingly at Teofil, like prosecutor at a trial, 'that you sided with Napoleon because you hoped thereby to restore the now long-defunct Polish state!'

'My reasons for joining the French army are my own!'

'The Polish-Lithuanian Commonwealth has been dead and mercifully buried nearly thirty years!' Teofil turned away in exasperation. Captain Semienko saw that he had won that round, a fact that would demoralise the others. Capitalising on his advantage, he started the build-up to the next round. 'Where are your wife and children?'

'Gone away. On a holiday visit.'

'Where?'

'Nibork. To stay with my son's godparents.'

'In Prussia? Do these – godparents – know of their impending visit?'

'It was arranged – some time ago.'

'Really?' Captain Semienko held out a gloved hand, and a sergeant placed a letter in it. Semienko opened it and held it up. 'This letter, written by you, was intercepted yesterday by our censors at the Prussian border. It advises a *Pan* and *Pani* Zaletnik, of Nibork, to expect your wife and two children forthwith.' Semienko replaced the letter in the envelope and handed it back to his sergeant. 'Perhaps our postal services are a bit on the slow side. How long ago did you write this letter?'

Teofil knew he was cornered, and Captain Semienko chalked up round two with a hint of a smile. 'It was a spur-of-the-moment decision,' he conceded angrily.

'When did they leave?'

'Yesterday.'

'So, they should be in Prussia by now.' Semienko's tone gave nothing away.

Teofil mentally calculated the possibility of Eloise and the children being intercepted at the border. It all depended on where the letter was discovered, read and acted upon. A cold shiver of fear ran down his spine at the thought of the four of them being taken off the coach for questioning. 'I sincerely hope so!' he sneered through his teeth, and immediately regretted it. Time and time again he had played into his enemy's hands with his attitude. Semienko was not to know one way or the other where Eloise and the children were, but in the psychological stakes the third round was again his, because he was now certain that Teofil had sent his family away in anticipation of trouble. If he had been innocent, he would not have been aware of any impending trouble.

Chrys had been listening in consternation to the exchange. Not for a moment did he think that Spytkowiec – calm, peaceful, trouble-free, pro-Russian Spytkowiec – would be harbouring any revolutionary sentiments. Even Teofil was surely too old for this patriotic stuff so beloved of students and young tearaways. It was time to come to the rescue. 'Well, Captain,' he said affably, 'if I – we – hear of anything, naturally we shall keep you informed.'

A bolder smile crossed Semienko's lips, suggesting there was more. 'I am only peripherally involved in this operation, *Panie hrabio*,' he said. His eyes sought out – and found – the beautiful ice queen that he had been told to look out for. Jolanta was standing apart from everyone else, aloof and still. 'You should address yourself to Colonel Arkady Petrovitch Osvetlensky. He is taking command of the garrison at Kaunas. He is being briefed on the administration of the Lithuanian region of the Kingdom of Poland.' He paused to read the expression on every face. 'I believe the Colonel has been a guest in this house,' he added.

There was a chain reaction of embarrassed looks on the faces of all but Jolanta. Her cold inscrutability could not be ruffled. But Chrys' could, and was. 'Well, indeed, yes, but only briefly,' he blurted. 'He spent Christmas with us – it must be – let me see – when was it…?'

'I was briefly engaged to Colonel Osvetlensky in the Spring of '21,' interrupted Jolanta without any sign of discomfort. 'Please convey to him my kindest regards.'

Captain Semienko, finding no capital to be gained from her forthrightness, mellowed momentarily and bowed formally to Jolanta. 'I would be honoured, *Pani hrabino*,' he said. Then he turned to Chrys. '*Panie hrabio*, I shall trouble you no further. Colonel Osvetlensky also trusts –' the word was laced with menace '– that he shall not be needing to trouble you further.

With that the platoon left, leaving a stunned silence before

Chrys broke it vehemently. 'What in heaven's name is going on around here?' he bellowed. 'We've never had any kind of trouble with the authorities at Spytkowiec! Never!'

'Then you'd better get used to it, Chrys,' replied Teofil, 'because it's coming to you whether you like it or not!'

'It's all your fault for coming here!' cried Chrys accusingly. 'You and your nationalist ideas! You bring trouble wherever you go, Teofil. This would never have happened if you hadn't come. I think you should leave!'

'All this has got absolutely nothing to do with me!' cried Teofil. 'If, as you say, you kept your ear to the ground you'd know.'

'What do you mean? Explain yourself!'

'Tell him, Inka,' said Teofil. 'Tell your father!'

'Tell me what?' said Chrys, taken aback and looking enquiringly at his daughter.

Inka returned his look 'No!' she said.

'Tell him!' cried Teofil angrily. 'Or I will!'

Inka froze with horror, then burst into tears. 'There's a cell –'

'I knew it!' cried Chrys triumphantly.

'No, you didn't,' sneered Teofil. 'You don't know anything! You merely play lord and master of all you survey, including my money. Go on, Inka.'

'I am a member of this cell,' sobbed Inka.

'Then you will leave it immediately!' said Chrys.

'I c-c-can't!'

'Why not?'

'Because she's the leader of it!'

Everyone turned. It was Jolanta who had spoken. 'Cousin Teofil is right, father. You don't know what's going on. Whatever happens around here you're always the last to know. You don't even know what Inka and I do. You say you keep your ear to the ground, but you only hear what people want you to hear.

That goes for us too. The whole of St Petersburg knew about the affair with Daniel Meadows, but you were the last to know. Inka's involvement with the Maliny cell was common knowledge, if you knew where to listen.'

'I didn't know you knew!' sobbed Inka.

'I wasn't going to betray you, Ineczko, if that's what you're worried about.'

'And why do you think I sent Eloise and the children away?' added Teofil.

'But this is outrageous!' thundered Chrys. 'Nobody ever tells me anything! Why wasn't I told these things?'

'Because you're a pompous, insufferable ass!' cried Jolanta passionately, before instantly blushing and turning away apologetically. Everyone looked at her in astonishment, because everyone knew that that was precisely the reason that he was never told anything. Until this moment she had made not the slightest comment on the whole Spytkowiec situation, believing it to be an exclusively Polish family matter. However, everyone else knew that she was absolutely right. Chrys was not a man to inspire confidence. In his book, everything had to be clear-cut, spelt out in black and white, and done through the correct channels, and these were not wide enough for any personal manoeuvrings or circumstances. Chrys ceased staring incredulously at his beautiful daughter, closed his mouth, and, with only a cursory glance at Jolanta, sat down heavily in an armchair.

'So, what do we do?' he said quietly.

Everyone followed suit and sat down, each in his or her habitual seat as for a family council, facing the straight-backed chair whence Maminka used to dispense wisdom and advice. Now everyone stared at the empty chair thoughtfully, perhaps wishing that her ghost would suddenly appear, a transparent apparition in black, grey and white, armed with answers and advice from the Beyond.

Teofil broke the silence. 'There will be revolution,' he said. 'There are cells and organisations in all the three Partitions that are just waiting for something to blow before following suit.'

'You know this for a fact?' said Chrys.

'I don't know any specific cells, but –'

'Then how do you know they will activate?'

Teofil sighed. 'There are cells everywhere, Chrys! There are about a dozen in Lithuania alone. Warsaw, Poznań, Kraków – even Lemberg. Nationalism is a growing creed, whether you and the Russians like it or not. One spark and the whole lot will blow.'

'Are you suggesting the spark comes from here?'

'I'm not suggesting it. I'm just saying that it most probably could. I believe the time has come. We've no choice but to ignite it, otherwise the Russians will, and then there really will be one bloody massacre.'

'So, what do you intend to do?'

'Inka has asked me to take charge of the Maliny cell,' said Teofil. 'There's a meeting tomorrow. I don't know what the outcome will be, but you'd better prepare yourself for war!'

III

It was a game of cat and mouse combined with hide and seek. In Mariampol and over the Russian border in Vilnius the security forces were maintaining a high profile, as if daring the opposition to show its hand. Those Vilnius detainees who came from Poland were 'repatriated' with much publicity to detention centres in Mariampol. Everyone believed that if there was to be an uprising it would be in Mariampol, in Poland, rather than Vilnius, which is in Russia. The prisoners were to act as bait. Security was tactically lax, as if to invite rescue raids.

'With a small band of half a dozen we could spring our people without any trouble,' said Inka. The cache of arms that was hidden in the forests at Maliny had been distributed among the members of the cell, who all risked death if these were found in their possession. They were all restless and twitchy, and raring for action rather than a nerve-wracking waiting game. The only action that Teofil sanctioned was to despatch a number of riders to other parts of Poland where there was known revolutionary activity. Their brief was to warn of an impending well-organised uprising in Lithuania, which should be a signal for a general call to arms by all Poles. But he drew the line at that, and refused to countenance an immediate attack.

'That's what they want us to do,' replied Teofil, who understood their fears. 'They're playing games to get us to act first. They've got military hidden all over the place, just waiting for us to move. We don't attack until we see what they've got lined up against us.'

Inka and some of the more reckless elements of the Unborn Future disagreed, and wanted to mount a raid independently, until Teofil pointed out that they would get caught and tortured to give the rest away. Agreement came, but grudgingly.

The Russians chose a wet, grey and very depressing day two weeks later to cast a psychological blow. The body of one of the detainees, a professor of history at Vilnius University, was found in the street in Mariampol. He had been beaten to death. Despite raging fury, Teofil still forbade action. Two days later, the bodies of two students were found in exactly the same circumstances, but still Teofil held back.

*****

On the first day of October came the catalyst that ignited the spark. Chrys' brother, Young Kaz arrived unexpectedly at Maliny with a new wife, whom he had married in Turin the previous month, in tow. It was supposed to be a surprise, and in that respect the ruse was more successful than he could have possibly imagined. Kaz and his wife disturbed some clandestine activities in and around Maliny. They did not see Kaz's approaching coach. Sensing trouble, he immediately turned his coach round and made for a military road block almost back at Mariampol, that he had passed earlier. There he informed the commanding officer that there were suspicious characters on his estate, and would they mind terribly investigating. The commanding officer assured him that it was no trouble, and galvanised his troops into action. The raid on Maliny was short and the battle fierce, and the unit returned to base having successfully mopped up an armed rebel band.

'It was only a small band, Colonel, about two dozen, all armed. There were no survivors.'

'Our losses?'

'None, Colonel.'

'Excellent!' said Colonel Arkady Osvetlensky. 'This is what we have been waiting for. 'They're bound to come out of the woodwork now!'

Arkady was right. In a forest clearing just off the Mariampol road, Teofil was holding a council of war before a crowd of some two-hundred armed rebels on horseback, with Inka beside him. He could no longer control the troops, who threatened to storm the garrison at Mariampol with or without Teofil's help or consent.

'We've been holding off for nearly a month!' cried a large and ferocious-looking peasant farmer with a scythe. He had been gathering in his late harvest when the call came. 'It's already October, and I don't fancy waiting till the snow comes!'

There was general agreement to this sentiment, and Teofil knew that he had to comply with their wishes, or there would be mutiny. And in this case, orders were not there to be obeyed, but treated as advice to be taken or left at the whim of undisciplined peasants, hotheads, or just thugs spoiling for a fight.

'All right,' Teofil conceded. 'We attack the garrison at daybreak the day after tomorrow. Stick to the agreed plan, and no survivors. Get the word out!'

The rebels nodded impassively, slowly turned their horses and left, some riding, some casually leading their horses in different directions. Teofil and Inka galloped back to Spytkowiec, their hearts in their mouths, and their minds honed, concentrated and incredibly alive to the task in hand. 'Cousin Teofil, this is it!' gasped Inka, drunk on the prospect of the battle. They rode in silence, for further talk was impossible.

Back at Spytkowiec Teofil and Inka walked straight into a merry family conference.

'Teofil! My dear uncle! Or shall we make it cousin? After all, we're exactly the same age!' gushed Kaz. The two men embraced each other, Kaz enthusiastically, Teofil perfunctorily. It has been said that some parents have two sons, while others have the same son twice. The latter was true of Chrys and Kaz. The newcomer was a replica of Chrys in every way, except that Kaz was nine years younger.

'I've been absolutely longing to meet you! Chrys has written so much about you! Pity I shan't be meeting your lady wife and the children. Hear they've gone on a spot of leave in Prussia! Still, never mind, some other time perhaps! Now, I want you to meet my wife, Maria Celestina! We only got married last month, you know!'

Maria Celestina was in her mid-thirties. She was large and buxom, with three chins and a perpetual grin that was almost a laugh. She had enormous brown eyes, rich, full lips and a vast quantity of curly, auburn-red hair.

'Cousin Maria Celestina,' Teofil first kissed her hand, then embraced her and kissed her on both cheeks. 'My heartiest congratulations to you both.'

'*Me piace molto,* Teofil,' said Maria Celestina.

'I'm afraid Maria-Celestina only speaks Italian,' said Kaz. 'She sings opera, you know! In fact, that's how we met. I first heard her at la Scala, that's Milan's great opera house, you know. She was singing Cimarosa's *The Secret Wedding*. Went back time and again, got to meet her, we fell in love, and here we are, a married couple! Do you like opera, Teofil? I'm besotted with it! It's the drama, you know. And talking of drama, amazing thing, there were some armed rebels at Maliny this morning, would you believe? Positive shock to the system, you know, when a chap comes home with his brand-new wife, to be confronted with a bunch of ruffians armed to the teeth and baying for blood! Had to ride back and report it, you know, but the Russkies managed to sort it out thank goodness, haven't seen if they did any damage, came straight here to say hello and get you all to meet Maria Celestina, I say, Chrys, it's good to be back again, it's been too long this time, how long has it been now –?'

Teofil was finding Kaz, as well as the occasion, wearing in the extreme. He had to exert maximum effort of will at least to look as though he was welcoming the newly arrived newlyweds. Kaz never once stopped talking, and the company got the benefit of the latest updates on Sardinian politics, the latest fashions in Louis-Phillippe's France, the latest operas to come out of Italy, and Maria Celestina's parts in them. There were endless comparisons between Europe's varying cuisines, with the Mediterranean coming out on top. Maria Celestina hung onto every word, even though she could not understand a word of Polish, and laughed at all the jokes, her bosom bodily in time to her guffaws.

Occasionally Teofil tried to catch Inka's eye, but she was being equally impassive, with only the occasional contrived hearty grunt to show that she was paying attention. Chrys listened, his face a fixed mask of a polite grin, as did Jolanta, whose statue-like presence would not have been noticed but for her stunning beauty.

Teofil suggested that Kaz and Maria Celestina should stay the night at Spytkowiec, to give the servants a chance to clean and air Maliny. What he really meant was to give him time to warn the cell members not to come anywhere near it. Kaz readily accepted the invitation.

*****

The next day Teofil and Inka rode to Maliny with some servants to get the house ready. Kaz was in seventh heaven, and went along with anything that was suggested. If he had noticed a certain coolness, a lack of overwhelming enthusiasm from the family, he did not show it. He continued to be his cheery, prattling self, little suspecting the turbulent thoughts that were churning round and round in everyone's minds. Chrys even suggested he stay at Spytkowiec, but Kaz insisted on moving on to Maliny, because he wanted Maria Celestina to see it, to accept it and to love it. He dismissed Chrys' regrets that Kaz had not warned him of his arrival, otherwise he would have made sure that everything was ship-shape and spotless.

'But then it wouldn't have been a surprise, what!' laughed Kaz.

By early evening Maliny was ready. The meetings of the cell had disturbed nothing, and it was just a question of cleaning, fresh linen, stocks of food and logs for the fire. Even though Kaz was willing to 'live like a gipsy', Chrys lent him his housekeeper to keep an eye on things.

That night, after everyone had retired, Teofil and Inka crept out of the house, sure in the knowledge that no one else at Spytkowiec knew of the plan to attack the garrison at Mariampol. They saddled the horses, and by midnight they were riding in silence through the forest. They noted with satisfaction that the moon was up and cast enough light to illuminate their path.

After a hard night-ride, the lights of Mariampol came in sight. Teofil and Inka slowly rode up onto a hillock overlooking the town. Down by the glistening river Teofil thought he saw some shadowy movement, and surmised that the foot units were in place. The church bell sounded five. Inka looked at its tall onion-domed spire, and also noted signs of movement below.

'Five o'clock. An hour to wait,' whispered Teofil.

Almost imperceptibly, a horseman rode up. 'Teofil Samojarski?' enquired the newcomer.

'Yes, that's me,' said Teofil.

'Call off the attack. Immediately.' His tone was restrained, though tinged with a strong hint of urgency.

'What do you mean?' came Inka's voice in the darkness.

The horseman turned at the sound of a female voice. 'Inka Barnicka?'

'What is this? Who are you?' came the reply.

'Never mind who I am. Just call off the attack at once. The

city is surrounded. There are twenty thousand troops, both horse and foot, positioned in the forests, and a further five thousand in the city, mostly holed up in the houses. There are cannons in the hills behind us trained on the city. They have been waiting for an excuse to pound the region into dust and rubble. The Russians have been trying to provoke an uprising to get you to show your hand. If you do, you'll play straight into Osvetlensky's hand. You'll stand no chance.'

'The whole of Poland will rise!' squawked Inka, trying to whisper and shout at the same time.

'There are no cells in Poland prepared to go along with you. Not at this time. Call it off before you all get killed, and Mariampol is wiped from the map!'

'How good is your intelligence?' said Teofil.

'Trust me. It's good.'

There was a pause before Teofil spoke again. 'We're calling it off.'

'No!' Inka cried, not attempting to whisper.

'Don't be a fool, Inka!' Teofil whisper-shouted. 'If what he says is true –'

'How do we know it's true?' Inka returned to whispering. 'He may be a Russian spy! I say the attack goes on!'

'Then it goes on without me!' Teofil turned his horse. 'I suggest it goes on without you, too, Inka!' With that he made off at a canter. There was no time for discussion, and he hoped desperately that Inka would panic and follow him.

'Wait! Cousin Teofil!' Inka's desperate entreaty was lost on the morning breeze, for Teofil was out of earshot. Inka turned to the newcomer. 'The attack goes on!'

'*Pani hrabino*,' hissed the rider through clenched teeth, 'There is still time! Call off the attack before you all get killed!'

'We will die for our Fatherland!' seethed Inka. 'Even if it takes the whole of the Tsar's army to do it!'

The rider sighed impatiently. It was obvious that Inka was battle-drunk, and that nothing would deprive her of the ecstasy of dying for the only cause she had ever believed in.

'It is, of course, your choice, *Pani hrabino*,' muttered the rider, restraining a raging fury. 'I'm only the messenger.' He turned his horse. 'With your permission, I should like to live another day to bear further messages on behalf of the Fatherland.' With a curt, cynical bow, he disappeared into the night.

Time passed, although Inka was now trapped in a timeless void of total mental and physical paralysis. Any thoughts of deviating from the plan simply never entered her mind, and she waited for the moment, to be marked by the first stroke of six from the church tower, in a religious trance. When it came, she fulfilled her duty immediately.

IV

Teofil arrived back at Spytkowiec before anyone was aware that he had gone, having thrown his weapons into a bush at the earliest opportunity. Inka had not followed him, as he had gambled on her doing. 'Stupid bitch!' he had muttered under his breath. He was angry that she had put him into the position of having to abandon her to her fate. There had been no time to discuss whether to abort the mission or go ahead, and even so Inka would not have been persuaded, which was why Teofil had decided to take the initiative. He cursed his cousin soundly for her decision to stay. At one stage he had stopped and waited for her along the road, and even considered going back to fetch her by force. Seeing no sign of the attack being aborted – no mass defections, no extra movement on the road or in the forest, Teofil decided that his was the Devil's alternative, turned his horse south and made for home, risking meeting one of the patrols that was purported to be surrounding Mariampol. Sure enough, he had been stopped by a small platoon manning a road block, but luckily, he was recognised by one of the soldiers, a Lithuanian whose father owned a small tavern in Mariampol.

'It's *Pan hrabia* from Spytkowiec,' he grinned, touching his forelock. 'Out for an early morning ride!'

That had seemed good enough for his colleagues, whose vacant peasant faces were concealed beneath the smart, Tsarist uniforms, and he had ridden on his way unimpeded.

Teofil stabled his horse and made his way to the Manor as casually as possible. The dawn by now was well advanced, and the servants would be about their chores, even if everyone else would still be asleep. In the Manor he met the servant girl lighting the fires. They greeted each other perfunctorily, and Teofil made his way up to his room, fell onto the bed with a sigh of relief, and considered his position.

He found it impossible to relax. Six o'clock, the signal for the start of the uprising, was now long gone, and his mind was firmly in Mariampol, wondering what was happening to Inka at that very moment. Was she still alive? Was she in pain, lying wounded in the gutters of the Lithuanian city? Had she been taken prisoner, to be interrogated by some sadistic Asiatic to whom all Europeans looked the same?

Mingled with concern for his hot-headed cousin was his concern for his own conscience. Had he the right to abandon her to her fate? It would certainly look like it when the dust settled. Again, fate would cast Teofil into the role of the hapless villain who always gets it wrong. Every situation turns out as a no-win situation – and he would without doubt get the blame for Inka's fate.

As usual Inka was not missed. The household stirred at about eight, and shuffled down to breakfast. Teofil was in desperate need of silence, but Chrys talked endlessly about Kaz and expressed his admiration for Maria Celestina.

'Damned fine woman,' he enthused, 'just what Kaz needs, a good, stalwart wife who will tame the reckless pirate in my brother!' Teofil smiled wryly at the thought of Kaz the reckless pirate. 'Time he settled down, you know. Chap can't spend his life gallivanting round the world eating and enjoying himself for ever. He's past forty, and it's time he assumed responsibilities!'

'You mean children.'

Chrys put down his fork and looked at the source of the remark. 'And what do you mean by that cynical tone of voice, Jolanta?'

'Just that,' said Jolanta, sipping her sweet black tea. 'Children. You've got to have children to leave...' she waved her hand all around '...all this to, don't you?'

'Well, there is that –'

'But you haven't got any children.'

'I've got you and Inka!' said Chrys, hurt.

'Hardly a suitable pair for the continuation of the Barnicki line as a fine, upstanding landowning family!' The bitter tone of her voice was lost on Chrys.

'You will marry one day!'

Jolanta snorted, finished her tea, and rose. 'Don't be naive, father!' With that she left the room.

'There's Inka!' cried Chrys after her, but Jolanta was gone.

'You'll probably find that there isn't,' said Teofil quietly.

'Isn't what?' said Chrys, returning to his scrambled egg, oblivious to the sinister tone in Teofil's voice.

'Inka.'

'She's probably gone off riding,' said Chrys.

'She's leading an insurrection at Mariampol.'

'Don't be an ass, Teofil. That nonsense is all finished with. I soon knocked all that rebel rubbish out of her!'

Teofil threw down his napkin and rose. 'You just don't know what the hell goes on around here, Chris, do you?' he cried angrily. 'I'm telling you that even as we speak, your daughter is at the head of a rebel army storming the garrison at Mariampol!'

Chrys expelled a mirthless guffaw. 'How can you possibly know that?'

'Because I've just got back from trying to get her to call it off before a hell of a lot of people get massacred and Mariampol is razed to the ground!'

Chrys' face became serious. 'You've been with these – these rebels?'

'Yes!'

'My God, Teofil! You're one of them! I should have known it!'

'There's a hell of a lot you should have known, except you bury your head in your – rather my – bank account, and you have not the slightest clue as to what is going on all around you!' There was a long silence, during which Chrys stared hard at Teofil, paralysed with disbelief. 'Here we are, on the brink of war and insurrection, with all Lithuania, and probably Poland, on the edge of an abyss, surrounded by half the Tsar's army, while you and Kaz prattle on as if you hadn't a care in the world!'

'I am a faithful subject of the Tsar as King of Poland!'

'Tell that to the Tsar!'

'My conscience is clear.'

'For God's sake, your daughter's leading an insurrection! When the soldiers come your conscience won't even get a look-in!'

The door opened and Tatiana entered. 'Good morning, everybody!' she said cheerily. 'A little fresh.' She noticed the suddenly impassive look on the faces of the two men. 'Oh dear, have I interrupted something?'

Both men answered simultaneously. Chrys mumbled, 'No, nothing,' while Teofil stated, 'Inka's in Mariampol leading an insurrection.'

It took Tatiana a long time to assimilate what Teofil had said. 'My God, Teofil!' she cried, 'Is this true?'

The morning lumbered past like a lump of lead. It was cold and overcast, and seemed endless as Teofil and Chrys waited for some – any – development. Tatiana automatically took her husband's part, and reinforced his views on every point. Jolanta edged herself back into the situation, and sided with Teofil in berating her father for his total ignorance and naivety, and her mother for not having any views of her own. The only thing that all four of them agreed on was a deep concern for Inka.

'You mustn't blame yourself, Teofil,' said Jolanta in answer to her cousin's conviction that he had betrayed Inka. 'No one's been more supportive of her than you! If she gets herself into trouble it's entirely her doing! When she makes her mind up about something, nothing – but NOTHING – will deflect her! I know! She's my sister.'

Chrys took the opposing view. 'It's all your fault, Teofil. Ever since you came to Spytkowiec you've been nothing but a bad influence on this house! And now you've turned Inka's head with your patriotism and new-fangled ideas!'

*****

At noon a small platoon of the Russian Cavalry arrived at the Manor. Jolanta stayed ensconced behind the curtains, while Chrys and Teofil went out to meet them.

'Cou- *Pan* Samojarski?' the soldier in charge, a familiar figure, saluted smartly.

Teofil stepped forward. 'I am Teofil Samojarski,' he said.

'I'm Captain Valery Semienko, of the Imperial Guard stationed at Mariampol. I believe we have already met.'

'I recall the occasion, Captain. You warned us of dissident elements operating in the area.'

'You should have heeded the warning. I have a warrant for your arrest, signed by Colonel Arkady...' his gaze fell on the icy figure of Jolanta, pale and monochrome, who had surreptitiously appeared from behind the curtain '...Osvetlensky.'

'On what charge, Captain?' said Teofil.

'Treason,' said Semienko. With his eyes still fixed on Jolanta, he signalled to his men to seize Teofil. '*Pan* Samojarski took part in a – slight disturbance – at Mariampol this morning.'

'Nonsense, Captain!' said Jolanta, stepping down the steps onto the gravel. '*Pan* Samojarski had breakfast here at eight. We all had a heated family discussion. When was this – disturbance?'

'At dawn, Countess.'

'Then he must have had a remarkable horse to convey him

here in time for breakfast, Captain. He certainly did not have the air of one who had just ridden two hours, having fought a battle.'

'Leave this to me, Jolanta,' interrupted Teofil, now held firmly by two soldiers. 'I shall have the whole thing sorted out with Colonel Osvetlensky.' He turned to Semienko. 'I am ready, Captain. Let's go.'

Semienko acknowledged Teofil's co-operation with a slight bow. Teofil shrugged off the two soldiers, and allowed himself to be ushered to a horse that had been brought for him, and mounted. The platoon immediately surrounded him. Captain Semienko turned back to Chrys, who had been speechless from shock and sheer disbelief.

'I require that neither yourselves, nor any other members of your household leave the estate until further notice.'

Chrys found his voice. 'Are we – under arrest?' his face was contorted with horror.

'Shall we say, temporarily confined, *Panie hrabio*. Regrettable, but necessary for your own safety. There may be some dissident elements abroad, who may pose a danger to yourselves. Purely a precaution.'

'But –'

'The Tsar insists!' Semienko over-dramatised the last word. Chrys read the menace in the other's voice, and surrendered without further question.

'Very good Captain.'

The platoon turned to go. Chrys called out, as an afterthought. 'Captain Semienko!' The Captain turned to face Chrys. 'What – what was the – outcome of – of this – disturbance?'

'Ah, I almost forgot,' said Semienko with only a pretence of deference. 'Please forgive me. So much to think of. The disturbance was quickly and efficiently suppressed, *Panie hrabio*. But it is my – sad duty to inform you of the death of your daughter, Countess Jadwiga. She fell victim to a bayonet charge in the opening minutes.' Chrys blanched visibly and swayed on his feet. Jolanta burst into tears, and Teofil gritted his teeth and closed his eyes in suppressed rage. 'You should really keep a better grip on your family, *Panie hrabio*. Trouble seems to follow those around you. Some of this trouble might rub off onto yourself one day. Perhaps soon, even. Please be warned.'

Captain Semienko bowed curtly and the platoon rode off at a steady canter.

*****

Apart from milling crowds standing around in concerned groups, Mariampol was relatively peaceful. Teofil noted the lingering smell of burnt powder in the chill autumn air, and some small damage to several buildings. There was a certain amount of litter in the streets, mostly clothing – as well as dark patches of dried blood in the dirt. All casualties had been removed.

'My cousin's body...' began Teofil, feeling sick inside.

'...will be returned to the family, *Panie hrabio*,' said Semienko, 'after the formalities and body counts have been completed and recorded.'

'Thank you.'

At the Garrison Teofil was placed in a single cell in the dungeon. As he looked about him, he reflected that he had known less comfortable places of detention in his time. There was a marble-topped table with a jug of water and a basin, as well as a bucket concealed behind a screen. A straw mattress and some blankets lay on the rough wooden cot. The barred window gave onto the courtyard of the Garrison.

His feeling was that the Russians intended to be as civilised as possible about the whole matter. Captain Semienko had treated him with some respect, had used his title, and the guards refrained from manhandling him, and maintained their distance, almost trusting him not to try to escape.

*****

Just after five o'clock – he recalled the clock chiming that very hour into the cold pre-dawn, such a short time ago – he was politely summoned and ushered into Colonel Osvetlensky's office. The Colonel rose to meet him.

'*Panie hrabio*, please,' he indicated a chair, 'sit down.' Teofil obeyed, rather than accepted, the invitation. He noted the pointed use of his defunct title. The Colonel dismissed the guards with a wave of his hand. 'A glass of vodka?'

'Thank you, no.'

Osvetlensky went to a small occasional table where a decanter and glasses had obviously been specially placed. 'It would help if you did. This is most unpleasant for me.'

'For me too, Colonel. How can I drink with my cousin's killers?'

'What can I say, *Panie hrabio*?' Osvetlensky poured two glasses regardless, and carried them over to Teofil. 'Circumstances have forced certain issues, and people like you and me are caught in the middle, bound by our respective loyalties. It was not as I would have wished.'

Teofil ignored the proffered glass. 'Did you order the bayonet charge?' he asked, 'knowing that my cousin was at the head?' Osvetlensky pursed his lips and breathed deeply, looked out of the window and exhaled, his breath quivering with suppressed emotion.

'Well, at least now I know.' Teofil relaxed. Osvetlensky placed the glasses back on the table and returned to his desk. Teofil leaned forward. 'Why?' he demanded, his voice oozing bitter venom.

'It was my duty.'

Teofil sat back and let out an exasperated grunt. 'Duty,' he muttered. 'The usual excuse that is dredged up for some of the worst crimes that have ever been committed.'

'The crime was your cousin's, *Panie hrabio*. My job is to maintain order in all the Tsar's lands.'

'She just wanted her country back.'

'And you sympathised. Please don't forget that!' Teofil ignored the statement. 'She went about it the wrong way,' continued Osvetlensky, rising again and retrieving his glass of vodka. 'Surely you must be aware of the Tsar's feelings? He favours Poland's eventual independence. He has discussed the question at great length with many leading Polish statesmen. It could have been just a matter of time, except that, with respect, hot-heads like your cousin spoil it all by enacting romantic ideals gleaned from heroic romances! The politics of the cheap, sensational novel! They show no long-term vision. What in God's name did your cousin intend to do with her independent Poland?'

Osvetlensky drained his glass in one go, and filled it again.

'Poland has to live with Russia, whether she likes it or not. There is no natural frontier, and enormous tracts of territory the size of France will be bloodily disputed till the end of time, unless Poland and Russia come to an accommodation. You cannot make an enemy of a neighbour that can invade your land and no one hears about it for two weeks! Your cousin wanted independence, and she wanted it now, whatever the cost!'

'The cost was too high.'

'Agreed.'

'You could have taken her prisoner. As an aristocrat and a woman, she deserved a better fate.'

'As an aristocrat and a woman, she was a potent rallying force. Apart from being a very special personality. The Tsar cannot afford a Polish Marianne baying for Russian blood. As a military man it is my duty – no, I shall not use that word – it is my strategy to eliminate such forces. Countess Jadwiga had to go. As a soldier and a veteran of Napoleon's wars you will understand my soldier's reasoning.'

'Oh, I do,' said Teofil. 'But there is another reason why she had to go.'

'Please explain, *Panie hrabio*.'

Teofil studied Osvetlensky carefully as he spoke. 'Revenge.' A barely perceptible shock wave crossed the Russian's face, which did not go unnoticed.

'Revenge, *Panie hrabio?*' the other almost smiled, 'how so?'

'You were aware how close my cousin was to – her sister.' Teofil swallowed awkwardly. After a long pause: 'Jolanta.'

The Colonel's face darkened perceptibly, and Teofil knew that he had grated against a raw nerve. As if summoned by telepathy, the two guards re-entered.

'Take *Pan hrabia* back to his cell,' he commanded.

V

The golden autumn gradually declined into a bleak winter, and life at Spytkowiec had become a nightmare. Chrys had sunk into a deep depression, and spent most of his time in his room, brooding. The events of that autumn had come as a complete shock to his system, as he realised that what he had thought of as his safe, secure little world, was in fact a hotbed of intrigue, deception and betrayal. What was more, he was riddled with guilt as far as his two daughters were concerned. He had placed one on a pedestal and adored her, while the other was forced to fend for herself, both physically and emotionally. Now, possibly as a result of his blindness and naivety, both had opted out of life – one committing emotional suicide, the other fulfilling her death wish. He was now finding it very difficult to come to terms with his past relationships with Jolanta and Inka, and was convinced that he was being punished for his failure as a father.

Tatiana made a valiant attempt at being supportive and helpful, but to very little avail. She had devoted her life to seeing no wrong in Chrys, automatically taking his side in every matter. She ensured that he had everything he needed, from a comfortable and luxurious home to total emotional fulfilment. Now she, too, was finding it difficult to cope with a situation that she never even dreamt could befall her paragon of righteousness that was her husband.

Only Jolanta found the necessary resources to keep life going. The servants increasingly went to her for their orders, as did the tenant peasants. She was the only one to whom it had occurred that Eloise should be informed of events. On the day of Teofil's arrest she wrote her a long letter, explaining the circumstances of both Inka's death and Teofil's arrest. She strongly advised her to stay at Nibork for the foreseeable future. Her timely flight from Russian Poland at a sensitive time had been noted, and it was possible that the borders were being watched for her return. She realised that the letter might well be intercepted by the censors, but short of a coded information sheet, there was no other way of imparting the news from a personal viewpoint.

Kaz made frequent social calls from Maliny, but his words of encouragement to his brother were largely empty of feeling or content, and fell on unreceptive ears. Besides, Kaz was totally tied up with Maria Celestina, and the couple went about their business of being newly-weds as though nothing unusual had happened to spoil their honeymoon. They even went to spend a few days in St Petersburg to take in some concerts and operas, which were beginning to find an enthusiastic public among educated Russians.

A fortnight after the insurrection Inka's body was returned. Permission for her burial at the Holy Cross Church at Mariampol was refused by the Russians, so she was interred at a private ceremony in the small cemetery of the Chapel of St Basil in Spytkowiec village. This was attended by an official from Mariampol, who made a note of all those who attended, with the result that half a dozen local peasants who turned up were later interrogated.

Half way through November, when the rain was beginning to sleet and even settle in patches of soggy white, Eloise and the children returned from Prussia. Jolanta rode out to meet them, and they embraced each other with the passion of players in a common tragedy. The ensuing days, even weeks, were spent in reliving the events of that autumn over and over again, and every possibility for gaining Teofil's freedom was discussed.

*****

At the beginning of December news came that Teofil had been taken to St Petersburg and tried for treason. The prosecution had demanded the death penalty. However, the extenuating circumstances that he had been trying to abort the Mariampol Insurrection had been taken into account. The soldier son of the Mariampol tavern-keeper had testified that at the time of the Insurrection he had seen and stopped *Pan hrabia* – the fact that his defunct title had been unofficially re-instated was not lost on Teofil – at the road block manned by his platoon, some considerable distance to the south of Mariampol. *Pan hrabia* had been riding towards Spytkowiec to the south, and had been unarmed. Teofil had maintained all along that he had not planned the raid, nor was he at Mariampol to take part in it; and the prosecution had been unable to establish any hard evidence of intent.

Teofil's effective non-involvement, as well as his nationalistic sympathies, were noted. But the evidence of his loose membership, and even leadership, of the Maliny cell had been established after a number of survivors had been interrogated. So, the death sentence had been commuted to thirty years' imprisonment in Moscow.

*****

1824 dawned very cold, and the Russian Orthodox Christmas a week later was as white as it could be. Spytkowiec was snowed in. Tatiana, a natural hostess, came alive in the preparation of the feast, helped by Eloise, who was anxious to help keep up spirits during the festive season. Even Jolanta added her weight to whatever cheer could be wrenched from the gloom.

Christmas dinner was a sad but splendid affair, and the conversation revolved around Christmas dinners past. Kaz and

Maria Celestina had been invited for the Christmas period. Two extra places had been laid, one for Inka, for whom a special prayer was said, and one for Teofil, to whom a special toast was drunk. There were further toasts to Christmases yet to come, with the hope that, with God's help, they will be happier. After dinner there were presents for Franciszka and Julek, as well as trinkets exchanged by the adults.

As the family sat round the blazing fire, mellowed by good food, vodka and finest French and Armenian brandy, Kaz spoke at great length about the St Petersburg cultural scene.

'We met this young civil servant at a soirée given by Prince Yevgeni Komarovsky – you may have heard of him – Chrys, a splendid fellow, and throws some superb balls to which he invites all the best people, you know. Anyway, this young chap's name was Mikhail Ivanovitch Glinka, who gave us some of his songs. A bit peasantish, but sheer heaven nonetheless. Good to hear the Russians coming up with some fine songs of their own. I told him so, and suggested he should write an opera one day. He was absolutely thrilled by the idea, and promised me one day he would! Anyway, Maria Celestina asked to see the music, and do you know, the two of them ended up doing a full concert of them for the multitudes!'

'I sight-read,' grinned Maria Celestina, showing that she had learned a few words of Russian, 'but no words! I no read Russian letters – very funny letters!' And she gushed with laughter.

'Maria Celestina sang all the songs to *aah*, as if it were a violin! Did you ever hear of such a thing? I say, I've got young Glinka's songs here,' continued Kaz. 'Fellow gave us copies, very decent of him. We thought perhaps Jolanta might play upon the pianoforte, while Maria Celestina sings? She's learnt the Russian words already, you know, and they are very beautiful. Chap will go far, mark my words. Jolanta?'

Jolanta was staring at the whiteness through the frosted

window, of the thick, silent snowfall against the black beyond, illuminated from the inside by the warm glow of the fire and candlelight. She was oblivious to the hearty prattling of her uncle and his wife. The name of Prince Yevgeni Komarovsky had re-ignited the smouldering memory of just one such soirée, to which an archangel had been invited, such a long time ago. That was after a fateful Christmas past that was forever etched upon her heart – the Christmas that her dashing young cavalier had come to celebrate the birth of Christ with her family. The Christmas that led inexorably to her own personal heaven and hell – from which she knew she would never emerge.

'Jolanta?'

Jolanta looked up absently, and her eyes focused past the beaming faces of her uncle and his wife, onto the flickering fire beyond. Seized with a sudden convulsion of emotion, she burst into tears and fled out of the door and up the stairs.

'The heavens!' cried Kaz in astonishment; 'I hope I didn't say anything –'

'It's all right, dear Kaz,' said Tatiana soothingly. 'Let her be. She has – memories –'

'Oh!' Realisation hit Kaz. 'You mean the business with –'

'She hasn't got over it yet.'

'Perhaps when she feels like –'

'She never plays the pianoforte anymore.'

'Never?'

'Never.'

'The heavens!'

That night was a never-ending torment for Jolanta, and she could not sleep. The snow was still falling heavily, and the silence, when not punctuated by the howling of wolves, was deafening. Jolanta had lived in a state of mental anaesthesia over the past months, but it had only needed one spark to bring her whole tragedy back into sharp relief. The name of Prince

Yevgeni Komarovsky conjured up the image of Daniel Meadows, yet it was uttered in the context of a boring account of a boring event by a boring person. This juxtaposition acted as a wrench that violently loosed the taps of Jolanta's passion, and she wept pitifully, alone, for the rest of the night.

Then there was the spectre of Arkady Osvetlensky, the real villain of the piece, even though Jolanta could not find it in her heart to hate him, no matter how hard she tried. It was he who had slain Daniel Meadows on a point of honour, and it was he who had ordered the bayoneting of her sister on a point of duty. It was also he who had arrested her cousin Teofil and had him put away for what might well be the rest of his life, again on a point of duty. Yet it was he whom she had once loved, then cast aside. She found it hard to hate such a man.

By morning she had wept all her tears, and spent all her passion, yet still she could not sleep. The cold dawn blurred her recurring thoughts and images, causing them to lose their gloss. Her tormented mind was exhausted, and other thoughts and images weaved in and out of her consciousness. Of these images, that of Teofil took over, and she reflected on his kindred spirit. Both were prisoners of destiny, each in their own way, each with the expectation that they will die in their own prisons. She knew she would never be free, but Teofil? Could he be freed by some perversion of honour and duty?

Perhaps.

By the beginning of February, the heavy snow that had buried Spytkowiec had largely receded, and the roads were passable once more. Kaz and Maria Celestina had returned to Maliny, and Spytkowiec was almost frozen in time, waiting for the winter to spend itself before spring breathes new life into its inhabitants.

'I'm going to ride into Mariampol today,' Jolanta announced at breakfast one sunny day.

'You can't!' said Chrys, 'we're not allowed to leave Spytkowiec.

You'll be arrested!'

'That is precisely why I'm going to Mariampol!'

'This is the height of foolishness, Jolanta,' began Chrys, but no amount of coaxing would reveal why Jolanta, who had reverted to her withdrawn, melancholy self, wished to go to Mariampol to be arrested. 'You're being totally unreasonable! 'I order you to come back this minute!'

But Jolanta was not listening. She had asked for a horse to be saddled, and had wrapped up warmly for a long, cold ride. With only a forced smile as a goodbye, she rode off, watched by an amazed audience.

Two hours later she was at the gates of the Mariampol Garrison.

'I wish,' she announced to the two guards at the gate, 'to speak to Colonel Arkady Osvetlensky!'

VI

Moscow. The Lubianka Prison, late afternoon. The heavy iron door clanged open and two guards stood on either side.

'You have a visitor,' said one.

Teofil rose gingerly from his wooden cot just as the handsome, smart figure of Colonel Osvetlensky strode in. He looked about him at the bare, cold cell with displeasure, and wrinkled his nose at the bucket, full to the brim with human excreta, in the corner. Then, casting a cursory glance at Teofil, he spoke. 'We will talk somewhere more congenial. The Governor's office in five minutes.'

With that he strode out again and the guards locked the door. Teofil sat down on the cot once more, wondering what this sudden brief interruption was all about. Time had ceased to have any significance for him. Five minutes? What was that compared to the five or six months (his counting had become lackadaisical) spent in this hellhole. In the event he waited for an hour and a half, sitting mindlessly on the edge of his cot, reasoning that there was no point in lying down if he was to be disturbed again in five minutes.

The sound of people shouting in St Peter's Square outside made him look up at the barred window above his head. He had never looked through it. It was out of reach. But the sounds of the outside world reached his ears at all times of day and night. All he could see was a bright blue sky, and the welcome warmth suggested that spring was making way for summer, and an end to the relentless numbing cold of the Moscow winter.

At length he was summoned and marched into an enormous and spacious office, lavishly furnished in the French style, and decorated with baroque gold leaf. Off centre and at an angle there was an enormous desk, at which sat the immaculately turned-out Governor of the prison, General Viktor Lubachevsky. By the crimson velvet-draped window Colonel Osvetlensky stood over a small, occasional table at which he was pouring three glasses of vodka from a silver decanter.

'So, we meet again, *Panie hrabio*,' smiled Osvetlensky. 'In very similar circumstances as the last time. Vodka?'

'Why am I here?' Teofil ignored the offer.

'To discuss the conditions of your freedom,' Osvetlensky timed the last word to coincide with the proffered glass.

Teofil, in his amazement, took it. 'I am to be freed?'

'Shall we say,' interpolated the Governor, 'that a limited amnesty, at our discretion, has been approved by the Tsar.'

'Am I on this list?'

'There are conditions,' said the Governor.

'I'm sure!'

'They are straightforward, *Panie hrabio*,' said Osvetlensky. 'You will undertake to return to Spytkowiec, devote your life to the rearing of your family, and instilling in them a respect for the Tsar and for Russian law. You will finance and help manage the estate as you have done before. Your assets in your bank at St Petersburg will be unfrozen so that you will have access to further investment in your ventures.'

'Your account will naturally be monitored for signs of spending that could be misconstrued as – contrary to the interests of Mother Russia,' added the Governor.

There was a long pause. 'Is that all?' said Teofil.

'You expect more?' said Osvetlensky.

Teofil did not answer. Then, 'What if I join an insurrection?'

'We have been assured that you wouldn't,' said the Governor
'By whom, for heaven's sake?' said Teofil.

Osvetlensky hesitated before speaking. 'You have a guarantor, *Panie hrabio*, who has personally vouched for your good behaviour.'

Teofil laughed mirthlessly. 'A guarantor? What fool would guarantee my good behaviour after all that came out at my trial? My views on the independence of Poland have been aired enough, haven't they?'

Colonel Osvetlensky went to the door, opened it, and nodded to somebody outside. Teofil rose to his feet as Jolanta, pale and impassive, yet as icily beautiful as ever, entered. 'Hello, Teofil, you look well,' she lied, successfully concealing her horror at Teofil's gaunt appearance. She noted the sunken eyes, the sallow, pasty skin beneath a patchy and unkempt beard. His clothes were filthy, and he stank of stale sweat, urine and excreta.

'Jolanta!' he gasped finally, 'what in God's name –?'

'You're to be freed, Teofil,' she continued. 'I assured Ark – Colonel Osvetlensky that you are not really a rebel, and that you would keep out of any further trouble.'

'*Pani hrabina* Barnicka has moved to Moscow, *Panie hrabio*,' said Osvetlensky. 'She has asked me to find her an apartment.'

'Moscow is such a beautiful city!' said Jolanta.

'Being posted here, I am honoured to be in a position to – protect *Pani hrabina*. And show her around, naturally,' said Osvetlensky.

'The Colonel has been very kind.'

'I consider it an honour,' said Osvetlensky. 'And a duty,' he added pointedly.

'We hope,' interpolated the Governor, rising from his desk, 'that the position is quite clear.'

Teofil, who had been following the clarification, obviously carefully dramatised and rehearsed, with his head going from one to the other, looked at the Governor, his mouth gaping wide open. Finally, 'Quite clear,' he mumbled, his eyes finally falling on Jolanta, looking for signs of the real reason behind the theatricals, but finding none.

'Excellent!' said the Governor. 'Now, perhaps we will drink a toast to a new future!'

This time Teofil drank. Events had overtaken him, and he no longer knew where his loyalties – and his duties – lay. His senses had been dulled by a long, freezing winter, in which he was plucked from the jaws of death at regular intervals to be warmed and revived only to suffer further in his cell. Yet now they were sharp and he was able to bring his position into some semblance of focus.

It was obvious that Jolanta had come to an arrangement with Osvetlensky in exchange for his, Teofil's, freedom. He had installed her in what was doubtless a luxury apartment, where he kept her as his mistress. And Jolanta had done this of her own free will. Why, Teofil asked himself. Why was she sacrificing her honour, her self-respect, her whole life even, to save him from dying in that stinking, freezing cell? The only answer, a cruel and self-indulgent one, that he could glean was that she had nothing further to lose, and wanted to use the one thing she had left, her beauty, especially in the eye of a beholder such as Colonel Arkady Osvetlensky, to save her cousin. Osvetlensky, in turn, could not afford to take back his ex-fiancée after the Daniel Meadows affair. However, he could continue the relationship with Jolanta as a personal whore without loss of honour. His, that is.

But why would Jolanta stoop to such depths? It was not as though they had been particularly close. Perhaps, in the fullness of time, he would find out the reason for her self-sacrifice. He emptied his glass in one draught, more grateful to Jolanta than he could ever express in words, and knowing that this was a debt that he could never repay.

*****

Teofil was duly released into Jolanta's care immediately. Osvetlensky had arranged for a carriage to take them to her apartment, where he was able to have a hot bath, a good meal, a shave and a change of clothing. Being in a state of shock, he could hardly bring himself to say a word all this time; it was almost as though he had just woken from a terrible nightmare, and could not entirely believe that he had returned to reality. Jolanta realised this, and was prepared to act out her role on his terms. After all, it was Teofil who was the object of the whole exercise.

It was several days later that Teofil finally came out with the question that he had been so reluctant to ask. 'What happens if I don't behave myself?' he said over a light supper of *pierogi* stuffed with cabbage, rice and meat.

'You don't really want to know the answer to that, Teofil,' replied Jolanta.

'I need to know, Jolanta,' he said earnestly. 'You know perfectly well I'm going to behave myself, and act like a good tsarist. Apart from anything else, I'm getting too old to embark on these adventures. Tell me.'

Jolanta put down her fork. 'I signed a confession that Inka's insurrection was jointly planned by the both of us, and that I stayed behind to lead a further insurrection in the event of the failure of Inka's.'

'My God, Jolanta!' cried Teofil, aghast. 'He can use that against you any time he wants to – and for any reason!'

'He would not accept less for your freedom.'

'Was it his idea?' Jolanta nodded. 'Bastard!' hissed Teofil. 'Some dashing young cavalier, eh?' He poked at his *pierogi* thoughtfully before continuing. 'But why, Jolanta? What purpose can this serve?'

'Your freedom, Teofil.'

'But what a price!'

Jolanta shrugged. 'I can pay,' she muttered noncommittally. They ate in silence for a while. Then, 'I love you, Cousin Teofil. No, don't misunderstand. Not that way. Not after Daniel. I could never love anyone again after Daniel. I love you in a…' she searched for a way to express herself '…an older cousinly sort of way. Brotherly and fatherly at the same time.'

'You already have a father, Jolanta. Don't forget that!'

Jolanta snorted. 'He's pathetic.' Teofil threw down his fork, rose, and tried to remonstrate with her, but his anger only made him choke. 'Wait!' continued Jolanta. 'Hear me out, Teofil! It's not that I don't love him. Beneath that bumbling, self-righteous exterior there wallows a sentimental family man. I know he preferred me to Inka, which luckily did not affect her as much as it affected me. That's why I've tried to give Inka that little extra that he couldn't give. But I loved her, and did not resent it. She was dumpy, horsey and not very attractive, but as far as I was concerned, she was my sister, whom I loved dearly. What I'm trying to say to you is that I didn't want to be loved because I was a perfect goddess. Perfect goddesses are adored, not loved and respected, and I wanted to be loved and respected because I was Jolanta Barnicka. Only you gave me that love, Teofil.'

'Not consciously, Jolanta,' replied Teofil, having finally cleared his throat. 'I took you for granted. You were my young cousin, pretty, intelligent, talented, and very good company.'

'Just what I wanted, Teofil.' Jolanta's eyes were laughing. 'Can you see that? You treated me as a woman and a normal human being.'

Teofil sighed. 'Nice of you to say so,' was the only thing, albeit inane, that he could think of to say. 'I won't let you down, Jolanta. I shall behave myself and refrain from drawing moustaches on pictures of the Tsar!'

'The Tsar already has lots of moustaches!'

They both laughed a lot at this, and went on to make more ribald jokes about the Tsar. The wall between them had crumbled, and they both realised that in this terrible game in which they were involved purely by dint of birth, they had found in each other a loving, true and trusted friend. The laughter died away and they gripped each other tightly in a warm hug that neither wanted to be the first to break off.

*****

Teofil spent two weeks at Jolanta's apartment, before Osvetlensky arranged for a carriage to take him home to Spytkowiec. A letter had been despatched to Chrys on the day of Teofil's release, advising him of his impending homecoming. Jolanta had done a good job on feeding Teofil up, taking him for walks in the parks, where he could enjoy the hot Asiatic summer, and a couple of visits to the theatre. He had put on weight; his eyes lost that sunken look and his complexion improved. A visit to a barber's resulted in a dashing cut of both hair and moustaches in the latest fashion. Osvetlensky had even arranged a complete outfit that was the latest vogue among the young, rich and fashionable bloods of Moscow that summer.

Both Osvetlensky and Jolanta came to see him off at St. Peter's Square. It was the first day of July, and the sun spilt its warmth onto Moscow out of a clear blue sky. The Kremlin, with the stunning domes of St Basil's gleaming in the shimmering heat, were, Teofil had to admit, the most beautiful architectural marvel that he had ever seen. How can a people that can build such world-shakingly beautiful monuments also become such an aggressive nation?

Teofil tore his eyes away from the fairy-tale vista. He and Jolanta looked into each other's eyes before embracing and holding one another tightly for a very long time.

'Take care, Jolanta.'

'You too, dearest Teofil.'

The driver of the coach and his postilion appeared and mounted. Osvetlensky took Teofil aside.

'You must hate me, *Panie hrabio*,' he said, 'but I would like to think that in a different climate we might have been friends. Close friends, even. Please do not think that we Russians are all barbarians. We have standards too. I do sincerely wish you, and your House, well. What has passed between us, and between Jolanta and me, was due to loyalties, passions and duties which placed on us such pressures as were beyond our personal control. Please understand that I still love her, yet this is the only way that I am able to express this love. I hope you will grow to understand.'

Teofil swung wildly between loathing and understanding. How can a people that can build such world-shakingly beaut – 'She has agreed to be your whore of her own free will for my sake, and I shall never forget that,' he said at last. 'But if you harm her in any way, or cast her off like a useless rag after you've finished with her, by your God and mine I swear, Osvetlensky, I shall kill you!'

'You have my word, as an officer and a gentleman, *Panie hrabio*.'

Teofil climbed into the coach. He looked first at Jolanta, who was trying to suppress tears in her eyes. He then gave Arkady a glance of pure hatred and disdain before gazing up at what he estimated to be the barred window of his old cell in the Prison. He held the gaze until the coach turned a corner, and St Peter's Square was lost to sight.

VII

Teofil arrived in the Market Square at Mariampol on July 15. It had been a long, eventful and arduous journey. The coach was waylaid by bandits on the road to Smolensk, although Teofil was fortunate in that he had virtually no possessions for the bandits to steal. One passenger, an aristocratic lady, was not so lucky. She lost her jewels, suffered a heart attack, and died. Transporting corpses across local customs checkpoints and road checks entailed considerable bureaucratic hassle, so she was strapped in her seat and passed off as living until the coach reached Smolensk, her home city, three days later. Much to everyone's relief, the body was collected by her family for burial.

Because of a band of renegades terrorising the road in the approaches to Vilnius, the coach driver made a detour south through Minsk. There the whole coach party was forced to spend four days, as there were no fresh horses available to continue the journey. Every horse in the area had been commandeered by the Military Governor for his campaign against the rebels. Even the coach horses were 'temporarily confiscated'. Eventually the coachman enacted a clandestine deal with a Volhynian horse thief, who, by a strange co-incidence, had stolen the coach's original horses from the Governor's stables.

Teofil was met by Eloise, Franciszka and Julek. The reunion was heartfelt and tearful.

'Dear tata! We never expected to see you again!' cried Franciszka, now a very pretty eleven-year-old with the first hints of an elegance and poise yet to come.

'I never doubted it for a moment, Franciszka,' said Teofil. 'And I was right!'

'What was it like in prison, tata?' cried Julek.

The boy had grown, and was certainly tall for his eight years, thought Teofil. 'It was horrible, Julek! Full of rats, toads and other unspeakable – THINGS!' As he uttered the last word, he made a playful lunge at the boy, who squealed in exquisite terror at the thought of indescribable monsters.

'Welcome home, my love!' whispered Eloise. The kiss was long and passionate. The children gazed, fascinated, until Franciszka poked at Julek with a disapproving frown, and they both turned away, guiltily.

The welcome at Spytkowiec was cooler. Chrys received Teofil standing in front of the empty fireplace in the drawing room. Tatiana had reverted to her submissive position, seated nervously on the couch just behind her husband. Kaz and Maria Celestina were also present, keeping a low profile opposite her.

'I suppose I should welcome you back with open arms, Teofil,' said Chrys, 'but I'm afraid I cannot bring myself to do it.'

'I didn't think you would, Chrys,' muttered Teofil, 'But it's good to see you, nonetheless.' He kissed his uncle on both cheeks, and felt the cold response.

'You in exchange for Jolanta is a hard bargain for me to bear.'

'She offered herself of her own free will.'

'You accepted her sacrifice. I will find that hard to live with.'

'And I suppose my serving a life sentence in Hell's anteroom in Moscow for my pains in trying to save Inka from herself has afforded you some good nights' sleep? Jolanta did this out of love for me. Would she have done the same for you?'

Chrys turned away. He had made his point curtly and clearly, and was not prepared to discuss it further. 'Dinner will be at eight,' he said impassively.

Dinner continued to be at eight in the years that followed.

Life at Spytkowiec continued much as before, with certain exceptions. Inka and Jolanta had both gone, although Jolanta wrote every week to Teofil. They were just gossipy news about life in Moscow. She avoided all mention of Arkady and concentrated on describing the social and cultural scene. Teofil noted her enthusiasm, and was pleased that, whatever the circumstances, at least she was alive once more. Chrys' jealousy was ill-concealed, and caused Teofil to ask Jolanta to address at least some of her letters to her parents.

Subtractions from the family, however, were balanced by additions. Towards the end of 1825 Eloise gave birth to Adam. Like Julek, Adam had fair hair, blue eyes and a pale complexion, in the true Samojarski mould.

'Your next one had better have black hair and brown eyes like me,' said Franciszka, pretending to be annoyed, and ham acting a deep huff. 'You've got to make a stand, mama, for the Terrassins!'

'Tata and I will see what we can do, darling!' said Eloise.

The day after the birth of Adam, Tsar Alexander I died during a visit to the Crimea. The whole of Poland held its breath. Two months later Kaz and Maria Celestina returned from a lengthy trip to Warsaw, which was awash with speculation. 'There are rumours about the succession,' said Kaz. 'It may not turn out as straightforward as one has been led to believe.'

'You mean it may not be Nicholas?' said Teofil.' At least we knew where we stood with Alexander. Better the devil you know, eh?'

'I hardly think you can compare the Tsar with the Devil, Teofil!' said Chrys reproachfully.

The days following the birth of Adam were marred by a plot, hatched in Warsaw, to depose the heir to the Russian throne, and its implications were far-reaching, not least to Spytkowiec, which was ever under close scrutiny by agents from St Petersburg. It was essential for the family to maintain a 'correct' stance – whatever that might turn out to be.

'Who's really supposed to succeed Tsar Alexander?' asked Franciszka. History was her favourite subject, according to Mr Samuel Greathorpe, the children's English tutor. Recently she had been showing a rudimentary interest in politics.

'Nicholas,' said Teofil.

'Constantine,' said Chrys. 'Tsar Paul had established the principle of primogeniture as far as the tsarist succession is concerned. Constantine is the eldest and inherits the throne.'

'Constantine the Wolf-Man!' Julek, who had been sitting at the table, drawing, turned his face to the ceiling, pursed his lips and gave a long, lingering howl, in imitation of the sounds he had often heard in the forests at night.

'Shut up, Julek!' cried Franciszka in exasperation. 'What does primo-whatever mean, tata?'

'Who is Tsar Paul anyway?' said Julek. 'I thought his name was Alexander!'

'Alexander's dead, silly!' Franciszka gave her brother a disdainful push. 'Tsar Paul's his father.'

'He must be dead, too!' cried Julek.

'Well, of course he's dead, stupid, otherwise Alexander would never have become tsar in the first place!'

'That's what I like to hear,' said Eloise, entering the room at that precise moment carrying Adam in her arms. 'The cut and thrust of heady political debate and discussion! What's the heated topic?'

'The question of succession!' said Franciszka haughtily, proud to be using a grown-up expression. 'Tell us, tata. And don't interrupt, Julek!'

Teofil smiled. 'When Tsar Paul died in 1801, he decreed that the eldest son should succeed. This is called primogeniture.' He watched Franciszka mouthing the word silently. 'Alexander was his eldest son, so he became tsar.'

'But Alexander hasn't got any sons,' said Franciszka.

'That's why the throne should go to his next brother, who is Grand Duke Constantine.'

Julek cut in. 'Constantine the Wolf-Man! How-w-w-w-w-ooo!'

'Shut up, Julek!'

'But Constantine, who is the Military Governor of Poland, and lives in Warsaw, has renounced the throne.'

'You mean, he doesn't want to be tsar?'

'He must be mad,' interrupted Julek. 'If I were the tsar, I'd…'

'That's right,' said Teofil, ignoring the boy. 'He prefers to stay in Warsaw. So, the next brother is Nicholas.'

'Is he going to be tsar, then?'

'Yes, except that there's a plot to make Constantine tsar, even though he doesn't want to.'

'What does Nicholas think about that?'

'It's making him very angry.'

'Gosh,' said Julek, 'are they going to have a fight? The Wolf-Man versus the Angry THING from St Petersburg! Grrrraaaagh!'

'Shut up, Julek!'

Julek, whose sound effect accompanied a frenzied bout of pretend sword fighting across the carpet, scowled and returned to his drawing.

'Who will win?'

'Nicholas.'

'What about Constantine?'

'He'll stay in Warsaw.'

'What about the plotters?'

Teofil shrugged. 'Who knows?'

'What's Nicholas going to be like?' said Franciszka.

'No one knows much about him, actually. We shall just have to wait and see.'

'I'll bet he's a fierce warrior, who will lead his hordes into battle and kill lots of Mongolians!'

'Shut up, Julek!'

'Show me what you've been drawing,' said Teofil.

Julek picked up his piece of paper and took it to his father. It was a charcoal sketch of a man with a wolf's head, set in relief against a background of conifers and an enormous full moon. The background was blurred and sketchy, but the attention to detail on the figure was meticulous. The military uniform was correct, with every button in place; while the hairy hands and the wolf's face betrayed a gentle humour, rather than a ravening beast.

'This is a very fine picture, Julek,' said Teofil, impressed. Julek had been showing signs of a rare talent for drawing from an early age, which had been nurtured by Mr Greathorpe, who was himself a more than adequate hand at watercolours. He had a particular gift for caricature, usually in charcoal, which he liked to smudge 'to get a blurry effect'.

'It's Constantine!'

Teofil laughed. Grand Duke Constantine was an ugly man, and was disrespectfully nicknamed Wolfman in certain quarters of Warsaw. Despite his short temper, he was actually a popular figure, who loved Poland and, especially, Warsaw. He was Commander-in-Chief of the Polish Army, which was why the plotters included a number of Poles. They considered him a better prospect than the unknown, surly Nicholas.

As the year drew to a close and 1826 dawned cold and damp, the matter of the succession was ruthlessly settled by Nicholas, which gave everyone a good inkling of the nature of the reign to come. The ringleaders of the Warsaw plot were hanged, and all those involved, who were mostly Polish and Russian aristocrats, were deported, along with their wives and children, to Siberia, many never to be heard of again. Constantine remained as Commander-in-Chief of the Warsaw garrison, as had been his wish all along.

Tsar Nicholas I had made his mark, and fear and a sense of foreboding gripped Spytkowiec.

VIII

Teofil's release from prison and return to Spytkowiec gained him growing popularity in the Mariampol region. His reputation had been enhanced by the 'Chinese Whispers' accounts of his adventures as a soldier of Napoleon. The fact that he was not an officer, as would befit a count, made him one of the people, a grass-roots warrior and a champion of the oppressed. Tales of his exploits in Egypt and the Middle East, his inheritance and altercations with Grocholski, his brief and aborted involvement with Inka's uprising, and his imprisonment in Moscow, all grew more colourful with each telling, and he reluctantly found himself assuming the mantle of folk hero.

'I never knew you stormed a Turkish brothel with a hand-picked force of mercenaries to rescue a beautiful, black-eyed maiden from a wicked and lustful Caliph,' said Eloise with a glint in her eye.

'Is that what Igor Bukowsky said?' grinned Teofil.

'He had it from Danilowicz.'

'He should know not to believe everything they hear from him. Danilowicz should stick to buying and selling horses, and leave the fiction to the novelists! Anyway, it was a Syrian brothel.'

'What's a brothel, mama?' Franciszka had come in at that moment.

'With people like Danilowicz around, my dear, you'll soon learn!' laughed her mother.

Franciszka wrinkled her nose, pulled a face and left.

It was the Spring of 1827, and the rain had not stopped for

two weeks. Teofil had intended to go and see Danilowicz anyway about a new saddle for Franciszka. Braving the pouring rain, he rode to Danilowicz's stables in the village.

'Good morning, *Panie hrabio*,' said the horse merchant, going out to meet him. By this time Teofil's title had been well and truly restored by the local population, to whom the Grocholski saga had passed into folk legend. 'How can I be of service?'

'For starters,' said Teofil with a smirk, 'you could spread the word that I didn't rescue just one beautiful black-eyed maiden, but six, and that my hand-picked mercenary force had to wait for me to have my wicked way with each maiden in turn, before I passed her on to them.'

'*Panie hrabio*, I was merely –'

'Exaggerating, is, I think, the word you're looking for, Abraham.'

Danilowicz shrugged and spread his hands. 'You're a romantic figure already, *Panie hrabio*!' he cried. 'People think of you as a hero – especially as you survived prison in Moscow! Mark my words already, you could go far in this community!' He led the way into his house.

'What do you mean, Abraham?'

'Have you not considered getting yourself elected on the Landowners' Council?'

'It's not my line, Abraham,' replied Teofil. 'I'm keeping my nose clean, and staying out of trouble. I need a new saddle for Franciszka. What have you got?'

'But that's just it! The Russians like councils as long as they have a portrait of the Tsar hanging in the chamber. You sit on the Council; they leave you in peace. Franciszka? What's wrong with the one I sold you?'

'She is thirteen years old, Abraham. She's outgrown the little one.'

'I'll buy it back off you in exchange...' Danilowicz hoisted a small, full sized saddle onto the table, '...for this one.'

Teofil turned the saddle over and felt it. 'How much?'

'We come to a price, heh? I don't cheat you. The Russians, yes, you, no. Anyway, what do you say? Once you're in the Council the Russians will say you're a good, upright citizen already! I put in a good word for you.'

'How much?'

'I'm telling you, on my mother's grave, they need men like you! Honourable men of the people!'

'How much?'

'You could bring justice for poor traders like me, they'll listen to you fifty marks.'

'How much, Abraham?'

'Fifty marks. Forty if you bring in the old one. Thirty if you stand for the Council. All right, twenty, you take it, bring back the little one, consider what I say, and give Franciszka a kiss from me, and tell her I want one back now she's thirteen! Ha! Ha! Ha!'

Teofil grinned and threw down twenty-five marks, and picked up the saddle. 'You'll have to ask her for that yourself, you old rascal!' he laughed. '*Shalom!*'

'*Shalom!*'

*****

That summer Eloise presented Franciszka almost with what she wanted. Michał was born with a luxuriant mop of dark hair, and a golden skin. But still Franciszka was not satisfied.

'He's got blue eyes!' she scolded jokingly. 'Mother! How could you do this to me?'

Eloise thought about Franciszka's good-natured outrage, but her thoughts were serious. There were, as far as she knew, no brown eyes in either Teofil's or her family. Her thoughts were drawn irrepressibly to the day before Maurice and Lenka left Czarne Lasy for France, ten long years ago. She had always had nagging doubts, but had managed to suppress them almost totally. Until now.

Teofil, meanwhile, had given a great deal of thought to Danilowicz's suggestion. Even though the old Jew, taking advantage of Teofil's easy nature, saw in him a hope of improving conditions for the merchant and artisan classes and might even speak for the serfs, whose emancipation had been on and off the cards for a long time now.

'Don't be an ass, Teofil,' Chrys had said. 'You know perfectly well you're not the type to sit on the Council! What good could you do?'

'What good do YOU do?'

'The heavens, Teofil! We get things done! Why, only last month we completed the Niemen canal project!'

'To take goods directly to the Baltic by waterway from the Kowno region. Very good, but who benefits?'

'The landowners, of course.'

'What about the peasants? The merchants? The artisans? What benefits do they get out of it?'

'What have they got to do with it? There were five thousand serfs drafted to dig the canal!'

'And where are they, now that it's finished?'

'The heavens, how should I know!'

'That's what I thought you'd say!'

Two factors went into Teofil's decision to stand for election to the Landowners' Council: Abraham Danilowicz's enthusiasm, and Chrys' pompous disregard for the ordinary people of the country. Having gathered support from among the horse-loving classes, Teofil got himself nominated and elected to the Council that September, much to Chrys' disgust. This was achieved with the help of Danilowicz, who, it seemed, had more sway with the local gentry than anyone would have believed.

'That Jew could get himself appointed to the court of the Tsar himself, with his gift of the gab!' said Eloise.

*****

Once on the Council, Teofil did not have to do much, other than irritate Chrys by his presence and block any projects that deprived the serfs in any way. The idea, a week after his election, of felling a 200-acre wood on one landowner's estate to increase grazing land was vetoed, because it was home to a woodman and his family, whose livelihood depended on it. This unheard-of act of consideration won Teofil the admiration of every underdog in the region, and many came to him, cap respectfully in hand, asking for basic rights. Teofil listened to everyone, and used individual tragedies to berate the insensitivities of his fellow councillors. The more popular Teofil became with the peasant classes, the more he was viewed with suspicion from some of the other members of the Council.

By the end of 1828, the Council was evenly split between the reactionary old guard who wanted to maintain the status quo, and to whom the basic needs of the peasants were totally irrelevant, and the more socially conscious set, who had read about modern western ideas of social justice and had heard of the word democracy. Over the months, the Council changed from a reactionaries' social club to a lively and often acrimonious debating society, in which the pendulum swung wildly from strict feudalism to open democracy at every meeting.

The final showdown between Teofil and Chrys was indirectly sparked off in the autumn of 1830.

Since his return from Italy with Maria Celestina, Kaz had been virtually retired from the diplomatic service to the Tsar. He was only too aware of the social stigma of having married an 'actress' – which was not done in aristocratic circles. However, he had salvaged some credibility by pleading aristocratic eccentricity. In more enlightened and artistic circles he had got away with it, but the hard establishment, including the Tsar, had considerable reservations about any further imperial appointment. He spent most of his time administering Maliny, writing his Memoirs about his life in Italy, as well as a series of essays reflecting the growth and spread of opera from its cradle in that country to the rest of Europe. He also travelled extensively, mostly in search of music and culture. On a number of occasions, he was summoned to St Petersburg to advise on diplomatic matters. It was in just such a capacity that he was summoned to the Russian court in the late Summer of 1830. Tsar Nicholas was concerned about growing unrest in Warsaw, and needed a diplomatic figure to be in place in the event of the unrest flaring up into a situation that might need unbiased mediation.

*****

Kaz arrived in Warsaw when the first leaves of autumn were beginning to fall. On this occasion he had left Maria Celestina behind, on the grounds that the Polish capital might well become a war zone before his mission was achieved. Maria Celestina had taken being left behind at Maliny with an italianate show of temper. She had become disillusioned with her husband, and had expressed a longing to get back onto the stage. Kaz, however, had expressly forbidden her even to think about it.

He took a house in the Krakowskie Przedmieście, and built up a high profile as an impartial observer. His first written report, on the first day of October, mentioned only bands of youths roaming the streets looking for Russian soldiers to taunt. Hardly the stuff for diplomatic encounters, Kaz directed his social life to soirées, concerts and the theatre rather than political and military conferences.

But even among the cultured classes, all was not as peaceful as he had first thought. Revolts in France and Belgium that year had awakened in a largely dormant Polish soul a reminder that the Fatherland was still under the Russian yoke. Hooligan action in the streets turned to earnest discussion about real insurrection. Kaz listened but did not comment. When the talk started coming from the ranks of the Polish Army, Kaz had to take note. He took further note when the voices of dissent rose even higher on the Tsar's proclamation that Polish troops were to be sent to Belgium to help crush the Revolution there.

By the end of November, the atmosphere on the streets of Warsaw was tense. Crowds of youths, many joined by soldiers, writers and intellectuals, gathered menacingly in the streets, and the Russian soldiers stayed in barracks, afraid to venture forth even in large numbers. Kaz, sensing that something was going to happen, summoned a carriage to take him to the Belweder Palace, the official residence of Grand Duke Constantine.

The Grand Duke received him in a state of panic.

'What's going on out there? How do you read this situation?' asked the Grand Duke.

'There are three factors for your consideration, Excellency,' said Kaz. 'Firstly, the street crowds are angry and numerous, but they have no weapons and could be subdued.'

'Can you talk to them?' said the Grand Duke, his whiskers quivering with terror. 'I want to avoid bloodshed.'

'No Excellency. They would not respond to talk. They are baying for blood.'

'The heavens! Secondly?'

'The Polish Army is staying put. They are playing loyal. For the moment, anyway.'

'So, they should be. I pay them enough!'

'Thirdly, and this is encouraging, the vast majority of the population are in no mood for rebellion.'

'Why? The crowds in the street obviously are!'

'Because they see no hope of success. They talk a lot, but are not prepared to take on the Tsar your brother. There would be too much bloodshed – ultimately all for nothing.'

'You mean –'

'I mean that they have no arms, and no leadership. They will bide their time – for a more suitable moment.'

The Grand Duke paced nervously back and forth across the Turkish carpet, deep in thought, his wolf-like face contorted with concentration into an ugly mask. He dismissed Kaz with an absent-minded wave of his hand. Kaz bowed and left the reception room, and joined a nervous and motley crowd of diplomats, officers, lawyers and soldiery, all talking in small groups, afraid of raising their voices above a murmur.

'What's happening?' said Kaz to the room at large. He sensed a nervous tension among the crowd. He was approached by General Zaręba, one of the Grand Duke's aides, a Pole whom Kaz had met on a number of occasions.

'There's something in the air, *Panie hrabio*,' said the General. 'There are rumours of action due tonight.'

'What kind of action?' said Kaz, almost casually. 'I cannot see any undue cause for alarm over and above what we have seen on the streets.'

'We have been advised that there may be a plot to storm the Belvedere Palace,' said the General. 'It may be just a false rumour, but we are not taking any chances. The guard has been doubled, and the Łazienki gardens are being patrolled all night.'

'The heavens, General!'

'May be open to us all tonight, *Panie hrabio*.'

IX

Krzysztof Żywiecki grunted with satisfaction. The night was bitterly cold, and the air was damp from a freezing fog that had been rising from the River Vistula, quickly obscuring his view of the brightly lit-up Belvedere Palace, a kilometre away to the west. The creeping lack of visibility was welcomed by Krzysztof, in whose mind every contour of the Palace was firmly etched. He knew exactly what to do, and was impatient to do it. His slim build and fine features belied his physical prowess, and his one surviving eye was eagle-like and observant, so nothing escaped its hard scrutiny.

His dedication had been fuelled from the days when he was a student at the Jagiełło University in Kraków. His first taste of Russian oppression took place exactly thirteen years previously, soon after the establishment of the Congress Kingdom of Poland. He remembered the occasion as if it were yesterday.

It was a cold November night, similar to this one, except then the pouring rain had not stopped for days. He was travelling to Warsaw in the company of a pompous Russian official and his wife, a Jewish merchant and a Pole with his French wife and four-year-old daughter. He recalled that it had been a rough journey, the rain having turned the post road into a quagmire, and the coach had been delayed. Just outside Warsaw he was forcibly taken off the coach by two Asiatic guards. The Russian officer in charge, seeing that he had been reading a book, had called him a clever bastard, ripped up the book and accused him of going to Warsaw to join the other Polish hooligans who had been rioting in the streets.

That had been merely typical of the kind of harassment that was meted out to any Pole who looked as though he might have an ounce of intelligence about him, especially a student. But it was the interrogation and subsequent term of imprisonment in a Russian jail that had hardened a resolve that was not even there when he had first set out from Kraków. His purpose had merely been to join a literary circle in Warsaw. He had emerged from jail only two years previously, with one eye, a limp, and a raging anger against all things Russian.

Now, ensconced with his motley rebel band among the shrubs and bushes on the banks of the Vistula, he peered through the fog, and saw clearly in his mind's eye the outline of the sumptuous residence of the Russian Wolfman whom he had vowed to kill, with his bare hands if necessary. He knew that similar bands were hidden in other parts of Warsaw, ready to seize key positions in the city. He peered upstream, where he knew the main body of the attack party would be well in place to storm the Arsenal beyond the Łazienki Gardens.

Krzysztof felt confident. He knew that the element of surprise was on the side of the rebels. The Palace only expected the usual street demonstrations, not a formal attack on the infrastructure of Warsaw. Certainly, he had seen no sign of extra guards on duty.

General Zaręba finished his glass of tea, excused himself from the group of officials with whom he had been conversing, and rose. 'Must see to the troops,' he said. 'We've got a whole company hidden here and in the Łazienki Gardens reinforcing the Palace guard, and they've never done this sort of thing before.'

'They're certainly well hidden, General,' said a Russian aide. 'I confess I haven't seen any more guards than usual.'

'That's how it should be,' smiled the General, making for the door. 'The element of surprise, eh?'

The hoot of an owl, which Krzysztof knew was not genuine, signalled the start of the attack.

'Right, you Russian bastard,' he whispered under his breath. 'Let's go.' Countless shadows arose, like wraiths from another world, all along the shrub-clad banks of the Vistula and the thickets of the Łazienki Gardens.

Silently they followed the seeping fog, splitting into two groups, one, with Krzysztof in charge of a unit of four men, making its way towards the Palace, while the other, larger group made for the complex of buildings that was the Arsenal. Beside one of the ornamental ponds in the Łazienki Gardens Krzysztof's unit surprised, and was surprised by, a unit of the Polish reinforcement force, maybe half a dozen strong. The two groups froze and stared at one another in silence for a seemingly eternal now, neither daring to move. It was as if reality had caught up with what had been effectively a war fantasy that had been enacted, around maps spread on tables in dozens of war-rooms over the past few weeks. Which Pole was going to be the first to kill another Pole? The rebels were the first to break the deadlock. They had anger on their side. Krzysztof was the first to move. As he drew his dagger from his belt, he simultaneously aimed a kick at the groin of one soldier, who clutched his genitals in agony, slipped and fell into the pond. A split second later he plunged his dagger beneath the ribcage of another, who, in turn doubled up and collapsed onto the ground. Krzysztof's attack activated the others, and within moments the army unit was neutralised. The rebels never knew how many fellow Poles were killed, and how many wounded. They gazed, stupefied, at what they had done.

'Come on!' hissed Krzysztof. 'They're done for!' He led the way at a crouching canter up the hill towards the bright lights of the Palace, now penetrating the swirling fog. He pointed to a first-floor window surrounded by creeping ivy. 'Up there!' he said.

The four shadowy figures only made the faintest rustling sound as they climbed up the ivy, two on each side of the chosen window. The woodwork of the window frames surrendered to the sturdy, steel daggers that all four carried.

*****

Kaz woke with a start. He had fallen asleep sprawled on a sofa. His bladder was full, and he needed to go and relieve himself. He rose, stiff from the awkward posture in which he had dozed fitfully, and made his way to the door. Most of the visitors were still awake, seated in small groups, talking in whispers, making the best of the tense, disturbed night. In the corridor outside, Kaz met General Zaręba. He had been checking out the guards who were in position at all the key points in the Palace.

The whole Palace was lit with more candles than usual. The General had decided to deprive any intruders of the luxury of darkness. Kaz made his way along one corridor after another, taking note of the increased soldiery that covered the whole building. He approached a young soldier standing guard outside a door. A split second before seeing him, the soldier had yawned profusely, before suppressing the yawn abruptly and jumping to attention.

'You're doing a damned good job, lad,' said Kaz encouragingly. 'Must be terribly tiring, standing guard all this time, eh?'

'Yessir,' said the soldier, bracing himself.

A chat might help, thought Kaz. Talking was often a good way to keep someone awake. 'Where are you from, lad?'

The soldier turned towards Kaz. 'Zamość, sir.'

'Damned fine city, Zamość. Went there with my wife once. Very historical. Some very fine buildings.'

'Can't say I'd noticed, sir. My parents an' me was too busy tryin' to make ends meet, sir.'

'Is that why you joined the army?'

'Only way a boy like me could get somewhere. You see, sir –' the boy suddenly relaxed his upright stance and let his rifle butt rest on the floor. He had obviously been torn between his duty as a soldier and a desperate need to talk to someone – anyone, about anything. But at that very moment the door, which was now behind him, opened. A man, aged about thirty, with a patch over one eye and a limp, grabbed the soldier by the neck from behind. Kaz looked on, hypnotised, as a flash of steel in the candlelight was followed by a spurt of blood ejecting from the soldier's throat. As the lad from Zamość fell to the floor, three more men emerged silently into the corridor. One of them grabbed the soldier's rifle a split second before it clattered onto the floor. The one-eyed man then flashed his dagger again, and Kaz doubled up and clutched at his stomach. A crimson ooze, glistening in the orange candlelight in the wall just beside him, seeped through his fingers, and he collapsed on the floor with an uncomprehending gurgle.

'This way!' indicated Krzysztof. The quartet silently made their way down the corridor, and disappeared round the corner.

The whole episode lasted maybe twenty seconds.

Kaz, in his agony, relieved himself there and then. The hurt was terrible, and he writhed in his own blood mixed with urine. A few moments later, gunfire broke out in the whole Palace, and in the Łazienki Gardens outside. But Kaz heard none of the screaming and shouting. The candles above his head began flickering in the draughts caused by doors opening and people rushing about. As he stared at them, the flickering flames first doubled in number, then increased in size to blurred haloes before fading into darkness. Rushing figures jumped, in both directions, over his hunched-up form, and the sprawled form of the soldier beside him, but Kaz knew nothing of this. Nor did Kaz ever know that the assault force which had mounted a full-scale assault on the Palace, had failed in its mission to assassinate the Grand Duke Constantine, in the name of free Poland.

The conspirators were killed or rounded up. Krzysztof Żywiecki, cornered and surrounded by a dozen guards, refused to be taken. He knew the mission had been betrayed, otherwise why were the Palace forces prepared? Why were they in place in such large numbers? Krzysztof fought with the rage of madness to the end, but he took a further half dozen soldiers with him before his strength, and with it his life-blood, ran out, and he surrendered only to blessed death.

Krzysztof Żywiecki never knew that the diplomat he had killed in the corridor of Belweder Palace was a cousin of that Polish patriot – with whose four-year-old daughter he had exchanged pleasantries on that fateful coach to Warsaw, all those years ago.

*****

News of the assassination attempt and the death of Kaz reached Spytkowiec a few days later. Chrys took the news very badly, and stopped just short of blaming Teofil for his brother's death.

'It's you and your kind!' he ranted, 'Call yourselves patriots! You go around killing and destroying whole families with your stupid notions! You never think about anyone but your own pathetic selves! You never consider the consequences! You might just as well have killed my brother with your own bare hands!'

It was the kind of wild, desperate argument that Teofil was not prepared to counter. He was just as upset by what had happened, even though he had thought of Kaz in much the same way as he thought of Chrys. But family is family, warts and all, and Chrys deserved his support. He tried to give it, but his efforts were largely rebuffed.

No one was more devastated by Kaz's violent death than Countess Maria Celestina Barnicka. Her hysterical outburst was followed by an angry sulk. She eschewed Spytkowiec and stayed at Maliny, where she seethed, alone, with unsuppressed rage at all things Polish and Russian.

'I go back to Italy!' she screamed at Teofil, who had gone to Maliny to see if there was anything he could do. 'I do not stay in this damned country a moment longer!'

She was as good as her word. She left Maliny in the hands of lawyers from St Petersburg, along with instructions that the estate was to be sold, as soon as the question of inheritance had been settled, and that the money should be transferred to a bank account in Milan that she was going to open specially for the purpose.

'I use it to finance my return to opera!' she cried. 'That will show you barbarians!' Her attempt at blaming everyone in Russia and Poland, and specifically Spytkowiec, for Kaz's refusal to allow her to return to opera, was seen as a hysterical outburst of sheer desperation, and was ignored.

The Russian Orthodox Christmas in January 1831 was a miserable affair at Spytkowiec, which was now firmly factionalised. Chrys and Tatiana virtually ignored Teofil, Eloise and the children, despite Teofil's genuine attempts to build bridges. Teofil's obvious yet unannounced support for the rebel Polish cause played a significant role in the rift, and pushed Chrys even further into the Tsarist camp.

There was an unspoken feeling that matters could not rest as they were, and that something was going to give, perhaps even sooner than later.

X

Throughout the opening months of 1832 chaos reigned in Warsaw. The November uprising had turned into a fiasco. The assault on the Arsenal had been initially successful, but because of a total lack of organisation, the insurrection crumbled. The Polish National Council, the puppet government of the Kingdom of Poland, led by Prince Franciszek Lubecki, assured the Tsar that the matter was a small, local problem, and that the Council would deal with it under Polish law. The Polish armies stayed, albeit on standby, in barracks. Everyone managed to keep their cool, with the exception of an angry rabble, who roamed the streets lynching anyone who might have anything to do with the Russians. The situation was being monitored day by day, but the crowds were leaderless, and did not have the support of the majority of Poles, who realistically could not see any insurrection succeeding. The National Council advised Grand Duke Constantine, and the Tsar, that patience would be the best policy, and that the whole thing would soon blow over without the bloodshed that everyone was so anxious to avoid.

General Chłopicki took over state security, and pledged co-operation with the Russians. He arranged safe conduct, for a very frightened Grand Duke Constantine and his court, out of Warsaw. This enraged Tsar Nicholas, who refused point blank to negotiate with Prince Lubecki and the National Council. He demanded unconditional surrender by the Poles, and made no secret of the fact that he wanted Poland to squirm. The National Council's reply was to vote that the Tsar be deposed as King of

Poland. The vote was passed.

Poland had unilaterally declared independence.

*****

Events in Warsaw dominated the first meeting after Christmas of the Landowners' Council in Mariampol.

'They're bloody idiots, every one of them!' cried Chrys. 'Seceding from Russia! Just as things were beginning to settle down, a bunch of your lot…' Chrys pointed an accusing finger at Teofil, '…blow Poland's chances of political and economic stability! There'll be all out war now!'

'I resent your continuous implications that I am personally responsible for every insurrection in Poland!' cried Teofil, angry at Chrys' endless and increasingly hysterical taunts. 'You know damned well it's got nothing to do with me!'

'Then whose side are you going to be on when the showdown comes, eh?'

'When the showdown comes, you'll be the first to know!'

The meeting ended in acrimony. Chrys stormed out of the chamber in a raging fury, climbed into his carriage and set off for Spytkowiec in a silent, silky snowstorm, without a backward glance. After he had gone Count Konrad Nabiesocki approached Teofil in the doorway of the building. 'You're not riding back in this weather, I hope,' he said. 'Why don't you stay in town at my house?'

Teofil, whose mind was seething with anger at his cousin's intransigence, looked at his friend Konrad and mellowed. 'Sounds like a good idea,' he smiled. 'Are you sure Kasia won't mind?'

'Perish the thought!'

Konrad and Kasia Nabiesocki were both in their seventies, and chose to spend most of their time in Mariampol, rather than at their estate in Nabiesock, near Kawaria. Since the estate, to the east, had been bisected as a result of the creation of the Congress Kingdom, Konrad had largely lost interest, and had left it under the administration of a manager, who kept it ticking over while allowing it to slide gradually into rack and ruin. In the event, Kasia was delighted to accommodate Teofil.

'Well, whose side will you be on, Teofil, when the showdown comes?'

They had dined very agreeably, after which Kasia had pleaded tiredness and had excused herself while Konrad placed another log on the fire, and brought out a bottle of French Cognac.

'You know perfectly well, Konrad,' replied Teofil. 'I'll be up there I suppose, brandishing a pitchfork, if necessary. Only I've got to keep my nose clean. Old Szulc is making a note of everything I say. I swear he's in the pay of the Russians. I've got to watch my tongue, and pretend to be a good boy.'

'There will be a showdown, Teofil.'

'I know.'

'The Tsar will not be merciful.' They drank for a long time in silence, staring at the blazing fire, and listening to the silent blizzard outside. 'You know the Unborn Future is reforming?'

'I hope they change their name. And their tactics.'

'Can we – they – count on your support?'

'I suppose so.' Konrad's slip, Teofil reckoned, was probably intentional.

'I mean – to lead.'

Teofil leapt up. 'Now wait a minute, Konrad! You know that's not fair! I'd be putting my head in the Tsar's noose just by being approached!'

'But you'd wield a pitchfork under a Polish banner?'

'Under it, but not in front of it!'

'You decline?'

'Yes.'

'As you wish.'

*****

The following morning dawned bright and clear, and the Lithuanian birch forests were a picture in black and white luminosity. Teofil thanked Kasia for her hospitality, and said goodbye to Konrad, mounted his horse – he preferred to ride rather than go by carriage – and set off for Spytkowiec. The leadership of the insurrection was not mentioned again.

The February meeting of the Council brought the news, triumphantly announced by Chrys, that a Russian army, 115,000 strong and led by General Diebitsch, was marching on Warsaw from the east.

'So, Teofil,' gloated Chrys, 'the showdown comes! Perhaps you will be so kind as to enlighten the Council as to whose side you will be on?'

'Why didn't you tell me this at home,' cried Teofil, furious at the games that Chrys was playing, 'instead of waiting to spring it on me in front of the Council?'

'Because the Council has a right to know!'

'And I have a right to decline to air my views in public!'

Teofil glanced at Konrad Nabiesocki, who immediately turned his eyes away. Both men were thinking that this was not the time to declare for secession. The remainder of the meeting was devoted to Chrys' attempts to veto Teofil's place on the Council, on the grounds that he was not, strictly speaking, a landowner.

He was outvoted, but only by a narrow margin. Many council members were for secession, but were not prepared to go along with it for fear of the Russians. So instead of showing their true colours, they opted for Teofil as unofficial spokesman for the undeclared principle of free Poland, while paying lip service to the Chrys Barnicki faction. With 115,000 Russian troops advancing on Warsaw, the lip service had to be seen to be effective.

'So, you see,' gloated Chrys, back at Spytkowiec, 'you don't have as much support as you think! And when General Diebitsch restores order in Warsaw, I think you will find your days on the Council numbered!'

The smirk on Chrys' psyche disappeared a week later, when news came that the Polish Army, less than a quarter of the size of the Russian force, had successfully blocked General Diebitsch's advance at Grochów, a small town just to the east of Warsaw. For the time being, at any rate, Warsaw was safe. This had the psychological effect of drawing loyalties out of their hiding places. Count Konrad Nabiesocki publicly declared for the Revolution, and was immediately followed by two thirds of the Council members, but still Teofil refused to show his colours. Not only that, but Mariampol, indeed the whole of Lithuania, came alive with demonstrations of support for the National Council in Warsaw.

'My carriage was stoned by hooligans on my way home!' cried Chrys, fuming with indignation on his return from a special meeting of the Council. 'There was hardly anyone at the meeting, and that was broken up by screaming hordes outside! What's it all coming to?'

The first hints of spring also brought news that General Diebitsch had retreated from the gates of Warsaw.

Teofil decided that the time was ripe to declare himself. He rode into Mariampol and made straight for Konrad Nabiesocki's house.

'We've been expecting you, Teofil,' said the elderly Count. 'We're all on the winning side now. You can declare for the Revolution, and no one will touch you. Even Old Szulz has fled to Vilnius.'

'I'm with you, Konrad.' The words were spoken with a resigned air of finality. 'Long live the fatherland,' he added with a sheepish grin.

Konrad's response was one of joy and relief. 'The revolution in Mariampol will unite behind you, Teofil! You will have to accept that, whether you like it or not!'

*****

There was a sense of euphoria in Lithuania, as Poles, Lithuanians, peasants and landowners joined the insurrection in their thousands. The official March meeting of the Landowners' Council was attended by all except Chrys and the pro-Tsarists. Chrys had declined to go, on the grounds of a fear for his life – a fear that was by no means groundless. Russians and pro-Tsarist locals were being beaten up, and even murdered, and most were now keeping very low profiles. Many had fled over the border, where they remained in hiding.

A Polish company that marched into Mariampol unopposed was given a heroes' welcome. Captain Valery Semienko, who was in command of the Mariampol garrison, a nominal force of only 500, surrendered unconditionally to the officer in charge of the Polish company, Captain Stefan Skrzypek. The surrender was peaceful and civilised. The terms were discussed over lunch, and the finer points were lubricated over a bottle of French brandy.

Polish and Russian soldiers got together, and a carnival atmosphere ensued. The streets of Mariampol were alive with soldiers in varying stages of good-natured alcoholic inebriation, and a thousand toasts to friendship between Russians and Poles were drunk. Teofil observed the celebrations wryly, marvelling at the irony of it all.

Captain Skrzypek remained sober enough to address the meeting of the Landowners' Council.

'The news for the Fatherland is excellent on all fronts,' said the Captain. 'The Russians have been defeated by our forces at Wawer, Dębe Wielkie and Iganie, while General Diebitsch's main army is holed up and isolated in Lublin. There's not a great deal he can do.'

'What about us, Captain,' said Konrad Nabiesocki, 'what can we do?'

'Two things, *Panie hrabio*,' said Captain Skrzypek. 'Firstly, a Revolutionary Council, with an elected President, must be formed to administer the Mariampol district. As temporary military commander here, I hereby appoint this Council to the task.'

'We accept, Captain,' said Konrad. 'And the other thing?'

'The formation of an armed militia that will take charge of local security. Under the terms of surrender the garrison building is placed at the Council's disposal. The Russians have been disarmed, and I shall leave a token force to supervise the changeover. I have Captain Semienko's assurance that the terms will not be violated. We were at the Military Academy together in St Petersburg. We are very good friends, and I can guarantee his word as an officer and a gentleman.'

'This shall be done. Will the Russians be repatriated?'

'No,' replied Captain Skrzypek. 'From midnight tonight they are to be confined to barracks until a formal peace treaty can be negotiated with the Russians, after which they will, naturally, be sent home. Needless to say, they are to be well treated, *Panie hrabio*. We are not barbarians.'

'Of course,' replied Konrad, and everyone nodded in agreement. The goodwill in the town was almost overwhelming.

Skrzypek's message was concise and straight to the point. After he left, the Council wasted no time in implementing his recommendations.

'There's no point in waiting till the April meeting, gentlemen,' said Konrad. 'I propose we elect at least a temporary President here and now.' After a thoughtful pause, he continued. 'I propose Count Teofil Samojarski.'

'I second it,' came a voice.

Teofil, who had been expecting this, did not move. 'I decline.'

Everyone stared at Teofil in total disbelief.

*****

'Why?' said an amazed Eloise later that night.

'I've had enough, Eloise,' replied Teofil, removing his boots. 'That's the real reason. I've fought enough over this damned country. I'm fifty-two now, and very little to show for it.'

'Your fatherland needs you, Teofil! Now more than ever. Think of what you, with your experience, could achieve in a new free Poland!'

Teofil sniffed, collapsed into his favourite armchair, and wriggled his toes, now bare and free of the constrictions of boots. 'Experience!' he sneered. 'I gave my youth to Napoleon, and my prime to Inka's Unborn Future. All I got out of it is sunstroke, frostbite, some nasty wounds, and six months in a Moscow prison!'

'So, what did you all talk about?'

'Konrad has agreed to keep things ticking over until they decide what to do. But he's too old. Otherwise, there's no President, no plans, no agenda. Just a mountain of indecision. At least the new Revolutionary Council meets every day. I'm sure they'll sort it all out eventually.'

'You know damn' well they won't!'

'They decided to hand the militia over to the Unborn Future. They're all out in the open now, anyway. They'll sort the garrison out without any trouble.'

'You do realise that if the Revolutionary Council don't take a firm hold of the reins, Chrys and his lot will.'

'The very idea!' Teofil snorted mockingly.

XI

Teofil dismissed Chrys too soon. The Revolutionary Council bumbled on, leaderless, for several weeks. It had achieved virtually nothing, apart from handing over the Garrison to the Unborn Future, who had mercifully dropped that name. At least security in the district was in competent hands. The Council members, largely landowners, farmers and aristocrats, still had the mentality of a social club. They had no political experience, and the idea of standing for a Presidency of a political outfit filled them all with trepidation. However, the population was reassured by the very fact that the Council existed, and placed its trust in it implicitly.

Teofil only occasionally attended, and then mostly in social capacity. Usually, he made some minor contribution to the proceedings, and sometimes, frustrated by the complete lack of efficiency and drive, was even tempted to take over, before checking himself. He was absent at the meeting, half way through May, when Chrys and a dozen stalwart pro-Tsarists turned up.

'I see Count Samojarski is not present!' he announced triumphantly. 'I take it the reins of office are beyond his capabilities!'

'What have you come for, Chrys?' asked Konrad suspiciously.

'To stand for office, Konrad. I note the chair of President is still vacant.'

'You would go against the Tsar?'

Chrys took no notice, but took a scroll from beneath his frock coat. 'But first,' he continued, unravelling it, 'I have here a proclamation from the Tsar, which I draw to the Council's attention.' He handed it to Konrad, who studied the Cyrillic script carefully. Chrys continued, 'In this proclamation to the people of the Mariampol district, Tsar Nicholas offers an unconditional amnesty to all those who renounce their treason, lay down their arms and renege on their illegal, insurrectionist and secessionist stance. No action will be taken against those who pledge loyalty to the Tsar, regardless of past actions.'

Konrad looked up from the scroll. 'May the Council take it that you and your faction have formally accepted this pledge?' he said.

'You may.'

'And you wish to stand for President of this Council in order to bring it back into the Russian fold?'

'That is correct. We are currently engaged in drawing up an agenda that will be acceptable to the Tsar.'

'You will find the task – difficult!' said Konrad, looking about him with a sarcastic smile. But no one else was smiling; with the Council disunited, and in the absence of any other candidates, the threat of victory for Chrys was very real.

'One must do one's duty,' said Chrys.

Teofil took the news of Chrys' intention to throw his hat in the ring with some alarm, which he tried not to show. 'It's a free country,' he commented over breakfast.

'You see, Teofil,' said Chrys, cutting into his sausage with gusto, 'our faction may be small, but we are united. We could take over the Council unopposed. It's just a matter of time, you know.'

'Good luck to you, Chrys,' muttered Teofil, trying to sound disinterested. The acrimony between Teofil and Chrys had died down considerably over the past few weeks. Teofil having declined to take part in politics, their relationship returned to a basis of civilised mutual loathing, rather than war.

The following day Teofil rode into Mariampol to attend the

Council, and walked straight into another serious crisis.

'Torture?' he cried. 'Are you telling me that the Militia have been torturing the Russian prisoners? Who made the allegations?'

'Genek Starski,' said Konrad. 'Poor lad was shaking with terror when he came to see me at my house. He said he didn't join the Militia to torture prisoners, and now he's deserted and is too frightened to go back. It seems they've been starving and beating the prisoners, and holding them in cupboards where they can't stand, sit or lie down for days at a time. We need you, Teofil! You can see for yourself we can't control this anymore!'

Without a word Teofil left the meeting in a rage, mounted his horse and rode to the Garrison. He stormed into the building past two sentries before they could stop him, and kicked open the door to the office of the self-styled 'General' Oleg Sosnowski, to the consternation of the two slouching soldiers guarding it.

'What's this I hear about the torture of prisoners?' he thundered.

Sosnowski rose nervously from his desk. Teofil noted with disgust how the man had changed. Once he had been one of Inka's most stalwart lieutenants, hard, disciplined and dedicated to the task of freeing Poland from the Russian yoke. Now his hair was dishevelled and he had not shaved for several days. The stained coat of his uniform was lying across his desk, beside a bottle, some empty glasses and a pile of papers. There were wet patches under his arms, where he had sweated.

'*Panie hrabio*,' he belched. 'An honour! Please –' he waved his hand at a chair.

'There is no honour here!' cried Teofil. 'Answer the question! Have you been torturing prisoners?'

'*Panie hrabio*!' Sosnowski grinned and spread his hands, 'we are not barbarians! Sometimes, you understand, it is necessary to punish –'

'Take me to see the prisoners!'

'Impossible, *Panie hrabio*,' Sosnowski scratched his nose

and winced. 'I cannot allow that. Only the President of the Revolutionary Council may authorise me to allow anyone to see the prisoners, and in the absence of a President, you understand, I am in charge within these walls. Those are the terms of the surrender, you understand – '

Teofil saw out of the corner of his eye that the two guards, reinforced by two large henchmen, whom Teofil recognised as the notoriously violent Kaunikas brothers, had entered the room, and were standing menacingly in the doorway. 'Oh yes, I understand! I understand very well! Now you understand this, General! When I return, I shall see the prisoners, and by heaven, if I hear of any ill-treatment, I'll have your balls crushed and stuffed up your arse! Understand?'

Before Sosnowski could reply, Teofil left, only pausing long enough to snarl at the Kaunikas brothers, 'Yours as well!'

*****

'They're shits, all of them!' cried Teofil to Eloise later. 'The Council, the Militia! The whole bloody lot of them! Napoleon was right! We Poles cannot govern ourselves! We're inefficient, we're corrupt, we're barbaric, we sell out, we betray, and we lick whichever arse might give us the least hassle at any given moment in history! Christ! Is there no end to this?'

Eloise remained silent, and let Teofil berate his country for the rest of the evening. Best to let him exorcise his rage, she thought. After a while he retreated into a furious sulk, and eventually calmed down and retired to bed. He turned over and went to sleep without a further word.

In the middle of the night, Eloise woke. 'What did you say?' she moaned. Her voice was swathed in sleep.

'I said I've decided to stand for President of the Council.'

'Good. Good.' Before she went back to sleep, she opened her eyes, and smiled with satisfaction at the dark.

*****

Teofil was unanimously elected President of the Revolutionary Council the following week. Chrys, furious, had withdrawn his candidature. Teofil immediately proclaimed a Revolutionary meeting in the Market Square for the following day, at noon. He spent his first night as President under Konrad's roof. At noon he was in the Market Square, wielding a scroll. He was accompanied by a group of some two dozen soldiers, armed with muskets and wearing very smart new uniforms. He received a rapturous welcome from a very large crowd.

'Citizens of Poland!' he announced from his improvised perch on the podium of the ornate, cast-iron and stone well in the centre of the Square. 'I speak to you as the new President of the Revolutionary Council of the district of Mariampol.' There was an approving roar from the crowd. 'I have here a proclamation from the Tsar!' He raised the scroll, and the crowd went silent. 'This document states that Tsar Nicholas offers an unconditional amnesty to all those who renounce their treason, lay down their arms and renege on their illegal, insurrectionist and secessionist stance. No action will be taken against those who pledge loyalty to the Tsar, regardless of past actions.'

Teofil lowered the scroll and looked about him. The crowd, bemused, remained silent. Teofil continued. 'I have summoned this meeting so that you, the citizens of Mariampol, may bear witness to my answer, as President of the Council, to the Tsar's most generous offer!'

With that, Teofil took a smouldering taper from one of the soldiers, and put it to the scroll. After a while, the scroll caught fire. Teofil held up the burning scroll for all to see. 'Our answer to the Tsar of Russia!' he cried. This was met by a hysterical outburst as the crowd went wild.

'Long live *Pan hrabia*! Long live the Revolution! Down with the Tsar! Russians out!' The cries and slogans turned to chants. There was no stopping the crowd in its outburst of euphoria.

When the scroll was just a wisp of ashes on the springtime breeze, Teofil turned to the soldiers, nodded, and together they marched off towards the Garrison.

This time the sentries at the gate were ready for them. 'Who goes there?'

'The President of the Revolutionary Council of the District of Mariampol,' announced Teofil.

'And the rest?'

'The Presidential Guard, as appointed by the Revolutionary Council.'

'Genek Starski? Jacek Szymanski? But – you're deserters!'

'Volunteers for special duty!' cried Teofil. 'Let us pass!'

'What is the purpose of your visit?'

'To investigate allegations of the ill-treatment of prisoners!'

'Permission to enter denied!'

At a signal from Teofil the two sentries were overpowered and disarmed in seconds, and Teofil led the way into the building. The two guards outside Sosnowski's office, who had listened with trepidation at the exchange outside, pointedly laid down their rifles and shuffled off, hands raised in surrender.

This time Sosnowski was clean-shaven, and dressed smartly in full uniform. He was seated behind his desk, on which papers were stacked neatly. He rose as Teofil entered. The Presidential Guard remained in the Hall outside.

'*Panie hrabio!*' he said, bowing, 'my congratulations on your election.'

'I wish to inspect your prisoners, General,' Teofil seasoned the rank with a sneer, 'because of allegations of ill-treatment!'

'By all means, *Panie hrabio*,' said Sosnowski. 'You will see that these allegations are unfounded. Please feel free to go where you will. Permit me to show you round.'

The tour of the cells and dungeons yielded allegations, though precious little sign of, torture. The prisoners looked well enough, although most told stories of beatings, starvation and confinement for days in cupboards and boxes in which they were unable to sit, stand or lie.

'Can't you see they are lying, *Panie hrabio*!' said Sosnowski. 'The Russians will say anything to incriminate the Militia and divide us! In certain cases, solitary confinement and some mild physical punishment is always necessary. But torture?' He shook his head.

Teofil was unable to find any evidence of bruising or broken bones, nor could anyone find any of the boxes or cupboards in which prisoners were confined.

'We'll leave it at that, for the moment, General,' said Teofil at length. 'But do not think this is the end of the matter. There will be regular inspections of prison conditions. Regulations will be drawn up by the Council, and these will be strictly adhered to. Understood?'

'Understood, *Panie hrabio*!'

Once outside, Genek approached Teofil. 'With your permission, *Panie hrabio*?' he said. 'I took the initiative to count all the prisoners, sir. There were 463 in all.'

'What are you saying, Genek?' said Teofil.

'There should be 485, sir.'

Jacek Szymański added his voice. 'There are 22 missing, sir. And that's not all. We all saw the Militia were there, but we none of us saw any sign of the Kaunikas brothers, or any of the others who did the worst things.'

Teofil looked at his troops. After Genek Starski's desertion in protest at what he saw as a betrayal of the Revolution, he was followed by others, mostly young and fired with idealism. Teofil saved them from being shot, the punishment for desertion, by getting them to volunteer for special duty as Presidential Guard.

As such, Sosnowski was unable to touch them, as they now enjoyed the protection of the Council. The whole first floor of the Council Building had been hurriedly turned over as their billet – considerably more comfortable than their quarters at the Garrison. They were given uniforms – special new designs, as yet unused, that had been sent from Russia on approval, and had been confiscated from the Garrison stores. The Presidential Guard had become, overnight, an elite corps.

'So where are they, these missing prisoners and torturers?'

'We can't figure it out, sir.'

'They can't just have disappeared, sir.'

'So, find them,' said Teofil.

'How, sir?' said Jacek.

'You're the Presidential Guard. You find them. I don't care how, but you've got a week. I want Sosnowski's head. And his balls. On a silver platter. Clear?'

Jacek and Genek looked at one another quizzically, as did the others. Then, with a big smile of dawning comprehension, they saluted smartly. 'Yes, sir, *Panie hrabio*, sir!'

Teofil sent his Guard marching back to their quarters in the Council Building. He watched them go and smiled. No officers, no hierarchy, just a tight togetherness that had cut its teeth on something called the Unborn Future. With a bunch like that, he felt he could take on the Russians themselves, if necessary.

XII

The following day Chrys attended the Council meeting, and dropped a bombshell that sent a shiver of fear down the spines of everyone present.

'I've just heard the news that the Polish Army has been defeated by General Diebitsch at Ostrołęka,' he announced triumphantly. 'Let's hope it marks the end of this ridiculous insurrection.' He paused for effect, before continuing. 'For your – our survival, I propose this Council be hereby disbanded as a token of loyalty to the Tsar, and immediately re-formed as a new administrative Council dedicated to the implementation of the Polish Constitution as recognised by the Tsar of Russia as King of Poland.'

'With you as President,' said Konrad.

'I shall stand for election,' continued Chrys. 'Those who vote for my candidature will do so in the full knowledge that their choice will be noted, and the amnesty implemented – with...' he cast a sideways glance at Teofil '...certain possible exceptions. For your own salvation, I would ask for a unanimous vote.'

Chrys sat down, crossed his legs, rested his chin in his fingers, and looked intently around him like a well-satisfied cat. He saw only impassive faces, and heard only a stunned silence. His eyes finally rested on Teofil, and a ghost of a smile alighted on his mouth.

'Ostrołęka?' said someone at length.

'In Mazovia. Between here and Warsaw.'

'What was Diebitsch doing there?'

'He must have broken out.'
'What about Skrzyniecki?'
'Who?'
'The new Commander-in-Chief, Prince Radziwiłł's replacement.'

General Skrzyniecki was considered by many Poles as a bad choice for the position. His view of ultimate victory over the Russians was a pessimistic one. He tried to play safe with his policy of talking first, fighting later. In this instance, instead of taking on the Russian armies while they were isolated and vulnerable, he dithered, thus allowing Diebitsch and the crack Guard Corps to link up near the village of Ostrołęka, in the Lake District, with drastic results for the Polish Army.

The dithering was not confined to the battlefield. In Warsaw, the President of the National Council, Prince Adam Czartoryski, was also undecided as to what to do next, fearing not only the wrath of Tsar Nicholas, but also a possible alliance between the three partitioning powers.

'At last, they're beginning to see sense in Warsaw,' said Chrys. 'Czartoryski knows they cannot win in the end!'

'Why not?' said Konrad. 'Our Army's almost as big as the Russians' – or at least it was until now – and we've got the motivation! And we've got French and American mercenaries and freedom fighters on our side. We could have kicked the Russians out once and for all! I blame the High Command.'

'What do you think, Teofil?'

All eyes turned to the President of the Revolutionary Council. Teofil had sat, immobile and expressionless, trying in his heart to come to terms with what had happened. The feeling that things were at last going his – and Poland's – way was rapidly evaporating, and he saw only a reversion to the heavy yoke of Russian rule poised to crush him once more into the dust. And this time he will take Jolanta with him. All the while, at the back of his mind, she was there, a beautiful reminder that he owed her his life, and that he had now betrayed her. While everyone around him had rushed headlong into Revolution, he had steadfastly stayed his hand, for her sake, until he was certain of victory. Now that certainty was gone, and he saw a bleak future with no hope. Chrys would be in the ascendant from now on, and his protection would have to be bought with further betrayal. Teofil would fall, and he would have to grovel at Chrys' feet, apologising further for bringing Jolanta down with him – and that on top of the Inka affair. He saw no way out of the impending situation.

It was a long time before he replied, and when he did, there was suppressed rage in his voice. 'I say we fight.'

Chrys burst out laughing. 'You must be mad, Teofil!' he cried. 'The cause is lost! Your free Poland is a myth once more! Cut your losses, shift your allegiance over to me, and I'll see what I can do to get us all off the hook!'

'I've got life in prison staring me in the face, Chrys!' said Teofil, rising, and pacing round the chamber. 'And I don't need your kind intercession to knock a year or two off my sentence! I'll fight! I've got nothing to lose!'

'But everyone else has,' said Chrys with a disdainful smirk.

*****

That night Teofil brooded long and hard at his predicament. 'I'm sending you and the children to Nibork again,' he told Eloise. 'Things are going to come to a head in Poland, and especially in Lithuania. The Prussians have been very supportive of the Revolution, and you should be safe there. We've got funds in Berlin and Königsberg, so you should be able to manage.'

'What about you, Teofil?' replied Eloise.

'I've got no choice. I've got to fight, to the end if necessary. If all else fails, I'll join you in Nibork.'

Teofil spent the next few days gathering support for the Revolution. He found that the majority of the Council was in favour of resisting Chrys' attempts to take over and effect unconditional surrender to the Russians.

'We've got a good army here, that could give any Russian force a hard time,' said Konrad, to general agreement.

Chrys' candidature for the presidency of a new, pro-Tsarist regime was put on hold. 'But only for the moment, Teofil,' said Chrys. 'Your days are numbered!'

*****

In the meantime, the Presidential Guard had come up with some very useful news. An old building close to the Garrison – which had been used as an arms dump in the past, and had been closed up five years previously, had been opened up again. Genek and a few others had been secretly spying on unusual comings and goings at the Garrison, and had seen prisoners, blindfolded and apparently unconscious, being carried into it, under cover of darkness, across a stretch of wasteland. Investigating further, they followed the figures, and tried to peer into a window from which a faint light was issuing.

'We couldn't see much, *Panie hrabio*,' said Jacek, 'on account of they'd draped a blanket across the window, but we could hear some right goings-on, people being beat up, an' moanin' and being sick an' all that sort of thing.'

'I reckon Sosnowski's turned it into an interrogation centre, where prisoners get done over,' said Genek.

'We hung about till someone come out, and it were them Kaunikas brothers.'

'We kept watch an' more were brought, blindfolded so's they didn't know where they were going.'

'Reckon that's why they were all vague, an' that.'

Teofil listened with mounting anger at what he heard.

'When they were all gone, we broke in to have a look, and there were these Russkies squashed into boxes, cupboards and gaps in the stonework. "We let 'em be", so's not to give the game away. Hope we did right, sir!'

'Absolutely. How many in Sosnowski's gang?'

'Reckon about a dozen or so. Hard to say being as it were dark, an' we might've counted some twice.'

'Do you reckon the Guard could take them?' said Teofil.

'Just try to stop us, *Panie hrabio*, sir!'

'I shall address the Guard in one hour. Tell them to expect action!'

'Yessir, *Panie hrabio*, sir!'

At ten o'clock that evening, the sixteen members of the Presidential Guard marched, fully armed, round Mariampol, attracting attention and making a great deal of noise. For all the world it looked like a straightforward bout of drill, probably designed to whip up morale among the population. In the dim glow of the street lighting, they presented an awesome, if rather romantic, picture. Indeed, many townsfolk, especially the girls, emerged to see the Count's Presidential Guard disporting themselves and showing off. Every smart move elicited loud banter, good natured cheer and some bawdy suggestions from the giggling girls. The boys played to the gallery, gradually making their way towards the Garrison, with the whole town following. The atmosphere was such that Ostrołęka might have been a million miles away.

The manoeuvres reached the square outside the Garrison, and within seconds every window was crammed with the staring faces of the regular militia, trying to make out what was going on outside. Most townsfolk were aware of the rift between the militia and those whom they considered as deserters.

'This is just a wind-up!' said a voice in the crowd.

'There's going to be a right ding-dong any minute now!' said another.

The latter was right. Suddenly a wild crowd emerged from the Garrison, wielding sticks, and charged at the Guard, laughing and shouting obscenities. The Guard, obviously expecting this, immediately scattered, keeping low, in all directions, some seeking the shadows behind houses, others losing themselves in the vast crowd that had built up. Within seconds, sixteen lads had seemingly disappeared off the face of the earth, leaving a bewildered crowd of militiamen not knowing which way to turn, and where to look.

The crowd turned on the militiamen, and mocked their military skills, or rather, lack of them, especially the girls. The atmosphere was one of youthful exuberance, which may have ended with not much more than a few black eyes, bloody noses, bruised prides and monumental headaches. The militiamen, like the Guard, played along with the crowds, joking and bantering, and flirting with the girls.

All of a sudden, the night was rent by the sound of gunfire coming from somewhere behind the Garrison. Everyone spun round. The Garrison gates were manned by eight of the Presidential Guard, who had seemingly materialised out of nowhere. They stood in a row, their guns pointing at the crowd, which suddenly went quiet. Teofil appeared in the doorway. 'Don't anybody move, or there will be bloodshed!' he shouted. 'I have to announce that my Guard and I have taken temporary charge of the Garrison. General Sosnowski has been relieved of command and arrested, as have several other members of the Militia, on charges of the abuse of authority. All soldiers will return to the Garrison now, on the understanding that my orders, and only mine, are to be obeyed until further notice.'

'So that's where the buggers got to!' said a militiaman. 'Clever sods!'

'Come on, let's get back!' The militiamen, as one, detached

themselves from the crowd and went back into the Garrison building. The crowd cheered them on.

The following day Teofil was formally requested by the Revolutionary Council to take command of all armed forces in the Mariampol district. Having accepted, he could legally institute court martial proceedings against eight men, including Sosnowski and the Kaunikas brothers. They were charged with betrayal of the Revolution, abuse of power, torturing prisoners, placing the security of the district in jeopardy at a time of insurrection, and of conduct unbecoming of the armed forces of the new, free Poland.

*****

During the trial, when several Russians, including Captain Semienko, were asked to give evidence, it transpired that there had been a hierarchy of abuse. Sosnowski had acted like a power-crazed petty tyrant soon after his appointment as Chief of the Mariampol Garrison. He had given vent to a vicious and sadistic streak, which he shared with the infamous Kaunikas brothers. The systematic torture of Russian prisoners started almost immediately, at first as punishment for such infringements as not saying 'sir', or showing disrespect with a look, or a gesture.

One Russian, who was crippled, had to be brought in strapped into a chair. He told the Court of the 'Crack', Sosnowski's *pièce de resistance* of barbarity. 'It is a wide fault in the heavy masonry of one of the walls in the building, *Panie hrabio*,' he said. 'It was probably the result of cannon fire, or subsidence. It runs irregularly from the floor to the ceiling. In some parts it's half a metre wide, in others half that. It's big enough to fit a man into it. I was forced in so that I could not move, but was also in a position where a jagged edge was pressing hard into my spine.'

'How long were you kept there?'

'Impossible to say, as I was blindfolded and without food or water. At one stage, I coughed, and my spine snapped.'

Sosnowski and the Kaunikas brothers were sentenced to death, and were shot in the Quadrangle by half a dozen volunteers from the Militia. The others involved were, by all accounts, merely obeying orders, but their activities were limited to occasional beatings, as well as running and fetching. They were sentenced to five years in prison – specifically among the Russians. Teofil reckoned that some private vendettas within the dungeons would be punishment enough. Altogether sixteen Russian soldiers who had been particularly ill-treated were escorted to the Russian frontier for immediate repatriation on compassionate grounds.

'Making plans to ingratiate yourself with the Russians when they come, I see,' said Chrys. 'You'll be hailed as a hero! Those sixteen will make glowing reports about your mercy and compassion!'

Teofil ignored the sarcasm. 'Just doing my duty,' he said.

XIII

The following week Eloise left for Nibork, in Prussia, with Franciszka, Julek, Adam and Michał. Teofil moved out of Spytkowiec, and stayed with Konrad and Kasia Nabiesocki at their Mariampol house. The elderly couple were glad of his company, and Teofil was pleased no longer having to share a roof with Chrys. He had lost all interest in helping him to manage the estate, and had withdrawn his financial support. From his new base on the spot, he was more able to exercise his duties as President of the still active Revolutionary Council, and Chief of the armed forces. For this he was advised by the Council to assume a military rank, which he refused to do, on the grounds that any rank to which he would be promoted could only be bestowed by the Polish High Command in Warsaw.

'We're still basically a bunch of rebels from the forests,' he maintained.

In June the first units of the defeated Polish army began to appear in Mariampol. They brought tales of repression that had already started in Poland. The wounded were taken in and cared for by townsfolk, despite reports that those who harboured Polish soldiers could expect to be executed.

By July the trickle had become a flood with the arrival of a reformed Polish army under General Giełgud. They re-grouped in Polish Lithuania and marched north. They crossed the River Niemen into Russian Lithuania proper. There they joined up with partisans, and gained control over an enormous swathe of Russian territory, from the Baltic coast to Vilnius and beyond.

They tied up the Russians enough to keep the Mariampol region still free.

Summer passed and Polish morale began its inexorable downward slide. The tables had turned, and the Russian war machine, under General Pashkievitch easily outmanoeuvred Skrzyniecki's remaining forces in the field. The Mariampol district, being remote from the heaviest war-zones, was a comparative haven of peace, although everyone was aware of the sword of Damacles that hung by a steadily corroding thread above the region. News arrived regularly – and it was always bad. Giełgud's forces in Lithuania were having a hard time as the Russians pressed ever harder to regain control. The summer ground on relentlessly, and everyone could only prepare themselves for the inevitable.

*****

September brought events to a head. First of all, Chrys disappeared. No one had any idea what had happened to him. At the same time the first minor Russian units began to infiltrate into Poland from Lithuania. The Garrison at Mariampol came under attack from one such small task force, but managed to repel it without too much difficulty. The second one was more successful. The force, 3,000 strong, marched out of Kaunas, crossed the River Niemen, and made for Mariampol. Half way there the force was beset by a band of some 200 partisans, who still ruled the roost in the region. The Russians stopped in their tracks and took up formal defensive positions on high ground behind the village of Brynie. This untypical over-reaction astounded the partisans. Few in number, their only aim was to inflict as many casualties as possible in as short a time as possible, before fleeing back into the forest. Taking on a Russian force in formal battle was never their intention.

Thus, having stopped the army, they had very little option but to see the fight through. They surrounded the hill, and despatched a messenger to Mariampol, requesting help from the Militia.

'I say we fight, Teofil,' said Konrad. 'These tiny Russian armies are pretty hopeless. Look at the last lot they sent against us. We thrashed them pretty soundly, and they ran with hardly a shot being fired. I say send the Militia, surround them, and eliminate them.'

'Why,' said Teofil. 'What's the point?'

'You're being defeatist!' replied Konrad angrily. 'Poland has the capacity to win this war, if only our leaders were not a bunch of defeatist ninnies! Now you're talking like one of them! The Lithuanian region, both in Poland and Russia, is still free, Giełgud's army still holds sway, and on Russian soil, to boot; and now a band of partisans have got a small Russian army cornered! What else do you want? Send in the Militia!'

Teofil did not have long to make up his mind. There was a limit to how long the partisans could hold the fort. Much to everyone's relief, he gave his approval for the Militia to move against the Russians.

He immediately went to the Garrison and called a conference with the leaders of the Militia, Karol Zmuda, Jan Górski and Piotr Piotrowski. Like him, they declined to use ranks, preferring to maintain the old, unofficial hierarchy of command they used in the days of the Unborn Future. Then, with the partisan messenger, a surly lad of sixteen called Muś advising on the Russians' position, Teofil outlined his plan.

Then he returned to the Council Building and called a meeting with the Guard, and explained what had happened.

'Tomorrow our Militia is going into battle with the Russians. I've explained the plan. You and I are staying behind to hold the fort.'

'Why can't we go too, *Panie hrabio*, sir?' asked Genek. 'We can fight as well as any of that lot!'

There was a murmur of agreement. Teofil shook his head. 'No,' he said. 'You never leave your garrison unguarded! That's just what the Russians want. There's more to this business than we think. I don't trust the Russians.'

There was disappointment on the faces of the Guard. The lads had formed themselves into an unofficial private army amongst themselves. Each skirmish in which they were involved boosted their self-esteem, and their confidence had grown to such an extent, that they began to consider the war as some sort of game.

At daybreak the next day the Guard watched, from their strategic positions in the garrison and the Council building, as the combined armed forces of the Mariampol district marched north. The army was some 2,000 strong, and consisted of the Militia, veterans of Ostrołęka with still some fight in them, and a sizeable contingent of volunteers. Word had spread of the impending battle, and further partisans came out of the woods to join the main force. It was a rag-tag army, some trained, some with not the first idea of warfare, some on horseback, most on foot. Some were intense idealists and patriots, and some were local lads spoiling for a good fight. About half were armed with some form of gun, but most wielded swords, scythes, knives on the ends of poles, and clubs. Carts full of provisions, arms and ammunition – as well as the lazy hitching rides – rumbled along, some of them breaking a wheel or an axle, thus blocking the rough road. By noon the company had reached the wooded slopes below the high ground where the Russians were still ensconced in their defensive circle. In the forest, the plan was outlined.

'You will be divided into three companies,' announced Karol Zmuda. He was a blacksmith, and a large, powerfully built man. 'All horse will remain hidden here in the forest, with Jan Górski. When he says charge, you charge. When he says kill, you kill. Understood?'

'What if he says run?' said a voice.

'Then you run, and we'll argue about it later!' said Jan Górski, riding up.

This was met with restrained laughter. The tension was mounting as the force realised that their first real battle was about to take place. Jan was a merchant who had travelled a great deal. He was a fine horseman, a swashbuckler and wit. He played hard, drank hard and fought hard, and was very popular with his troops.

'Piotr, take Muś with you and assemble the partisans round the western side of the hill, to the valley with the stream. From there you will mount an attack on the Russian positions. Your task is not to take the hill, but to lure the Russians from their positions down into the valley. As soon as they counter-attack, you retreat.'

'What if they don't follow?'

'They will if you scarper like frightened rabbits!' Another ripple of laughter followed, even from Piotr Piotrowski, a lugubrious gravedigger and sacristan at the Church of the Holy Cross, whose only joke ever was that war was good for business. 'The Russians don't know the Militia's here. Let them think the partisans have bunched up for one suicide attack. When you run, keep on running, we want them all off the hill. When they're all off, I move in with the main body behind them, and we harvest Russian arse hairs with our scythes. At the same time the cavalry comes down the hill to beat the shit out of their flanks. Understood?'

'Perfectly,' said Piotr, moving off with the partisans. 'Come on, then, and let's measure up bodies for coffins!'

This time no one laughed.

For what seemed like the hundredth time Teofil set off from the council building to the Garrison. He had deployed half the Guard, with Genek in charge, at the garrison, and the other half, under Jacek, at the council building. Thus, the two key buildings in Mariampol were defended by a minute but well-armed and idealistically fired force. The streets, like the council chamber, were deserted. Apprehension reigned in the town among both townsfolk and the council members, as everyone opted to await the outcome behind the closed doors of their homes.

At the Garrison he checked with Genek that everyone was in place before returning to the council building. He sat at the empty table, and waited. For what? He had no idea, apart from a gut feeling that the Russians were up to something, and that their ruse was to lure the Militia out of Mariampol. He sent out scouts to watch all approaches from the east, but there was no sign of any Russian force, either in the woods or the roads. Unable to keep still, Teofil rose and looked out of the east-facing window onto the street below. On an impulse, he crossed the chamber and looked out towards the west, and that was when he saw what he had been waiting for. A small Russian force, perhaps two dozen strong, was sprinting up the street, keeping to the sides of the buildings for cover.

'How the devil did they get on that side?' hissed Teofil. Then he shouted, 'Attack coming from the west!'

A dozen figures suddenly appeared as if from nowhere, and redeployed themselves in the west-facing windows of the building. Immediately there was the sound of gunfire. Teofil picked up his rifle and positioned himself at his window, and fired. The Russians effected two flanking movements, and soon the building was virtually surrounded. The Guard had the advantage of cover, and scored a number of casualties off the Russians, whereas in the Council chamber the only casualty was the chandelier, which crashed heavily onto the table.

After a while the Russians ceased firing and withdrew. In the sudden silence Teofil heard further gunfire in the distance, from the direction of the Garrison.

'To the Garrison!' Teofil shouted. 'Go!'

'Do we abandon the building?' said Jacek.

'Sod the building!' cried Teofil. 'Get the bastards from behind!'

Jacek gathered his group together, and they made their way at a run towards the Garrison. Teofil saw them go, then, with a final look at the Council Chamber, he ran down the stairs, out of the front door, and straight into an ambush. A dozen armed Russian guardsmen jumped out, seemingly from nowhere, and blocked his way. Teofil turned to rush back into the building, but found his way barred. His rifle was taken from him before he could react. Anger, rage, frustration, hatred, all welled up inside him, but failed to get a grasp of Teofil's psyche. He had seen it, felt it, all before. There was no further point. He relaxed, closed his eyes and hung his head, admitting to himself finally that he had lost his last war with life.

'The *dénouement, Panie hrabio*,' came a familiar voice. 'You knew it had to come this way.'

Teofil looked up. Beyond the impassive faces of the soldiers stood the imposing figure of Arkady Osvetlensky.

'I knew, Colonel,' he said calmly.

'General.'

'Congratulations.'

'We will talk. Please,' Osvetlensky indicated the door with his hand. Teofil turned and walked in, followed by the soldiers, their rifles pointed at him. Slowly Teofil walked up the stairs and into the chamber, knowing that as of this moment, his position was dissolved.

Seated in the presidential chair at the head of the table, partly obscured by the wreckage of the chandelier, was Chrys.

'I kept it warm for you,' said Teofil.

'You knew I would get it in the end?' said Chrys. 'You've lost, Teofil, but I salute you for trying. Please sit down.'

Teofil and Arkady both sat down, while the soldiers, at ease stood guard at the door.

'I take it there's been a deal,' said Teofil, looking from Chrys to Arkady, both seated next to one another, on the other side of the chandelier.

'The arrangement benefits you, too, Teofil,' said Chrys.

'You mean you've got a couple of years off my 30-year prison sentence?' said Teofil.

'Let me make your position clear, *Panie hrabio*,' said Arkady. Your forces have suffered total military defeat, both here and at the village of Brynie, to the north. You fell into the trap we set, even though you obviously realised it was a trap. But the small force that you doubtless took to be a company of Russian rabble was in fact my hand-picked guards battalion who have served under me in Moscow and St Petersburg. They now occupy the whole of this region of Poland. I should also add that most of Giełgud's army in Lithuania has now crossed into Prussia, where they have laid down their arms.'

'My Guard...' began Teofil.

'...are holed up at the Garrison, their ammunition spent, surrounded and awaiting your command to surrender,' said Arkady.

'They will die before that!' cried Teofil, finding enough anger in his heart to defend his beloved Presidential Guard.

'That can easily be arranged.'

Teofil mellowed. 'All right, he said. 'Will they be spared? They're young lads.'

'That also can be arranged. I think you may consider the Insurrection over. General Pashkievitch is taking Warsaw even as we speak. We just need to discuss terms.'

'There are terms?' said Teofil mockingly. 'Perhaps a year's remission from prison!'

'There is no need for you to return to prison,' interpolated Chrys, who had been sitting in silence with a smug expression on his face. 'I have secured your freedom from General Osvetlensky, on certain conditions.'

'Immediate and permanent exile, *Panie hrabio*, from Poland,' said Arkady. 'I suggest perhaps you should join your family in Nibork.'

'Jolanta?'

'Is safe and well. The position remains unchanged. I shall convey to her your best wishes.'

'And if I return?'

'A death sentence has already been imposed on you by the Tsar for your part in the Insurrection, in your absence, if necessary,' continued Arkady. 'Should you step onto Polish or Russian soil, you will be immediately arrested, and the sentence will be carried out.'

'What about my money?'

'I shall arrange for half of it to be transferred to a bank of your choice in Prussia.'

'Half?'

'The other half will cover expenses incurred by you on Spytkowiec through your actions. It will also pay for your safe conduct out of Poland,' said Chrys.

Teofil could only shake his head in disbelief. 'Why are you doing this to me, Chrys?' he asked.

'Well, you are family, Teofil,' said Chrys. 'Blood is thicker than water. I'd hate you to be executed.'

Teofil wondered if Chrys spoke in pompous innocence, or pure malice. He never worked out which it was.

*****

The following day the heavy hand of the Tsar came down hard on Mariampol. Since the first light of dawn Teofil had been listening to the firing squads, as he lay in a cell at the Garrison. He wondered what had happened to the Presidential Guard, especially Genek and Jacek.

During mid-morning his escort, the same guards who had captured him the day before, came to collect him, and together they mounted in the Square outside. Only Arkady came to see him off. He saluted Teofil, and proffered his hand. 'I wish you well, *Panie hrabio*,' he said. 'As I have said before, in a different set of circumstances, perhaps we might have been friends.'

Teofil ignored the hand. 'In a different set of circumstances, General, I might have strangled you with my bare hands! Please kiss my cousin's arse for me next time you see him!' He turned to his escort. 'Right, lads, take me to the promised land of Prussia!'

He spurred his horse and made off, westwards, with the soldiers following on behind.

Part Five - 1836

I

'Königsberg,' said the Englishman. 'Finest city on the Baltic Sea. It originally grew around the Castle, which was built in 1155 by the Teutonic Knights, and a hundred years later the city joined the Hanseatic League...'

Franciszka Samojarska, 22 years of age, well brought up and 'finished' at *Frau* Weber's Academy for Young Ladies in Königsberg, smiled politely, as she had been taught to do. She knew everything about the city that she had grown to know and love while at the Academy, but thought it totally unnecessary to correct the Englishman. The Castle, she knew perfectly well, had been built in 1255, not 1155. Her brother Julek, 18 and rebellious, could not have cared less, and took no notice. He preferred to stare pointedly out of the carriage window and pretend to watch the River Pregel flowing beside the post road into the outskirts of East Prussia's main port and city. Built on an inlet of the Baltic Sea, it was now bathed in the warm glow of the late summer evening.

'...the city, as you can see, is built on high ground on either side of the River Pregel, or, Pregoła, as the Poles call it...'

Franciszka looked up and caught a nostalgic glimpse of the Academy half hidden among the trees on the north side of the river. The Englishman had been boring the occupants of the carriage in his execrable German with a potted history of the Teutonic Knights, and no one was more pointedly bored than

Julek. His insolent stance, however, went totally unnoticed.

'...on the site of the fishing village of Steindamm, but after its destruction by the Prussians in 1163 – no, 1263 it must have been, when it was rebuilt on its present site – did I say the Castle was built in 1155? I really meant 1255...'

Franciszka and Julek glanced at one another, smiled mirthlessly and squinted. It was their childhood secret code look of exasperation. Apart from them the Englishman's audience consisted of a staid, elderly Prussian couple who maintained a deadpan expression throughout the lectures, and a blond, bespectacled young Swede who, although he only knew one word of German, listened intently to his every word with an interested smile on his face, constantly nodding and uttering '*Ja*' every few moments.

'...did you know that from 1457 onwards it was the residence of the Grand Masters of the Teutonic Order, but only until 1525, when it became the seat of the Dukes of Prussia. However, in 1618...'

Franciszka's eyes, her politeness having finally given up on her, became glazed as her mind wandered over events since her father's life had taken a different turn. Five years had elapsed since the Uprising and her father's expulsion from Lithuania. Teofil's exile had been a mixed blessing. On the one hand he had again lost a home where he had begun to set down roots, yet he was glad to see the back of Chrys Barnicki and everything that he stood for. His one true regret was that he would probably never again see Jolanta, that tragic and enigmatic girl who had sacrificed herself on the altar of his behalf. He dreamed that one day he might go some way to redressing the balance of her selfless act.

*****

Very soon after he had joined Eloise and the children at the

Zaletniks' in Nibork, Teofil had rented the Lodge on the estate of Baron Helmut von Heimdall, an impoverished Prussian nobleman reduced to working as a clerk at the Foreign Ministry in Berlin. General Osvetlensky had been true to his word, and had transferred half of Teofil's funds from St Petersburg to his Berlin account. So, the family was reasonably well off – to the detriment of Chrys, who was now virtually bankrupt and relying on excessive loyalty to the Crown of St Petersburg for his survival. That, Teofil reflected with a measure of smug satisfaction, was no longer his problem. On the threshold of 60, he had quietly resigned himself to seeing out his days on foreign soil – as had countless Poles before him.

Teofil's main concern was the education and future of his children. Franciszka's two years at Frau Hummel's Academy were very happy and successful. She emerged a witty, intelligent and socially extremely acceptable young lady, full of a kind of elegant charm and *chic* that one might associate with Paris rather than Prussia, and fluent in Polish, Russian, German and French. She was just short of being stunningly beautiful, and the times when she lacked an entourage of hopeful young studs – held firmly at bay by the formidable Frau Hummel – were few and far between.

Julek was sent to Almsbury College in Yorkshire, England, run by the Benedictine Order for the education of British Roman Catholic upper- and middle-class boys. Almsbury was one of the new breed of so-called public boarding schools that modelled themselves on Vienna's prestigious Theresianum. It offered a total education covering not only the basics of language and mathematics, but also all the academic subjects, arts and sciences, as well as health through physical education, artistic accomplishments and social graces. The intended end product was a finished, educated English gentleman. Julek, who had left Almsbury that summer, had not fitted into that category. Although fluent in English and academically brilliant, he could in no way be described as an English gentleman. His undoubted charm, affability and essential Polishness were unencumbered by the restrained English stiff upper lip. His highly rated talent for landscape painting, the ability to manage ungentlemanly quantities of alcohol without having his wits unduly impaired, and an anarchic, anti-authoritarian streak had earned him the nickname PK – short for Polski-Konstabulski – in good-natured mocking deference to his emulation of the fashionable English painter, John Constable. His best friend at Almsbury was Stanford McWhirter, the son of a Scottish industrialist, who did, paradoxically, turn out a perfect English gentleman. He proudly described to Julek the Scottish capital's famous Medical School, where he intended to study to be a homeopathic doctor, and inspired Julek to do likewise. And so Julek once again plied the familiar post road from Nibork to Königsberg, once more to board HMS the *Star of Skye* bound for Aberdeen, and thence by road to Edinburgh for the start of his medical training. This time Teofil decided to let Franciszka go with him, for no other reason than to spend a year in Edinburgh 'in search of fame and fortune – and, hopefully, more' – to quote her own words.

There was also a vague plan for her to travel to France at some stage to stay with Maurice and Lenka at Frontillac, their vineyard near Libourne, in Saint-Emilion country. *Chavelet et fils* was the brand name of their small but successful enterprise. The *fils* was Jan-Pierre, the bearer of a characteristic mixture of French and Polish spellings – who was born in July 1816, in Geneva. This was as far as the Chavelets had got after leaving Poland: because of extensive flooding in Central Europe, they were stranded there for nearly three months. The floods had brought mayhem and disease in their wake, and Geneva, like many other cities, was hit by an epidemic of typhoid. Lenka fell victim to the disease, and gave birth to Jan-Pierre during its most virulent stage. Maurice managed to find excellent medical care in the city's hospital, which was so overcrowded that the doctors were scarcely able to keep up with the spread of the epidemic, that Maurice had resigned himself to the loss of both wife and child. By some miracle, or perhaps because of the care shown to the Chavelets by the kind and devoted Dr. Louis Pierreault, Jan-Pierre was born alive, if by no means well. Dr. Pierreault's care extended to Lenka, who suffered a long and terrible period during which she was unconscious for much of the time. Eventually, to Dr. Pierreault's relief and satisfaction, her temperature dropped. She managed to rally and begin to devote herself to her new-born son. She called him Pierre after the Doctor. As winter approached Lenka had a relapse, and the Chavelets found themselves back at Square One, relying on the considerable skills of Dr. Pierreault once more.

Thus, the Chavelets did not arrive in Frontillac until the following May, by which time both mother and son had fully recovered from a traumatic year.

Teofil and Maurice corresponded regularly, and the open invitation to Franciszka had been of very long standing.

*****

Meanwhile, in Edinburgh, lodgings had been arranged for Julek and Franciszka with Mrs Mary McIntyre, a homely widow and family friend with a house overlooked by the Castle, who was well-disposed to young people, especially students.

*****

The sun was low over the Estuary when Julek and Franciszka boarded the *Star of Skye*.

'Welcome aboard, Mister Julek sir,' said Captain Grymsdyke, who instantly recognised his regular tri-annual return passenger of the past five years.

'Hello, Joshua, you old sea salt,' bantered Julek. 'I trust you have arranged some suitably foul weather with which to torment your helpless and captive charges on this voyage. I want you to meet my frightfully responsible sister, Franciszka. She's been briefed to chaperone me in case I disgrace myself on foreign soil and besmirch the good name of Samojarski.'

'Delighted, Miss,' said the Captain. 'May I count on the pleasure of your company over dinner this night?'

'You may, old fruit, and you shall tell my sister of your piratical adventures on the high seas over a brandy, while I tell you of my plans to become Honorary Dismember of Edinburgh's Worshipful Society of Bloody Butchers, and saw the limbs off innocent people.'

Beneath her bemused smile at Julek's affected teenage pretentiousness, Franciszka blanched at some of the true implications behind the medical profession.

The *Star of Skye* sailed at dawn. Julek, having seen it all before, chose to remain in his cabin, but Franciszka was up on deck to watch the port of Königsberg and the Castle recede into the sunrise while the ship emerged from the Pregel Estuary into the Frische Haff lagoon, and sail on, past the maritime town of Pillau on the northern promontory guarding the entrance to the lagoon, and into the olive-tinged colourlessness of the Baltic Sea.

II

Franciszka was totally unaware that that very morning, 700 kilometres away in Vienna, Jerzy Grocholski woke in his rat-infested prison cell to the fact that he was no longer a Count. The fact had also been established that he had never been a Count in the first place.

'It's a very sordid and unpleasant case, Excellency,' said Ludwik Mendel.

'Then why has it taken twenty years to come to light?' replied Prince Clemens Metternich, Imperial Minister of the Interior, to his special agent appointed to investigate corruption in high places throughout the Austro-Hungarian Empire.

'There is, Excellency, a nest of lawyers, Jewish lawyers, whose activities have aroused suspicions in the past. Despite many checks their papers have invariably been in complete order.'

Metternich leaned back in his chair. 'So what are they supposed to have done?'

'That's just it. Their practice is completely legal, respectable and above-board, except in one particular department in which fortunes have changed hands, with the lawyers creaming off massive percentages. The buying and selling of titles.'

'But that's impossible, Mendel!' cried Metternich, slapping his desk with the palm of his hand. 'Austrian titles are all on record! They can be checked.'

'It appears to the contrary, Excellency. Since all titles are hereditary, and all progeny of a title themselves bear the same title, you have to admit that there are a great enough number of titles for the occasional one to become, shall we say, misplaced, or even replaced. Especially in places not within the immediate sphere of influence of Vienna, such as Dalmatia, Moldavia or the Galician outback. A well-forged signature will pass the most stringent scrutiny, and many of our officials in these places are lackadaisical in their administration.'

'I see. So, what are the facts behind this…' Metternich picked up a document on his desk and looked at it '…Grocholski case? A Pole, I take it.'

*****

Jerzy Grocholski's tenure of Sarenki had been an unmitigated disaster from every point of view. First, he had resigned from his position as Chief of Security for the region as a first step towards self-gentrification, and had taken up residence at Sarenki. Despite making conciliatory noises and dispensing largesse, the villagers accepted neither his bribes nor himself as the lord of the Manor, and their displeasure was plain for all to see. The first to come up hard against him was Father Józef, who on the very first Sunday of Grocholski's residence delivered a sermon in which he ranted against the 'new evil presence in our midst which must be mercilessly excised and returned to the slimy mire whence it had come, thus restoring Sarenki to the care of Almighty God…' this time Father Józef did shake his fist at the roof of the church '…the only true authority as to who should be the earthly lord of the Manor around these parts!' The sermon went down a much-needed treat, and had re-instated Father Józef's credibility, which had suffered a considerable setback after the Kazio Gruszka fiasco following the massacre of the three fugitives.

Father Józef's arrest the next day by a band led by Bogusław Filipowicz, who was still on the security payroll at Nowy Sandec, and summary transportation to the prison there, was Grocholski's first major mistake. He was consequently summoned to the Lwów office of Count Ferdinand von Steiger, the Deputy Governor of Galicia, to explain his reasons for arresting and imprisoning a harmless but bombastic priest. Grocholski's claim of gross disrespect towards a loyal servant of the Habsburg Empire was dismissed as preposterous. 'Render unto Caesar what is Caesar's, and to God what is God's, *Panie hrabio*,' the Governor, who was a Catholic, had said. He was comparatively new to his post, liked fair play and a quiet life, entertained no prejudices against Poles, and had no idea about Grocholski's newly acquired circumstances. 'And as for being a loyal servant of the Habsburg Empire, I am told that you have now resigned from your post as Chief of Security of the Nowy Sandec region.'

Grocholski had no answer to these points, and so Father Józef was released and returned to the bosom of his delirious flock, who saw the incident as a welcome early slap in the face for the usurper in their midst.

Grocholski's next mistake was to try to take Kazio Gruszka on as his trusty, paid side-kick in the village. The disgraced and, it must be said, apologetic old farmer had been making a good recovery from his beating when Grocholski called on him to express concern. This expression was reinforced with a fat envelope, 'an advance on your position as my estate manager.' The envelope was seized enthusiastically by Frania Gruszka. 'My husband is not well enough to make decisions as yet, *Panie hrabio*,' she said. 'We shall discuss this matter when he is fully recovered.'

A fortnight later Kazio was on his feet again, and was in a position to reply, through his wife, to Grocholski's offer.

'My husband regrets, *Panie hrabio*,' she said, while her husband sat in a chair with a deadpan look on his face, 'that due to his severe beating he will be unable to work again. He is incapacitated.'

'Incap-incapacitated,' muttered Kazio.

'But I have already paid you…' said Grocholski.

'Incapacitated he is, as you can see, *Panie hrabio*,' continued Frania, 'and unable even to look after our own holding, let alone *Pan hrabia's* estate, and we have no savings…'

'No sav-savings,' muttered Kazio.

Grocholski was about to demand the return of his envelope when he recognised the piece of theatre that had been prepared for his benefit. The envelope was nowhere to be seen. 'Very well,' he sighed, resigning himself to the loss of a sizeable bribe. 'I wish you well. If there's anything I can do –' He tailed off, knowing that he had already, unwittingly, done it.

Thenceforth the Gruszkas, still under a cloud of suspicion, lived quietly, maintained a very low profile, and avoided all contact with Grocholski for fear of further retribution.

*****

Life at Sarenki, Grocholski eventually realised, was not all it was cracked up to be. Even though he had become a wealthy man through his numerous dealings over the course of two decades of bribery and corruption, it was not easy to live among people who loathed and ignored him. Even Father Józef, having made his initial personal comment, reinforced it perfectly by ignoring his very existence. The largesse that Grocholski had initially dispensed in an effort to buy loyalty had been taken readily enough, but had not been acted upon. In the spring following his acquisition of Sarenki, he had appointed Zygmunt Karłowicz as estate manager. Karłowicz was a former deputy of Grocholski's from Nowy Sandec who was basically a decent fellow with a good eye for business. He could certainly be trusted to look after the estate while he, Grocholski, migrated to Baden, the spa town just to the south of Vienna, in search of a more exciting, less provincial way of life, where his past was unlikely to catch up with him. There Count Jerzy Grocholski developed a taste for gambling, at which he cheated, drank, which he did to excess, and womanised, from which he derived an income. He used to dupe naive young women into parting with their money for various nebulous investments of his own creation. His activities did nothing to enhance the good name of the Polish aristocracy among the wealthy Austrian patrons taking Baden's waters.

By 1834 he had acquired and lost several fortunes. Aged 60, he had long since abandoned the pursuit of women to finance his debauched lifestyle, and had been living off capital from his accrued fortunes and income from Sarenki. He was down to the clothes he was standing in at the Casino, and, as a last resort, staked Sarenki in a final bid to get himself out of serious debt. His adversary was Hans von Schaftesberg, a major in the Austrian army, and the stakes were the best of three hands, the same whereby he had won Sarenki from Teofil nearly two decades previously. It only took the Major a four of diamonds, a veritable bargain, to acquire Sarenki.

Or so he thought.

And so, Count Jerzy Grocholski became yet another penniless Polish aristocrat destined to wander the four corners of the Empire in search of survival.

The transference of the deeds of Sarenki was placed in the hands of Sachs & Spielberg, reputedly the best lawyers in Vienna to deal with in such cases as may lead to too many questions being asked. Jakob Spielberg took on the brief, and learned of the suspicious circumstances surrounding the transference of both title and property from Count Teofil Samojarski to that of Jerzy Grocholski. Spielberg had heard the name Grocholski before, when he was still a young lad from the Jewish quarter of Minsk, in the Russian Empire, and studying international law at the University of Vilnius. His hot-headed older brother Boris, who had already qualified as a lawyer, had gone first to America, and then back to Vienna, where he had involved himself with a dissident faction bent on establishing democracies, like the United States of America, throughout Europe.

In the course of his campaigns for freedom Boris had been misguidedly involved in the assassination of the Imperial Inspector of Agriculture in Galicia, Count Leopold von Loebl. He and his two co-plotters had been given to understand that von Loebl was a Habsburg agent ruthlessly seeking out dissidents in the Carpathian region to denounce to the authorities. Spielberg also learned that his brother Boris had been caught and executed in a barbaric manner by one Jerzy Grocholski of Nowy Sandec. He put two and two together, and decided to investigate the case thoroughly, and established that it was the same Grocholski who had been responsible for Boris' murder. Spielberg also discovered that the transfer of the deeds to Sarenki was, to all intents and purposes, perfectly legal and above board, but that the title transfer was fraudulent, being that of a still-born son of a registered but unnamed Ruthenian count in 1791.

Spielberg had a friend, a fellow Jew, in the Ministry of the Interior by the name of Ludwik Mendel, to whom he confided his suspicions of legal malpractice, and the matter was further investigated over a number of months at the highest levels. It was also discovered that a scheming and ambitious young deputy at the Imperial Agricultural Inspectorate for Galicia, one Gottlieb Schultz, had put about the story that his superior, Leopold von Loebl, was a ruthless secret dissident hunter. Schultz had assumed that it would be just a matter of time before von Loebl would be assassinated by some hothead, and he, Schultz, would step into his office. At first everything had gone according to plan, and Schultz had achieved his aim.

On September 1 1836, Grocholski was tracked down by Spielberg to a squalid boarding house just outside the Glacis in Vienna. He was denounced, arrested and promptly stripped of his title. Also arrested were Gottlieb Schultz, by now fully fledged Minister of Agriculture for the whole of the Empire, and one Stanisław Warewicz, the Kraków lawyer who had set up the deal. All were awaiting charges of forgery and corruption.

III

Mrs MacIntyre was a veritable earth-mother. She was larger than life – both literally and figuratively, and appeared always to be bustling around her 'boils and grills' as she jokingly referred to the young lads and lassies that constituted her lodgers, mostly students at the Medical School. There were six in all. Apart from Julek and Franciszka, there was another surly and withdrawn fellow Pole by the name of Ząb, who refused to divulge his Christian name, and seethed with an exquisite hatred for Russia and all things Russian. Having arrived in Edinburgh almost immediately after the Uprising, he was now in his final year, and had started to formulate plans to return to Poland as a fully qualified medic. His ambition was to help his fellow countrymen when the next Uprising came – which he was convinced would be soon. Julek's early attempts to be friendly were rebuffed. Ząb found Julek's banter and good-natured buffoonery irritating beyond belief, so Julek decided that life was too short, and abandoned all further effort at getting through to him.

Then there was Claire Fraser, the daughter of a Minister of the Church of Scotland, from the Isle of Lewis, beneath whose severe dress and austere lifestyle there showed, like the hem of a frilly petticoat, hints of a wild streak which Julek had decided would be worth investigating at some later stage.

There could be no greater contrast than the two other boys, both new students that year, who completed Mrs MacIntyre's stable. The first was Sir Charles Carnethie, whose father's estate in the Highlands was a haven for politicians, artists, painters and musicians from all over the world, and Hamish Fergusson, who had dragged himself out of the slums of Glasgow in pursuit of a better world. Despite their vastly differing circumstances, Charles and Hamish became firm friends during their first term together, their common bonding factor being a passion for music: Charles being a fair pianist with a penchant for the delicate elegance of Mozart and Chopin, while Hamish, though no performer, was a devotee of Bach, whose more robust, Germanic utterances he would listen to at every available opportunity in the churches and concert halls of Glasgow.

Julek Samojarski threw himself wholeheartedly into his studies at the Medical School. Perhaps his closest friend was Stanford McWhirter to whose house in Queen Street he became a frequent visitor. Franciszka embarked on learning to speak English by being helpful to Mrs McIntyre around the house, which gave her plenty of opportunity for English conversation. She was also a frequent and welcome visitor to the McWhirter house, where her company was particularly appreciated by Stewart, Stanford's older brother. He was an Old Boy of Almsbury, now 25, and being groomed as his father's successor in running the family business.

'You know Stewart is madly in love with you,' said Julek to his sister as they strolled in the Botanical Gardens one unseasonably glorious autumn day.

'I know,' she replied quietly.

'Well?'

'Well, what?'

'Well, what are you going to do about it?'

'Nothing.'

'Nothing? Why?'

'I don't want to encourage him.'

'Why ever not? Good-looking fellow. Decent family. You

could do worse.'

'I know.'

'So?'

'I don't fancy him.'

'Ah.'

The additional help of readily available books and newspapers, and the company of those young people whom Mrs McIntyre, in chaperone mode, would allow access to her, ensured that by the end of Julek's first term at the Medical School she was virtually fluent in English. She spoke it with a Scottish Lowlands accent tinged with Polish, which she was told never, under any circumstances, to try to correct, as it was utterly charming and seductive.

The damp Scottish autumn ushered in a cold and snow-bound winter, and with it the Christmas festive period. Charles invited Julek and Franciszka to spend Christmas and the New Year at Carnethie Castle, his father's ancestral home on the shores of Loch Venachar in the Scottish Highlands near Callander.

'The Pater will be absolutely delighted to have you,' Charles said to Julek and Franciszka. 'He's terribly keen on Poles, you know. Ever since '31 it's been the thing to have at least one Pole in one's house party, you know, especially if he's got tales to tell of adventures and derring-do against the dastardly Russians.'

Charles' father – 'the Pater' to Charles – was Lord Duncan, the ninth Earl of Carnethie. He was an enlightened and philanthropic politician and Member of Parliament for Kingston, Surrey, where he spent most of his time fighting on behalf of oppressed minorities.

'The Pater's still on about the Polish Question, you know,' continued Charles as the family carriage crunched out of Stirling and along the road to Callander. The weather was beautiful and the horses were well able to cope with the thick, crisp snow that covered the ground. The blinding whiteness of the woods dotted about the landscape, all brilliantly etched against the clear, cloudless blue sky reminded Franciszka of her Lithuanian childhood at Spytkowiec. 'When he first took up politics over twenty years ago, he became interested in foreign affairs. He went to Vienna with Castlereagh as a minor official for the Congress in Vienna back in '14, got involved with the Poles and supported their claim to have their country back. Now he's doing his bit again for all you lot that have come over here after '31, making fiery speeches in the House and writing to the Times about it all. He has a lot of support, you know. I say, do you like Chopin?'

Both Julek and Franciszka had heard of the brilliant young Polish pianist who had recently embarked on a tour of Europe, but have never heard him play.

'Pity. Did you know that when he learnt about the news of the troubles in Warsaw there, he got on the next coach back to Warsaw to be with his family and to fight, but after a few staging posts decided not to go back after all.' Charles raised the topic over a welcoming dram of whisky, served by a very old and arthritic retainer by the name of Hanson, before a blazing log fire in the Great Hall at Carnethie Castle.

The talk of Chopin made Franciszka cast her eyes on the Broadwood grand piano, built of walnut inlaid with rosewood, which stood, open, in the corner beneath a portrait of the Seventh Earl of Carnethie. Charles followed her gaze, and walked over to the piano. He ran his fingers lovingly along its woodwork, sat down at the keyboard and broke gently into a Chopin Mazurka. 'He was told to go to Paris and be an ambassador for his country through his music,' he continued as he played. 'Apparently he's a bit frail, not the stuff of your usual ferocious Polish warrior.' At that moment a large Irish wolfhound suddenly filled the Hall, barking excitedly. Charles stopped abruptly. 'I say, PK, isn't she a magnificent beast?'

It was a moment or two before Julek realised that Charles was talking about the piano, and not the dog, which he pointedly ignored. The dog was followed by a large man in a kilt, with bushy eyebrows, a ruddy complexion and a veritable mane of wavy white hair. He made straight for the piano. Charles got up. 'Hello, Pater,' he said.

'Charles! Good to see you,' replied the other, shaking him heartily by the hand. 'Did you have a good journey? Snow's not too bad, but they expect more over the next few days. Now,' Lord Duncan Carnethie looked over his son's shoulder, 'you must be Franciszka; and Julek. *Moje uszanowanie Państwu!* Welcome to Carnethie. Don't mind Baldwyn – down Baldwyn! I say! Down, sir! – his Bach is worse than his Bite-hoven! Ha! Ha!'

Charles impatiently repulsed Baldwyn's frenzied advances and managed to introduce Julek and Franciszka to 'my father, the Pater, whose musical jokes, like his Polish, are far, far worse even than his speeches in the House. But nothing is quite as bad as that confounded hound from hell! He should be put down forthwith!'

*****

Later that evening they were joined for dinner by Elizabeth, Lady Carnethie, who had returned from helping out with pre-Christmas preparations at the house of a local family with eight children, two of whom were ill. She was a slight woman with a breathless manner and darting eyes that gave a false but endearing impression of being permanently apologetic. 'The Mater likes to do her bit for the locals, you know. It helps the Pater's credibility as a champion of the downtrodden,' said Charles.

The few days leading up to Christmas were spent walking the great Carnethie estate in tow of the formidable Baldwyn, or along the banks of Loch Venachar, or, when the weather was discouraging, gathered around the piano listening to Charles playing Mozart, Clementi and Chopin.

On Christmas Eve the official house party arrived, some two dozen souls, among them local luminaries and officials, McLintock the estate manager and his wife and grown-up son, and two Members of Parliament. Also present was one Stefan Sulechowski, the London representative of the Polish government-in-exile. This was led by Prince Adam Czartoryski at the Hotel Lambert in Paris, with whom Lord Duncan had close links. Finally, Hamish Fergusson arrived from Glasgow, and was introduced, as were Julek and Franciszka, as friends from the Medical School in Edinburgh. Everyone must have been briefed about Hamish, as no one enquired as to what his father did, much to Hamish's relief. Unlike Julek and Franciszka, whose parents and their circumstances were of supreme interest to all. Julek found himself in his element, regaling his audience with tales and anecdotes from Lithuania and Prussia, as well as his school days at Almsbury.

'Great pity about Alexander and Daisy,' said Lord Duncan adding several drops of 12-year-old Laphroaig to his gigantic crystal goblet and covering it with his hand 'to entrap the nose, what!'

'That's Uncle Alex, PK,' said Charles in reply to Julek's quizzical look. 'Got some land in the West Indies, and grows sugar.'

'My younger brother,' said Lord Duncan, momentarily contemplating the glowing amber liquid breathing gently under the palm of his hand. 'Owns nearly a hundred Africans, you know. Made several fortunes out there,'

'I thought slavery had been abolished,' interpolated Franciszka.

'Alex never let that kind of thing stop him!' Lord Duncan led the chorus of guffaws that burst forth from the gathering like a geyser.

'Uncle Alex and Auntie Daisy have always managed to spend Christmas here with us,' said Charles.

'But with this plague raging in the West Indies, and half the blacks kicking the bucket like flies, had to stay to keep the plantations on course,' said Lord Duncan. 'Hard to get replacement labour since the abolition, you see.'

Julek blanched. He had vaguely heard about the slave labour of captured Africans and was horrified that here was a man who actually owned a hundred of them, and seemed proud of the fact. And this is Great Britain? Civilised and enlightened Great Britain? Lord Duncan took his hand off the glass of Scotch, turned to face Uncle Alex and placed an arm about Julek's shoulders. 'Splendid chap, Julek. Polish, you know. But you'll like him for all that. I've always had a soft spot for foreigners and their strange ways.' Lord Duncan took the nose of his gigantic crystal goblet, and deemed the moment ripe to take the taste. 'To absent friends.'

'Absent friends,' came the echo.

*****

On Christmas Day the whole party drove in convoy to attend the service at the Church of the Holy Trinity in Callander. The Christmas feast that followed, which was prepared and served with the help of extra staff from among the locals, and overseen with military precision by the ancient but still robust Hanson, was a splendid affair, with goose and venison the order of the day, washed down with inexhaustible quantities of Champagne, the finest Bordeaux wines, brandy and Scotch whisky. Julek and Franciszka noted wryly the extra place setting, in deference to the Polish tradition, in case Jesus came to the gates, disguised as a homeless pauper, to test Man's charity.

'Supposing some ne'er-do-well layabout knocks, Duncan,' said Stephen O'Farrell, MP for South Dorset, 'would you let him in?'

'Yes, how do you distinguish a tramp from Jesus in disguise?'

added McLintock the estate manager.

'A good point,' said Lord Duncan. 'Mercifully, it's never happened, although I've only observed this tradition since the Polish Uprising. That's when I first heard about it. A quaint idea, I must say. Alex loved it. How about you, Julek, have your people ever had a tramp call on their charity over the festive period?'

'Go on, PK,' said Charles, 'give us one of your tales about Polish peasants!'

All eyes turned to the young Pole, who no doubt had further tales to tell of romance and skulduggery than those with which he had already regaled the guests during the course of the day. His anarchic streak tempted him to come up with that preposterous story about such a tramp who, having feasted and drunk to excess, proceeded to run amok with a meat cleaver, bent on mass-murder of the rich, only to be finally restrained, beaten up and tied up by the big, muscular Ukrainian parish priest by the name of Father Józef, who made the man see the error of his ways by shaking his fist at the ceiling and invoking God's wrath and retribution in the fires of Hell. Such was the priest's power of persuasion that the man embraced contrition, changed his ways and became a priest himself. Franciszka had heard the story before, originally told during *Wigilia* by seven-year-old Julek in full creative flight, before a horrified Chrys Barnicki. Franciszka saw it coming, and pre-empted her brother. 'Never in our family,' she said. 'Although…' she winked at Julek '…I often do wonder what would happen if the homeless, hungry tramp might turn out to be a mass murderer with a meat-cleaver.'

Julek's pointed glare and set jaw accused his sister of spoiling his story.

After dinner Charles entertained at the piano with a selection of festive airs. Estate manager McLintock, who had a fine, tenor voice, gave renderings of some Christmas carols, while Franciszka, accompanied by Sulechowski, who vamped a little on the piano, was persuaded to sing some Polish ones, to everyone's delight. Charles then returned to the piano to play some Mendelssohn Songs without Words and Chopin Mazurkas.

'What exactly is a Mazurka?' said Mrs McLintock in a broad Highland accent. 'Is it a dance of some kind?'

'It's one of the two main Polish dances,' said Julek. 'The other being the Polonaise. You dance the Mazurka when you're drunk, and the Polonaise when you're sober!' With that he drained his whisky in one gulp and held his glass out for more. There was a momentary stunned silence, in which Franciszka threw her brother a severe reprimand with her eyes. 'So, which one shall we all dance?' said MP O'Farrell. 'Are we drunk enough yet for the Mazurka, or shall we have a go at the Polonaise?'

This evinced a peal of laughter round the company. 'Then I'm a Mazurka man meself, if anyone would care to join me!' It was not clear as to who said that, but everyone drained their glasses in one gulp and rose as one, demanding Charles to play, and Julek and Franciszka to teach the steps of the Mazurka. Before long, Carnethie Castle reverberated to the swirl of the Mazurka as Julek and Franciszka led the by now well-lubricated company round the Hall in Poland's national dance. To this were added steps which owed more to *ceilidh* than the banks of the Vistula. Sulechowski was also able to vamp some of the traditional folk Mazurkas, and McLintock, who, as were several others, wearing a kilt, brought his bagpipes and played along.

Any subtleties of ethnic cultural cross-fertilisation were lost on all concerned, but no one cared. Christmas was going with a swing-without-frontiers.

Later that night, Franciszka sat in her room writing a letter home, which she did every week. She described her stay at Carnethie Castle, the Christmas visit to church, the feast, and the music and dancing afterwards. She expressed how much she missed her family, especially at this time of Christmas. She signed the letter, added the usual tear-drop, and waited until it dried, leaving the tiny, tell-tale stain, before sealing it.

IV

Major Hans von Schaftesberg of the Austrian army was unable to find a buyer for his estate in the Carpathian Mountains, even at bargain rates. In the first place, Sarenki was in dire need of repair and investment. Also, it was in the middle of nowhere, and off any established beaten track. As an inveterate gambler with debts amounting to a small fortune, the Major was desperate to get rid of his white elephant in the Galician outback and see the colour of some real cash. He was spending his Christmas recovering in Vienna's *Allgemeine* hospital from a severe beating by a Hungarian wine merchant from Sopron, to whom he owed a considerable sum of money. It was there that he had a visit from a slight, dark man with black eyes, a black beard and a black cloak.

'Don't be alarmed, Major,' said the visitor, who obviously constituted a frightening sight to the battered and bruised soldier as he emerged suddenly from a troubled and painful sleep. 'My name is Spielberg. Jakob Spielberg. I am a lawyer.' He placed his visiting card on the pillow.

'I shall pay,' gasped the Major, wincing with pain. 'I shall get the money early next week.'

'I very much doubt that, Major. You will not pay anyone anything. You have got no money, and no prospects whatsoever of getting any. Which is why I am here.'

Before he could explain further, Spielberg burst into a coughing fit which went on for several minutes. A concerned nurse brought him a glass of water which did little to alleviate his evident distress. The Major studied his coughing visitor with some measure of curiosity. He was perhaps in his fifties, and wore a pallid expression through which his extremely dark colouring showed wanly. His black eyes were sunken, but still exuded the doleful look of a melancholy yet compassionate man. Curious, for a Jew, thought the Major. 'So why are you here?' he groaned when the rasping paroxysm had subsided. 'Who are you representing?'

'A good question, Major. You, perhaps. I may be in a position to help you in your predicament. How much do you owe?'

'That's none of your fucking Jewish business!'

'Part of my fucking Jewish business, Major, lies in buying and selling property. Some of it in the Galician outback. I understand you have such an estate to sell. How much are you asking for it?'

Major von Schaftesberg swallowed. 'You want to buy Sarenki?' he asked incredulously.

'I might be interested. If the price is right.'

'One hundred and fifty thousand thalers. It's worth twice that. In cash.'

'You owe eighty thousand.'

'If you knew, why did you ask.'

'I will give you eighty thousand for Sarenki. Cash.'

'Fuck off.'

'Very well.' Spielberg rose and swiftly walked out of the ward.

'Wait!' croaked the Major, hoisting himself up on his elbow. But the lawyer was already gone. 'Shit!' he added, sinking back onto his pillow. The visiting card attracted his attention. He picked it up and squinted at it.

A week later Jakob Spielberg was in his office in Rauhensteingasse going through his correspondence, and smiled wryly when he found a note from Major Hans von Schaftesberg asking for an appointment. The address was given as the Army Barracks at Schwechat, to the south east of Vienna. So, the

Major has recovered from his enforced stay in hospital. Perhaps, reflected Spielberg disdainfully, his next visit to hospital might be connected with his duty to Emperor and country, rather than to the game of chance.

The meeting was set for 10 o'clock on the morning of January 10. The Major arrived punctually, his horse having successfully negotiated the heavy drifts that lay between Schwechat and Vienna's city centre. His bruises were still plain to see. 'All right, eighty thousand,' he said without preamble. Spielberg opened his mouth to utter a greeting, and express polite satisfaction that the Major had – largely – recovered from his – er – wounds, but, seeing the seething anti-Semitism in the Major's body language, he decided against it.

'Sit down, Major.'

The Major sat. 'This is sheer robbery,' he cried. 'You've got me over a barrel. I've got no choice. A hundred and twenty thousand.'

Spielberg looked intently at his client. 'There is always choice. You survive or you go under. Eighty thousand. Do you wish to proceed with the sale?'

'I'm here, aren't I?'

Drawing up the paperwork and formalities took the best part of two hours, and included the fetching of eighty thousand thalers in cash from the bank on the corner. When the final signatures were signed, the deeds handed over and the cash counted and folded neatly into a large leather pouch – with the compliments of Sachs and Spielberg – the Major rose and made for the door without saying a further word. At that very moment the door opened and a group of a dozen or so men entered, led by a man who introduced himself as Samuel Sachs, partner in the firm. Another closed the door behind them and stayed there, ensuring no one else would enter – or leave.

'I represent the interests of these gentlemen, Major,' he went on, 'who are suing for the return of moneys owed –'

He did not get any further. The Major lashed out in desperation with the leather pouch and made a scramble for the door, but was totally outnumbered and overpowered. The Hungarian wine merchant from Sopron, who had put him in hospital over Christmas, this time needed only a restraining grip round the Major's throat to ensure that the pouch was handed over to Sachs.

*****

Several days later, at the Hofburg, Chancellor Metternich picked up the Grocholski file. 'Any further developments on this one?' he asked.

'An interesting outcome, Excellency,' replied Ludwik Mendel. 'As you know, Grocholski had gambled his estate away to a Major Hans von Schaftesberg.'

'A soldier?'

'Stationed at Schwechat. The Major is an inveterate gambler, owing a great deal of money. He found no takers for Sarenki.'

'That's the estate in the Carpathians at the centre of the business?'

'Indeed. In the end he was forced to sell it for a song to Jakob Spielberg in order to pay off his debts.'

'The lawyer dealing with the case? What does a Jewish lawyer want with a crumbling estate in the Carpathians?'

'Spielberg is an extremely wealthy man, who is dying of consumption. Sarenki issues waters which, according to legend, have certain healing properties, especially for respiratory problems.'

'A spa!' cried Metternich. 'Spielberg is buying himself a private spa!'

'It's more than that. It's where Grocholski murdered Spielberg's brother, Boris. He wants to establish a medical centre for the treatment of consumption in his brother's memory.'

V

By a curious quirk of astrological configuration, July 14 1837 was an exceptionally auspicious date in the Samojarski story. On that day, in Sarenki, Father Józef Baraniuk dropped dead in the courtyard behind his church. It was a blazing hot day. He was about eighty years old and sawing timber for repairs to the roof.

*****

On that day Julek and Charles happened to be in London with Lord Duncan. Term had finished at the Medical School at the start of July, and the two students wanted to catch the last of the London season before everyone repaired to the country for the shooting. It was Julek's first visit to the English capital, and he had been looking forward to it enormously, especially in the wake of the accession to the throne of eighteen-year-old Princess Victoria, following the death of King William IV on June 20. There was a heady sense of excitement and anticipation in the air, and London was vibrant with concerts, plays and dinners. That evening, the two young men attended a dinner party with Lord Duncan at the London home of piano manufacturer James Broadwood; Lord Duncan intended to purchase his latest model for his London house in Dover Street. Also present at this dinner was a small, shy and frail foreigner who spoke no English, although he was able to converse with Broadwood and one other lady guest in French. He was exquisitely, almost foppishly, dressed, and was introduced as Monsieur Fritz. After dinner, Monsieur Fritz was asked to play the piano, which he did, to everyone's delight. He played Chopin with a rare delicacy and that legendary intimate touch that very quickly gave away his true identity.

'My God, PK,' gasped Charles, 'it's Chopin!'

'Of course, it's Chopin,' replied Julek. 'You play this Mazurka yourself. Only not as well.'

'No, I mean it is Chopin. I recognise him from the pictures. That man is Chopin!'

The lady seated next to him was the one who had spoken to the pianist in French. She touched Julek's sleeve. 'Sir Charles is right,' she whispered with a knowing smile. 'It is Monsieur Chopin. I have met him before, and have heard him several times in Paris. He's supposed to be incognito, but he doesn't fool anyone. Doesn't it sound like droplets of water falling into a pond of lilies?'

Although Julek was unable to close his mouth from awe, he remained uncharacteristically speechless for the rest of the evening, even though he was the only person present who might have spoken to the great man in his native tongue. As it was, his only future anecdote would be about the occasion when he almost met Fryderyk Chopin.

*****

On that day, which happened to be Michał Samojarski's tenth birthday, his father received a letter at his home in Nibork from a Jewish lawyer from Vienna by the name of Samuel Sachs stating that he, Teofil, had inherited Sarenki following the death of his partner, Jakob Spielberg, the brother of Boris Spielberg, who was illegally executed there by Grocholski in 1813. The letter, addressed to Count Teofil Samojarski, was a complete mystery to Teofil, who had no idea whatsoever as to the fate of either Sarenki or Grocholski. What was more, he didn't care. He had craved, and finally achieved, a quiet life, so this news came as a shock.

'What are you going to do?' said a very bemused Eloise. 'This is so unexpected.'

Teofil stared long and hard at the letter before replying. There was the faintest hint of excitement in his voice when he did so. 'I suppose I'd better go to Vienna to see what this is all about.'

'Do you want me to come with you?'

'No. It would be best if I sorted this out by myself. The paperwork will be horrendous, and there'll probably be Grocholski to deal with, as well as this Spielberg person, whoever he is. You look after Adam and Michał. It will all ultimately be for their benefit.'

*****

Also on that day, at Frontillac, at his father's vineyard on the banks of the River Dordogne, Jan-Pierre Chavelet celebrated not only Bastille Day, but also his twenty-first birthday. Half a dozen close friends from the community attended and watched as Maurice opened the six bottles which he had originally laid down for his son when he was born, but the 1817 Saint-Emilion turned out to be undrinkable. Dinner, served *al fresco*, was accompanied by some younger vintages, on which the young Monsieur Chavelet got very drunk.

*****

And yet again on that day Franciszka set off for France with Mr and Mrs McLintock. Lord Duncan's estate manager's brief was to travel to Bordeaux, taste and select the best vintage wines, and arrange for a shipment to stock up the cellars of both the Castle and the London house in Dover Street. Like Julek, Franciszka had become very close to the Carnethies, ever since that memorable 'Mazurka Christmas', as it eventually came to be known in family legend. She had finally accepted the Chavelets' invitation to stay at Frontillac, at least until the *vendange* – the autumn grape harvest, after which she would return home to Nibork. It seemed like the perfect opportunity to travel together.

It was pouring with rain as the Carnethie carriage, with Mr and Mrs McLintock aboard, pulled up outside Mrs McIntyre's house to pick up Franciszka to take her the short distance to Edinburgh's port. There they boarded the *Star of Strathclyde*, sister ship of the already familiar *Star of Skye*, which had originally brought Franciszka to Great Britain. Under the captainship of Elijah Grymsdyke, brother of the equally familiar Joshua, the *Star of Strathclyde* sailed from Aberdeen to Bordeaux, by way of Edinburgh and London, laden with wool, cloth and whisky. On her return voyage she was laden with wines destined for the cellars of Britain's numerous *cognoscenti*. She was known in these circles as the Claret Clipper.

Their first port of call was London. The ship docked for three days, which gave Franciszka the opportunity to see Julek, who was staying alone at Dover Street, as Charles and his father had gone to spend a few days with friends in Hampshire. Julek told her all about how he almost spoke to Chopin, and together they managed to squeeze in a play at Drury Lane and a Philharmonic Society concert at the Hanover Square Rooms. The programme included music by Mendelssohn.

'Who knows?' said Julek, 'we might catch a glimpse of the new Queen. She goes there regularly, you know. She plays the piano and adores Mendelssohn.'

They were disappointed in that respect, although the concert was excellent.

On July 19 the *Star of Strathclyde* sailed at dawn, and Julek came to see Franciszka off.

The McLintocks learned that among the passengers who boarded in London was one Henry Cottershall. His father lived in Bordeaux, where he ran an export company: Bordeaux's flourishing wine business was largely in the hands of English enterprise. Henry was about twenty-five years of age, good-looking and witty. Franciszka was attracted primarily by his eyes, which were blue, sparkling and full of gentle humour, and his fair, curly hair, which was big and chaotic as it was tossed about by the warm summer sea-breezes that blew across the English Channel. Franciszka and Henry exchanged glances with only the barest hints of mutual acknowledgement; anything more might have been considered unseemly, especially in front of Mrs McLintock. Unlike her husband, who was a man of the world not averse to bending the odd rule of etiquette, she came of stauncher Scottish Presbyterian stock, and would have brought her chaperoning duties into instant play at the merest hint of communication. Captain Elijah Grymsdyke had introduced Henry to Mr McLintock as a possible business contact, but Mr McLintock, perhaps in deference to his wife, chose not to introduce the handsome Henry to Franciszka.

'Damn these English niceties,' she cursed to herself.

Fate, however, took a different line. On the third day out, during a summer storm in the Bay of Biscay, Franciszka was out on deck, exhilarated by the salty spray, the heaving mountains of water and the hot, howling wind. All of a sudden, she came into violent contact with a lurching body that had been trying to get into the interior of the cabin. It was Henry, glazed of eye and grey of face and not in control of his legs. He hove amidships into Franciszka, and both fell in an ignominious heap on the soaking deck. He then threw up copiously all over her already soaking cloak. Cleaning herself and Henry up as best she could, she managed to drag him inside and deposit him onto the bed of his cabin. Her instinct then was to administer to the unfortunate fellow further, to at least take off his boots, lay his head on the pillow and wipe his brow; but then she weighed seemliness against charity, Mrs McLintock's disapproval against her approbation, and finally decided to let him be, and left.

Franciszka saw no more of Henry Cottershall until the ship had turned the *Pointe de la Coubre,* and was sailing up the wide Gironde, the long estuary into which emptied the Rivers Garonne and Dordogne. At the head of the estuary lay Bordeaux, capital of France's premier wine growing region, where English was very much the language of commerce. Franciszka gazed at the low-lying left bank, and its little towns, chateaux and villages with names that activated the taste buds of the countless British lovers of good claret.

'We've just passed Saint-Estèphe, and we should be passing the Pauillac region very shortly.' Franciszka turned to find Henry at her elbow. The glazed eyes and grey expression were gone, and his fair mane was again tossing about chaotically in the wind that blew in off the bay. 'Although I confess, I'm more of a Saint-Emilion and Pomerol man myself, rather than the Médoc. They're further inland, on the other side of Bordeaux, you know.'

'I know,' Franciszka smiled. 'That's where I'm bound. A family friend owns a vineyard there, near Libourne, and I shall be staying with him.'

'Really!' cried Henry. 'What is the name of this vineyard? Do I know it?'

'It's called Frontillac.'

'You don't mean old Chavelet's place, do you?'

'Yes. Maurice Chavelet. He is a friend of my father's. They're both veterans of Napoleon's wars.'

'Well, this is a turn up! I know Monsieur Maurice well. And Madame Lenka. And that son of theirs, Jan-Pierre. A strange chap. I import their Saint-Emilions, you know.' Henry suddenly squared up to Franciszka. 'I say, may I introduce myself, as nobody else will. I'm Henry Cottershall. I work for my father who has offices in Bordeaux. We're in the wine business. Arthur

Cottershall – and Son. That's me!'

Franciszka proffered her hand. 'Franciszka Samojarska,' she said. 'How do you do, Mr Cottershall.'

'Not Polish by any chance?'

'Indeed yes.'

'Like Madame Lenka. But there is something Celtic about your accent.'

'I have been living in Edinburgh for a year.'

'Ah, that explains it. Very charming, if I may say, and somewhat exotic.' Henry stared awhile at Pauillac passing. 'Perhaps – perhaps one day you might care to dine with us in Bordeaux. Along with Monsieur Maurice and Madame Lenka, naturally. My father would be absolutely delighted.'

Franciszka smiled. 'That would be very nice, Mr Cottershall. Thank you.'

'I didn't knae ye ken Mr Cottershall, Franciszka!' Mrs McLintock's tone was just this side of disapproving.

Franciszka's smile remained firmly fixed as she looked up to see her chaperone walking towards them. 'Mr Cottershall and I bumped into one another during the storm, Mrs McLintock,' she said. 'He was not very well at the time.'

Henry was suddenly taken aback. 'Oh, yes. Indeed. No, I wasn't, was I? It was frightfully embarrassing. Please forgive me, it was most remiss of me, remiss – Miss Sam – Sam – oh dear, these Polish names, you know…'

'Franci…'

'Samojarska,' interrupted Mrs McLintock with a quiver in her voice. She was obviously thoroughly enjoying Henry's discomfiture. 'It's quite simple when you split it up: *Sam – oh – yar – ska!*'

'Yes. Quite. Miss Samojarska. Please accept my profuse apologies, and thank you for your kindness under the circumstances,' burbled Henry. 'It shall not happen again.' He made as if to move off.

'Unless we meet again on the high seas,' laughed Franciszka.

'Which is highly unlikely,' said Mrs McLintock coldly. 'Come, Franciszka, it is time to prepare for the docking. Mr Cottershall.' Mrs McLintock nodded curtly to Henry and made off at a business-like pace towards the cabins. Franciszka exchanged a warm smile with Henry, and followed her.

The Claret Clipper duly docked and disgorged its passengers onto French soil.

'Franciszka! *Mon Dieu!* It cannot possibly be!'

Franciszka turned towards the cry. She did not recognise the jolly, smiling, grey-haired little barrel of a man with twinkling brown eyes who was bearing down on her with arms outstretched. After all, she was only a toddler when Maurice had kissed and hugged her goodbye at Czarne Lasy, over two decades ago. Now, recognising her instantly, he kissed her again, on both cheeks, and hugged her tightly for a long while.

'Uncle Maurice!' she said. 'Uncle Maurice you were then, and Uncle Maurice you will now continue to be!'

There followed hearty introductions on the quayside as Mr and Mrs McLintock handed their charge over to Maurice, who also shook hands with Henry Cottershall. He had come over to say hello and how nice it was to see Monsieur Maurice, and also to have met the McLintocks – and Franciszka, of course – and to express the hope that they would come to dine – and talk business – with his father in Bordeaux. And maybe Monsieur Maurice would care to come too with the family – and perhaps bring Franciszka. All this was taken in good cheer, and mutual visits were enthusiastically promised. Even Mrs McLintock, now that her chaperoning duties were over, positively encouraged the contact between Henry and Franciszka.

'She stopped young Henry from falling o'erboard during a storm, ye ken,' she confided to Maurice. 'Dinna they make a lovely couple?'

'Absolument!' said Maurice inanely, gazing in awe and wonder at the lovely young woman that his best friend's little girl had grown into. *'Absolument!'*

And so, as Franciszka climbed into Maurice's buggy for the 30-kilometre drive to Frontillac, the McLintocks accepted the offer of a ride in the carriage that Henry's father had sent to pick him up, and were dropped off at the Hotel d'Angleterre.

'You know where we are, Mr Cottershall,' said Mr McLintock. 'We would be delighted to see you and your father for dinner one evening; next Thursday, perhaps?'

The business contact established, Henry bade the driver continue to his father's large town house in the city centre, close to the place de la Comédie.

VI

Frontillac stood in 15 hectares of vineyards close to the River Dordogne, some five kilometres from Libourne. The house could have claimed *chateau* status had the owner aspired to such heights, but to the Chavelets it was just *la Maison*. The two-storey, six-bedroomed mansion had belonged to Auguste Charpentier, a close friend of Marcel Terrassin's father, who had been finding the vineyard difficult to manage on his own. His wife had died during the closing stages of Napoleon's campaigns, leaving him, aged 67 and without progeny, to mind the farm on his own. A mean streak, in conjunction with deep regrets that he had no sons to leave the vineyard to, precluded the employment of local labour, so both house and business began to enter rack and ruin. When Marcel had written to him from Kraków about a young veteran, experienced in the wine trade and restoring old properties, and his Polish wife, who were looking for a new life in the new France, Auguste's creaking instincts told him to engage the couple. He suggested the posts of estate manager and housekeeper respectively, especially if, coming from the wilds of Poland, they would work for a pittance.

Maurice and Lenka saw Frontillac as a kind of Sarenki-substitute, and embarked on their new adventure with great enthusiasm and efficiency, despite the meagre salaries. Most importantly, they were able largely to exorcise Grocholski from their lives and regain their faith in the future, especially after the traumatic circumstances of Jan-Pierre's birth in Geneva a year before their arrival.

They found that beneath old Auguste's mean and crusty exterior there still lurked a mean and crusty interior, but tinged occasionally with bouts of sentimentality of which he seemed thoroughly ashamed when they surfaced. They grew to ignore the old man's constant nagging and complaints, which they found to be totally insincere. They knew that Auguste had actually grown to love them as his own flesh and blood, although he had a strange way of showing it. What was more, he constantly complained about 'your noisy brat can't you keep him in the barn,' and yet Lenka frequently caught him at the baby's cot, stroking his cheek with his finger and cooing Bordelaise airs at him. At the end of the day, Auguste had become so used to being mean and crusty that he found it impossible to change, despite his latent better instincts. Maurice and Lenka saw through him easily, humoured him, and took any bait that he threw at them with a levity bordering on disdain. The *modus vivendi* worked, and all their neighbours were amazed that there was someone actually capable of dealing with the cantankerous old eccentric with such ease.

One evening in the spring of 1830 Auguste suffered a heart attack seated at table after dinner, and died, aged 82. He left Frontillac to the Chavelets, as well as instructions on where to find an enormous hoard of cash stashed away in various mattresses, buried chests and wall cavities dotted around the property. The cash dated back to pre-Revolution times, so only some of it was actually worth anything. What was left, however, was enough to pay for some badly needed restorations to *la Maison*. Business since then had been good, thanks in no small way to the British taste for Bordeaux wines, especially since Maurice had signed a contract with Arthur Cottershall & Son very soon after Auguste's death.

*****

It was shortly after six o'clock that Lenka served a lavish dinner in Franciszka's honour on trestle tables set out beneath an enormous pergola in the garden of *la Maison*. The evening was hot and balmy, and Franciszka had her first taste of *al fresco* French cuisine, specifically of the Bordelaise region. She was overwhelmed by the richness and unfamiliarity of the fare: the artichokes, the asparagus, the *foie-gras* with truffles, the roast duck in the thickest and tastiest sauces imaginable, the delicious and meticulously prepared pastries made with fruits whose names Franciszka did not know in any language, and the greatest array of cheeses she had ever seen, all washed down with the finest vintage 'house wines' that Maurice proudly produced and poured.

Conversation revolved around the Napoleonic campaigns as Uncle Maurice nostalgically regaled Franciszka with tales of adventure specifically illustrating the deep friendship that existed between him and her father.

'Can't you talk about anything other than the war, papa. It's getting on my nerves.'

Franciszka looked up from her pastry. Jan-Pierre had been virtually silent ever since she had arrived, and she wondered whether he was moody, or just naturally shy. He was small, like his father, with a mop of thick, dark hair which he wore short. His complexion had the delicate smoothness of a Polish country girl, yet tinted with a swarthy colouring which took well to the southern sun, giving him a healthy, outdoor air. But behind his glowing brown eyes lay some kind of smouldering passion which Franciszka could not immediately identify. He was, she had to own, extremely good-looking, although frighteningly so. Her tentative but friendly overtures evinced only the barest level of response, almost verging on the insolent. Then there was the remark Henry Cottershall had made. 'And that son of theirs, Jan-Pierre. A strange chap,' he had said. Shelving the idea of getting through to him, she threw herself whole-heartedly into Maurice's reminiscences over dinner, often interrupting to ask specific questions about her father. The conversation eventually led to Sarenki, but it was soon obvious that neither Maurice nor Lenka really wanted to talk about it. Franciszka knew the whole story, including the Grocholski affair, although Maurice had stopped short at the part that Lenka had played in his deliverance. And so, the talk returned inevitably to the wars.

'Jan-Pierre,' said Lenka sternly, 'how could you! Franciszka is our guest, and she should surely be made aware of the close friendship between her father and yours!'

'But it's getting to be a bore!'

'Maybe to you,' interpolated Maurice. 'I know you've been forced to listen to my stories for years, but this is all part of Franciszka's history. You have no right to talk in such a manner in front of her.'

'Why don't you tell her about the Grocholski business?' retorted Jan-Pierre. 'Now that's a story worthy of a Stendhal novel. And it's true!'

A look of horror alighted on Maurice and Lenka's faces. 'Jan-Pierre!' cried Maurice. 'That's enough! See, you have embarrassed Franciszka.'

'Franciszka looks to me as though not a lot would embarrass her.' He flashed his brown eyes at her and let drop a hint of a smile. 'Franciszka is a woman of the world! The whole of Europe is her oyster! Tell me, Franciszka, what embarrasses you? We need to know so that we can draw the line as to topics of conversation. Just like the lines generals draw in the middle of a field before a battle.' Jan-Pierre stood up and placed his right hand, Napoleon-like, into his jacket. *'Messieurs!'* he intoned theatrically. *'Voilà la ligne de démarcation!'* He described a line in the gravel with his foot, and jigged from one side to the other. 'This is your side – and this is our side! At the signal, we all charge, cross the line and kill one another! *Voilà* your war, papa! A good game. Very exciting.'

'Jan-Pierre!' Maurice leapt to his feet, his face dark with rage. 'You will leave the table this instant!'

Jan-Pierre took no notice, but walked over to Lenka and put his arm round her shoulders. 'Tell me, dear *maman*, are the battlefields of the bedroom also thus demarcated? A line drawn down the middle of a sheet, perhaps? This is your side – and this is my side! At the signal, we both charge, cross the line and – and then what? In fact, who? *Voilà la question!* Perhaps Franciszka would care to hear of your war experiences, *non*? Perhaps it is your turn to reminisce? *Hein, maman?*'

Lenka burst into tears, leapt up and fled into the house. Maurice, after throwing his son a look of pure rage, ran after her. Jan-Pierre watched them go, then calmly sat down again, took a sip of his wine and resumed eating his pastry in silence. Franciszka sat glued to her chair, mouth open and fork in hand, and found herself unable to move. She listened intently for what seemed like an eternity to the deafening sound of the cicadas, before deciding to take this bull firmly by the horns.

'You bastard!' she muttered.

'Fine language for a well-brought-up Polish girl,' said Jan-Pierre.

'It's probably the only language you understand. What have your parents done to deserve being utterly humiliated in this manner?'

'You don't know the half of it.'

'Enlighten me!'

'One day.'

'As you wish.' She drained the last of her glass, rose, and walked towards *la Maison*.

'Franciszka,' said Jan-Pierre. Franciszka stopped in her tracks but did not look back. 'I didn't mean to embarrass you. I'm sorry.

I like you. I'd like to be friends with you, if that's possible now.'
Franciszka went indoors without a word or a backward glance.

VII

The following day an extremely strained atmosphere hung over Frontillac. Maurice and Lenka tried their best to smooth things over, but the spectre of their son's behaviour dominated every moment at *la Maison*. Their embarrassment and mortification were plain to see, especially as far as Lenka was concerned. Franciszka saw in her a warm-hearted, rather mousy, prematurely grey-haired little lady with a pleasant face and smiling eyes, who bustled quietly about the house with the minimum of fuss and bother. Overnight she had turned into a hand-wringing, apologetic woman with a grey face and sunken eyes that seemed not to focus on anything. Maurice was trying to put a brave face on matters. He put his arm round Franciszka's shoulders. 'We consider you as family, *ma chère*,' he said. 'As you can see, we have certain problems. I am sure you will understand. After all, your father and I were as brothers – perhaps even more so. I miss him terribly, especially when –' his voice trailed off and his eyes gazed into the distance. 'How would you like to go for a walk this morning? It is only ten minutes to the River. It is very pretty. Then I can show you some of the vineyards. Jan-Pierre can deal with whatever needs to be done. At least he is utterly reliable on that score.'

Jan-Pierre was acting as though nothing had happened. He had reverted to his surly self – yes, reflected Franciszka, that was the correct word, not naturally shy, as she had originally thought – speaking only when spoken to, and then mostly in monosyllables. He was up very early going about his tasks in the vineyards and the *caves*.

'He works very hard at the family business,' Maurice told Franciszka as they reached the grassy banks of the Dordogne. He is utterly devoted to it. They are his life's passions – wine and Frontillac.'

'What caused last night's episode, Uncle Maurice?' said Franciszka.

'Jan-Pierre has been a grave problem for Lenka and myself. Even as a child he has been difficult. Very disobedient and rebellious. His mother had a hard time bringing him up. Perhaps she spoiled him, but I think not. He was a beautiful child, you see. Everyone doted on him, but he did not endear himself to people. He had not the gift of charm. You have noticed this, naturally. Lenka saw the dangers, and tried to make it up to him by showing him what was perhaps excessive love. She devoted herself entirely to him, gave him all the attention, the hugs and the kisses. But he found it hard to reciprocate. Then, in a final attempt to teach him about what true love means, she told him her greatest secret, which she had kept hidden in the deepest recesses of her soul.'

'The Grocholski affair?'

'The Grocholski affair. We had put it behind us. All this…' he indicated the vineyards on the slopes above the riverbank with his hand, '…was supposed to be a new start for us after the horrors that took place at Sarenki.'

'Horrors?'

'No doubt your father has told you?'

'About the Grocholski affair? Yes, he told me about the three fugitives that were horrendously killed, and how he lost Sarenki – and his title – to him in a life-or-death game of cards. He also told me how you were involved and arrested by Grocholski, but that you managed to escape from prison.'

'Ah, but did he tell you how I escaped?'

'He may have done, but I don't remember any details, except that you fled to Kraków, where you met up with your love, Lenka, and ended up in each other's arms. You were considered quite a hero, having outwitted the evil Grocholski!'

'Ah,' said Maurice. They walked on for a while. The morning sun was gaining heat. Fish were jumping in the river, and a dragonfly flitted among the reeds growing on the bank, reminding Franciszka of the Polish tongue twister that she enjoyed imposing on non-Polish speakers. *Chrząszcz brzmi w czcinie*. The dragonfly is buzzing in the reeds. She found it amusing to hear them struggling with those onomatopoeic strings of consonants.

'There's more, isn't there?' she said at last.

'Yes.' Maurice told her the full story.

'My God!' said Franciszka when he had finished. 'No wonder. It would be enough to drive any normal boy off the rails!'

'She should not have told him. She re-opened the can of worms, and has thrown away the lid. We are at our wits' end. And there's another thing.'

'Do I need to know?'

'You're family, Franciszka. You should know – everything.' There was a slight hesitation in his words, as yet another thought alighted on his mind, a momentary, involuntary image that flitted through his consciousness: a moonlit night in June 1814 – Czarne Lasy – Eloise – brown eyes. 'He's convinced Grocholski was his father.'

'But surely, that is impossible! Surely, the dates…'

'…fit in his mind. He is a deeply troubled young man. He thinks he is twenty-four years old. Two weeks ago, when we celebrated his twenty-first birthday, he was celebrating his twenty-fourth. It was a dreadful day. Our guests – you know, local friends and neighbours, humour him for our sakes, but they all think he is very strange. Even the wine we had laid down for him when we arrived was undrinkable. An omen, perhaps. He said that it was proof, because that wine would not have lasted 24 years. All his birthdays since he was told the truth have been dreadful. He has convinced himself that we have lied to him about his age to cover up the fact that Grocholski was his father. You see, Franciszka, Jan-Pierre thinks he's the son of a whore and a mass-murderer.'

*****

Over the next few days, the atmosphere loosened up a little as Maurice and Lenka made Franciszka feel more and more as part of the family. The bonding process took place far quicker than anyone would have dared to imagine. Jan-Pierre was almost civil to her, and occasionally she caught him giving her a strange look which might have been a shy smile. 'Either that, or he's undressing me with his eyes!' she thought. The thought at first disturbed her, but then – on the other hand – she smiled to herself wickedly.

On one occasion he caught up with her in the hallway of *la Maison*. 'The other evening' he said, 'I shouldn't have said those things.'

There was something about Jan-Pierre that brought out the aggressive in Franciszka. She again took this bull by the horns. 'No, you shouldn't have! But then you're a mindless idiot, and you did!'

Jan-Pierre opened his mouth to speak, but failed to find either the words or what to say with them. He gave up and settled for 'Sod you, then.' He turned and made off the way he had come. Franciszka let go the bull's horns. They felt soft. 'Wait!' she said.

Jan-Pierre turned. 'I didn't know the full version of the Grocholski story.'

'That's what I thought. Afterwards, that is.'

'My father kept it from me. Not quite the sort of thing a well-brought-up Polish girl should know. But you're wrong about your age. You're twenty-one.'

'I'm twenty-four. They're trying to cover it all up. All of them. The neighbours and all that lot. They're all in league together. How do they know how old I was when we first arrived? I know these things. It's instinct. I feel things, you see. Voices and things. Nobody understands.'

'Then how come you weren't around when I was? You were born in Geneva. I'm definitely older than you. Your mother was pregnant with you when you left Czarne Lasy. I vaguely remember your father kissing me good-bye and telling me to be a good girl.'

'You're in this with them!'

'How can I be? What would I gain by lying to you? My father would have spoken about you if he had seen you.' Jan-Pierre lifted the corner of the carpet with his boot, then smoothed it out again. The horns crumbled. 'Trust me, Jan-Pierre,' she said. 'You've got to trust someone.'

Jan-Pierre played with the carpet again. 'Sod you,' he said, and left.

*****

A week later the Chavelets received a visit from Arthur and Henry Cottershall, with Mr and Mrs McLintock in tow.

'A courtesy call to one of our most cherished producers,' said Arthur. Maurice and Lenka promptly invited them to dinner.

Dinner was a jolly affair, during which Maurice brought out his finest wines to taste, although no business was discussed over the meal. Instead, Henry was in fine form, disporting himself and his charms for the benefit of Franciszka, who now had nothing to fear from Mrs McLintock, and the obvious fact that he was making a play for Franciszka dominated the ethos of the occasion, to everyone's evident delight.

'Are you fond of opera, Mademoiselle Samojarska,' enquired

Henry.

'Indeed I am, Mr Cottershall, what I have seen of it in Königsberg. Mozart's *The Marriage of Figaro* springs to mind as a delightful experience, although I found Rossini's *The Barber of Seville* quite memorable.'

'But that is incredible,' said Henry, 'they're reviving *The Barber* at the Grand Theatre in Bordeaux next week! Perhaps M. Chavelet would permit me to invite you to join my father's party at a performance? My Aunt Prudence – she's father's sister – and Uncle Willie, and their daughter Verity from England, who've just arrived on the Claret Clipper, will also be there. As, of course, will Mr and Mrs McLintock. We would consider it an honour!'

Arthur grunted his approbation. Franciszka raised an eyebrow at Maurice, who nodded with a smile. 'I would like that, Mr Cottershall. Thank you.'

*****

The evening at the Opera was a great success. Aunt Prudence and Uncle Willie were heavy duty opera enthusiasts, and pronounced the performance superb. Their daughter Verity, aged eighteen, was appreciative enough, although Mr and Mrs McLintock both found it difficult to hide the fact that they were a little bored by all that singing. Mr McLintock possessed, as had been shown at Christmas, a fine tenor voice, but his musical interests did not go beyond traditional Scottish airs. Afterwards the company dined at the Hotel d'Angleterre, and Franciszka was offered a room for the night at the Cottershalls' house in the rue des Remparts, where Uncle Willie, Aunt Prudence and Verity were also staying.

The following day a carriage was ordered to take Franciszka back to Frontillac. Henry emerged from the house to see her off. 'A memorable evening, Franciszka,' he said. They had slipped effortlessly into Christian name terms. 'May we meet again?'

'Yes. I'd like that.'

'Perhaps a ride into the Médoc? Very pretty countryside, and the wines are excellent.' Franciszka looked doubtful. Henry read her misgiving. 'I would suggest Verity rides with us, as well as Monsieur Poussard.' Henry giggled.

'Who is Monsieur Poussard?' asked Franciszka.

'Monsieur Poussard – Monsieur Guillaume Poussard is a wine-grower. A very good one. He is madly in love with Verity, and we are all waiting for him to propose marriage.'

'A good prospect, then?'

'If you call a vintage, fruity but elegant 1775 bachelor with a *chateau* and a vineyard in Margaux a good prospect.'

'That makes him – in his fifties! The older, more mature type of man, then. Does Verity love him?'

'Verity loves *chateaux* and wine. So do Uncle Willie and Aunt Prudence. It would be a good match. Monsieur Poussard is a delightful man, charming and considerate. And he enjoys riding. How about you, Franciszka. Are you the type that prefers the older, more mature type of man?'

'That is a pointed question, Mr Cottershall,' laughed Franciszka, accentuating the Mister. 'I shall reserve judgement until I have met one.' Henry looked sadly at his feet. 'However,' she continued, 'I am most happy drinking a good, young wine that has something fresh and honest to offer the taste bud.'

Henry looked up again and smiled. 'So, that's settled then. We explore the Médoc on horseback! Till we meet again.'

'I look forward to it. Goodbye, Henry.' The carriage drove off.

VIII

'Do you like him?' said Jan-Pierre.
'Who?' said Franciszka.
'Henry Cottershall. He obviously lusts after your body.'
'Does that matter to you?'
'Doesn't make any difference to me one way or another.'
'In that case, I do like him. He's very nice.'
'What a stupid expression. Nice. Doesn't really mean anything, does it.'

The bull's horns appeared. Franciszka grabbed them. 'Look, if I say that Henry Cottershall is nice, then that is exactly what I mean. I've been to finishing school, so I know the meanings of words. If you have a problem of any kind with semantics, go and read a book or two. You might even learn something. If, on the other hand, you're just jealous, with your mind firmly fixed on a romp in a haystack and a grope at my knickers, then you are barking up the wrong tree!'

'You should be so lucky,' muttered Jan-Pierre, and sloped off into the vineyard. Franciszka looked after him, shook her head and smiled mirthlessly. The horns crumbled away.

The ride in the Médoc was the most romantic episode in Franciszka's life, in which she luxuriated in a delicious sense of freedom. She initially stayed at the Cottershalls' before being picked up, along with Henry and Verity by M. Poussard and taken to *Les Sèverines*, his *chateau* on the banks of the Gironde. The four of them, along with Jacques, M. Poussard's henchman, set off at first light, and watched the wan sun penetrating the early morning mist rising off the river, casting an eerie light on its reedy banks. They rode inland towards the undulating slopes of the Haut Médoc, by which time the sun rode high and hot in a clear blue sky. At noon they stopped to picnic off *foie gras, patisserie* and Sauternes, taken in the shade of a small copse overlooking the vineyards. Franciszka and Henry, free and unencumbered, rode mostly side by side, and talked a great deal. She told him of her father, his relationship with Maurice, of her Polish and Lithuanian childhood, and of life in the orbit of the Prussian city of Königsberg, and, more recently, her Scottish sojourn. Henry, in turn, told her of his early life in London before his father had set up his business in Bordeaux, and how his mother had died of consumption when he was only five years old. There was an easy-going, friendly bond developing between them, and Franciszka gave full vent to feelings of exhilaration as she rode beside this charming, attentive and handsome young man, whose smile made her glow with every fibre of her body. The party returned, exhausted but happy, to Les Sèverines in time for dinner *al fresco*, washed down, naturally, with Margaux vintages.

That night Franciszka lay awake in her room, gazing at the crescent moon in the star-spangled sky, and wondered why she was still tingling deliciously all over.

*****

'*Mon Dieu,*' said Maurice to Lenka in the kitchen two days later, 'Franciszka is in love!'

'Does it show?' said Franciszka sheepishly.

'Of course, *ma chère!* You have a silly grin on your face – the far-away look Lenka had back in Sarenki – before the –'

'It's the way you toy with your food,' interrupted Lenka with a smile.

'And you don't hear a word of what is being said to you.'

'It all depends on what is being said to her,' said Jan-Pierre who at that moment walked into the kitchen and poured himself a large tumbler of wine. 'If I were to say to you that Henry Cottershall is only interested in getting into your knickers, you'd pay full attention. Wouldn't you, Franciszka.'

'Jan-Pierre! What a dreadful thing to say to Franciszka!' cried Maurice as Lenka fled from the kitchen in tears. 'And in front of your mother!'

'Why don't you give up, Jan-Pierre,' sneered Franciszka, holding the horns again. 'You know you'll never get into mine. Ever. You have lost before you've even started.'

'Franciszka –' began Maurice, a shocked look on his face.

'I'm sorry, Uncle Maurice, but I think that is the only language Jan-Pierre understands. I've seen the way he looks at me. He's only interested in my body, and he can't bear the thought that I might – just conceivably – be interested in someone else's!'

'My dear Franciszka!' Jan-Pierre spread his arms out, spilling some of the wine onto the floor, as Maurice's shocked look jumped to his young guest, 'what on earth gave you that impression? I was only anxious about maintaining your honour and preserving your virginity! I may presume, may I not, that, being a well-brought-up Polish girl, you are a virgin? Oh, cruel maid! How can you treat your devoted benefactor so?'

With that he left abruptly, drinking from the tumbler as he went.

'*Quelle éloquence!*' cried Maurice after him. 'He talks for weeks in monosyllables, then comes up with speeches! What is the matter with the boy?

'I will talk to him, Uncle Maurice,' said Franciszka. 'Sometimes he listens to me.'

Franciszka was right. Over the following days she spoke to Jan-Pierre in what she thought was his own language, using words and expressions that no 'well-brought-up Polish girl' would normally use, and found that her ploy worked. While she veered from hard-hitting to gentle understanding, Jan-Pierre veered from obscene bluster designed to shock, to awkward apologies verging on grovelling; from utter disdain to total deference, as if to a goddess. Eventually, they found a turbulent but working *modus vivendi* which Maurice and Lenka could hardly believe.

'I think you're the only one who can get through to him,' said Maurice. 'What is your secret, *ma chère*?'

'I've no idea, Uncle Maurice,' she replied. 'It's just that I feel – a kind of empathy with him. It's as if there were something of me in him, and that there is something of him in me. It's very difficult to explain. Do you understand at all what I am trying to say?'

Maurice replied slowly and deliberately. 'Yes, *ma chère*, I believe I do.' Again, the thought alighted on Maurice's mind, a momentary, involuntary image flitting through his consciousness: a moonlit night in June 1814 – Czarne Lasy – Eloise – brown eyes. 'I believe I do,' he said.

*****

September turned, and the early autumnal golds turned everyone's attention to the impending *vendange*. The grapes were rich and full, with the promise of a good vintage to come. Franciszka was by now spending a great deal of her time in Bordeaux, where her relationship with Henry was going from strength to strength under the watchful auspices of his father. He was enthusiastically aided and abetted by Aunt Prudence, who also made a big thing of enthusiastically aiding and abetting the romance between her daughter Verity and the charming M. Poussard. Paradoxically, the greatest bonding appeared to be between Uncle Willie and M. Poussard, who both shared a great enthusiasm for opera and hunting, which they discussed in enormous detail and insatiable passion at every available opportunity over a bottle or two of

Margaux.

Equally paradoxically, Franciszka's bonds with Jan-Pierre also went from strength to strength, although the direction of their relationship was anything but romantic. Jan-Pierre appeared to have found in her a confessor, a counsellor who understood him, whereas Franciszka embraced the challenge of nurturing what was obviously a tormented soul consumed for some deep, hidden reason by insecurity and self-loathing. Lenka often watched them going off into the vineyards together, always apart, never close enough to touch, and wondered where she had gone wrong with her son's upbringing.

Maurice gazed at the young people with a mixture of joy and doubt, and always recalled that June night 23 years ago, and again speculated for the millionth time whether Franciszka was his. He also wondered for the millionth time whether Eloise had also speculated similarly over all those years. The brown eyes – they were exactly the same shade as those of Jan-Pierre, and yet, in every other way, they were so different.

*****

In October the *vendange* was in full swing, and many migrant workers were enlisted to help bring in the harvest. When the last of the grapes were gathered in there were feasts and celebrations throughout the region. The town of Saint-Emilion organised a great open-air feast at which all the local specialities were served, along with the best local wines. Four bands were engaged, a Spanish flamenco outfit that was doing a tour of the *vendange* parties, as well as a Basque ensemble which, along with a French group from Libourne, provided music for dancing, while a string quartet played music by Gossec, Haydn and Boccherini for the more sedate, cultured members of the community. The festivities lasted well into the warm, balmy night. Henry Cottershall joined the Chavelets' party: his father, Uncle Willie, Aunt Prudence and

Verity had accepted M. Poussard's invitation to a small ball at Les Sèverines, which unfortunately coincided with the festivities at Saint-Emilion. Jan-Pierre was on very good form, to everyone's delight and relief. Whatever he said was, not surprisingly, laced with some degree of sarcasm and outrageous innuendo, but it was witty and good-natured, and even Lenka found herself able to appreciate his undoubted contribution to the fun of the evening. Franciszka, seated between Jan-Pierre and Henry, noticed not the slightest hint of animosity between the two young men, and even felt curious vibrations emanating from Jan-Pierre not only of approval, but even blessing towards her relationship with Henry.

After the sumptuous dinner, Franciszka smiled an apology at Jan-Pierre as Henry whisked her off to dance to the Basque band as it played exotic airs from the Pais Yvasco and the mountains of Navarra. It soon became obvious that Henry and Franciszka would be dancing the night away, so Jan-Pierre got up, looked for, and found, a girl with whom to do the same. This was not difficult, because most girls immediately fell for his smouldering charms and found his anarchic and irreverent attitudes a distinct turn-on.

Meanwhile, the wine continued to flow and everyone was thoroughly enjoying themselves and lost all track of time. Finally, the weeks of hard work caught up with Maurice and Lenka, and they cast about for the youngsters to round them up for the ride back to Frontillac. They caught sight of Henry, wandering around among the revellers with two glasses of wine in his hand, and called him over. 'Have you seen Franciszka, *Monsieur* Maurice?' he said.

'I thought she was with you, Henry,' replied Maurice. 'We were just thinking about driving home.'

'*Monsieur* Maurice is very tired,' added Lenka.

'I only left her for a moment to fetch another couple of

glasses of wine,' said Henry. 'Perhaps she's gone somewhere with Jan-Pierre?'

'We only saw him a moment ago dancing with the Bernardine girl from Chouet, but he seems to have disappeared.' Maurice caught sight of the girl in question passing close to their table. 'Giselle, have you seen Jan-Pierre?' he called over to her.

'I've just been dancing with him, M. Chavelet,' she replied, 'but he said goodnight because he had to go home. I thought he'd be with you.'

'Well, there's no sign of him anywhere.'

'If you want to get away home, M. Chavelet, please do so,' said Henry. 'Leave Jan-Pierre and Franciszka to me. I shall find them and bring them safely to Frontillac in my carriage. You have my assurance.'

'Very well, then, Henry. That would be very good of you,' said Maurice.

'Anyway,' Henry smiled broadly, 'there's still a couple of dances left in me! The night is yet young!'

Maurice and Lenka agreed to the plan, bade Henry a good night, lit the lantern of their buggy, spurred the horse and set off back to Frontillac.

Dawn was breaking when a commotion in the cobbled yard in front of *la Maison* woke them. Maurice rose quickly and ran to the window. By the faint light of the first break of day he could just make out Henry alighting from his buggy, carrying a bundle in his arms. '*Monsieur* Maurice! *Madame* Lenka! Please come! Help me!' he cried.

Maurice and Lenka quickly draped themselves in their dressing gowns and rushed downstairs. In the hallway they met Henry, who gently placed the bundle on a chaise longue by the door. Lenka lit a candle, which she held up, and the sight that met her eyes made her drop the candle and cover her mouth to stop herself crying out. Maurice picked the candle up. It was still lit.

'Mon Dieu!' he cried, aghast. 'Who has done this?'

Sprawled on the *chaise longue* was Franciszka, barely conscious and whimpering weakly. Her dress was torn virtually to shreds and she was covered in blood and bruises.

'Who has done this?' repeated Maurice. Lenka was dumbfounded and unable to move or to utter a sound.

'I had to do it, *Monsieur* Maurice!' wailed Henry, quivering from head to toe. 'I couldn't allow it to continue! Oh, my God, *Monsieur* Maurice, you must see that I had to do it!'

'You – you did this to Franciszka?!' cried Maurice, his face contorted with rage.

'I – no, of course I did not do this to Franciszka, *Monsieur* Maurice, but I couldn't allow it to continue! I – I killed him! My God! What have I done? I killed him! He violated Franciszka! I have never seen such wickedness – such violence – such – such –'

Henry swayed, lost his balance and fell to his knees. Maurice took him by the shoulders and shook him hard. 'Who? Whom did you kill, Henry? Who did this thing?'

'I stabbed him with a carving knife – from the roasting lamb. I left him bleeding, don't you see. He violated Franciszka – would have killed her had I not – not – my God, *Monsieur* Maurice, I have killed your son – may I be forgiven – I have killed Jan-Pi –'

IX

'Your passport is not valid, *Herr* Samojarski.'

Teofil waved his arms in frustration. It had taken six weeks of bureaucratic hassle to get this far – the gates of Vienna – only to be told that it had all been for nothing. Two days after he had received Samuel Sachs's letter, he had gone to Königsberg to apply for permission to travel throughout Prussia. As a refugee from the 1830-1 Uprising, he had been officially 'interned' – granted residential status – but only within the Königsberg region. Twice this permission had been refused, but perseverance and the intercession of Baron Helmut von Heimdall, his landlord, had finally paid off. Despite his lowly position at the Foreign Ministry in Berlin, the Baron was able to pull a few strings, and got Teofil the necessary permit, which would be valid until the last day of August. The Baron also gave him the name of a senior official in Berlin who might hopefully issue him a valid travel document for the Austro-Hungarian Empire. Teofil went to Berlin and found that the official's willingness to help was in direct proportion to the amount of 'expenses' that would be incurred. Teofil's initial 'offer' would ensure that he received the document within two months of application. After some uncharacteristic street-market haggling, a sum was arrived at that would ensure a 'fast-track' process that would take two weeks. In the meantime, Teofil had to return to Nibork and await the arrival of the document by post.

It arrived on the morning of August 30, a month after his initial application.

The following day found Teofil, who had been ready to depart at a moment's notice, at a checkpoint at Rawicz, on the border of the Grand Duchy of Posen and Silesia.

'Your permit to travel throughout Prussia expires tonight,' said the official. 'Where are you bound for?'

'Vienna.'

'You are some distance from the frontier. You will never make it.'

'I might if you just let me go on.' Teofil pressed a wad of banknotes into the official's hand.

'On the other hand, it might be possible. God speed, *Herr* Samojarski,' grinned the official, waving the carriage through.

Teofil stayed that night at the Golden Goose in Breslau's Market Square, a first-class hostelry where formalities were lax, and no one even bothered to ask him for his papers. The following morning, September 1, these papers were no longer in order. Teofil dreaded having to show them, but it was only at the frontier mountain town of Glatz, famous for its spa, that he was asked to produce them.

'Your papers are not in order, *Herr* Samojarski,' said the frontier guard. 'Your permit to travel throughout the Kingdom of Prussia expired yesterday.'

'So, what are you going to do?' said Teofil petulantly, 'send me back to Nibork?'

'I'm afraid that I shall have to detain you pending investigation.'

Teofil's frayed temper frayed some more. 'But I'm at the frontier now!' he cried. 'Why not just expel me from Prussia and be done with it?'

'I'm sorry, *Herr* Samojarski, but regulations clearly state –'

'What regulations?!'

'What is the problem?' A third voice had come into play.

Ah, thought Teofil. A superior officer with an ounce of sense, with luck. 'It seems my travel permit has expired. I take it I must leave Prussia immediately,' he said as politely as his seething nerves allowed, pointing ahead.

'You have a passport, sir?'

Teofil produced his international travel document, which the official scrutinised. 'Have a safe journey, *Herr* Samojarski,' he said with a smile, 'and a pleasant stay in Vienna.'

Teofil closed his eyes tightly and sighed with relief. Glancing back as the carriage crossed into the hills of the Austrian province of Moravia, he saw the superior officer talking firmly to his underling. Perhaps telling him that life is really too short to take regulations too literally.

After that it was plain sailing until the gates of Vienna.

'What do you mean my passport is not valid? I only received it two days ago!'

'That's as may be, sir, but it is not valid until tomorrow. See, the date states quite clearly: September 2. You will be well looked after for a night at *zum Schwarzen Adler*.' The official pointed to the post hotel almost opposite.

Teofil looked heavenwards. At least he was not going to be sent back. The following morning his trunk underwent a thorough customs inspection before he was allowed to enter Vienna with it, but there were more checkpoints on the way. Teofil found himself having to fill in countless forms, stating age, religion, marital status and object of journey. Written proof of financial solvency was waived on the production of a case full of currency, considering that he was not intending to stay very long. Various forms had to be filled in and presented to various offices in Vienna itself within twenty-four hours.

*****

'Alas, *Herr Graf*,' said Samuel Sachs, 'the Empire is in the grip of such stringent bureaucracy as would beggar belief. I am sorry that you have had such trouble coming to Vienna, but I am afraid that is par for the course these days. Metternich is terrified of dissent within the Empire, and fears revolution above all else, you see. He has such a hold on everyday life as to make life quite difficult at times. There are arrests with ill-treatment in custody. There is imprisonment without trial. Metternich's agents are everywhere. My advice to you, *Herr Graf*, is to accept the inevitable. Visitors to our city show dissent or disrespect at their peril.' He took a sip of his coffee and washed it down with a mouthful of water. 'Mozart died in this house, you know. Up on the first floor.'

Teofil looked around. They were seated in one of Vienna's numerous coffee houses in the Rauhensteingasse, next door to the offices of *Sachs und Spielberg*. The coffee, Teofil noted, was excellent. He took a sip and recalled Jolanta playing Mozart at Spytkowiec. Such a long time ago. He wondered whatever happened to her. 'Whatever happened to Grocholski?' he asked.

'He is languishing in jail. He will probably not be brought to trial, but just left to rot. It would take too much man-power, you see, to pursue a penniless Polish fraudster. The important thing, *Herr Graf*, is that your title has been restored to you. In fact, you have never lost it. You are also the owner of Sarenki once again.'

'Have you been there?'

'No. But Jakob has, naturally. He retired there as soon as he had bought it. He was a very sick man, *Herr Graf*. He retained Zygmunt Karłowicz, who used to manage the place for Grocholski. A very able and conscientious man, by all accounts. Also, old *Frau* Gruszka, a local farmer's widow, came in to look after him. Jakob wrote very highly of her. He said that her name meant pear in Polish, and that she was shaped like a pear!' Sachs burst into peals of laughter, which turned into a series of strangled gasps. Tears came into the old Jew's eyes. '*Mein Gott, Herr Graf*, but I do miss him so. A fine man. A sensitive soul. Jakob Spielberg. He took the waters, of course, but ultimately to no avail. They gave him a Christian burial, you know. There was this crazy parish priest who tried to convert him to what he called the side of Good. Old Jakob went along with it to please the old priest. It was all the same to him. There's just the one God, and that's it. It never mattered to Jakob how you addressed Him, as long as you acknowledged him. Hebrew, Latin, whatever. He's dead now, too.'

'Father Józef?'

'Yes, that was his name. Józef Baraniuk. He must have been well into his eighties. Nineties, even. A remarkable priest. And human being.'

Teofil was silent for a few moments savouring a vision of Father Józef shaking his fist at the sky and threatening Jakob with every tribulation in Hell if he did not embrace the only God truly on the side of Good. 'But why did Jakob leave Sarenki to me? Had he no children – or relatives?' he said.

'As I said, Jakob was a sensitive man. But he was alone in the world. I believe he fully understood your stance in the Grocholski affair. He saw you as a good man who stood up to evil, and lost. Maybe he needed to compensate you for it. Sometimes we all need to recompense to expiate some evil.'

'Is a medical centre in memory of his brother Boris a prerequisite of this legacy?' said Teofil after a pause.

'By no means. It is yours to do with what you will. However,' Sachs summoned a waiter for more coffee, 'Sarenki needs investment. You are a rich man, I understand, but if I may point out two things for your consideration, *Herr Graf*. Firstly, consumption is one of our century's greatest evils. It consumes all before it. If the waters of Sarenki can be harnessed to combat this dreadful disease, the investment would be worthwhile. Secondly, Sarenki is within the sphere of influence of Kraków, which holds one of the greatest concentrations of Jews in the world. A medical centre dedicated to the memory of a Jewish freedom fighter would be very well patronised by the Jews of Kraków, many of whom are extremely rich. Now I know full well that the aristocracy does not speculate. It is bad form to do so. However, if money were to flow freely into an enterprise without it being fought for, shall we say, you would be exonerated from being a dealer, which is what we Jews are for. I predict a very prosperous future for you and your family. And, of course, for Sarenki. You have a son at the Medical School in Edinburgh, I understand.'

'You are very well informed, *Herr* Sachs.'

'It's what I do, *Herr Graf*. I deal in facts as well as money.'

'Is this relevant?'

'It could well be. If Sarenki is to become a major medical centre in Central Europe, it will need medical staff. And a fully qualified doctor to run it. I have heard that Edinburgh leads the world in consumption research.'

'You are very shrewd, *Herr* Sachs.'

'I am a Jew, *Herr Graf*. I see many things that Christians do not. But I do not seek a partnership with you. It would not be – seemly, either among your people or mine. However, a certain understanding based on mutual respect and honesty is another thing. I would very much like to do something for you. You have proved yourself a sensitive, unbiased human being. One definitely on the side of Good, as Father Józef used to say. Jakob saw that, and that is good enough for me.' The waiter brought the fresh coffee. Teofil and Sachs picked them up. 'Thank you, *Herr* Sachs. So, to prosperity. Your good health, *Herr Graf*.'

Teofil inclined his head slightly and smiled. The opening strains of Mozart's A major Piano Sonata edged past his mind as the two men drank their coffee.

X

Teofil, who had never actually set foot in Vienna before, found the capital of the Habsburg Empire very beautiful and vibrant, but claustrophobic in the foetid heat of the Central European late summer. The magnificent city centre, dominated by the Hofburg complex and the Cathedral of St Stephen, was surrounded by the Ramparts, known as the Glacis, with its promenades along which the bourgeoisie disported themselves in the evenings wearing the latest fashions. The buildings, often up to six storeys high, were tall, and the streets were narrow, and the sun seldom gained access to the cobbled pavements, where pedestrians and carriages vied for supremacy. There were no trees to be seen anywhere, apart from the open parks, like the Prater. Otherwise, the only place where one could breathe with any ease was the Graben, the wide and airy central street lined with smart shops selling the latest fashions and rich fabrics, furnishings and fancies to those who could afford them. Coffee houses and restaurants abounded everywhere, many of them meeting places of artists, musicians and – the politically aware young, fired by the modern ideas that echoed Revolutionary France, or imported from the United States of America. They discussed politics in these places at their peril. Teofil soon learned to spot government agents, who sat alone and casually moved to eavesdrop on the conversations of any group of young people.

'There is a genuine fear among all the population that any remark, however innocent, might land them in trouble,' Sachs had explained. 'So, people only go out to show themselves off.

Any serious debate and discussion take place strictly behind closed doors.'

Teofil's only concern was to regain access to Sarenki. For this he needed a valid passport, permits to travel within the Empire, and a residential permit. Sachs had initially pointed him in the right directions, and Teofil spent his first week in Vienna being ushered from pillar to post, and from one office to another. His frustrations were exacerbated when it was discovered that one of the forms he had laboriously filled in to enter Vienna in the first place had been lost, and the bureaucracy involved in setting this to rights took a whole week. By the middle of September, he was weary, foot-sore, frayed of temper and no nearer to his goal.

On September 20 he was refused a residential permit. On September 21 he was refused a travel permit within the Austrian Empire. On September 22 he was expelled from the Austrian Empire – effective within 24 hours – on suspicion of being a French, a Prussian, a Russian spy or Polish Freedom fighter. The police could not make up their minds which. On September 23, having given up, packed his trunk and set off for the Prussian border, he was refused permission to leave Vienna as he had no travel permit for the road to Moravia and the Prussian border at Glatz. His loss of temper caused him to be arrested and locked in a customs office. On being asked if there was anyone in Vienna who might vouch for him, he mentioned Samuel Sachs. At first this name was rejected on the grounds that Jews could not vouch. However, in the absence of any alternative whatsoever, a young captain who Teofil thought had an ounce of common sense agreed to send for Sachs.

'*Herr Graf,*' said Sachs to Teofil four hours later, 'I had no idea you were having such problems! You should have told me. There are ways, you see. As I have said before…' he cast a sarcastic glance at the bemused captain '…our bureaucracy has gone mad. However …' he took the elbow of a small, well-dressed man with a curt manner and darting eyes, who had arrived with him, '...I would like you to meet *Herr* Ludwig Mendel. He is a friend of mine, and well placed to help you with the matter in hand.'

Ludwig Mendel showed the captain a paper credential which had the immediate effect of making him jump smartly to attention. 'You shall hand *Herr Graf* Samojarski to the care of my department in the Ministry of the Interior immediately.'

'Yes, sir!' said the official.

'See that his personal effects are sent to – where was it you were staying, *Herr Graf*?'

'Zum Schwarzen Adler, in Mariahilf,' said Teofil.

'See to it.'

'Immediately, sir!'

Ludwig Mendel's interest in the Grocholski affair had been personal right from the start, and he felt an exquisite loathing for both him and everything he stood for, as well as a strong sympathy towards this somewhat maverick Polish aristocrat who had effectively lost everything for the sake of a Jew. At least that is what it looked like to him, although in fact Teofil would have done the same for any fellow human being. Mendel felt that the least he could do was to ensure that Teofil's title was officially re-established, and that he was granted full citizenship and an Austrian passport without any further delay.

Teofil's spirits immediately improved, and he spent the following week actually enjoying Vienna. He took leisurely walks along the Glacis, watched the world go by from the coffee-houses, went for a long walk in the Prater and visited St Stephen's Cathedral. He took in a performance of Donizetti's *Lucia di Lammermoor* at the Kärntnertor Theatre, and took a carriage to sample the waters and the gaming tables at Baden.

On October 1, through the machinations of Ludwig Mendel, he was invited to Court and presented to Emperor Ferdinand at the Hofburg. 'His Imperial Majesty is a little simple, as you are no doubt aware,' Mendel had said to him beforehand, tapping his head with his forefinger. 'Whatever you do, you must humour him, and answer all questions regardless of their content. Otherwise, he might get upset. You will actually find him very pleasant and affable, poor man, because he is always so anxious to please.'

Teofil knew, as did everyone else, that due to inbreeding, the Habsburg genes had become severely diluted, and several members of the Dynasty were simple-minded and had physical and mental deformities. The Emperor himself had an enormous forehead, and Teofil wondered whether the anecdote was true that his favourite pastime was to roll around the corridors of the Hofburg ensconced in a waste-bin. For all that, the Emperor engaged Teofil in some in-depth discussion on sledging. Teofil's advice – such as it was – on the finer points of the sport were noted with great enthusiasm. 'See to it that *Herr Graf* Samojarski accompanies us into the hills when the snows come,' he said.

'Yes, your majesty,' said someone, before the matter was quietly forgotten.

The golden Central European autumn was at its zenith when Teofil climbed into the carriage bound for Kraków and Lwów, and experienced a frisson of apprehension at the prospect of seeing his real home again. With one significant reservation: he found it impossible to imagine Sarenki without Father Józef.

XI

'Franciszka is in no fit state to travel anywhere,' said Maurice to Mr and Mrs McLintock. 'She shall stay with us until her father decides what to do for the best.'

Two days had passed since the fatal stabbing of Jan-Pierre. Maurice, unaware of developments on the Sarenki front, had immediately written to Teofil in Nibork explaining that Franciszka had been savaged by a bear during an excursion into the Pyrenees. He added that she was stable, but would require considerable care and attention, which he and Lenka would be giving her while awaiting instructions as to what further course of action should be taken. Henry Cottershall, who remained at Frontillac in a state of shock, confused and incoherent, had been duly arrested, charged with murder and taken, not resisting but sobbing hysterically, into custody in Bordeaux. The McLintocks drove to Frontillac as soon as they had heard the news. Having left behind a dossier of orders with Arthur Cottershall for a wide selection of wines from the Médoc, Saint-Emilion and Sauternes, they were set to return to Britain, with Franciszka, the following week, on the Claret Clipper.

That fateful morning the local physician, Doctor Mereau, had been immediately summoned to tend to Franciszka. She was bathed, bandaged and put to bed by an extremely distraught Lenka, who had become a turbulent volcano of conflicting emotions which she found hard to cope with. She never left Franciszka's side, and Lenka's deep and genuine concern for her was counteracted by the mixture of sorrow and rage at the violent loss of her only son. This loss, in turn, was counteracted by a deep sense of guilt resulting from a strong feeling that it was perhaps all for the best, and she found herself asking whether she had actually loved – or hated – Jan-Pierre. She had never consciously considered the possibility that she might have hated her son until now: how could he have done this terrible thing to a girl – any girl, let alone the only girl who showed any signs of understanding for his tormented spirit. It was unforgivable. What was more, it was she, Lenka, who had given birth to this monster, and that in itself was a cross she found very hard to bear. Curiously, she felt nothing whatsoever for Henry, the thoroughly decent and eminently suitable suitor of Franciszka, whose shock at what had befallen the girl that he obviously loved led him to take all leave of reason and commit an act of murder.

As for Maurice, he again resigned himself to nurturing and lovingly caring not only for the beautiful girl whose birth was for him an impenetrable enigma, but also for a deeply disturbed wife.

The McLintocks, shocked and subdued, duly returned home armed with a letter for Julek, in which Maurice explained everything in detail. 'Julek should know the full facts,' he had told the McLintocks, 'whereas Teofil should be spared the gruesome details, for the time being at any rate.'

*****

October was drawing to a wet and windy close when one bleak evening during supper a bleary-eyed and haggard young man arrived on the doorstep of Frontillac. 'Monsieur Chavelet?' he said in English-accented French.

'Oui, je suis Maurice Chavelet.'

'Je suis le Comte Julian – Julek Samojarski.'

It seemed the most natural thing in the world for the two men immediately to embrace each other warmly. Unlike Franciszka's,

Julek's French was accented, the result of his English public-school education. 'Franciszka – is she –?'

'She is recovering as well as can be expected, Julek,' said Maurice. 'She is sleeping at present. Lenka is with her. She stays with her virtually all the time. She should not be disturbed at this time. Perhaps some supper?'

'Yes – thank you. That would be nice.'

'You have travelled far today?'

'From Limoges.'

'A fair distance.'

'Especially considering the weather.'

'It is foul. But we usually have a pleasant respite during the first week of November. Some soup?'

'Thank you, M. Chavelet.'

'*Oncle*. Uncle Maurice. It is what Franciszka calls me. You shall do likewise. Your father and I were as brothers.'

'I know.'

Later that evening Lenka, who had taken her supper on a tray in Franciszka's room, came down and took Julek to see his sister. 'She is awake. I told her you had arrived. She wants to see you.'

'Julek,' said Franciszka, a smile of recognition alighting on her dry, colourless lips, 'how lovely to see you!'

Julek was momentarily taken aback. His first sight of his bed-ridden sister confirmed his worst fears. Her wounds had largely healed, and only the discoloured remnants of bruising were still visible, as were some scars which fortunately looked as though they would not be permanent. She looked like a heavily-sedated ghost, pale and frightened, yet the sight of her brother brought an instant flush to her cheeks and a light into her eyes. The transformation took a few moments to register.

'Franciszka,' he said, kissing her three times on the cheeks, 'I came as soon as I heard. How are you?' It sounded to Julek an inane thing to say, but no other words came.

Franciszka turned away and a sadness wetted her eyes. She said nothing. Julek turned to Lenka, who shrugged and shook her head. 'We are doing what we can,' she said softly.

'Does *Tata* know?' said Julek, turning away from his sister. 'He has gone to Vienna. I don't know whether you are aware of this.'

A look of consternation crossed Lenka's features. 'No, we didn't know. We wrote to him immediately at Nibork.' Her voice dropped to a whisper as she led Julek away from the bed. 'Not the full facts, of course, only that she had had an accident – an altercation with a bear in the mountains. We thought –'

'So, he won't have heard anything at all?' said Julek. 'Unless *Mamusia* had read the letter and written to him in Vienna. You see, he has regained his title, as well as Sarenki.'

At that moment Maurice entered the room. 'Sarenki?' he said, 'what is this about Sarenki?'

Julek turned back to Franciszka. 'We've got Sarenki back, Franciszka,' he said. '*Tata* went to Vienna to finalise matters with the lawyers. He may not have heard about what has happened to you.'

Franciszka, who had been trying to follow the conversation with her eyes, suddenly looked tired. Lenka took Julek by the elbow. 'I think she should rest now, Julek. It has been too much. Perhaps in the morning –'

Over coffee in the kitchen, while Lenka stayed in Franciszka's room, Julek learned from Maurice that she had been severely traumatised. Four weeks had elapsed since her violent rape, most of which was spent in complete withdrawal. She lay in bed and acknowledged no one, spoke no word, ate or drank nothing, and stared pointedly past Lenka or Maurice out of the window. Occasionally she would come down to earth and act like a normal invalid, saying that she was hungry or thirsty, or that she wanted to get up and sit in the garden. It seemed as though she were trying hard to return to reality, but these spasms only lasted an hour at the most before her eyes glazed over again, and she seemed to retreat once more into her private world of total negation.

The following morning dawned bright and sunny. The expected Indian summer had arrived a few days early, unlike Teofil's letter to Maurice, written in Vienna six weeks previously, which arrived late. Maurice read it out aloud before Julek went up to see Franciszka, who again came alive at the sight of her brother.

'It's a beautiful morning,' he said, trying to sound positive. 'Shall we enjoy the sunshine in the garden? *Tata's* letter about Sarenki has just arrived. I shall read it to you.'

Franciszka's eyes lit up. 'Yes, please!' she replied. 'If Aunt Lenka can help me get dressed. It's about time I got up. I've got to face things, Julek, haven't I?'

'Absolutely!' said Julek, flabbergasted at the transformation. 'You're doing so well! I'll go and get Aunt Lenka.'

'What does *Tata* say?'

'I'll read it to you when we're in the garden.'

In the event, Franciszka's return to reality was short-lived, and she retreated once more as soon as an excited Lenka arrived to help her dress. Her father's letter lay by her bedside, unread by her, for several days.

'But it's a definite step in the right direction,' said Maurice. 'You have obviously shown her the beginnings of a new lease of life. Perhaps time, the great healer –'

Julek took the opportunity to write to his mother, re-iterating what Maurice had written to Teofil four weeks previously, adding that he was prepared to bring Franciszka home as soon as she was fit to travel, but that in the meantime he would stay with her at Frontillac until he heard either from her or from his father. He was prepared to miss the autumn term at Medical School in order to make sure Franciska was safe and recovering from her ordeal.

*****

Maurice was right: time was a great healer and, slowly, Franciszka began to show definite signs of recovery. She read her father's letter and expressed great satisfaction with the contents. She and Julek would go on walks along the Dordogne or through the now desolate and monochrome vineyards where once the Chavelets' livelihood bloomed and blossomed so greenly and profusely until the *vendange* that none of them would ever forget. They talked of life in and out of Prussia and Lithuania, and Julek told her of his holiday time adventures after a summer season spent in London, doing the social rounds, and visiting Carnethie Castle, shooting grouse with various political figures, Polish activists and musician friends of Charles Carnethie's'.

'Now that I'm acknowledged by everyone as Count Julian Samojarski,' he had said, 'I have a further 'Polish' anecdote with which to regale my spellbound listeners!'

'The heavens preserve us from any more of your tales!' smiled Franciszka. 'I wouldn't mind, except that you embellish them with your own version of the truth!'

'It's all part of my Slavic charm!' riposted Julek.

Franciszka gave her brother a loving hug. 'If you say so, brother dear,' she said.

It was only when they were sitting in the garden, and Julek had mentioned an episode involving fellow student Claire Fraser, that Franciszka's eyes glazed over and she retreated into herself once more. Julek had been right about Claire when he had first expressed his suspicions that beneath that outwardly severe aspect there lurked a wild streak that would be well worth investigating at some point. That point came shortly after the beginning of the new term, when both Julek and Claire had been invited to a harvest ball at the McWhirters' house in Edinburgh.

Julek found that Claire was by no means averse to a dram or two of whisky, after which she happily managed to dance most of the night away with him. It was in the wee small hours of the morning, after a small string of stolen kisses in the library, that she confided in him that if her father had known that she had gone to a ball and drunk whisky he would have blown his top and made her return to Lewes for good.

'As a minister of the Kirk he considers all balls to be rituals of Satan,' she giggled. 'And as for drinking whisky and dancing the night away – and kissing – and with a Roman Catholic to boot –' By this time Julek had noticed that Franciszka was no longer listening, and he realised, just in time, that any mention of a romantic or sexual encounter was anathema to his sister. 'Shall we go in?' he interrupted himself, unable to think of any other way to change the subject.

On December 1 two letters arrived in Frontillac, both addressed to Julek. The first was from Mrs McIntyre who forwarded a very stiff and formal letter from the medical school informing him that unless he had a satisfactory explanation for his absence, expulsion would be considered.

The second was from Nibork. 'It's from my mother.' Julek turned as white as a sheet. 'My father's dead,' he stammered. 'We are to go immediately to Vienna and report as soon as possible to a lawyer called Samuel Sachs at his office in Rauhensteingasse, where everything will be explained.'

Julek immediately sat down and wrote two letters.

XII

The first snows were dusting the high rooftops when the diligence from Munich rumbled into Vienna. The customs formalities were as bureaucratic and irritating as ever, although Maurice and Julek managed to cope with the endless searches and hassle without too much difficulty. They finally booked in, as advised, at the Zum Schwarzen Adler Hotel in the Mariahilf area of the Austrian capital, as the winter darkness encroached on the crisp whiteness of the snow.

'*Herr Graf* Samojarski, we have been expecting you,' said the innkeeper with a formal bow and a quizzical look at Maurice. 'As well as your sister. Is she not –'

'My sister has not been well enough to travel. But I would like a room for Monsieur Chavelet, who was a close friend of my father's.'

'Of course, *Herr Graf, Monsieur* Chavelet,' he nodded to each in turn. 'I am Wolfgang Wölfl. May I express my deepest sympathy on the loss of your father. He was a most valued and agreeable guest. It is a terrible loss. Naturally I have kept his effects safely.'

'Have you any idea what has befallen my father?'

'Ah,' replied Wölfl, 'so you have not heard?'

'Nothing, except that he has died.'

'In that case, *Herr Graf*, I feel I should let *Herr Sachs* explain everything to you at the appropriate juncture. It would not be seemly for me to venture a speculation. Your mother the *Gräfin* arrived yesterday with your young brothers, but they have gone into town to see *Herr* Sachs, and are not expected back before supper. Meanwhile, if there is anything we can do…'

'Thank you, *Herr* Wölfl, there is nothing at present.'

'Let me see you to your quarters.'

The rooms at the Zum Schwarzen Adler were warm and comfortable, dominated by the beautifully tiled stoves in the corners. Julek found his room was next to that of his mother, a spacious one where two extra beds had been installed for Adam and Michał. A maid was busy unpacking their trunks. The room designated for Franciszka was given over to Maurice, and both men retired to sort out their belongings and to rest after their journey.

The clock on the tower of the Church of St Margarethe was just striking six when a carriage pulled up outside. The snow was not yet thick enough on the ground to muffle the sound of the wheels. Maurice, whose room overlooked the street below, leapt to his feet and hurried over to the window. He had spent the past hour lying awake, his heart pounding uncontrollably at the prospect of seeing Eloise again. Franciszka – brown eyes – June 1814 – Jan-Pierre – Grocholski: resurrected images which had haunted him throughout the cold, ten-day coach trek from Libourne.

All the way through Lyon, Basle and Munich, these images were still churning round Maurice's fevered brain like mental leeches that sucked at his very life blood, and would not let go. He had no reason to accompany Julek to Vienna, except to support Teofil's family at this tragic time. Franciszka had felt unable to face the journey, so it was decided that she should stay at Frontillac with Lenka. Now Maurice watched as Eloise, hooded and well-clad against the cold, alighted, followed by the two boys, and made her way into the building. Maurice came away from the window and stared at a hunting print hanging on the wall, undecided as to what to do. Should he go down and meet them? Or should he wait until Julek came to fetch him? How would they greet each other? Politely or lovingly? How would he react? Would his embarrassment and confusion show?

His reverie was interrupted by a noise on the landing outside followed by the door bursting open and two boys charging into the room and vying for priority in giving him a hug.

'Uncle Maurice! Uncle Maurice!' they cried in Polish. 'We've been dying to meet you! *Tatuś* never stopped talking about you!'

Maurice returned the hugs with much relief and bemusement. 'Hello, you must be Michał and Adam!' he replied, also in Polish, 'so which is which?'

'I'm Adam!'

'I'm Michał!'

The individual identities did not register. At that very moment Eloise stepped into the room. Their eyes met, and a momentary flicker in Eloise's brown eyes betrayed her own reservations about the meeting.

'Maurice. It is good to see you again. How have you been?' She had chosen the polite route, and spoke in French. No hugs or kisses. 'Prospering in my own way. And you?'

'Busy. With these two.'

'Fine boys. Handsome, too. A credit to you.'

'They are a great joy to me. And your son? How is Jan-Pierre? And Franciszka?'

At that moment Julek appeared. He barged boldly between them and addressed Maurice. '*Mamusia* has not been able to see *Herr* Sachs today, but we are all to meet him at his office tomorrow at noon,' he cried with as much heartiness as he could muster. 'But now that we have all met, why don't you boys go and have some fruit cordial in the kitchen, and look at the hunting trophies, while *Mamusia*, Uncle Maurice and I have a glass of wine and catch up on one another's news?'

Julek threw Maurice a knowing look. They had agreed to tell

Eloise the whole truth, and had decided it would be better if the boys were not in on it. The telling fell on Julek, his first duty as new head of the Samojarski family. He poured three glasses of refreshing Neusiedlersee wine slowly into three glasses, as if putting off what he had to do for as long as possible. When he finally began, he did not find it pleasant. He hated the look of sadness and horror that unfolded on his mother's face as she listened to the graphic but honest description of the rape and mutilation of her beloved daughter, and of the killing of the tormented and disturbed Jan-Pierre by the affable yet ultimately doomed Henry Cottershall. The expression of mortified incomprehension on the face of Maurice whenever Jan-Pierre's name was mentioned did not register with Julek, neither did the fleeting, questioning looks exchanged by Maurice and Eloise.

After the telling of the story there seemed nothing more that anybody could say. The long, empty deafening silence was broken only by the ticking of the grandfather clock in the corner and the crackling of the log fire in the cosy lobby, as all three stared into their untouched glasses, somehow fascinated by the reflection of its flames in the green-tinged golden liquid.

'I wonder what happened to *Tatuś*,' said Julek. All three wondered what had happened to Teofil, and the question was superfluous, but its sheer inanity acted as a catalyst to break the deadlock. Suddenly, Eloise burst into an uncontrollable fit of tears as the full set of implications finally registered. Julek and Maurice both leapt to their feet, but Julek got to her first. Mother and son held one another tightly as Eloise gave full vent to the agony of her situation. Maurice looked on with a concerned expression, yet glad that the onus of comforting her had not fallen on him. He would not have known the correct ratio of politeness and passion required for the comforting mixture. Then Adam and Michał ran into the room.

'*Mamusiu*, they're the biggest antlers we've ever seen –' Adam broke off. '*Mamusiu*, are you all right?'

'*Mamusia's* very upset, Adam,' said Julek. 'You see, we still don't know what happened to *Tatuś*.' His tone changed to one of hearty affability. 'But we shall know everything tomorrow. In the meantime, let's have supper. I must say, I'm getting very hungry.'

As if on cue, Wölfl entered. 'Would *Herr Graf* and *Frau Gräfin* care to take supper?' he enquired.

'That would be most agreeable, *Herr* Wölfl. What would you recommend?'

'*Frau* Wölfl has made a cauldron of *Szekelyer kaposzta*, a favourite speciality of hers from her native Hungary. It is a pork goulash with diced cabbage.'

'Sounds excellent!' cried Julek. '*Szekelyer kaposzta* it will be!'

'Very good, *Herr Graf*.'

Julek had taken masterly charge of the situation, and had managed to diffuse all the underlying emotional currents that were sparking off in different directions. Eloise had calmed herself down, and gazed in admiration at her eldest son. The youthful bluster was now tinged with a certain maturity that she had not seen before. The tone that he had set out for the rest of the evening meant that Maurice and Eloise did not get a chance to talk together, which was something they both needed to do. When, at the end of an excellent meal, Julek announced bedtime in preparation for a busy day ahead, everyone obeyed without question. Julek, Eloise noted with a strong element of pride, was definitely growing up and into his new role as head of the family.

The following day brought more snow, and the Samojarskis ordered a carriage well in advance, and arrived promptly at Rauhensteingasse with a minute to spare. Samuel Sachs was waiting for them. Julek seized the role of head of family and spokesman with the same mastery as he had acquired the day before, and made all the necessary introductions. Sachs was profuse with sympathy and condolences and hand-wringing. 'I have heard a great deal about you, *Monsieur* Chavelet,' said Sachs. '*Herr Graf* used to recount tales of your adventures together in the old days with Napoleon. You will miss him terribly, I think.'

He then turned to the boys.

'I'm eleven,' replied Adam to Sach's enquiry.

'And I'm ten,' added Michał.

'Well, boys, you will have to learn to be strong for your mother,' said Sachs. 'This has been a terrible thing to have happened to your dear father. A wonderful man and, I am proud to say, a good friend, although of all too short a standing.'

'What has happened to my husband, *Herr* Sachs?' There was a measure of stark control in Eloise's voice.

'Perhaps over a cup of coffee next door, *Frau Gräfin*,' Sachs extended his arms to shepherd the family out of his office. 'It is more – amenable than an office.'

Sachs ushered everyone into the coffee house next door. 'Mozart used to live in this house.' Sachs avoided mentioning that he had died there too. 'I find his life forces still present. A consolation for me when times are hard.' Sachs ordered coffee and pastries, and fruit cordials for the boys. 'On November 23 your husband, *Frau Gräfin*, was killed by *Zbójnicy* who waylaid the coach in the Beskid Hills in the Moravian hinterlands.'

'My God! *Zbójnicy*!' cried Eloise in horror.

'Who are the *Zbójnicy*, Tatusiu?' said Michał.

'Mountain bandits' replied Adam, pre-empting Julek's reply. 'They rob people on the roads. I have heard *Tatuś* talk about them. They're supposed to be very fierce and merciless.'

At that Eloise burst into tears. Maurice raised a tentative arm towards her, but was pre-empted by Julek, who rose from his seat, went over to her, knelt at her feet and held her close. 'W-what – how –?' she sobbed.

There was a respectful pause before Sachs replied. 'He was on his way back from Sarenki, which, as you know, my late partner *Herr* Jakob Spielberg had left to him in his will. *Herr Graf* had gone there to re-establish his ownership. He stayed a month. That is the last that I have heard from him.'

'Then how –?' began Julek.

'There was one survivor, a Viennese furniture manufacturer by the name of Himmel. Friedrich Himmel. He has a factory near the Prater. He managed to escape unscathed into the hills, whence he observed the massacre. There were perhaps a dozen assailants, all armed with rifles and guns. They spared no one.'

'What happened to this – Himmel?'

'He managed to return to Vienna by the next coach in a state of considerable shock, and reported the matter to the authorities. They have sent an armed unit into the area to seek out and destroy this gang, who, it seems, had been responsible for a number of similar incidents.'

'And he actually witnessed these – these bandits murdering my husband?'

'*Herr* Himmel and your husband had exchanged visiting cards,' continued Sachs after a slight pause. 'It seems that your husband had been interested in *Herr* Himmel's products for his estate, and had expressed a wish to keep in touch.'

'How did you come to know of this, *Herr* Sachs?' said Eloise.

'Your husband mentioned my name in conversation. *Herr* Himmel felt it his duty to contact me, the only person in Vienna who effectively knew him.'

'M-my husband's body…?' stammered Eloise.

'Has not been found, to my knowledge. The incident took place in a remote region, and *Herr* Himmel was not able to identify the site. Besides, the robbers had initially forced the coach off the main route, obviously to confuse pursuit.'

'And the authorities…' began Maurice.

'Are doing everything they can.'

'My God,' groaned Eloise, 'What are we going to do?'

'We must go to Sarenki immediately, and finish what *Tatuś* had started,' said Julek resolutely.

'A wise decision, *Herr Graf*,' said Sachs. 'Sarenki is, after all, once again your home now, is it not?'

XIII

Zygmunt Karłowicz, the self-appointed estate manager of Sarenki, and Julek raised their glasses of Old Pankracy. Age had not abated the brewer of this legendary firewater, who was now at the rusty gates of his ninetieth birthday, and still brewing. 'My father often used to recall that he had always been Old – with a capital O – as if it were part of his name,' said Julek, 'even when he was a youngster.' He raised his glass. *'Na zdrowie!'*

'Na zdrowie!' replied the other. They both downed the clear, warming liquid in one.

It was a cold, crisp Christmas night, almost idyllic in its perfection. An almost full moon lit up the heavily snow-clad landscape of the Carpathian foothills, making the flickering yellows and orange ambers of the fires and lamps shining from the windows of most of the cottages in the village almost superfluous. Julek had escorted his mother, with Adam and Michał following on behind, to Midnight Mass. This had been celebrated by the recently appointed Father Józef Godny. 'He's young, bland, awfully nice and harmlessly ineffectual,' Karłowicz had confided in Julek, 'but for all that he's firmly on the side of Good, as the late, lamented other Father Józef used to say. But the late, lamented other Father Józef he isn't.'

The Samojarskis were watched intently by the whole population of Sarenki, all of whom, including the old, the infirm and the blind drunk, had turned out that night to see their re-instated Lord of the Manor celebrating the birth of Jesus Christ as it should be celebrated – with a real *Pan hrabia* and his family in their front pews, where they belonged. Over twenty years they had the ghost of Grocholski and a dying Jew as figureheads of their community, and now they were united in their welcome of the one true figurehead – the handsome and forthright young Count Julek Samojarski, cutting such a lofty and imposing presence in their midst.

After Mass Julek and Karłowicz stayed up 'for a last snifter', while Eloise packed the boys off to bed before retiring herself, leaving the men to their final contemplative drink. It had been, both men agreed, an emotional week.

After the meeting with Samuel Sachs in Vienna, Julek had immediately written to the estate manager at Sarenki, explaining the situation, and notifying him of his family's plans to travel first to Kraków, and thence to Sarenki. Sachs had also made Julek aware of plans, as initially conceived by his father and Jakob Spielberg, of establishing a medical centre at Sarenki, an idea that Julek took to with great enthusiasm, although he had reservations about naming it after a Jew. 'You know perfectly well that neither my father nor I have any prejudices against Jews, *Herr* Sachs, but there are many who have,' he said.

Maurice had decided to return to Libourne, and to make such arrangements for Franciszka as he would see fit. He left with a certain sense of relief. Such conversations with Eloise as he could snatch without Julek present had been inconclusive, and there was nothing in her demeanour to suggest anything other than that he, Maurice, was a dear and close family friend, with whom her daughter was currently staying, albeit under terrible circumstances. Brown eyes never entered the equation. He had been worrying about nothing.

Julek, his mother and brothers had duly arrived in Sarenki in a snow storm a week before Christmas, and had presented themselves at the Manor to a warmly welcoming Zygmunt Karłowicz.

'*Panie hrabio*,' he had smiled. 'Such a pleasure. About time, too, if I may say.'

Julek found the estate manager to be an affable, portly little man in his late fifties. He had very little hair and a slight squint. His smile was disconcertingly one-sided, which gave an insincere look, although Julek later found out that his mouth was partly paralysed as a result of a fight in his younger days when he used to work for Grocholski. A small scar was visible only to careful scrutiny. Karłowicz lived frugally at the Manor. He occupied the kitchen and the room beside it, which he had made warm and cosy, while *Pani* Frania Gruszka 'did' for him. The rest of the house, Julek noted, was not in very good condition, and required attention, especially in those places where a leaking roof had caused damage. For all that, he and *Pani* Frania had managed to open up, clean and prepare two further rooms for the return of the *Hrabiostwo*.

Karłowicz did not need to exert a lot of pressure to persuade Julek and his family to stay at Sarenki over Christmas, more as a gesture of intent towards the villagers rather than for festive reasons.

'I realise, *Pani hrabino*,' he said to Eloise in passable French, 'that you have nothing to feel festive about, but this is your home, and the villagers don't know you. For twenty years they have lived in a kind of limbo, and the time has come to re-establish the natural order of things. Please stay until the New Year.'

*****

Over the next few days Julek, his mother and brothers were plied with condolences, as everyone came to express pleasure at the return of the Samojarskis to the bosom of their fold. They spoke fondly of Teofil's far too brief a visit just over a month previously, and had been looking forward to that day when the whole family would be reunited once more in their true home.

Wigilia had been a wistful but ultimately successful affair, improvised in the kitchen of Sarenki by Karłowicz in collaboration with *Pani* Frania. The widow of the hapless Kazio Gruszka had re-invented herself after the death of her husband of a stroke a decade previously. She had assumed control of, rather than been hired for, the running of Sarenki, which she had come to regard as her domain, especially as it came with a tenant in the shape of Zygmunt Karłowicz, one-time paid lackey to the most hated man ever to impose himself on the community, but now a pleasant and amenable man still just in his prime. Her devotion to both estate and estate manager was total and uncompromising – often to the irritation of the latter.

'I swear that she has her eye on me as a prospective husband, *Panie hrabio*,' muttered Karłowicz one evening after *Pani* Frania had set off for home, her daily duties completed. 'If only she were twenty years younger, then, perhaps –' his voice tailed off, as did his thoughts.

Pani Frania had come up with a creditable feast considering the circumstances. *Barszcz* made from that year's beetroots from the Gruszka farm was followed by a handsome carp donated by Little Irek, who had caught it especially for the returning Lord of the Manor. Although now at the threshold of 30, he was still known as Little Irek, formerly the Old Father Józef's favourite altar boy. He had now taken over the pig farm from his father, the outspoken Big Irek, who was now chair-ridden and suffering from senile dementia.

The Samojarskis stayed at Sarenki until the Feast of Epiphany on January 6, by which time Julek had made his very positive mark on the community. He announced the impending formal return to the way things used to be, with the Samojarskis in their rightful inheritance, and of Julek's intention to complete his studies at the Edinburgh Medical School. He also announced plans for the development of Sarenki as a spa, with the hiring of medical experts and advisers to test the waters, in accordance with the wishes of his predecessor, Jakob Spielberg. All this, Julek promised, would bring a new era of common prosperity and optimism for Sarenki. These projections were all met with great enthusiasm tinged, however, with a certain set of reservations.

'Teofil was more one of us than this one,' said someone. 'Still, I'm sure that beneath that haughty lordship there must be a bit of the bolshie old Teofil about him.'

Eloise had won the hearts of everyone, who admired her enduring 'frenchness' – and accent – she spoke very little Polish – as well as her dignity and poise in the face of the tragedy of the loss of her husband. The boys, needless to say, sought out, and found, peers with whom to play in the snow and explore the woods. Zygmunt Karłowicz was officially re-hired as the new estate manager, with a brief to turn Sarenki's fortunes around, do all the necessary repairs to the Manor, restock and develop farming, and generally prepare for the return of the Samojarskis. His brief was re-enforced with the promise of extra pay dating back to the death of Jakob Spielberg, his last paymaster. The development of the spa would commence fully only after his qualification at Edinburgh, and would be put on hold for the time being.

The New Father Józef led the farewell delegation as the *Hrabiostwo* climbed into Karłowicz's coach. It was driven by Little Irek, at his own insistence, for the journey to Nowy Sandec, where they would find public transport to Kraków – and back to Nibork.

*****

On the day of their departure a bedraggled, elderly man with a straggly beard, sunken eyes and frost-bitten hands staggered into a small house just outside a remote village in the hills to the north of Olmutz, in Austrian Moravia. He was amply clad in a dirty, torn but thick fur greatcoat and strong, sturdy, mud-bespattered boots. As he lurched across the room, his legs buckled under him, and he collapsed on the floor. The owner of the house, one Antonin Przybyl, rushed over to him, and cradled his head in his lap. His wife, whose name was Jarmila, immediately brought a jug of *slivovica,* which she forced between his cracked lips.

'Please – please help me,' croaked the man, trying to focus his eyes, which would not stop blinking. 'My name is – I am – Count – Count Teofil Samojarski.'

*****

Also, on the same day, at Frontillac, Franciszka went up to Lenka, who was cleaning the flagged kitchen floor. 'Aunt Lenka,' she said, with a quiver in her voice and a tear in her eye, 'I think I'm pregnant.'

Part Six – 1838

I

Eloise Samojarska and the boys returned to Nibork towards the end of January 1838 after a cold and circuitous route through Prussia, avoiding Russian territory. Snow lay thick on the ground, and made progress difficult. Almost as soon as he had arrived, Julek set off for Königsberg, where he knew that *The Star of Skye* was due to sail. Joshua Grimsdyke was not likely to consider some characteristic rough weather in both the Baltic and North Seas as reasons to abandon his habitual voyage to Aberdeen. Julek was now totally focused on completing his studies at the Edinburgh Medical School and establishing his health spa at Sarenki, and had delegated the responsibility of the move to his mother. Eloise's brief was to wind up their affairs in Prussia, pack, transfer the bank accounts to Kraków, and send all the family effects on to Sarenki to the more than capable care of Zygmunt Karłowicz. Then, with the arrival of spring, she was to bid farewell to the Zaletniks and set off with Adam and Michał to take up residence as the Lady of the Manor in the absence of the student Lord of the Manor.

*****

What Eloise had no way of knowing was that the true Lord of the Manor had materialised on the doorstep of Sarenki in the middle of a severe snowstorm three weeks after the family's departure. It took both *Pani* Frania and Karłowicz a good few moments before they recognised the thin, emaciated figure that stood at the door, his lacklustre eyes fixed on the blazing log fire in the kitchen beyond.

'But – but we all thought you were dead, *Panie hrabio!*' gasped *Pani* Frania after Teofil had removed his fur hat and greatcoat. 'My God! But what has happened to you?'

'It's a long story, *Pani* Franiu, which I will tell you after I have had a glass of – I take it that's Old Pankracy in that jug –'

It was. Teofil immediately downed three shots, after which his lacklustre eyes assumed a new life. *Pani Frania* took his coat, sat him down in front of the fire, ladled a large portion of *bigos* into a bowl, accompanied by a large chunk of rye bread, all of which Teofil attacked with a ferocious vengeance. This pleased both *Pani* Frania and Karłowicz, who watched his every mouthful intently, not wishing to hurry him. 'As I said, it's rather a long story,' he said finally, sitting back and stretching out his legs towards the fire.

*****

Teofil's long story in fact began with his arrival in Sarenki during the closing days of the golden autumn that had blessed central Europe that year. The whole village had come to the Manor as soon as they had heard of his return to take up residence in what everyone considered to be his rightful place. He met and established warm relations with Zygmunt Karłowicz as well as with the New Father Józef Godny. It was a brief visit, aimed primarily at re-establishing his newly official presence at Sarenki, in which he had a full run-down on the Grocholski years, and found that it had been a period of stagnation, as the usurping Lord of the Manor had, mercifully, virtually abandoned his domain in favour of the fleshpots of the Viennese circuit. Then they had felt sorry for Jakob Spielberg. Many found the fact that he was a 'good' Jewish lawyer a modern concept that was difficult to cope with. Racial intolerance was almost a way of life in Eastern Europe, with Jews and Gipsies the prime victims. However, his doleful warmth, as well as his terminal illness, added to the fact that he was, after all, the brother of the ill-fated Boris, whose grisly death was still etched indelibly on many local psyches. Besides, anyone following Grocholski as tenant of the Manor would automatically qualify for at least a modicum of respect.

At the same time, Teofil met some new faces, as well as old faces that were new when he was there last. He was pleased to see Henryk Staruch, son of the old wastrel Jan Staruch, and recalled how as a twelve-year-old he had sneaked into his stable to play with his horse, Mazurek, when he had first arrived at Sarenki with Maurice twenty-five years previously. He had given the boy the job of looking after Mazurek, which inspired Henryk to take on horses as a career. Over those years Henryk had become a superb horseman, and had established a saddler's workshop at Nowy Sandec and stables at Sarenki. He also bought Irek's buggy to ferry people to Nowy Sandec, and even as far as Lwów or Kraków.

Teofil also remembered Bogumił Małosielski and Cisia Benarska when they were still children. They were now married, Bogumił was a roofer and thatcher, and they had a very pretty daughter, Honorata, who was, very obviously to anyone in the village, the specific object of adoration by Witold Sienkowski.

Old Pankracy was Older than ever, completely toothless, and still making his fire-water for everyone's benefit. He had a standing order for a barrel a week which was delivered regularly by Henryk Staruch in his buggy to the White Eagle in Nowy Sandec. Teofil, in turn, updated everyone on Grocholski's situation, prompting many to wish him 'a long life rotting in his Viennese dungeon.'

At the end of the first week of November, when the weather turned more wintry, Teofil decided to return to Nibork and prepare for the permanent move before the snows of winter would make travel difficult. Because of an early snow-storm, which caused drifts in the Beskid Hills, he was delayed in his departure, and had to spend three days in Kraków, kicking his heels. Also delayed was a jolly young furniture manufacturer from Vienna by the name of Friedrich Hummelstein, who provided some cheerful company during the wait. Seated one evening after supper over a few glasses, Hummelstein told Teofil about how he was taking over the family business, from his ageing father, while Teofil, by now a little drunk and in high spirits, told him – as well as the whole inn, who could not help but overhear – the story of his reclamation of his estate at Sarenki. The whole matter was in the hands of a Viennese lawyer by the name of Samuel Sachs whose office was in Rauhensteingasse. Teofil further expressed a wish to do business with Hummelstein, as Sarenki would need to be extensively refitted and furnished over the coming months. Teofil and Hummelstein exchanged visiting cards.

There was no reason whatsoever why Teofil should have taken any notice of an insignificant patron drinking quietly in the corner of *Zum Schwarzen Adler*, who glanced momentarily at him before going out into the night. Had he done so, Teofil would undoubtedly have recognised him.

*****

Three days later, half-way through November, the weather again changed for the better, and the Vienna diligence was set to depart at daybreak. Apart from Hummelstein, who sat by the window opposite Teofil, there were seven other passengers. As the coach rumbled off southwards into the Beskid Hills, which formed a natural frontier between Galicia and Moravia, Teofil and Hummelstein continued to develop their friendship with bantering conversation and anecdotes, all laced with laughter and jollity, with the other passengers joining in. It promised to be a pleasant and congenial journey for all.

It was on a remote stretch of hilly terrain in the Bielsko region, some ten hours out of Kraków, with the light failing, that the coach was ambushed by a gang of *Zbójnicy*, some dozen mountain bandits, all armed with guns and knives. A sniper first shot both the driver and the postilion, whereupon the rest of the riders took control of the horses, and led them off the track and down a steep slope. As the coach rumbled, out of control, down the slope, the door swung open and Hummelstein fell out. Teofil tried to grab him, but it happened so quickly that there was nothing either of them could have done. A moment later one of the bandits rode up against the door and looked into the coach. Teofil and he recognised one another instantly – despite a lapse of two decades. It was Filipowicz, Grocholski's henchman in the Nowy Sandec days. Older, still clad in furs, but no less vicious in appearance and attitude than he had been then. There was no sign of Hummelstein. Before Teofil could gather two strands of wit together, the coach crashed into a boulder and overturned. Teofil, thrown clear, experienced a searing pain in his side, followed by a knock on the head which momentarily dazed him. In the chaos that followed, he watched in horror as the bandits opened fire, shooting or stabbing everyone except him. Finally, Filipowicz rode up to Teofil, jumped off his horse, and kicked him in his side, exactly where the excruciating pain was.

*****

'I doubled up in agony,' said Teofil as Karłowicz recharged his glass. 'It still hurts.' He winced as he felt his side gingerly. 'Anyway, I soon gathered that Filipowicz was the leader of this gang. He pointed a finger menacingly at me and told these two men to tie me up really tightly.'

*****

One of these men was a burly, blond-haired Czech and another, a large, bovine *Góral* with one eye, a loping gait and a perpetual, toothless grin. While they tied him up, Teofil glared at Filipowicz, who watched the process with a leering grin. 'So,' he said, 'we meet again, *Panie hrabio*. You are looking well on your good fortune.' He leaned down and pulled a knot particularly tightly. 'But I think we have unfinished business still.'

'I can't think of any business with you that I would wish to pursue.'

'There is always business to be done with the aristocracy.'

'I should have known I'd come across you again,' replied Teofil, wincing from the pain.

'It was meant to be, *Panie hrabio*. Fate just needed a little prod from me. You were going on so much back at the Bear Inn that you didn't see me.'

'You were there? So you knew I would be on the coach?'

'News travels fast, even in the mountains.'

*****

Karłowicz topped up Teofil's glass. 'So, this operation must have been planned for your benefit,' he said.

'Obviously. After that arguments broke out among the bandits,' continued Teofil.

*****

The *Zbójnicy* ransacked all the trunks and personal belongings, and unharnessed the horses. The bodies were unceremoniously manhandled and dumped over the edge of a ravine. Teofil strained to look about him, hoping to see some sign of Hummelstein, but it was getting too dark. The bandits did not seem to be aware that one of the passengers had eluded the massacre. Part of him was disappointed, as Hummelstein might have helped to attempt some sort of escape, while another part was glad, knowing that he was safe, and probably in a better position to get help anyway. Finally, the grinning *Góral* and the burly Czech with enormous blond hair, whose name, it transpired, was Vlad, hoisted Teofil onto one of the horses and they all set off along a barely visible path leading further into the mountains. The pain in his side was excruciating, but there was nothing Teofil could do about it. After about an hour the gang pitched a camp in a rocky clearing beside a cave in a hillside. It was almost completely dark. Teofil found himself dumped unceremoniously just inside the cave, along with all the other bandits. It was freezing cold, and Teofil spent the night shivering and counting the minutes until daybreak when, he assumed, the party would continue on its way to whatever destination it was bound. He tried to listen to what the gang, who were huddled over a small fire further inside the cave, were saying, but they were talking in whispers and muttering, mostly in Czech. Finally, there was silence, broken only by someone snoring.

By the time daybreak finally came, Teofil was almost paralysed with cold. The urine that he had been forced to pass in the night had frozen down his legs, which had lost all feeling. Filipowicz and Vlad gathered up their forces and once more led the way further into the mountains. After about six agonising hours spent trying to keep his balance on horseback, no easy feat with his hands tied behind his back, the pain in his side and the uneven terrain that the horse had to negotiate, the party reached its destination. The gang's hideout was a village, hidden away in a remote valley, from which Teofil thought he could see the craggy outline of the distant High Tatras to the east. There were women and children around, and plumes of smoke rose from each cottage, testifying to a permanence not usually associated with a bandits' hide-out. His hands still bound, Teofil was bundled into a freezing hut, a storage dump of sorts, and further tied to a thick, wooden beam where he was finally left all alone.

*****

The next day Teofil woke from a fitful sleep to overhear a snippet of conversation between Filipowicz and Vlad. It was in Czech, but he understood enough to make him sick with worry.

'But I still think it's worth a try,' he heard Filipowicz saying to Vlad. 'If it doesn't work, we'll just kill him.'

'I thought we were going to kill him anyway?'

'Let's see what happens first, shall we?'

With this nebulous threat hanging over him, Teofil tried hard not to panic, and to keep hold of his faculties. He had plenty of time to do so. The days passed agonisingly slowly, with no relief from the biting cold and the pain in his side. Each day he was fed stale bread and ewe's cheese by the grinning *Góral*, who appeared to have been given the job of jailer. Teofil looked at him closely, wondering whether trying to open some form of communication with him might be a wise thing to do. The *Góral* was certainly a man of few, if any, words. One morning, a week into his captivity, and with no sign of Filipowicz or anyone other than the *Góral* taking any notice of him whatsoever, he decided to act. 'Hey, Baca,' he said, pronouncing it Batsa and trying to sound cool and casual. 'What am I doing here, man? Why wasn't I killed with the others?

The *Góral*'s grin disappeared. 'Man!' he said. 'You smart! You know *Góral* talk! No one knows my real name! Everyone calls me Wół. You call me Baca. Nice expression to call a man. I like that. You one smart aristocrat!'

This was going to be better than Teofil had imagined. *Wół*, pronounced *Voow*, was obviously a nickname. It meant ox in Polish. It figures, thought Teofil. He was definitely ox-like, slow and vacuous. Teofil had taken a chance: Baca is a very common expression among *Górals*, meaning mate, chief, squire, or any other friendly appellation. He played the advantage. 'Where you from, then, Baca?' he asked, trying to be friendly enough to gain the slow-witted *Góral*'s confidence. 'I can call you Baca? Or would you prefer Wół?'

'Nah. Don't like Wół. I'm not an ox.'

'What's your name, then?'

'Nah. You don't wanna know that, man. *Góral* name. Yukh!'

'Right.' Despite the pain in his side, which had got to a dull, numbing stage, Teofil smiled at him. 'So, where're you from, Baca?'

Baca looked out of the window towards the east. 'Folks come from Zakopane. You know it?'

It was a clear day and Teofil, following his gaze, could definitely make out the high crags of the Tatras, the home of the *Góral*s. 'I've heard of it. They say it's very beautiful.'

'It's shit, man! It's all cold shit. It's just fucking mountains. My folks were poor. Cold and nothing to eat.'

Teofil decided to try psychology. 'You're not like the others, Baca. You look like a good guy to me. So, you were poor and cold. It's not a crime to be poor and cold.' Baca, Teofil noticed, was listening. 'You don't need to kill, you know. Why not just be a robber? There's enough to go round, you know, without killing. It's not wrong to steal to live.'

Baca rolled his eyes as he pondered this possibility. 'They aren't going to kill you, man,' he said at last. 'Least not yet.'

Teofil was interested. 'Why?'

'Not supposed to tell you, but Filipowicz says he knows you. You could be useful, he says, being an aristocratic an' that, he says.'

Teofil was interested. 'In what way?'

'Man, I talk too much,' was the reply. The *Góral* shrugged and wiped his nose on his sleeve.

II

Slowly, as the endless days went on, Teofil managed to open up Baca's limited mental faculties, and discovered, a little bit at a time, that the big blond Czech, Vlad, had also been one of Grocholski's thugs in Nowy Sandec twenty years previously.

*****

'Down the years Filipowicz had maintained his close friendship with Grocholski,' continued Teofil, now fully relaxed with his feet stretched out towards the fire. 'He had on a number of occasions fenced stolen goods for him on the streets of Baden. Filipowicz had been saddened and shocked at his former leader's arrest and demotion. Then, while in Kraków two weeks previously, Filipowicz had further learned on the tavern grapevine of my re-instatement at Sarenki, which was high-profile gossip at all echelons of society. It was all my fault – me and my big mouth at the Bear Inn in Kraków! How could I have missed him? It was then that Filipowicz had formulated a wild plan which necessitated keeping a close watch on comings and goings at the post office, to glean when and where I would be travelling next. This was standard practice among the *Zbójnicy,* who often targeted specific victims. I gradually learned that the plan was to find and kidnap me and use me as a bargaining counter for the release of Grocholski. So, aware of the delay of the diligence due to bad weather, they both kept their ears and eyes open, until finally Vlad found me at the Bear Inn, talking loudly to a young Viennese businessman. Vlad reported to Filipowicz, and the plan was laid, and the rest of the gang notified.'

Teofil further gleaned from Baca that Vlad had gone to Vienna, pretending to be an emissary from the bandits, offering Teofil's life in exchange for the release of Grocholski. This news threw light on the disturbing snippet of conversation that Teofil had overheard at the start of his captivity.

'Vlad's got this cousin who works in the kitchens at the Ministry,' continued Baca, 'who fixed hostage deals if Vlad ever caught someone important.'

'How can he do that?' asked Teofil incredulously.

'Don't know. Didn't ask.'

Teofil had visions of secret meetings between Czech kitchen workers and justice ministers in the dark alleys of Vienna, and began seriously to fear for his safety. Over the next few days, he developed something akin to a meaningful relationship with Baca, who talked of his childhood in the Tatra Mountains, where he was perpetually cold and hungry. Teofil assured him that, if what he had said was true, the Ministry – whatever that was – would certainly do a deal, and that he, Teofil, would be released. 'When all this is over, Baca, come and see me in Sarenki and we'll down some Old Pankracy together and talk about this time and have a laugh!'

'Man! I'd like that!'

'I know! You can have a job on the estate. Help manage the place. You'll be paid fairly. No more robbing. You could go straight.'

Baca's grin increased and made him look almost frighteningly ugly. *'Człowieku!'* he beamed, 'Man!'

After another few days, Teofil asked Baca to loosen his bonds because he had lost all feeling in his hands. The *Góral* obliged. The next day the bandits were all gone on a raid, leaving him in charge of their captive. Teofil seized the opportunity to ask

Baca to remove the ropes altogether. 'They're killing me, Baca,' he said. 'Anyway, it's time we trusted one another. I shall be free soon. We're friends, aren't we?'

*****

'Baca obliged,' said Teofil, 'and we ended up sitting together in the hut, in a semblance of total mutual trust. For the first time since my capture, I was able to use my own hands to feed myself. I told him nice things about Sarenki, Old Father Józef, New Father Józef, my family back in Nibork, Maurice, Old Pankracy, the Gruszkas – always avoiding any mention of the Grocholski affair. In this way I lulled Baca into a false sense of quiet security. With feeling returning to my numbed wrists, I reached out and seized a large piece of timber lying on the ground, leapt up and hit Baca hard across the head with it.'

*****

Making sure that Baca was out cold, Teofil wasted no time. He made for the door, opened it surreptitiously, and looked out. The village was completely quiet, and only the thin spirals of smoke issuing from the chimneys testified to any life; otherwise not a soul was to be seen anywhere. Snow lay thick all around and the sky was a uniform slate grey. It was, Teofil estimated, mid-afternoon. Making absolutely sure that he was not seen, he made off in the direction of a wooded thicket just beyond a hovel on the edge of the village. By the time he reached this cover he realised that he had left footprints in the snow, although he reckoned that the women and children were highly unlikely to give chase, and neither would Baca, when he finally came round.

As for the rest of the *Zbójnicy*, there was no knowing whether they would be back before dark, but by the following day he would have put some considerable distance between himself and the village. Emerging from the thicket on the far side, he fixed his gaze on the rugged horizon and made for a wooded slope in the indistinct distance. Teofil had no idea where he was, or where he was going: there was nothing but mountains all around. It was bitterly cold, and he just kept going, trying to get as far from the village as he could. There was no sun at any time to navigate by. His only possible point of reference was the High Tatras mountain range, which he may or may not have caught a glimpse of at the start of his captivity. They would have been to the east. He couldn't even be sure that what he had seen was, in fact, the Tatras. It may have been clouds, or an optical illusion, but it was his only chance of gaining some sense of direction, so he tried to keep going north, hopefully towards Galicia. As he never actually saw the sun, either rising or setting, he was able to estimate the points of the compass as to the different shades of grey cloud cover. Apart from that, he could only guess.

Teofil spent a week blundering around the freezing mountains trying to find some form of human habitation, or at least temporary shelter. It snowed on and off, so he at least had the satisfaction of knowing that his footprints would have been erased. Fortunately, he had his greatcoat, which offered some protection against the penetrating cold and the icy winds that blew off the mountains. He was on the verge of despair, staving off a deep urge just to lie down and embrace oblivion, when he thought he saw a thin spiral of smoke coming from the floor of a valley. With hope re-ignited, he pulled himself together and peered into the distance. Through his iced eyelashes he saw it: a small village clinging to the slope of a hill.

III

'How I managed to get to it I still don't know,' said Teofil. 'All I remember, apart from the pain and the cold, is staggering into the first house I came to, and collapsing on the floor.'

'So, you didn't die of exposure in the mountains, *Panie hrabio*,' said *Pani* Frania Gruszka, cutting another slice of *babka* onto Teofil's plate. Teofil looked at her with an amused twinkle which alighted in his eye, the first one for many a day. Vividly he recalled their first meeting, when he went up to the Gruszka farm to investigate the embezzlement on his estate. He recalled her hovering, embarrassed, wringing her hands and wiping them nervously on her pinafore from feeding her poultry. Now, beneath the same pinafore she was still wearing the same long, pleated black skirt covering black boots, the white blouse with billowing sleeves and the heavily embroidered black bodice, in the manner of the peasants of the Kraków region. On her head she still wore the red scarf, knotted at the back.

Now, two decades later, only the etch of the lines on her face testified to the passing of twenty years; as well as the depth of the eyes, the weary stoop, and the quiver in the voice, all of which she tried to suppress for the benefit of her *Pan* Zygmunt by adding a liberal zest of hearty bustle.

'The owner of the house, a retired wood carver, and his wife took me in,' continued Teofil. 'They were Czech. Antonin and Jarmila Prybyl. A kinder couple you wouldn't find anywhere. The Prybyls fed me and looked after me for a full month, by which time I'd recovered enough to be on my way.' Teofil paused with a thoughtful look on his face. 'I gave them the only thing of any value that I had,' he continued.

'I'd bought a diamond ring in Vienna for Eloise, and kept it in a secret inside pocket of my greatcoat. The bandits never found it. I was determined not to part with it, even though I was originally tempted to bribe Baca with it. But in the end, I decided he was, after all, just another murderous bandit, and he got what he deserved.' Teofil paused, and thought of the grinning *Góral*. Did he really mean what he had just said?

At the time, he recalled, he did feel sorry for Baca. Poverty, he had said, was not a crime. 'But the Prybyls were another matter,' he continued, mentally dismissing his compassionate moment. 'At first they refused the present, saying it was far too much, but in the end, Antonin accepted it as surety, when I told him I would return soon to pay them something towards my stay, after which he insisted that he would be returning it.'

'I take it you will not go back to reclaim it?' said Karłowicz.

'The Prybyls saved my life. It was only a ring. I can afford to replace it. Their kindness was beyond price. They fixed everything for me.'

Old Antonin had lent Teofil a horse and rode with him as far as Bielsko, which was on the post road. As there would not be another coach for two days, Teofil put up at *zum Heiligen Kreuz* post hotel while he pondered his next move: Antonin had insisted on paying the hotel bill, and all expenses, in full. It was there that Teofil learned from the innkeeper the full sequel to the story of his capture.

'There was no deal, I take it?' said Karłowicz.

'What do you think? Vlad's offer – through the mediation of his cousin in the kitchens of the Ministry – was readily accepted. Too readily, if the truth be known.'

*****

Vlad's idea, when he presented himself at the back gates of the Ministry of Justice in Vienna, where the kitchens were, was to pretend to be betraying the notorious gang of *Zbójnicy* that had been terrorising the Galician-Moravian outback, by leading the authorities to the camp where Count Samojarski was being held. The condition was that Grocholski should be released and allowed to accompany them, escorted by no more than six armed guards as security, in case of treachery. When the camp was in sight, Vlad and Grocholski were to be allowed to disappear, while the armed guards, with the element of surprise in their favour, could storm the camp and kill everyone. Then – unofficially, of course – they could raid the coffers where all the loot was stashed, and there would be no one to ask any questions. What Vlad didn't divulge was that the bandits would in fact be waiting for them, ready and armed to the teeth. There were over a dozen of them, and they knew the terrain well, so the odds were very much in the bandits' favour.

The authorities' representative in this instance, whom Vlad's cousin went to fetch, was Chief Prison Officer Zoltan Kis, a specifically promoted Hungarian thug whose underhand dealings and treatment of the prisoners was equally specifically of no concern to the authorities. Prison Officer Kis' plan differed from Vlad's only marginally. The moment the camp came in sight, Vlad and Grocholski would be shot in the back, and the two-dozen strong and fully trained Austrian Army unit secretly shadowing their tracks would open fire, storm the camp and raze it to the ground, and kill all the inhabitants, including, if necessary, Count Samojarski, before raiding the coffers where all the loot was stashed. It would also rid the authorities of Grocholski without recourse to lengthy and expensive legalities, and Count Samojarski would have been an unfortunate victim caught in the crossfire.

At first everything went according to the common plan. As

soon as the camp came in sight, Prison Officer Kis' plan came to the fore, and Vlad and Grocholski knew no more about it. The ensuing shoot-out was short and fierce. The Army unit lost not one man, and there were no survivors in the village, man, woman or child. The village was put to the torch after having been thoroughly looted.

*****

'So that was the end of Grocholski,' concluded Teofil. 'And Filipowicz. Can't say I'm sorry. I would have pulled the trigger myself.'

'They don't dither, these Austrian army lads, do they?' said Karłowicz.

'Vlad and Filipowicz were idiots to have even considered the idea! I mean, how important were Grocholski and I in the scheme of things? A small-time criminal and a Count from the Galician outback?'

Teofil reflected momentarily on his own unimportance in the corridors of power at the Hofburg in Vienna. 'But I can't help wondering about Baca.' Teofil sighed at the recollection of the pathetic, slow-witted Ox. 'I can't really help feeling sorry for him. You know, if I had given him that job here, I'm sure he would have turned out to be a completely loyal and devoted worker. We shall never know. Anyway,' he continued after a pause, 'after all that I couldn't make up my mind what to do next: to get to Vienna, to go back home to Nibork, or to come back home to Sarenki.'

Teofil gazed absently at the fire for a good while. It now needed a poke. *Pani* Frania saw the line of his gaze, attended to it and added a log. 'In the end,' Teofil muttered, 'I decided to come back to Sarenki, mainly because that was the direction the next coach was going.'

'We're glad you did. You do realise that your family have been here?' said Karłowicz after a pause, during which glasses were recharged.

Teofil looked up excitedly. 'My God! Why didn't you tell me?'

'What, and spoil your story? They arrived a week before Christmas, and left on the Feast of the Epiphany for Nibork. They'd heard all about your – death – from Samuel Sachs. He'd summoned them all to Vienna, ostensibly to hand over the inheritance of Sarenki. I must say, your son Julek is a credit to you. A fine fellow who took to his responsibilities as – forgive me – new Lord of the Manor with courage and fortitude rare in one so young. We persuaded them to stay over Christmas.'

Teofil paused to digest this information. He opened his mouth to speak, but then reconsidered. A great deal had happened since the summer. Many journeys had been undertaken, and many letters had been written and sent, but perhaps not read. Events were overtaking one another at an alarming rate, and the post – having to contend not only with the weather, but also with a vast, pan-European circle embracing Nibork, Edinburgh, Frontillac, Vienna, Sarenki and Lugano– simply could not keep up. To go back to Vienna? To write to Nibork, or to go there? To write to Edinburgh? To Frontillac? To tell everyone to stay put? Or to summon everyone to Sarenki? It was one of those situations that could lead to paths being crossed in opposite directions without anyone being aware of the fact.

Teofil's two-month adventure with the *Zbójnicy* was over. Sarenki was his. The *bigos* and vodka had lifted his spirits considerably, but had done nothing for his capacity for making decisions. *Pani* Frania had gone to prepare a room for him, only recently vacated by Julek and his young brothers. The pain in his side was tormenting him as before, but at least he was no longer cold, he was well fed, and at home.

Home! A confusing word, taking all things into consideration. He had never really known the meaning of the word.

Suddenly, he felt desperately tired again. And old. He closed his eyes and allowed his mind to wander a little. So Julek had taken his responsibilities as new Lord of the Manor with – what was it Karłowicz had said? – courage and fortitude rare in one so young. Good. Let him sort it out.

Teofil smiled to himself, and decided to do absolutely nothing.

*****

400 kilometres away, at the Ministry of the Interior in Vienna, Ludwig Mendel was updating Prince Clemens von Metternich on the latest state of play on the Imperial corruption front.

'Should there be an official investigation into this?' said the Minister.

'It would serve no purpose, Excellency,' replied Mendel. 'It has all been very convenient. It is really quite irrelevant that Grocholski and Vladimir – there seems to be no record of a surname – were shot in the back. Just hearsay. If I may suggest that the report states merely that following an anonymous tip-off a unit from the Schwechat battalion identified and stormed the hideout of a gang of bandits in the Moravian-Galician border region, and that all the bandits were wiped out in the shoot-out.'

'What about Samojarski?'

'He didn't appear to have been there. His body was not found. But then, there was no one to identify a body.'

'He may still be alive?'

'One would hope so. We shall find out in the course of time. Both his title and his estate have been duly restored. I understand from his lawyer, Samuel Sachs, that he intends to take up residence there once more.'

'Samuel Sachs? Isn't he one of those Jewish lawyers involved in buying and selling titles?'

'There has been no evidence that we've been able to uncover. Certainly not in recent years. In fact, it was Sachs and his late partner, Jakob Spielberg, who laid bare the Grocholski case.'

'Clever bastards, you Jews.'

'And useful, Excellency, you must admit. I recommend no further action on that front.'

'Has Count Samojarski a residential permit?'

'And full citizenship, Excellency. You recall you signed the papers on –' Mendel fumbled through the file.

'I recall nothing of the sort, Mendel, but never mind,' interrupted Metternich. 'I shall take your word for it. I think we can now consider the Grocholski case closed. Coffee?'

'Thank you, Excellency.'

IV

It was Monday; a bitterly cold, misty and monochrome February dawn, but it still did not stop the old man from assuming his habitual perch on the small, rotting wooden platform on the edge of the River Dordogne just upstream from Saint-Emilion. He would have claimed, had he been asked, never to have missed a morning's fishing in sixty-six years, ever since that first time, when he was just ten years old, that his father had introduced him to its joys. On this occasion the tug at his rod was something much heavier than the expected carp. He pulled at his line, and in the wintry half-light he noticed that it had become entangled in the clothing of a human body floating on the river.

'*Merde,*' he muttered, dropping the rod in consternation. He fumbled for it, and managed to retrieve it before the current could claim it. At first, he just held on, indecision freezing his reactions. '*Merde alors!*' he repeated, holding the rod tightly, unable to move. But help was on its way: his wife of half a century had just emerged from their cottage fifty metres away, with a chunk of bread, butter and a pot of hot coffee.

'*Mon Dieu!*' she cried, assessing the situation immediately. 'It's a body! Do something, Claude! Don't just stand there like a stuffed scarecrow! Pull it in! It might still be alive!' With that she put the breakfast down on the bank, grabbed the rod, and together they pulled the heavily clad body onto the bank. Claude just stood and stared, holding the rod, his mouth open and his eyes agog, while his wife struggled to disentangle the line and turn the body onto its back. 'It's a woman!' she cried. 'Go immediately into town and fetch the Constable. And the Doctor!' Claude made no move. 'Go!' Claude blinked, emerged from his stupor with what felt like a superhuman effort, dropped the rod and made off, constantly glancing back at the body and the breakfast in turn. 'Go on, you old fart! Get on with it!'

As her husband staggered into Saint-Emilion as quickly as his arthritic legs would carry him, his wife inspected the body for any sign of life. There was none. The woman was perhaps in her mid-forties. She was small, had mousy hair gathered beneath a thick bonnet, and a friendly, not unattractive face behind the stark, staring eyes. She gave the appearance of obesity, although this was probably due to the numerous layers of clothing and the fact that she was undoubtedly bloated with water.

An hour later Dr Mereau and Constable Dubois were supervising the loading of the body onto a cart by two men for transportation to the town precinct. Dr Mereau immediately identified the body, and pronounced drowning as the cause of death. 'It's Mme Hélène Chavelet, the wife of Maurice Chavelet of Frontillac,' he told the Constable, who duly made a note of the fact in his notebook. 'She was Polish-born, and known as Madame Lenka. You may recall the tragic killing of her son by the young Englishman last autumn, during the *vendange*.'

'Ah, yes. I recall the case. A nasty business. The Englishman is still being held for the crime as far as I know. Are you – were you acquainted with the deceased?' said the Constable.

'I knew the Chavelets well. Madame Chavelet has not been well recently. In fact, ever since the murder. She suffers – suffered – from melancholia. I have attended her as well as the young Polish lady who has been staying with them since July.'

The Constable noted the facts. 'Would that be the young lady at the centre of the murder – the one who –?'

'Yes.' Dr. Mereau declined to elaborate.

'At – the – centre – of – the – murder,' muttered the Constable as he wrote. 'Very well,' he continued, 'we shall take the cadaver to the precinct for the formalities before handing it over for disposal. Perhaps I could ask you, Monsieur le Docteur, to call on M. Chavelet and tell him his wife's dead, and that he'll be able to pick up her corpse when we're done with the formalities.'

'Yes, of course,' said Dr Mereau, thinking of more sympathetic ways of putting it. 'I shall do it right away.'

Constable Dubois accompanied the cart back to Saint-Emilion, while Dr Mereau climbed into his buggy and set off in the opposite direction. Claude and his wife watched them go. The old man then picked up his rod and peered into the pot of coffee as he made for his little wooden platform on the bank.

'It's gone cold,' he said.

'I'll make fresh,' said his wife.

Maurice was drinking steaming coffee by the kitchen stove when Dr Mereau arrived. He had been awake since three o'clock. Franciszka was still asleep, and he was loath to disturb her.

Maurice leapt up. 'Lenka!' he said as soon as the Doctor entered, 'have you seen Lenka? She's disappeared. I haven't seen her since Friday night, when we went to bed! My God! Monsieur le Docteur!' Maurice grabbed the Doctor by the lapels, 'something dreadful has happened to her!'

'Calm yourself, M. Chavelet!' said Dr Mereau, grabbing Maurice by the shoulders and pushing him into his chair. 'Sit down! Calm down. There is something I must tell you.'

'Lenka's dead!' There was a pause. The Doctor bit his lower lip and sat down. 'I knew it! It's true, isn't it?'

The Doctor took a deep breath. 'I'm afraid so, M. Chavelet. Her body was pulled out of the river near Saint-Emilion an hour ago.'

Maurice burst into tears and howled hysterically. 'Lenka! My Lenka!' The Doctor watched, and did nothing. The beginnings of grieving, he knew, took many forms, and had to take their course.

'W-what's happening?' said a quiet voice, which somehow penetrated Maurice's cries of anguish. The Doctor rose and went to the doorway where Franciszka stood in her nightgown. She was shivering. He ushered her outside into the hallway. 'There has been an accident,' said the Doctor, placing his greatcoat about Franciszka's shoulders. 'Madame Chavelet – she's…'

'She's dead!' The Doctor nodded. Franciszka closed her eyes tightly. 'How?'

'She drowned.'

'I guessed so.'

The Doctor looked at Franciszka and wondered at her calmness and poise. She was now four months gone, and it was beginning to show. She stared up at the ceiling for a good while, before going straight into the kitchen, where she knelt at Maurice's feet and hugged his convulsing body to her. 'Uncle Maurice,' she sighed. 'Uncle Maurice.' No other words came. Doctor Mereau could only watch and hover. He reflected on the tragedies that had been piling up on this family ever since he had known them. The troublesome Jan-Pierre, his grisly murder, his rape of the daughter of a family friend, their guest, her resulting pregnancy, her trauma, and Madame Lenka's deep bouts of suicidal depression. There could be no doubt in the Doctor's mind that she had thrown herself into the river. He had almost seen it coming, as indeed had Franciszka.

Lenka had never got over Jan-Pierre's killing, and her guilt at not regretting it had been eating away at her psyche like a cancer. For she had finally reconciled herself to the truth that she had never loved Jan-Pierre in the first place, and that his death – albeit violent – had been a relief to her. This overwhelming feeling even overshadowed her concern for Franciszka and her plight, and she found herself wallowing in seas of self-pity almost to the exclusion of the tragic girl in her care. The Doctor had observed the three-way relationship, Maurice, Lenka and Franciszka, embarked on a never-ending carousel of mutual destruction, spinning faster and faster out of control. Now one of the carousel's three horses had broken its fitting and been hurled into the void.

One down, reflected the Doctor with an unwanted touch of cynicism, and two to go.

Over the weeks leading into the approaches of spring, Maurice and Franciszka became increasingly close. They relied on one another in every way, both emotionally and in the daily running of the vineyard. Their mutual care and support effectively helped to keep them both on a fairly even keel. Maurice had even found a certain perverse relief in Lenka's death, in many ways akin to the perverse relief that Lenka herself had felt on the death of Jan-Pierre. He had been watching his beloved wife slowly disintegrating emotionally into the severe suicidal depression, whose beginnings dated back two decades to the Grocholski affair. It was brought violently to the fore after a dormant period by her guilt at having given birth to a monster that she had tried, but ultimately failed, to love. There had been, it seemed, no escape from her predicament other than death.

Maurice's immediate instinct was to throw himself wholeheartedly into working the vineyard in preparation for the year's growth, but his first constructive act, two days after Lenka's death, was to write to Julek in Edinburgh, informing him of Lenka's death and of Franciszka's pregnancy, and offering – indeed, begging – to see her through the coming ordeal. He added that, having lost both his wife and son in terrible circumstances and quick succession, he felt a strong need to devote himself totally to something positive, and the nurturing and redemption of the ravaged daughter of his closest friend seemed the obvious course of action.

At least, that is how he put it, because by this time Maurice had firmly convinced himself that Franciszka was his own daughter, and, in his own mind, he felt himself best qualified to nurture her and bring about her redemption. He asked Franciszka to add an insertion of her own to the letter, but she refused, maintaining that she was unclean, and that Julek would no longer want to be associated with her. None of Maurice's entreaties or reasoning bore any fruit: Franciszka had built a wall of guilt around herself that only Maurice had been allowed to penetrate.

V

Three weeks later Maurice received a heartfelt letter from Julek, in which he said that he had returned safely to Edinburgh, and had resumed his studies at the Medical School with renewed vigour. He agreed unconditionally to Maurice's offer, and thanked him for being such a good friend and support for the family. He promised to come to Frontillac as soon as it became possible, in order to persuade his sister not to cut herself off from the family that loved and cherished her despite the dreadful events that had happened. He had also written to his mother, passing on the gist of Maurice's letter. He knew that his mother would worry to the point of panic as to what should be done about Franciszka, especially in the context of the move to Sarenki. But having seen at first hand the strong bonds that had been established between Franciszka and the Chavelets, he strongly recommended that she should stay at Frontillac, for the time being at any rate, and trust to the kindness and care that Maurice would bestow on her.

The real bombshell came, however, one morning in March, in the form of a letter from Poland. 'My God, Mrs McIntyre!' he gasped over breakfast, 'it's from my father! He's alive!'

Teofil, having decided to stay put at Sarenki and do nothing, had, after all, written to Eloise, Julek and Maurice, chronicling in detail his adventure with the *Zbójnicy*, and expressing his intention to stay at Sarenki and await the arrival of Eloise and the boys. He further re-iterated Julek's status as Lord of the Manor. *'Karłowicz had referred to you as a fine fellow who took to his responsibilities as new Lord of the Manor with courage and fortitude rare in one so young,'* Teofil had written. *'Well, Julek, that's good enough for me. I am old and tired, and I want you to take over. Just let me have my own quarters when you start work on the health centre, and I shall be happy. God bless you, my boy.'*

Julek decided that another month of study would have to be sacrificed. He wrote back to his father announcing his intention to travel to Poland at Easter. *'As Lord of the Manor, as you put it, dear Tata, I stipulate that Easter this year should be marked by a grand family reunion of the Samojarskis at Sarenki,'* he wrote. *'I charge you, as my second-in-command and man-on-the-spot, with arranging it. Collude with Karłowicz and Pani Frania and spare no expense.'* He added, as an afterthought, his intention to visit Frontillac *en route,* although he did not elaborate any further.

Julek also wrote to Maurice and Franciszka, asking them both to come to Sarenki. *'I know that Franciszka will refuse, and that you will decline, but if there is anything that you, dear Uncle Maurice, can do to persuade her to come and join the family that loves her so dearly, it would mean so much to all of us.'*

With some considerable help from Stanford McWhirter, Julek managed to catch up on a backlog of studies that he had missed during the autumn and winter, with the added awareness that he would miss out on even more during Easter. The two young men burned many a candle at both ends as they sat together in Stanford's study at his father's Queen Street house, smoking and drinking whisky and setting the world to rights; or, more likely, poring over case studies, patent medicines and anatomical diagrams.

*****

It was the early spring, and the evening was wet and windy. The London Representative of the Polish Government-in-exile, Stefan Sulechowski and his new wife, Jenny Sanderson, *née*

Sulechowska, the daughter of a Polish-born Oxford don, were passing through Edinburgh *en route* for a honeymoon in the Highlands that was to culminate in a stay at Carnethie Castle. Stanford's parents, Sir Robert and Lady Sarah McWhirter, had decided to throw a Polish-oriented dinner party in their honour. Apart from their two sons, Stewart and Stanford, Julek and Claire Fraser were also invited. Julek and Claire had been spending a great deal of time together, aided and abetted by Stanford, whose sense of romance, which usually appeared either non-existent or dormant, was brought to the fore by the volatile idea of a liaison between a Roman Catholic Polish Count and the daughter of a Presbyterian minister from Skye. The party was completed by Ann Lonnegan, the pretty, fair-haired older daughter of a shipping agent from Glasgow, and Stanford's love interest at the time. She was also, perversely, Irish and a Roman Catholic. Stanford's dubious sense of romance was not shared by Sir Robert, who accused him of manipulating people and prejudices just to make a statement of some kind.

Although by no means critical of either of the liaisons, he foresaw enormous difficulties, should Julek's friendship with Claire reach the ears of her father. As for Stanford's friendship with Ann, he reckoned he would get over that at the appropriate juncture and embrace good sense and a nice, Protestant girl instead. Only Stewart lacked a female counterpart. Lady Sarah, well aware of the depression that had been haunting her elder son for several months, had not invited anyone to fill that seat. Only Franciszka would have done that.

*****

'It's all thanks to Burke and Hare, you know, that you've got those drawings,' said Sir Robert over dinner one evening. Everyone waited with bated breath for further elucidation, but none came as he sharpened his carving knife and addressed the wing rib of beef that Tavistock had brought in and placed in front of him at the head of the table with meticulous concentration and attention to detail. Strange, thought Julek, how the British put so much drama and theatre into cutting up meat. There was also something about Tavistock that frightened Julek and sent shivers down his spine; he had always thought that the cadaverous old butler looked like Death, and moved without a sound; and he had just materialised from the ether at Sir Robert's elbow.

'Burke and Hare?' said Jenny Sulechowski. She had chosen not to feminise her surname in the Polish way as it would only cause confusion. 'I've heard of them. Weren't they hanged for murder some years ago?'

'Do you not know the full story about Burke and Hare?' said Sir Robert to the beef. 'Didn't you ever tell Jenny about Burke and Hare, Stefan?'

'I don't even know myself,' said Stefan.

'They say,' added Julek conspiratorially, 'that it was Burke and Hare who founded the Edinburgh Medical School!'

'Even though they didn't do anything of the sort,' said Stewart, 'but at least they put it on the map!' He was being charming and affable, and putting on a very good show, which did not go unnoticed by either his parents, or by Julek. Stewart had been deeply shocked, even traumatised, by what had happened to Franciszka. He had made no secret of the fact that he was deeply in love with her, and had been visibly upset when she left for an extended stay in France. When his reservations were justified, he was inconsolable for a very long time. However, with support from his parents, his brother, and latterly Julek, who were all extremely sympathetic, he had managed to pull himself together by the turn of the year. Although he had by no means got over Franciszka, he had resigned himself to living with a brave face and stiff upper lip.

'You've heard of Robert Knox, of course,' continued Sir

Robert.

'We all have,' said Julek.

'He was the famous anatomist,' added Claire. 'He lived here in Edinburgh. His work is part of our curriculum.'

'Indeed, indeed.' Sir Robert threw the girls a wry glance. Perhaps, he thought, the subject of anatomy was not a suitable one over dinner in front of respectable young girls from Oxford, Ireland and the Isle of Skye.

'Well,' interrupted Stewart, rising to the bait, 'he used to buy dead bodies to study, and did not ask too many questions as to where they came from.'

'So, do tell me about Burke and Hare, Sir Robert,' said Stefan.

'Not really a suitable topic at dinner, Julek,' replied Sir Robert, assessing the best place to make another incision into the crispy side of the Aberdeen Angus, 'especially with ladies present.'

Lady Sarah looked at the girls in turn, and they all burst out laughing. 'If you don't tell, Robert, then I shall ask Claire to do the honours!' cried Lady Sarah, 'I'm sure she's dying to!'

Sir Robert cut another slice before answering. 'Very well,' he grinned at Claire. 'I can see you're a tough lass of few sensibilities and squeamishness. Ha! These shortcomings and flaws of character will put you in good stead in relating to our wild and unprincipled Polish guest!' Julek accepted the bantering accolade with a smile and a bow. Claire wiped her lips with her napkin and winked at Julek, who then turned his attention to Stefan and Jenny, and noted what a good-looking young couple they were. Stefan was approaching thirty, dark, handsome and urbane. He sported an air of quiet, youthful confidence as befitting a peoples' statesman-in-the-making. Jenny was perhaps in her early twenties. Her curly, blonde hair, classical features and wide, alert blue eyes gave the impression of great intelligence and insight. Sir Robert, who had attended the wedding in London, had described her then as a 'damned fine woman by Jove!'

'William Burke was a criminal from Ireland,' Sir Robert pointed westwards with his carving knife as he launched into the story with almost indecent relish. 'On the run, most probably. He came to Edinburgh – must have been about twenty years ago. He lodged with another dubious Irishman by the name of William Hare, who ran a boarding house. The story goes that about ten years previously one of Hare's lodgers, an old army pensioner, died. This was the time of the body snatchers. The so-called Resurrectionists. They used to raid graves and steal the corpses of the freshly deceased…' Sir Robert made a series of intricate incisions around the bone '…to sell. There was a market for dead bodies among doctors, scientists and…' he pointedly looked at Julek, Stanford and Claire in turn '…medical students. Anyway, they approached Robert Knox with the body. He was, as Claire had pointed out, a leading anatomist in our city. He gave them seven pounds ten shillings for the corpse. This is an excellent claret, Stewart. Is it from the new batch, or have we had it since '33?'

Sir Robert had stopped carving to taste the wine that had been decanted and surreptitiously poured for him by Tavistock. He usually left the choice of wines to his eldest son, whose passion was Bordeaux, the city, its environs and its wines, although he reserved the *droit de seigneur* to taste Stewart's choice, which he did for dramatic effect. More British theatre, thought Julek wryly. 'It's from the new batch shipped in the autumn, father. Saint-Emilion '29.'

Sir Robert added a few more eulogies before continuing. 'Anyway, Burke and Hare decided that this was a good way of making money. So, they hatched out their grisly plan.' Sir Robert momentarily concentrated on the excision of a large piece of gristle, which he placed on the side of the carving board. All eyes were on him as he did so. 'They lured unsuspecting travellers to the boarding house, where they first plied them with drink, and then, when they were good and drunk, killed them by suffocation.'

Sir Robert paused to take another sip of wine. 'In that way,' he continued, 'the corpses were not damaged, and were thus suitable for being carved up and experimented upon. Please begin.'

He had finished carving, and had distributed the beef onto everyone's plate. Julek awoke from a reverie. He had stopped listening. He was staring at his glass, which reflected the candlelight in its rich, ruby redness, thinking about Saint-Emilion, Frontillac, the Claret Clipper and Franciszka. He looked first at Stewart, then at his portion of rib with disappointment, which he suppressed. Why, he asked himself, did the British burn their marvellous Scottish beef to a cinder? Ideally, he preferred his beef in the Tartar fashion – raw and minced, although he very happily settled for severely underdone.

'Besides,' continued Sir Robert, 'they might have ended up with blood everywhere, which might have constituted evidence. Then they sold the dead bodies to Knox, who paid up to fourteen pounds for a good cadaver in excellent condition. A perfect consort to the beef, Stewart, this '29. A marriage made in heaven.' It's only food and drink, thought Julek. A marvellous nation, the British, but yet so – somehow so –

'Two years they kept it up,' continued Sir Robert. 'Then the police got wise. They must have got careless. Anyway, they were found out and arrested for murder. Hare turned King's evidence, and blamed the whole thing on Burke. Burke was found guilty and hanged here in Edinburgh at the end of January 1829. That's the year of this wine, Stewart. They'd done away with at least fifteen people. I recall it well. It was pouring with rain, and it was the day that I concluded that business deal with Johnston's of Newcastle.' Noting that no one expressed an interest in Johnston's of Newcastle, Sir Robert went on. 'Hare was freed, but the whole population was up in arms against him and gave him no peace. In the end, he couldn't stand the persecution any longer, and disappeared.'

'So, what happened to him?' said Julek.

'No one knows. They say he disappeared off to England somewhere.'

Julek grinned. The British! The English. The Scots. There's no nation like them anywhere. He reflected that Poles had always looked to Italy for art and culture, to France for food, wine and lifestyle, and to Britain for fairness and politics.

Because Julek and Claire had been spending a great deal of their time together, Mrs McIntyre could not help but notice the stars in their eyes, and found herself unable to decide whether to approve or not. On the one hand, their relationship appeared innocent and totally harmless: two young people breathing the fresh air of the Scottish springtime together. On the other hand, however, she shared Sir Robert McWhirter's reservations about the religious differences. Should this romance of occasional handholding and stolen kisses lead to something more serious, there would be insurmountable problems leading to far-reaching consequences.

The matter was put on hold two days after the dinner at Queen Street, when Julek kissed Claire goodbye, and boarded the Claret Clipper for the first leg of his journey to his new domain.

VI

Franciszka's pregnancy was kept a secret, although Maurice knew perfectly well that he would not be able to keep up the deception indefinitely. Dr Mereau visited frequently, and found himself increasingly acting as confidant and counsellor to both of them, especially to Maurice, whom he came to regard as a good friend. They had, after all, known one another ever since the Chavelets first arrived at Frontillac. From the very start he had asserted his unconditional support for both of them, and warned of the impending scandal when her pregnancy became apparent, and that they would both have to prepare themselves for the ostracism to come. His visits to monitor Franciszka's condition soon became invitations to dinner, which Franciszka, who had embraced the job of housekeeper with enthusiasm, always prepared.

One warm and sunny evening two weeks before Easter, Franciszka served coffee in the dining room before excusing herself, as usual, claiming tiredness, leaving the two men to their cogitative late Cognac.

'She's definitely showing, Maurice,' said Dr Mereau. They had recently slipped into Christian name terms. 'You will both have to face it sooner or later. There will be talk.'

'I agree, Phillippe,' replied Maurice. 'We shall find a way somehow. What's done is done, and we're hoping that people will understand. There's nothing we can do to stop the gossip, but at the same time, this is my home, my livelihood, and Franciszka is –' Maurice stopped abruptly. Was he really going to say, 'my daughter?' He pursed his lips and remained in deep thought for a good while. Dr Mereau patiently refilled the glasses. 'May I speak frankly, Phillippe?' Maurice said finally, ignoring his refilled glass.

'We've known one another long enough, Maurice.'

'I am almost certain that Franciszka…' he glanced at the door, which, he noted with satisfaction, was closed '…is my daughter.'

'*Mon Dieu*, Maurice! What are you saying?'

Maurice took a deep breath, settled back and closed his eyes. After a long pause, he spoke. 'It was the summer of 1814. Czarne Lasy. A perfect moonlit night. I remember it so clearly, almost as though it were yesterday. There has not been one day since when I have not thought about it. Teofil had a great deal on his mind at the time, and could not cope with life very well.'

'The Grocholski affair?'

'The Grocholski affair. He had lost Sarenki, and had been living permanently on the edge of a seething rage that he could not control. I have known him a very long time. He could not always find that inner strength that most men have when times of trial come. I have seen him go to pieces before. He began drinking, and it all got seriously out of hand. He spent most of his time in the drinking dens of Kraków, and virtually ignored Eloise, who just didn't know which way to turn.'

'So, she turned to you, *hein*?'

Maurice sipped his Cognac and gazed at Dr Mereau across the rim of the glass. 'It was the night of his mother's funeral,' he said. 'Two months previously, you see, he'd somehow managed to pull himself together. He'd even stopped drinking. Things went back to normal, and Eloise, of course, was delighted. Then, on June 19 1814 his mother died, and Teofil went back to square one. On the evening of the funeral, he rode to Kraków and embarked on a drinking spree that eventually lasted a full week. Eloise was again plunged into despair. It was past midnight when she fled in her nightgown from the Lodge, where they were living, and ran, barefoot, to the Manor, where Lenka and I had a small apartment on the top floor. She shouted to me, and threw stones up at my window, but succeeded only in waking up the whole garrison of French soldiers who were stationed there. Thinking something terrible had happened, I rushed downstairs to take over and defuse the situation.'

'I think I can guess the rest,' said the Doctor.

'I dismissed the sergeant who had emerged in his nightshirt to investigate. Then I opened the main doors, and found Eloise fraught and shivering uncontrollably. She had obviously been crying. She made her way up the stone steps. I led her into one of the reception rooms coming off the hallway and lit a candle. There hardly seemed any point, as the moonlight was very bright. She immediately remonstrated with me. No candle, Maurice, she said, put it out. Well, she was in a terrible state, so I did as she asked. Then the tears came. In floods, like a dam bursting. She threw her arms around me and held me tightly. You know, with passion. I didn't know what to do. *Mon Dieu*, Phillippe, this was not what I wanted. It was not as it seemed. Yes, I did hug her, but my hug was warm and sympathetic. I held back. But before I knew it, our mouths met, and we were kissing. My mind was utterly confused. The kiss was passionate, long, and somehow, you know, I felt I didn't want it to stop. My heart was pounding like Napoleon's artillery, and my head was in a whirl of panic and indecision.'

Maurice looked in the Doctor's face for signs of censure, disapproval, condemnation even, but found none. 'These things happen, *mon ami*,' was his inane reply to Maurice's quizzical look. It was accompanied by a shrug.

'Maybe it was the moonlight, *n'est-ce pas?*' continued Maurice, also inanely.

'And you made love to her in the moonlight?' The Doctor

appeared unconcerned.

'It was one of the most wonderful experiences of my life, Phillippe. May I be forgiven, the faithless adulterer that I am. I have made love to my best friend's wife, and enjoyed it beyond comprehension. I have fucked a lot in my time, Phillippe. I have also made love on occasions. But I have only touched the stars with one woman, and it wasn't Lenka. Eloise. The moonlight. I could almost hear it, you see. Like silver chimes and violin harmonics in unison. Her body was like an ancient Greek statue of polished marble in the Syrian ruins. Such beauty, gleaming, scented with that heady perfume of femininity, yet at the same time cold and colourless. A study in textured light and shade. God's work of art. Masterpiece. It was an extraordinary, almost mystical experience. And yet, one that could not be replicated. Ever. It was unique. A cosmic one-off. It could never happen again.' Maurice stared at the Cognac glass. 'Can you understand?'

'Were you – are you in love with Eloise?'

'I don't know. I shall never know. What is love, anyway? It seemed somehow as though a whole life's love had been condensed into half an hour. A concentrated essence. She came and she went like a shooting star. Maybe there are as many kinds of love as there are stars. Some lasting forever, some fleeting, transient, but intense.'

'Does Teofil know? Or suspect?'

'Absolutely not!'

'And Eloise?'

'I don't know. I looked for the signs in Vienna, but she was giving nothing away.'

'I presume she might still be Teofil's?'

Maurice pursed his lips. 'Teofil would certainly know if she wasn't!'

'You realise that if Franciszka is yours the baby will almost certainly be deformed.'

'Yes.'

'Be prepared, *mon ami*.'

'How?'

Dr Phillippe Mereau shrugged and pursed his lips. He had no answer to that question.

*****

The following day a buggy drew up on the cobbles outside. Maurice, thinking that Dr Mereau had called again, climbed out of the vat that he had been cleaning. He stopped short, his mouth open.

'Julek!' he cried. 'What are you doing here? Come in! Come in!' The two men embraced excitedly. 'Franciszka will be delighted –' Maurice's voice trailed off, and he became subdued. 'Perhaps it might be difficult.'

'She is well?'

'Outwardly, perhaps. Within? Hm.' Maurice shrugged and pursed his lips as they walked into the house. 'She has gone for a walk by the river. She throws a flower into the water every day. For Lenka.'

'I am sorry, Uncle Maurice. Really. Such a terrible tragedy. I have come to see how you are. Both of you.'

'You are very kind. We are coping. And you? How are the studies?'

'I am a little behind, but managing. As you know, my father has abdicated in my favour. I am now Lord of the Manor, as he calls it. Very inconvenient, in some ways, but he's had enough. I am on my way to Sarenki for the family Easter. Will you and Franciszka be coming?'

Maurice poured two glasses of wine. 'Try this '29, Julek. It's exquisite.'

Julek read the label and raised an eyebrow. 'I already have,' he said. He inspected the colour, contemplated the nose and sipped with ostentatious slowness, pursing his lips and swirling it round in his mouth before swallowing it. He was learning fast from the British. He thought of the dinner at the McWhirters'. Claire. Stewart. He drank. 'So, will you come.'

'Alas, no,' said Maurice. 'Franciszka has settled into a kind of acceptance of the way things are. It is a narrow acceptance, which excludes her family. She will only allow me and Dr Mereau within the walls of her existence. Her shame will not permit contact with the outside world.'

'We are not the outside world.'

'That is the whole point. To her you are. Family, or not. That is what makes it so much more difficult.'

'Even with me?'

'We shall see.'

At that moment Franciszka entered the room. She took one look at Julek, and her face contorted slowly until it exploded in tears. She fled from the room. Julek rose to go after her, but Maurice restrained him. 'Leave her, Julek,' he said quietly. 'She is not yet ready. Time, you see. You must give her time. It is a great healer.' He said the last as though he did not really believe it, and the insinuation was not lost on Julek, who, after a moment frozen in an awkward, half risen posture, relaxed himself back into his chair. 'My God, Uncle Maurice! What is happening to us all?'

Maurice agreed with Julek's suggestion that he should be on his way first thing in the morning. His visit had obviously distressed Franciszka, and he had no wish to prolong the agony. 'We shall be all right, Julek,' said Maurice at the parting. 'She will come to realise that your visit was because you cared. Kiss your father for me, will you. And Eloise, of course.'

VII

Easter 1838 at Sarenki was a splendid affair. Eloise and the boys had successfully wound up all their affairs in Nibork, and had set off just as the first blossoms started to appear on the trees. A new spring, a new beginning. Sending all their effects on, Eloise first called on the Zaletniks to say their goodbyes, and to hope that one day they might venture forth and travel to Sarenki for an extended visit.

'I would dearly love to, *Panie hrabio*,' said *Pani* Zaletnikowa, 'but you know how it is, trying to get Mr Zaletnik off his fat backside even to go into town, lazy stick-in-the-mud that he is!'

Pan Zaletnik's excuse was that he had always wanted to travel, but *Pani* Zaletnikowa had soon knocked those notions on the head shortly after they married, and now he was too old anyway.

Eloise and the boys arrived at Sarenki on a cold and windy afternoon in late March, followed two days later, in glorious spring sunshine, by Julek.

'A good omen, *Panie hrabio*,' beamed *Pani* Frania, kissing his outstretched hand. Julek permitted himself a certain degree of aristocratic aloofness, so as not to appear quite as 'democratic' as his father. 'May the sun always shine on your incumbency of the Manor.'

He arrived impeccably dressed, having stopped on the way in Kraków to buy new clothes, as well as a silver-topped cane, which he wielded with a debonair carelessness that he had picked up in Scotland. 'One has to look the part when one comes to take one's rightful place at one's inheritance,' he had muttered to his overjoyed father. 'Besides, one's got to make it quite clear to the peasants who's who, in case they get stroppy and over-familiar with one.' Teofil grinned. He knew that beneath his son's affected, aristocratic bluster, picked up at that English public school, there lay only a modest amount of perfectly harmless and healthy snobbery. The rest was theatre.

Julek also arrived with a veritable consignment of Saint-Emilion and Pomerol wines, some of which he accepted from Maurice as an Easter gift to the family, while the rest he insisted on paying for in full. 'Maurice wanted to give it all away, but he's not a charitable institution, and he's got to live. Besides, he has your daughter and...' Julek paused indecisively, but failed to find the right word '...to support.'

The whole village turned their efforts to welcoming the true, rightful, Polish, Catholic, honest, (the list of adjectives was long and varied) *Hrabiostwo* back to the bosom of its people. Teofil appointed himself to the final task of his incumbency of Sarenki, that of restoring the Manor to a semblance of what it should be. After two decades of virtual neglect, Karłowicz and *Pani* Frania, as well as artisan members of the community, had galvanised themselves into a hive of cleaning, repair work and general tidying up. The gardens were weeded and undergrowth cleared. Everyone accepted Teofil's abdication, and wished him a long and happy retirement.

Easter week arrived, and New Father Józef Godny came as much into his own as he was likely to. Without recourse to passionate invocations, blessings, curses and admonitions, or shaking of fists at the heavens, he preached the story of Christ's passion, death and resurrection with restrained fortitude and dignity.

On Good Friday Teofil risked the censure of Father Józef and persuaded Julek to have a *Śledź*. This custom, in which all the men folk get together in the evening to eat *śledź* – that is, pickled herrings – washed down with vodka, while the women prepare the Easter feast and the children paint the eggs, used to have Old Father Józef firmly at the centre of things, and drinking everyone else under the table. 'The good Lord Jesus liked his booze as much as the next man,' he used to growl, glaring at the ceiling, 'except in his day they didn't have Old Pankracy, so he had to make do with wine, which is crap, and when they ran out of the stuff, he came up with some of his own miracle hooch distilled out of plain water, but had he known better he'd have plumped for vodka instead of wine, that's for sure!'

Father Józef was not actually against *Śledź*, but reminded those intending to take part *'to think about the death on this sacred day of Our Lord Jesus Christ, who fed the seven thousand with four loaves and six fishes* (to his congregation's amusement, he could never remember the actual numbers) *so offer up this feast of fishes, bread and – and liquor – to His glory and pray for the forgiveness of sins and the resurrection of the body, which we are about to celebrate.'* The men folk in question went along with this admonition in the sure knowledge that their intentions, which were good, would inevitably falter as the evening wore on. Among the participants sitting round the dining room table were Teofil, Julek, Karłowicz, and Little Irek, who asked to bring his father, the senile but placid Big Irek, who quietly and surreptitiously drunk himself into a stupor. Father Józef arrived, blessed the feast that *Pani* Frania had prepared, allowed himself two glasses of vodka and a small plateful of herring pieces with black bread before excusing himself *'to attend to God's work.'* After his departure the evening quietly degenerated into a thoroughly congenial party.

On Easter Sunday Father Józef celebrated Mass, after which everyone returned home for the *Święcone,* the Easter Feast. Little Irek had prepared a specially cured ham, which he presented to the new Lord of the Manor, 'in homage!' Julek tried to pay him, but Little Irek refused. 'Let's just say,' he said, with a big grin on his face, 'that *Pan hrabia* owes me!' He also knew, as did Teofil, that beneath Julek's aristocratic bluster there lay only a modest amount of perfectly harmless and healthy snobbery. He was right. Julek was, at heart, just one of the lads. 'Very politic to be in with the management,' he later told his uncomprehending father.

Pani Frania surpassed herself in coming up with a magnificent *Święcone*, for which she baked sweet *babka*, and cooked new potatoes tossed in butter and dill, and fresh spring vegetables. Julek decanted four bottles of Maurice's eight-year-old Saint-Emilion. A toast was drunk to 'absent friends and family', and even the boys were allowed half a glass each.

There followed a long silence as everyone spared a thought for Franciszka and Maurice, in the sure knowledge that the gesture was being replicated at the other end too. Julek then took his place at the head of the table, at which sat Eloise, Teofil, Adam, Michał and Karłowicz. On Teofil's insistence, *Pani* Frania also had a place at table, with the family. 'You can't expect the poor woman to eat in the kitchen all on her own, Julek,' Teofil had said. 'It is Easter, and she's done a lot for us.' Julek sniffed, and agreed, on only a tiny dose of sufferance.

The painted eggs had been brought out and displayed in all their glory in six wooden bowls carved in the mists of time by Staś Sieńkowski, interspersed among colourful bowls of spring flowers. Over the week Julek had supervised Adam and Michał, as well as a number of children from the village, in the painting of the eggs. Julek's reputation as an artist had preceded him, and the village children had been the first to benefit from his talents. He did several eggs himself, turning each one into a work of art, giving the children a practical art lesson by painting his own eggs in the manner of Turner and Constable, as well as portraits of everyone in the family after Rubens and Holbein. In front of him, in all its pink, black and white glory, was Irek's ham, which Julek carved with all the style and theatrical aplomb that he had learned from Sir Robert McWhirter. Adam and Michał were highly amused.

'You carve like a swordsman from those tales of old, going forth to rescue maidens in distress!' laughed Michał. 'He has just slain the dreaded Transylvanian Ham-Dragon, which has been breathing fire and terrorising the Moldavian Virgins on the Black Sea coast!' added Adam, in full mock-fantasy flight.

Easter Monday morning was marked by a veritable onslaught on Sarenki's maidenhood, as all the youths, armed with buckets of perfume-imbued water, drenched every girl they came upon in the course of the traditional custom of *Śmigus*. Anticipating this annual event, Julek had purchased a small barrel of Provençal perfume while passing through Lyon. He handed it over to the lads, who made full use of it in the traditional manner. He then threw caution to the winds, let drop his airs, and joined the lads in hunting down girls, who were happy to be drenched in French fragrance, as opposed to the customary cheap scent. Also, it lingered on them for the rest of the day.

Later, Julek was sitting on a fence, sharing a bottle of fruit cordial with Witold and Jacek, the two sons of carpenter Henio Sieńkowski, nephew of Old Staś. Witold, now 20 and good-looking, cut quite a dash in the local youth scene. He was also hopelessly infatuated with eighteen-year-old Honorata, the daughter of roofer Bogumił Małosielski and his wife, Cisia. They were laughing, joking, and discussing the relative merits of the village girls. Witold, in a clumsy, lateral attempt to draw Julek's attention to the object of his dreams, was recommending Honorata to Julek's attention, when the girl in question, along with a small bevy of giggling friends, sprinted teasingly past in the direction of the woods. She flashed Julek a dazzling smile as she passed. The gesture was noted with suppressed consternation by Witold, who put on a brave face. 'There you are,' he said. 'That's Honorata. What did I tell you? You'd certainly be in with a chance.'

'I'd be taking unfair advantage!' laughed Julek.

'Why not?' said Jacek. 'If she's willing!'

'I think our new Lord of the Manor is basically shy,' said Witold with a hint of mockery in his voice. 'What do you think, Jacek?'

'Could be he has a girl in Scotland, to whom he has sworn to be faithful!' replied Jacek, who was the same age as Honorata. What he lacked in good looks he made up for with his steady charm and wit.

'I don't believe it!' laughed Witold, suppressing a flicker of jealousy that passed through his psyche. 'Do you have a girl in Scotland, Julek?'

Julek's guard went up. 'Do you have a girl in Scotland, *Panie hrabio*!' corrected Julek.

There was a moment's silence during which all banter evaporated. 'Sorry, *Panie hrabio*,' said Witold in a friendly, but respectful tone. 'Does *Pan hrabia* have a girl in Scotland?'

Julek grinned, and the banter returned. 'That would be telling!' he said. 'Come on. Let's go. It's time for lunch.'

The three young men got off the fence and walked towards the village. Honorata and her friends watched them go from the edge of the wood, fragrant and disappointed.

The village lads, meanwhile, had learned a lesson in class parameters. They knew it was important to know exactly where they stood, and how far they could push familiarity.

The following day Julek said his goodbyes to everyone and set off back to Edinburgh. Again, Henryk Staruch took him to Nowy Sandec in his buggy. Witold and Jacek joined the crowd to see him off, as did Honorata. 'He can't wait to get back to his girl in Scotland,' teased Witold, pointedly, so that Honorata would hear.

'What's her name, *Panie hrabio*?' cried Jacek.

'Claire!' cried Julek over his shoulder. As the buggy disappeared down the track Julek waved without looking back, and did not see Honorata start and bite her lip.

VIII

Julek reached Edinburgh in the middle of April. He was met at the port by Stanford McWhirter with his buggy, and they arrived at Mrs McIntyre's in the middle of a crisis. Mrs McIntyre was standing by the mantelpiece in the drawing room, clutching a letter, her face pale and drained of all colour. Claire Fraser was seated in an armchair, crying into a handkerchief. Charles Carnethie stood over her, wondering whether to put a re-assuring arm round her shoulders or to maintain a respectful distance.

'Mrs McIntyre!' cried Julek, 'What has happened? Claire?'

'I have a letter here, Master Julek,' said Mrs McIntyre with a tremor in her voice. 'It appears that I must give you notice to leave my house.'

'Leave your house, Mrs McIntyre? I – I don't understand? What is it, Claire? Has something happened?'

'The letter is from Claire's father,' interpolated Charles, coming over. 'It concerns you and Claire. It is not good news.'

'He accuses me of running a den of iniquity,' said Mrs McIntyre, obviously controlling a welling rage in her heart. 'Would ye believe! My house a den of iniquity, Master Julek! He will nae allow his daughter to share a roof with agents of the Devil, he says, and that ye must leave.'

'Leave, Mrs McIntyre? What's this about agents of the Devil and dens of iniquity?' said Julek, looking perplexedly about him.

'It's all because you're a Catholic, and living here.' Everyone looked at the source of the remark. Ząb, the surly, Russian-hating Polish student had just entered the drawing room. 'In her father's eyes that makes this house a den of iniquity, and you, Samojarski, are an agent of the Devil. Once again religion rears its ugly head and spreads the doctrine of bigotry and intolerance throughout the world.'

Julek looked closely at Ząb, wondering whether he had, after all, found an ally of sorts in this withdrawn and unsociable fellow-countryman of his. 'What do you mean, Ząb?' he said.

'Well, it's obvious, isn't it?' said Ząb, stepping forward. There was a hint of a sneer in his voice. 'You, a Roman Catholic, have been showering your amorous attentions on the daughter of a Scottish Presbyterian Minister, and you expect a medal for it? I've seen trouble coming right from the start. I'm not blaming you, mind. I like Claire. She's a nice girl, but you were naive beyond belief, both of you, if you expected to get away with your affair. Isn't that right, Mrs McIntyre?'

'Well, it had occurred to me –' began the landlady, fingering the letter in her hand nervously.

'It had more than occurred to you, Mrs McIntyre,' said Ząb insistently. 'You openly commented on it right from the start. Not in front of Samojarski, of course. Nothing good will come of young Master Julek you said, bestowing his attentions on young Mistress Claire you said, mark my words you said there will be tears before bedtime. And you were right, Mrs McIntyre.'

'Ay, but that dinna qualify my house to be called a den of iniquity, Master Ząb.' Mrs McIntyre correctly pronounced the name *Zomb*, which, she had learned, was the Polish for tooth. Its bearer still refused to divulge his Christian name, on the stated grounds that he did not consider himself Christian. He blamed the hatred between Poles and Russians on their respective religions: he found Roman Catholicism and the Russian Orthodox creed totally incompatible bedfellows – or even neighbours. 'There's a latent streak of cruelty among Orthodox Catholics,' he had often said. 'Who else would be prepared to go to the great lengths and trouble that it takes to flay their victims alive? At least the Roman Catholics don't go in for such mindless sadism. That's one thing in your favour, Samojarski!' His tone betrayed the fact that he was speaking from experience. Whenever the Inquisition or the Reformation were mentioned, however, Ząb would just shrug his shoulders and assert that one god of bigotry and intolerance was much like any other god of bigotry and intolerance.

*****

As time went by Ząb continued to be a total mystery to everyone in Edinburgh. He had wholeheartedly embraced atheism as a young boy at the time of the Uprising. His family came from Lublin, where he had witnessed numerous atrocities committed on the Roman Catholic Poles by the mainly Ukrainian Orthodox Catholic troops, who were hell-bent on extracting their own brand of revenge against the nation that had, until recently, ruled them oppressively for centuries. And rubbed their faces in the mire, as Old Father Józef used to say.

Among these atrocities were the torture and massacre of his family. His father, a doctor, was dissected to death with his own scalpels, as was his mother. His teenage sister was raped by some two dozen drunken soldiers before being flayed while still alive, again, with her father's scalpels. They were egged on by a well-spoken and educated Russian officer. Ząb had watched it all from a wardrobe in which he had hidden when the soldiers first broke into their house. The careful and systematic removal of his sister's skin while she was still alive and screaming hysterically ironically mirrored his father's profession, which he had made up his mind to follow. This was despite the fact that on many occasions his father, too, had caused unspeakable suffering to patients in the course of some healing process or other. By this seemingly nebulous blurring of Good and Evil, young Ząb had decided then that there was no God.

After that, Ząb survived his teenage years on the streets, first of Lublin, then of Warsaw, where he ended up dossing in various ruins with various other radicalised, orphaned, feral teenagers who lived by robbing and stealing – often specifically from churches and Russian institutions. On a number of occasions, the gang's hideout was raided by the Russian security forces, but most of the gang had, by this time, learned the arts of survival in the chaotic mazes of Warsaw's rooftops, alleyways, tunnels and ruined buildings, and few ever got caught. Those that did never lived to describe what befell them at the hands of their oppressors.

Because of his name, Ząb became known literally as 'The Tooth', a sobriquet which he adopted, as it sounded tough in its animal menace. A tooth was something that bit, and he had developed a burning ambition to bite, and to bite hard. He wanted to grow up to be tough and resilient, a hard man to be feared and respected, especially by Russians.

By the time he had turned eighteen he realised that he would never become a physician unless he changed his lifestyle. How he emerged from his life of petty crime is not on record. Ząb was reticent and secretive from the start, and refused to discuss his past with anyone. He considered the matter strictly his own, and no one else's business.

All that Mrs McIntyre knew was that he arrived one day in Edinburgh, enrolled at the Medical School and found lodgings with her. He appeared to be in possession of sufficient funds, so any questions about his past were purely of a politely speculative nature. Mrs McIntyre came to consider his former circumstances as none of her business. Ząb's reticence won him no friends, which did not worry him in the least. He worked very hard at his studies, read a great deal and attended every operation and autopsy that he could. Professionally he was considered a model student with excellent prospects.

Otherwise, he preferred his own company, with the possible exception of Claire, with whom he was known often to spend up to ten minutes in social and medical conversation. Charles Carnethie tried constantly to get through to him, and the McWhirters often invited him to dinner, all without any success whatsoever. Julek had given up on him from the start, considering any further overtures beyond the initial ones a total waste of time.

*****

'Still,' Ząb looked intently at Julek, 'it's your problem. Not mine.'

With that he turned, glanced at Claire with what might have been a fleeting look of sympathy, and left the room, leaving Julek convinced, after all, that he had not found an ally. He turned to Mrs McIntyre. 'I have no choice, Master Julek,' she said, a note of desperation in her voice. 'The Reverend Fraser threatens to recall Claire home and abort her studies unless...' she looked for, and found, the relevant passage in the letter '...*you cleanse your den of the iniquity of the influence of Satan, and expel all the Devil's agents and return your house to the care of the Lord and the spheres of righteousness.*'

The spheres of righteousness. A variant on the side of Good, as specified by Old Father Józef, reflected Julek momentarily. 'One man's Good is another's Righteousness,' he muttered under his breath, 'I wonder which is which.' No one ventured an opinion. 'So, you wish me to leave, Mrs McIntyre,' he said aloud.

'Nae, Master Julek,' wailed Mrs McIntyre, 'I dinna want ye to leave, but I don't have an option, d'ye see?'

'Neither do you, Julek,' added Charles. 'He's found out about you and Claire, and will have none of it. He's a Scottish Presbyterian minister, for God's sake!'

'For *whose* sake?' said Julek angrily, glaring at Charles, who waved a hand and turned away. Julek, frozen with a seething rage, continued staring at Charles' back.

'You'll have to go,' added Stanford, 'or you'll lose her.'

All this time Claire had been sitting, perched on the edge of the armchair, sobbing uncontrollably into her handkerchief. Now she looked up. 'Never!' she cried, rising. 'I'll never let you go, Julek! I don't care what my father says! He's wrong!' Julek dragged his eyes away from Charles' back, went over to her and for a few moments they held one another tightly. 'I can't let him go, Mrs McIntyre,' she cried. 'I – I love him!'

'I ken,' said the landlady tenderly. 'That's why Master Julek must leave. It's the only way you can stay together.'

'What do you mean?' said Julek.

Mrs McIntyre suddenly regained her composure. 'I shall give the Reverend Fraser the satisfaction of throwing ye oot of my house,' she said. 'With righteousness re-established, Claire can continue her studies. You, Master Julek, will seek alternative lodgings. But not too far away, ye ken.'

'But, where can I go? I don't know of any –'

'I know! Why don't you stay with us, Julek?' interpolated Stanford. 'I'm sure my father would be glad to have you around. Our house is big enough.'

'My thoughts precisely,' said Mrs McIntyre, turning to Stanford. Julek thought he detected a hint of a smirk on the landlady's face. 'I shall appoint myself chaperone of Mistress Claire and assure her father of my dedication to the cause of…' she grinned pointedly at Claire '…righteousness! That should put the Reverend's mind at rest. Then,' Mrs McIntyre was beginning to enjoy herself, 'I shall feign a certain blindness –'

'I'm not sure you should be aiding and abetting a rift between Claire and her father,' interrupted Charles, turning round and facing Mrs McIntyre. He had been listening attentively to the exchanges without saying anything. 'The Reverend Fraser is bound to find out if Julek and Claire, with or without your connivance, Mrs McIntyre, continue on their course of deception.'

'What do you mean, connivance, course of deception, Charles?' cried Julek angrily.

'Come, Sir Charles!' cried Mrs McIntyre, taking the bait. 'Canna ye see they're in love?'

'But he's a Roman Catholic and she's Presbyterian, Mrs McIntyre,' said Charles. 'Whatever you say, there will be a clash. Of cultures, traditions, family ties, deep-seated convictions, not just religion. There's far more to it than that. I just hope you know what you're letting yourself in for, Julek.'

A look of pure rage inflamed Julek's eyes. 'Yes. I do,' he said through his teeth. 'I am letting myself in for – no, Claire and I are letting ourselves in for – a long battle against bigotry and intolerance. Ząb is right. It may well be a battle we will lose, unless our friends, family, and those we trust will fight with us. Claire and I love one another, and what's more, we both believe in the One Christian God, even though we may have different ways of worshipping Him, and asking Him for his blessing on our love. Nothing – I repeat – nothing will stand in our way! And that includes you! Do you understand, Charles?'

'Have it your way, Julek,' said Charles quietly. 'I am on your side, but don't say I didn't warn you.' With that he turned on his heel and left the room.

IX

Sir Robert McWhirter did not approve of his son's plan to allow Julek to lodge with him. In fact, he was quite vehemently against it. 'Think what you're doing, Stanford,' he cried. 'I've got some standing here in Scotland, and I have no desire to fall foul of the Kirk. No disrespect to you, Julek, but you must understand my position. If it ever came out that I am plotting against a minister of the Church of Scotland I could be ruined!'

'I don't see how, father!' replied Stanford. 'All I'm suggesting is that Julek stays with us as my guest. Claire and the Reverend Fraser have nothing whatsoever to do with this.'

'Of course, they have! The whole of Edinburgh knows about their affair! The whole of Edinburgh will now know why he has been thrown out by Mrs McIntyre!'

'Come on, father, you know that's a gross exaggeration. Neither Claire nor Julek have ever given anyone cause for the slightest suspicion of scandal!'

'They were seen kissing at the harvest ball.'

'So was I. With Ann Lonnegan. And she's Irish!'

'That's different!'

'She's still Catholic!'

'She's one of our Catholics!'

'Father! Come on!' snorted Charles.

'I must go! It's past nine o'clock. I shall be late for my appointment with the Chancellor!' Sir Robert, already wrapped in his cloak against the howling gale blowing down Queen Street, recognised the stupidity, uttered in frustrated haste, of his last remark. He grabbed his hat and cane, stormed out of the house without a backward glance and climbed into his carriage. Stanford, Julek, Stewart and Lady Sarah watched the coach trundling off towards the city centre from the shelter of the doorway.

'He'll come round,' said Stanford closing the front door.

'I don't think so,' replied Julek. 'Look, Stanford, I really don't think I should –'

'Nonsense,' interpolated Lady Sarah. 'Leave him to me, Julek. As Stanford said, he will come round. He's got a lot on his mind at the moment. We should all love to have you here. You know that perfectly well.'

'Frightfully fashionable, to have a Polish Count staying with one, you know,' said Stewart, trying to make light of the matter.

'Precisely!' said Lady Sarah. 'You shall be our tame Polish aristocrat.' She led the way from the hall back into the drawing room. Once inside, she turned, barring the way. 'However,' she added, looking intently at Julek, 'there will have to be conditions.'

'Conditions, Lady Sarah?'

There was an expression on Lady Sarah's face that Julek had never seen before – a hard, uncompromising look that cast a menacing shadow over her normally soft, clear features. 'Claire Fraser will not come within hailing distance of this house. Her name will not be uttered at any time when there are other people present. You will at no time give the impression that you are seeing her. As far as the world at large is concerned we are not aware of any relationship that you may be involved in. Do you understand, Julek?'

'Yes, of course, Lady Sarah,' said Julek, glancing at Stanford, who smiled. 'I quite understand. I shall give you no cause for concern. I promise you. The last thing I want is to be a burden to you in any way.'

Lady Sarah's expression softened. 'You will never be that,

Julek. We are all very fond of you, as you well know, and we know you love Claire dearly. But I cannot afford to let Sir Robert be compromised in any way whatsoever. I know I can rely on you.' Lady Sarah turned and walked into the drawing room, letting the three young men follow. 'Just one thing,' she added, 'don't trust Charles Carnethie.'

'Charles?' said Julek. 'But he's my best friend – along with Stanford, of course. I'd trust him with my life!'

'I wouldn't, if I were you.' Julek looked at her intently, but said nothing.

In the event, Sir Robert did, in the end, agree to allow Julek to stay at Queen Street, on the conditions set out by his wife. They had discussed the matter at great length, and had decided on the correct definition of the word 'righteousness'. The deep friendship between Julek and the McWhirter house had to be respected, and the young Pole was fully entitled to their total support. What was more, Love, they decided, should be given rein to conquer all, especially the forces of bigotry.

And so, on May 1 Julek moved into Queen Street, and was given the room next to Stanford's, which had thitherto served as a repository for hunting and fishing gear. The question of rent was not even raised, as befitting titled persons from whichever country: Julek did not offer, and Sir Robert did not request. Mrs McIntyre was brought in on the plot, and needed no persuasion to follow the conditions. She duly wrote to the Reverend Fraser admitting the error of her ways and assuring him that the young Pole had been given notice, and that she would personally oversee Mistress Claire's moral well-being and righteous influences.

For Julek and Claire, however, life took on a distinct turn for the worse. They were forced to meet only clandestinely, and chose the Botanical Gardens as the venue for their trysts. Gone were the days, and nights, when they would pore over anatomical drawings and case notes, pausing occasionally for a kiss and a cuddle on the sofa. Gone were the days when Claire would be invited to dinner, or a ball, at the McWhirters'. All previous such invitations were logged purely as social events with no specific connotations whatsoever.

Julek heeded Lady Sarah's advice not to trust Charles. He saw the wisdom of this advice when he reflected on Charles' innate opposition to their relationship. He began to wonder whether Charles was a Scot first, then a friend, rather than the other way round. He chose neither to give him the benefit of the doubt, nor to cause him to have to put his loyalties to the test. He gave Charles the impression that he had begun to lose interest in Claire.

'Really, Charles, you were right. I see very little future in a union between two such disparate and conflicting religious beliefs and traditions,' he told him during a late spring weekend at Carnethie Castle. Realising that his remark sounded awkward and contrived, he added, preening his hair theatrically. 'Anyway, I want to see what other fishes the sea might have to offer.'

'I'm glad you've seen sense, Julek,' replied Charles. 'It would have been bad enough battling it out with the Reverend Fraser, but a marriage would have been a recipe for disaster, don't you agree, father?'

'Absolutely, old boy,' said Lord Duncan. 'Are you two coming for a walk with Baldwyn?'

'Absolutely not!' replied Charles, making for the piano with his new volume of Mendelssohn's *Songs without Words*. Julek followed eagerly.

*****

As the wet Scottish spring turned imperceptibly into a wet Scottish summer, Stewart McWhirter, having ostensibly got over his infatuation with Franciszka, fell for Lady Jane, the daughter of Lord and Lady Walford Gilchrist. Lord Gilchrist owned a

Castle near Pitlochry, in Perthshire, a plantation in Jamaica, and a house in London, at which he threw a Whitsun Ball to launch their fourth, and by all accounts the prettiest and most accomplished, daughter. Jane had thick, jet-black hair, skin the texture of white porcelain and smouldering dark eyes. At the fortepiano she played Scarlatti Sonatas and accompanied herself in William Wallace songs. She drew miniatures, which were highly complimented by none other than John Constable, whom she met on one occasion, shortly before the painter's sudden and untimely death the previous year. She was obviously also smitten by the handsome and urbane Stewart McWhirter. Their mutual attraction was extremely well viewed by all concerned, and a glittering Scottish marriage was widely speculated upon on all the Highland estates.

*****

At the end of July, when London Society began to migrate to the Highlands for the shooting, and all the students at the Medical School prepared to leave for their vacations, Lady Jane Gilchrist made a detour to Edinburgh to stay with her older sister, Mary, now Mrs Wilfred Wilberforce, the wife of a wealthy Edinburgh timber merchant some 20 years her senior. The beginning of the holiday and shooting season was mercifully blessed with exceptionally warm weather, and the McWhirter boys planned a fishing trip, scheduled for Wednesday July 25, out on the Firth of Forth for a selected party of close friends. This included Lady Jane Gilchrist, Wilfred and Mary Wilberforce, Ann Lonnegan, and Julek. Ann brought along her younger sister, Philomena, ostensibly as a match-making exercise for Julek's benefit, in order to reinforce the deception that he was free of any romantic entanglements. Philly, as she was called, was fluffy, featherweight and on the giggly side, but very pretty. She had a wicked sense of humour, masses of curly, honey-coloured hair and enormous green eyes that seemed perpetually filled with wonder. Philly was quite excited at the idea of being in on a secret plot, and found the whole idea of aiding and abetting an illicit tryst at sea extremely romantic. One could say that she was in love with Love. The party was completed by Grant Burke, a contemporary of Stewart's at Almsbury who was reading Law at Oxford. A confirmed bachelor and misogynist, his only passions were his native city of Bath, the law, sport and Mendelssohn.

At least, that was the passenger list that the McWhirter boys chose to reveal. In fact, Claire Fraser was also secretly included, in contravention of the agreement with Sir Robert and Lady Sarah. This caused some serious reservations on Julek's part, although Claire had no misgivings, and was prepared to throw caution to the Firth winds in order to be with Julek.

'Look, Stanford,' said Julek, 'I know you and Stewart mean well, but if your parents were to find out, you'd both get into serious trouble, and I'd be out on my ear from your house. And that's even before the Reverend Fraser – and half of Scotland – gets in on the act and starts baying for my blood!'

'I assure you, PK –'

'And what about Mrs McIntyre? Have you considered how this might compromise her position?'

'Relax, PK,' said Stanford, 'Mrs McIntyre promises to see and hear nothing. We're all on your side, and we'd like you and Claire to have a lovely day together before you – indeed, all of us – part for the vacations. As far as everyone else is concerned Claire has arranged to go on a celebratory end-of-term picnic in the Pentland Hills with the Farishes. You know how fond the Farishes are of Claire.'

'Yes, they're a charming family, and very supportive, but Mrs McIntyre…'

'…will know nothing,' said Stanford. 'As far as Mrs McIntyre is concerned the Farishes will collect her in their buggy. In fact, it will be a buggy hired by me, but Mrs McIntyre will not know that.' Stanford paused before continuing in a quiet voice. 'They will bring her back the following day. Anyway, no one's going to find out unless one of us spills the beans, and I can't see that happening, can you?'

'Well, no, but someone might see us together,' said Julek.

'At the crack of dawn? In Portobello?'

'Is that where we're sailing from?'

'On the *Sally Jane*.'

The elderly but still very serviceable fishing smack the *Sally Jane* was captained by a gnarled, weather-beaten and hairy old seadog by the name of Malcolm, aided by a large, silent, barrel-shaped boatswain who appeared not to answer to any known name, and a big, soft, slobbery golden retriever which always answered to the name of Bo'sun.

The three buggies, the Wilberforces', the McWhirters' and the one hired to pick Claire up from Mrs McIntyre's, all arrived at daybreak, and the party cast off soon after. By midmorning they had passed the islands of Fidra and Craigleith off North Berwick and were heading towards the Isle of May, where the Firth of Forth finally opened into the North Sea. The plan was to circumnavigate the Island and return to port in time to eat the day's catch for supper at the Puffin's Nest, a rude but congenial hostelry on the seafront at Portobello, where Stewart and Stanford had taken rooms, and hired the kitchen and its staff, for the night. There was a little wind, and the Firth was just a little choppy, but nobody minded as the atmosphere was one of much cheer and bonhomie, lubricated by as many flasks of Scotch whisky as there were men on board.

Julek and Claire gravitated towards the bow. Their hands slipped naturally one into the other on the gunwale. 'That's my land over there,' said Julek, staring straight ahead into the rising sun.

Claire ignored the remark. 'By the way,' she said, 'what do you mean I shall be taken back tomorrow?'

'Just that,' replied Julek casually. 'Stanford reckoned it would be too late to take you back after supper, and has taken a room for you.'

'At the Puffin's Nest?'

'Yes. He has taken rooms for everyone.'

'A room for you and a room for me?'

'I suppose so. I haven't checked.'

'Have Ann and Jane rooms of their own?'

'I – I don't really know, Claire,' said Julek, obviously uncomfortable at this interrogation.

'I say, this is jolly. What are you two being so frightfully clandestine about?' Wilfred had staggered up to them, waving a chicken leg in one hand and a bottle of Bordeaux in the other. He stumbled and almost fell. 'Bit choppy, what?'

'Wilfred, have Stewart and Stanford taken separate rooms for Ann, Jane and myself?' said Claire.

'Separate rooms?' chortled Wilfred. 'Goodness, no! This whole voyage has been plotted as a prelude to…' he waved the bottle at the sun, '…a stint at the bosun bosom of Aph Aphro tidy Aphrodite! A spell of hanky panky! The materrrr-ialisation of Love's sweet dream by Jove! But I wax poetic, dear Claire! Happens when I partake excessively of the fruits of Bacchus – oh bugger! It's fallen in the water.'

Claire was no longer listening to Wilfred, who was pointing at his bottle bobbing on the waves. She had turned back to Julek. 'The Bosom of Aphrodite?' she said pointedly as Wilfred staggered off to join the others. 'A spell of hanky panky! The materialisation of love's sweet dream? Whose idea was this, Julek?'

'Not mine!' said Julek assertively. 'It was all Stanford's idea. I would never have come up with such a thing myself!'

'No?' said Claire.

'Of course not!'

'Why not?'

Julek failed to notice the hint of a smirk on Claire's face. 'Because it's not – seemly!' he finally said.

'Does that mean you don't want to share a room with me?'

'Of c-course not! The v-very idea.' Then he noticed the smirky smile and the penny dropped. 'Well – I suppose – now you come to mention it – oh! that's my homeland over there. I wonder what they're all doing right now.'

Their hands met once more on the gunwale, and they stared at the nothingness of the eastern horizon.

In the event not all that much fishing took place. Most of the party could be relied on to shoot fairly straight and with enthusiasm on a grouse moor, but few had any real urge to sit for hours with rod and line, hoping for a bite from a creature that they couldn't even see. Everyone paid some lip service to the nets and lines, with which they toyed, getting them, and themselves, into tangles, and enjoying the sheer buffoonery of extricating themselves. Every so often the large hamper, containing ham, cold chicken, rye bread, fruit and cakes was raided, and the contents washed down from a case of Bordeaux from the McWhirter cellars. Wilfred Wilberforce became very drunk and soon dropped off to sleep. Only Grant Burke showed any passion for the actual fishing, took no notice of the high jinks, and concentrated on the matter in hand. By the time the *Sally Jane* had rounded the Isle of May he had caught enough mackerel single-handedly to feed a whole platoon.

The *Sally Jane* had reached her furthest point from port, and had turned her bows for the homeward tack when the light changed, and dark, menacing clouds materialised as if from nowhere in the sky above. The thunderstorm suddenly descended and threatened only perfunctorily before releasing its full force directly over the island. The wind followed suit, and its sudden rage was terrifying in its ferocity. An enormous wave hit the *Sally Jane* hard amidships, causing havoc and mayhem on board. Grant Burke was knocked off his perch in the stern and fell into the embrace of the wave. Wilfred woke from his stupor only to stagger and fall into the sea. Mary lunged after him, missed her footing, and followed him. The two threshed about in the swell as Mary tried to keep her husband afloat. The women screamed. The men shouted. Malcolm yelled orders that no one except the boatswain understood: he had switched to Gaelic. No one was in a position to do anything about the ones who fell overboard, as everyone was primarily preoccupied with finding a secure place where they might hold onto something, as wave after wave battered the helpless boat, driving her towards the rocks of the Isle of May. Julek, who found himself holding a hysterical Philly close to him, watched, horrified, as Stewart failed to hold onto a wooden beam, which was slippery and too thick to hold firmly, and was thrown overboard. His cry of anguish was abruptly aborted.

After what seemed like an eternity, but was in effect only about twenty minutes, Julek, who had been looking round for Claire while gallantly hanging on to Philly with one arm, and holding the base of the mast with the other, suddenly let go of both. The ketch hit a rock, which caused the mast to break from its fixture and hit him hard across the head as it fell, and he knew no more.

X

The next day, like everywhere else in Europe, Frontillac sweltered in a heat-wave. Maurice returned home from his morning in the vineyards, hot and sweaty, to find that Franciszka was not there, and lunch had not been prepared. He was accompanied by Frédéric Ferrole, his manager, whose wife, the bustling and eminently sensible Lucille, acted as the local mid-wife – a useful connection in view of Franciszka's pregnancy. Frédéric had lost his job as manager of a vineyard near Pomerol after the proprietor's death on Easter Sunday, and was immediately taken on by Maurice, who knew him by reputation as a quiet, efficient, middle-aged peasant who knew everything there was to know about wine growing and management. He lived in a house just 3 kilometres away.

The two men found Franciszka's absence very strange, because she always had lunch prepared for the two of them at the dot of noon every single day without fail. She had got up early that morning, prepared breakfast and seen Maurice off as usual into the vineyards, where he met up with Frédéric.

'Franciszka!' he called. There was no answer. Leaving Frédéric in the kitchen, he went upstairs to her room, and found her bed still unmade, but no sign of her anywhere. 'Franciszka! Where are you?'

He went downstairs again. '*C'est très bizarre,*' he said. 'This is not like Franciszka.'

'Perhaps –' Frédéric shuffled his feet nervously, 'perhaps – the baby –? It is due any day, *Monsieur* Chavelet.'

Maurice was only too well aware of the fact. He had considered hiring Lucille to be with her during this time, but Franciszka had been absolutely adamant that she wanted no one except Doctor Mereau attending to her. Doctor Mereau made a point of calling in at Frontillac at every available opportunity to check that everything was in order.

'But that's no help whatsoever if the baby arrives when there's no one in the house,' Maurice had said, but there was just no reasoning with her.

'Perhaps we should search the grounds,' said Frédéric. 'She may have gone out, and even given birth among the vines somewhere? It is a possibility!'

'*Oui, bonne idée,*' said Maurice. 'You take the east fields and I'll try the river.'

'Very well, *Monsieur* Chavelet.'

With that they parted in opposite directions. Maurice walked briskly towards the river, his eyes fixed directly ahead of him. He had a strange sensation of being pulled along. He looked to neither left nor right; it was almost as though he knew exactly where to find Franciszka.

His instinct was right. Ten minutes later he found her, exactly where he had expected to, at her favourite spot, from which she threw a flower into the river every single day for Lenka. She was lying, barely conscious, sprawled among the reeds on the grassy bank, partly in and partly out of the lapping waters of the Dordogne. An occasional whimper issued from her chapped mouth, and her breathing was crackling and erratic. Her clothing was in total disarray, soaking wet, torn, muddy and bloodstained. Her hair was tousled, matted and wild, and covered her face, which was the colour and texture of mottled marble, dripping with perspiration. Her lower torso was uncovered and undignified, and those parts which were not actually in the water were caked in blood which had dried hard and crusty in the hot sun.

She had obviously been there for quite some time, and had tried to clean herself up as best she could before complete exhaustion overcame her and she lost consciousness.

Beside her, also half in and half out of the water, lay a small purple and blue body which, on closer inspection, seemed to be a stillborn baby, partly resting on the dried offal of the afterbirth. The hairless cranium was enormous and dome-like. The eyes, one of which was only just visible through a tiny slit, were out of alignment, and there was no nose and no jaw. The arms were short stumps, like fins, with three fingers at each end. There was no way of telling whether it was a boy or a girl: there were no sexual organs whatsoever that he could see. Maurice stood, mesmerised and shaking, swaying gently and irregularly. His mind, unable to take in the horror of the scene before him, completely focused on the swarms of flies in attendance. He listened with rapt concentration to their buzzing as though it were a symphony. Then, after an age, a howl, unbidden, issued from his mouth in a rising crescendo, and he fell to the ground on his knees and sobbed uncontrollably in a hysterical falsetto.

'Franciszka! *Mon enfant!*' he wailed, cradling the now unconscious Franciszka to his breast. '*Ma fille!*'

A hand rested gently on his shoulder. '*Monsieur,*' said a quiet voice. Maurice opened his eyes and looked up. How long he had been in a fitful daze he could not tell. He was only aware of an utter stillness broken only by the buzzing of flies and lapping of water. He returned with an effort to reality. There were two men on the bank, one leaning over him and Franciszka, the other sitting in a rowing boat in the river. 'What is happening *Monsieur?* May we be of assistance. It is evident you are in need of it.'

Maurice stared at the flowing river for a while. 'It is my daughter,' he croaked at last. 'Her baby – she gave birth – we are from Frontillac –' Maurice pointed vaguely in the direction of *la Maison*. 'Perhaps I could prevail on your goodness –'

'Of course, *Monsieur*,' said the man closest to him. 'I will help you take your daughter to the house.' He turned to his companion. 'Irenée, row into town and fetch the Doctor –'

'Doctor Mereau,' said Maurice. 'It must be Doctor Mereau…'

'I know him,' said Irenée, pushing the boat out onto the river once more. 'I'm on my way.'

'…and the Constable,' added Maurice. 'Tell them to come at once to Frontillac. The girl is unconscious and in a very bad way, and the baby –' he looked properly for the first time at the baby and his voice choked, '– the baby – *Mon Dieu!* – the baby is – d-dead!'

Back at *la Maison* Frédéric had been to fetch his wife Lucille, and was already there when Doctor Mereau and Constable Dubois arrived at Frontillac within one minute of each other.

'Maurice!' cried Doctor Mereau, rushing through the door, 'what a terrible tragedy! Where is Franciszka?'

Maurice vaguely indicated the stairs. He was seated at the kitchen table with Frédéric, Lucille and the man from the boat. Frédéric had taken the liberty of placing a bottle of Cognac on the table and pouring out four shots. Only Maurice had not touched his glass. It had not occurred to him to do so. Doctor Mereau took a not entirely disinterested look at the bottle, then made off upstairs, taking the stairs two at a time, followed by Lucille.

At the same time Constable Dubois entered with an air of pompous dignity that contrasted wildly with Doctor Mereau's lack of it. He was accompanied by Irenée. '*Messieursdames*,' he stretched out his hand to Maurice, who ignored it and continued to stare at his glass of Cognac. The Constable withdrew it. 'We meet again in unpleasant circumstances, Monsieur Chavelet. I understand that there has been a death. Where is the corpse?'

'A terrible tragedy, Constable,' Frédéric, seeing that his

employer was in no fit state to undergo any kind of interrogation, took charge. 'Monsieur Chavelet's daughter has given birth to a stillborn baby by the riverside. Doctor Mereau is upstairs with her now.'

The Constable took out his notepad. 'And you are, *Monsieur*?'

'Frédéric Ferrole. Estate manager.'

'And my name is Giraudon. Etienne Giraudon. Monsieur Irenée Juspin and I are rivermen, and we were rowing past when we noticed Monsieur Chavelet and his daughter. And her – baby.'

'Frédéric – Ferrole – Etienne – Giraudon – Irenée – Juspin,' said Constable Dubois, writing in his notebook. He turned to Maurice. 'I was not aware that you had a daughter, *Monsieur*,' he said.

Maurice looked at him blankly. 'I – I haven't, that is, I didn't until – until – un –'

'Can't you see that Monsieur Chavelet is distraught, Constable,' said Frédéric, coming to the rescue. 'Can the interrogation wait until the main facts have been clarified?'

'We suggest you come with us to the river,' said Etienne.

'Is that where the dead baby is?' said the Constable.

'Yes,' replied Irenée. 'But I suggest we wait for the Doctor to come with us.'

'Perhaps,' Maurice was able to summon enough wits about him to reach for his glass, '*un petit gout* – *un* Cognac?'

'That is very civil of you, *Monsieur*,' said Constable Dubois. 'I don't mind if I do.'

Frédéric did the honours and everyone downed the much-needed shot of liquor.

'Very hot weather we're having,' said Constable Dubois. No one said anything. 'Most unusual.' There was the sound of movement upstairs. Everyone stared up at the ceiling. 'They say this heat-wave is spread throughout Europe.' After another long silence, broken only by the Constable clearing his throat, a bluebottle flew noisily in through the window. 'There are probably flies all over your dead grandchild by now. Was it a boy or a girl?'

Maurice suddenly burst into a fit of suppressed sobbing. Frédéric placed an arm around his shoulder. 'There, there, *mon brave* –' He scowled pointedly at the Constable, who looked quizzically from one to the other of the men present. The strained atmosphere was relieved by Doctor Mereau coming back down into the kitchen. He made straight for the Cognac, poured himself a stiff shot, and downed it before speaking. 'Franciszka will be all right,' he said. 'She is in a dreadful state, but there is no permanent damage. We have washed her and patched her up as best we could, and given her a sleeping draught. She is sleeping soundly for the moment. Madame Lucille shall stay with her.'

The Constable opened his mouth to speak. 'And now,' continued Doctor Mereau, pre-empting another possibly tactless remark, 'the Constable and I will need to see the baby. Maurice?'

'I – I cannot, Phillippe,' sobbed Maurice. 'I – I'm in no state to –'

'We'll take you, Monsieur le Docteur,' said Etienne.

'We know exactly where it is,' added Irenée.

'Good,' said the Doctor. 'We'll take my buggy. We'll need a sheet.'

The four men squeezed themselves into the Doctor's buggy, and they set off across the vineyards to the riverside, where they found the remains of the baby exactly where Etienne and Irenée said they would be. They both knew what to expect, but the sight that met the eyes of the Doctor and the Constable caused them both to stop in their tracks and stare in undisguised horror.

'*Mon Dieu!*' gasped Doctor Mereau under his breath. 'She's his!'

'Who is whose?' asked the Constable.

The Doctor ignored him and squatted down to examine the baby's body. He turned it over, and the flies disappeared, only to return a few moments later. Despite them, the Doctor looked into the only good eye, and into the opening of the mouth. He listened to the baby's chest, then he examined the genital region, and shook his head.

'It's deformed,' said Constable Dubois. 'Just as well it was stillborn.'

'That's right, Constable,' said Doctor Mereau finally, standing up. 'I declare this baby boy died of natural causes. Stillborn.'

'Boy?' asked Irenée.

'Yes. He was born with no genitals, but he would have been a boy. There are ways –' He stopped and choked back tears.

'May I record his death of natural causes?' said the Constable, taking out his notebook.

'Yes. Natural causes.'

'Death – by – natural – causes,' wrote the Constable in his book. 'And the deceased's name?'

Doctor Mereau exploded. 'Holy Mother of God, Constable!' he cried, 'how in Heaven's name should I know! Ask his mother! On second thoughts, don't! She's already been to Hell and back!'

'So what should I write in my report?'

'Just write: Mother: Countess Franciszka Samojarska; stillborn son: Unnamed! Got that?'

'How do you spell Samo whatsit?'

By the time the four men returned to the house with the baby wrapped in the sheet that Maurice had provided, Lucille Ferrole had installed herself in Franciszka's room. Maurice had recovered enough to thank Etienne and Irenée for their support and kindness, and offer them another shot of Cognac before letting them go on their way. Constable Dubois, having written down in his notebook whatever his superiors required him to enter, also gulped down a Cognac, authorised Maurice to dispose of the corpse as he saw fit, and departed. Frédéric then excused himself to deal with vineyard matters left over from the morning.

Maurice and Doctor Mereau went into the salon with the Cognac bottle, and settled themselves into their usual armchairs.

'She's mine, Phillippe,' said Maurice. 'Franciszka's my little girl.'

'It would appear so. How do you feel about it?'

'Happy.'

'Really?'

'Really.'

'What about the baby?'

Maurice paused and took a sip of Cognac. 'Nature took its course, don't you think?'

It was Doctor Mereau's turn to take a long, thoughtful sip of Cognac. 'I think not.'

'What do you mean?'

'The baby's lungs were full of water.'

'So? She gave birth beside the river.'

'The baby was drowned, Maurice.'

'*Mon Dieu*, Phillippe!'

'Perhaps that is why Franciszka declined to have anyone to watch over her. Perhaps she knew. But rest assured, Maurice, it will be recorded as a stillbirth. Perhaps now you and Franciszka –' his voice tailed away and he pursed his lips. 'You must find yourselves a life.'

The next day, on the same spot by the river, the baby was baptised Francis Maurice Irenée Etienne Samojarski by Abbé Vassigny with Dordogne water. Then he was buried there in a tiny coffin after a short ceremony. A simple flat stone, with an inscription by Irenée Juspin, who was a dab hand with a hammer and chisel, was put in place a few days later.

XI

On the day after the interment of baby Francis Samojarski, a thousand miles to the north, Stanford McWhirter sprang to his feet off the rock on which he was perched, and pointed westwards. 'They're coming!' he cried excitedly. 'Rescue's on its way!'

Julek stirred, lifted himself up on his elbow, smiled, and fell back onto the mossy grass, his head pounding, his lips parched and his hair matted with blood. Claire, who had been lying beside him, sat up. Two days previously Julek had been woken in a wet, rocky cove by a wet, slobbery tongue licking his face. Behind the tongue was a big, wet golden retriever with enormous brown eyes, matted fur and a wildly wagging tail. Behind the wagging tail crouched Claire, wearing a concerned expression on her face. 'Down, Bos'un, good dog,' she had muttered weakly and ineffectually. Claire patted Bos'un on the head and gave Julek a hug. 'Thank God you're all right, Julek,' she said. Her feelings were echoed by the others.

The *Sally Jane* had wrecked herself on a rocky promontory of the Isle of May. With the exception of Wilfred and Mary Wilberforce, and Grant Burke, everyone else managed to scramble ashore without major injury. Except for Stewart, who had seen Julek floundering, unconscious, on the water, and had succeeded in hauling him to shore, at the expense of a couple of ribs, broken against protruding rocks during the struggle. And Philly had suffered a minor gash on her leg. Julek's dizziness, violent headache, double vision and drowsiness suggested concussion. All the others only suffered minor cuts and bruises.

For the remainder of that day, the survivors tried to come to terms with the tragic outcome of what was meant to be a pleasure trip – followed by a stint at the Bosom of Aphrodite. Suppressing feelings of impotent rage, they tried to make themselves as comfortable as they could, sharing the rocky coastline, low cliffs and grassy banks of the island with some very bemused puffins. The storm had passed as quickly as it had come, and the afternoon was once again hot and sunny. Malcolm and the boatswain, aided and abetted by Stanford, as well as hindered by Bos'un the golden retriever, managed to clamber onto the wreck of the *Sally Jane* to see what provisions could be salvaged. The food hamper had been washed away, but the case of Bordeaux, which had miraculously survived, had shed three bottles which were bobbing about in the water. None of the whisky flasks survived.

'Enough for a dram or two apiece,' said Malcolm, trying to keep up spirits: by now thirst had become a problem. 'Save us frae being too sober till they send rescue.' He assured everyone that it would just be a matter of time before the *Sally Jane's* absence was noted, and help is sent. Malcolm also did not need any persuasion to say a few words of Christian solace on behalf of those who had perished, which he did with all the confidence of having done so on many previous occasions. He then went on to curse his 'wretched an' senile ol' hag of a tub an' may ye ne'er rust in peace!'

The two nights that the party spent on the island were as cold as the days had been hot. Stewart was virtually immobile and in great pain all the time, with Lady Jane, shaken, but otherwise completely unhurt, in constant attendance. Philly had managed to bandage up her leg from material torn from her dress, and Julek felt reasonably comfortable just as long as he remained still and in a horizontal position, with his head resting in Claire's lap. Malcolm and the boatswain preferred to keep a respectful distance, feeling guilty and angry at the same time that such a tragedy should have occurred to the 'quality' under their auspices.

Now, awakened from a fitful slumber by Stanford's cry, Julek again tried to lift himself up off Claire's lap, but this time his whole being was convulsed with a spasm of nausea. His thirst was overpowering and his tongue felt like a scouring pad. He fell back onto the rocks, bumping his head again. He winced and retched momentarily before relaxing once more on his back, drinking in the welcome goodness of the hot sun in the western sky and Claire's tender caresses.

A large ketch arrived and moored in the inlet where the party had camped, and there were more than enough hands to help everyone get on board. In addition, there were baskets of bread, cold chicken, dried fish, oatcakes, several bottles of much needed fresh water – and two bottles of Scotch whisky, all of which were attacked and demolished within minutes by the hungry and thirsty castaways.

Among those on board the ketch was a Presbyterian minister, the Reverend William Robson, and Charles Carnethie. 'Julek!' cried the latter, 'when I heard that the *Sally Jane* hadn't returned, I was so concerned! Especially in view of the storm! My goodness, Stanford, what a spectacle that was! Never seen anything quite like it! Glad to see you're all right! Stewart, you look awful! We shall get you into hospital as soon as we dock. In the meantime, just hold on, and you'll be fine. And what about the girls? Claire?' His voice became suddenly quizzical and subdued as he saw her approach Julek, while at exactly the same moment the Reverend Robson came up. 'Claire,' he said. 'Not Claire Fraser? D'ye nae remember me, lassie? I ken your father well.' A look of recognition alighted on Claire's face, and she glanced at Julek and smiled nervously. 'Ay, I hadna seen ye for months!

I've seen ye grow up frae a wee bairn, an' look at ye noo! I hear you're studying medicine now at the School? A fine vocation. And what brings ye to this isle o' puffins?'

By now there was a great deal of jostling and crowding going on as the shipwrecked party was manoeuvred on board the swaying and tossing ketch, making conversation – and standing still – difficult. 'By Jove yes,' interpolated Charles as Stewart was carried on a stretcher past him. 'I didn't know you were with this party? This is a surprise!'

'Yes, Stanford invited me at the last minute,' said Claire nervously. 'To make up the numbers.'

'Ah, to partner Julek, I presume?' laughed Charles mirthlessly. 'Of course, you two know one another!' he added sarcastically.

'So, who is this young man, Charles?' said the Reverend Robson.

'This is my excellent friend Count Julek Samojarski,' said Charles. 'May I introduce you to the Reverend Robson.'

'How do you do, Reverend,' moaned Julek. 'Forgive me, but I have a dreadful headache, and feeling disorientated.'

'Of course, of course! I understand ye suffered a heavy knock on the head when the mast collapsed! We shall get ye to hospital as soon as we dock.' A puzzled look alighted on the Reverend Robson's bushy brow. 'Ye're nae the Polish lad at the Medical School, are ye?'

Julek and Claire looked at one another, and opened their mouths to speak, but no words came from them.

'Julek, dearest, please help me, I'm in absolute agony. My leg is killing me!' It was Philly. She jostled her way up to Julek and hung herself around his neck. 'I'm sorry about this, Reverend, but Julek has been such a tower of strength to us all, especially me; and that despite the knock on the head that he received when the mast broke. He was holding me so tightly, would not let go. He saved us both. And as for Claire,' Philly reached out and squeezed Claire's hand, 'she has suffered a terrible loss, Reverend. I'm really sorry about Grant, dear Claire. I know how close you were. Please excuse us.'

With that Philly and Julek allowed themselves to be whisked off by two seamen to join Stewart in the cabin, where beds had been prepared for those in need.

'By Jove, Philly, you're a trump card!' muttered Julek.

'You can give me a kiss in return.'

Julek obliged.

When everyone was on board and settled for the return tack, the Reverend Robson was asked to conduct a formal service of remembrance for Grant Burke and Wilfred and Mary Wilberforce. When he asked for prayers for Claire, the daughter of his very good friend the Reverend Menzies Fraser, whose tragic loss of her beloved Grant she would now have to bear with courage and fortitude, a number of eyebrows rose in bemused puzzlement, notably that of Sir Charles Carnethie. He threw an angry look at Claire across the crowded deck, which did not go unnoticed by her.

Julek was due to sail to Königsberg on the following Sunday, the first leg of his journey to Sarenki, where he had planned to spend the summer vacation, but Dr Johnstone Leightonstone, had categorically forbidden it. The McWhirters' physician of long standing, who had attended to both Stewart's broken ribs and Philly's gashed leg, prescribed complete rest for all three of them of at least a month. Curiously, both Stewart and Julek found this restriction quite welcome. Stewart loved his native city dearly, and was often homesick when away from it. Besides, Lady Jane was at hand. She had been persuaded to stay at Carne House, the Wilberforce residence some twenty miles to the west of Edinburgh, where Wilfred's elderly parents appreciated her companionship after the death of their son and daughter-in-law.

*****

Julek, on the other hand, was suffering a certain amount of nervous and physical exhaustion and sat down to write a long letter home. His trips to and from Europe, his lapsed studies, the Claire business, Franciszka, the Sarenki inheritance, all contributed to an overload of his mental and physical make-up. He now planned to spend his time quietly at Queen Street, catching up with a still sizeable backlog of medical studies. He had, in addition, branched out into the study of beneficial waters from various spas; this was in connection with Sarenki, and the health spa that he was planning to develop. He had already received considerable help from the late Grant Burke, who had been a native of Bath, a modern city that had evolved around its healing waters since Roman times. Grant had been regularly sending him any literature on the subject that he could lay his hands on.

He also gave Julek the address of his cousin, Stephen de Villiers, who was considered an expert on beneficial waters, notably those of Bath.

'Stephen has turned part of his house in the Royal Crescent into a laboratory, where he analyses the waters, studies their chemical make-up and makes various volunteers drink it to see which of their various ailments could be alleviated,' Grant had said. 'Could be a useful contact for you when your spa project comes up.'

Julek agreed, and made a mental note to follow it up. He had promised himself a leisurely visit to the city at some stage of the vacation – his condition permitting. 'After all,' he told Stanford over breakfast one morning, 'a chap with concussion is perfectly entitled to go and take the waters, if only for his health!'

Julek's greatest regret, however, was the absence of Claire. She had returned to Skye for the vacation, and they never even had a chance to kiss goodbye properly – let alone enjoy a 'stint at the Bosom of Aphrodite'. At Portobello everyone had been whisked off pretty promptly to their respective buggies and welcoming committees, watched by a sizeable proportion of the population of Edinburgh, who had all turned out to gawp at the safe arrival of the Isle of May Castaways.

*****

During the first week of August Charles called round to invite Julek and Stanford to Carnethie Castle for the Inglorious Ninth, a kind of unofficial Prelude to the Glorious Twelfth, which marked the start of the grouse shooting season. The Ninth was a new invention of Charles'. 'It's primarily a bash for all those friends of mine who enjoy a summer spell on the moors, but prefer music, literature, and the cut and thrust of debate and sexual encounters to shooting deers and grice.' Charles' contempt for blood sports of any kind included distorting sporting terminology. 'One of its advantages being that people don't overstay their welcome, and leave by the time the killer squads arrive! Hamish has already accepted, and I've also asked Ann and Philly, and they're both very keen to come,' he said, looking pointedly at Julek. 'Philly specially asked if you were going to be invited. I think you're onto a good thing there, Julek. Smart girl, Phluffy Philly. You know, I never for a moment suspected that you and Philly – you know – the fishing trip and all that –'

'Well,' said Julek, donning a theatrical hint of smirk, 'we have only just started seeing one another, so to speak. The fishing trip was our first real outing together, you know.'

'You certainly looked like a well-established pair, old man,' grinned Charles. 'But then, you Poles work quickly, don't you, as far as affairs of the heart are concerned. Not like us ordinary mortals!'

'No more than any other nation,' said Julek nonchalantly. He was not fully recovered from his knock, and hoped that Charles would stop labouring the subject; the strain of keeping up the pretence would ultimately prove too much, and he was very afraid of letting the deception slip. 'Anyway, it's just a casual bit of mutual diversion.'

'And there I was, thinking that you and Claire had got together again!'

'Let's change the subject, Charles.'

'Oh. All right. If you say so,' conceded Charles, foiled in his attempt to update himself on Julek's love life. 'So, I can count on you for the Ninth.'

'Absolutely.'

'I've got some new Chopin you might be interested in.'

XII

The Inglorious Ninth turned out to be something of a glorious washout. The weather broke as if on cue, and it poured with rain every single day. Charles' Carnethie's party included Stefan and Jenny Sulechowski, who had been invited for the Twelfth, but had agreed to come early to take advantage of some cultured young company, as the average age of the 'killer squads', as Charles had so colourfully described his father's hunting guests, on this occasion mostly senior statesmen and Members of Parliament of very long standing, hovered around the half century mark. Also invited, by Lord Duncan himself, was Jenny's best friend, Flora Chalmers, a talented soprano with operatic aspirations. She had ostensibly been invited 'to make up the numbers', which in effect meant a partner for Charles.

'Damned fine filly, that Flora, Charles,' he had told his son. 'Time you learned to ride. So, saddle yourself with her and stirr-up your loins, me lad! Ha! Ha! Ha! Come, Baldwyn.'

Charles winced at his father's attempts at humour, and sniffed. He had never had much success with women, whom he found daunting in the extreme, especially if they were beautiful. Julek had never in his life seen a young blood as awkward and tongue-tied as Charles in the company of any attractive woman who was not spoken for. With those that were, he could be witty and charming, as long as there was no hint of obligation on his part to make any kind of overture. He was at ease with all married women, unattractive women, and any other women who were unavailable in any other way. Flora made up with her warm and friendly personality what she lacked in looks: her eyes were too far apart, she wore her mouse-coloured hair short and straight, and her teeth protruded slightly. For all that, she had a very attractive, rounded figure, with a full bust and, as estate manager Mr McLintock had been heard to comment, 'child-bear-ring hups'. Lord Duncan had high hopes that Flora might just be the filly on which his reticent son might learn to ride, and Flora, in turn, hoped for a moneyed, landed connection to launch her on an operatic career.

That left only Hamish Fergusson without an invited partner. It would not have been socially possible to set him up with any girl from the Carnethie circle. His background would not have permitted it, and both the Carnethies and Hamish himself were well aware of the implications, and laboured under no illusions. From the start Hamish had been accepted by the Carnethies without reservation not only as a good friend of Charles, but as a valuable human being in his own right. Lord Duncan's lifelong championship of the dispossessed, the disadvantaged and the underdog was well-known, and even the most blinkered, unenlightened and class obsessed bigot had to toe the Carnethie line on Carnethie home territory whether they liked it or not. Hamish had in fact found his own partner in the shapely shape of Jeanette Foulds, the schoolteacher in the village, where Lady Elizabeth played a large part in the community. Jeanette, a bright, intelligent redhead with green eyes and a cheery smile, was always made to feel very welcome at the Castle, where she was often found in Lord Duncan's library, helping to catalogue his collection of manuscripts, music, prints and rare books.

The first day of this Ninth was spent avoiding taking Baldwyn for long walks in the pouring rain, and excuses ranged from reading, exploring the library, playing and listening to the pianoforte, or just talking, smoking and putting the world to rights without recourse to any fresh air other than the inevitable penetration of draughts that were a feature of all country houses. After a lively dinner of Scotch broth, Aberdeen Angus beef – mercifully rare in Julek's estimation – and treacle pie, Lord Duncan and Lady Elizabeth excused themselves and retired. Then raucous charades, light music, dancing, drinking and smoking gradually gave way to modest flirting, hand-holding, all enhanced with some modest kissing and cuddling, all well on the correct side of seemliness.

Bed-time was instigated by the midnight chime from the grandfather clock in the drawing room. Jeanette walked home in the dark, which she was quite used to do, and Hamish went to bed alone. Stefan and Jenny Sulechowski, recently married, had again been given the Arabic Room, where the sumptuous décor and drapes exuded an exotic and very romantic atmosphere, and had constituted the climax to their Highland honeymoon earlier in the year. Stanford and Ann retired to their respective rooms in the sure knowledge that they would meet again at some appointed time later that night, most probably in the equally exotic Chinese room, which had been allocated to Stanford: it boasted a four-poster double bed. Julek, who had been flirting disgracefully with Phluffy Philly all evening, did not consider that he was actually giving her any kind of sexual encouragement. Philly, however, did not see it that way. It was during the shipwreck, when Julek had held her tightly at the mast before it broke, that she became aware of his strength, courage and manliness. She was the Damsel in Distress, and he was the Knight in Shining Armour, and she became increasingly confused as to her fluctuating feelings. But she told herself that she was just being silly, and chose to support Julek in his love for Claire, and play the role that had been assigned to her. However, during the course of this evening, in the very welcome absence of Claire, she became aware of a closeness growing between them, and she found herself pondering the seemingly increasingly realistic possibilities of replacing Claire in his affections. But when Julek retired perfunctorily, wishing everyone a goodnight of equal strength, she watched him go with a look of bitter disappointment.

That night Philly lay awake, unable to sleep and tormented by passionate feelings and erotic fantasies. She caressed her virgin breasts, and wondered desperately what the Bosom of Aphrodite was really like. Every time she heard some clock chime one, then two, then three, she believed herself more and more in thrall to – in love with, even? – Julek, until finally, as the first glimmer of dawn showed in the eastern sky beyond her window, she dropped off into a fitful sleep.

The next two days differed from the first day only inasmuch as that Philly was not being as fluffy as she had been before. No one really noticed a dimming of her eyes, a quietness of demeanour and an absence of laughter, with the possible exception of Charles. Julek had continued flirting as before, totally unaware of the turmoil he was causing in his young admirer.

On the night of the Eleventh, after everyone had retired exactly along the processes established on the previous two nights, Philly decided that if Julek will not come to Philly, then Philly would go to Julek. Her heart was pounding with a heady mixture of passion and apprehension, as she considered the implications of the Bosom of Aphrodite. The poets wrote highly of it, writers have written novels about it, and lovers have died for it. And now, she, Philly Lonnegan, aged eighteen, would sacrifice her virginity for it. She had heard that all men are possessed with a natural sexual urge, especially where any attractive women are concerned. Her father had told her so. 'Beware of men,' he had warned her, 'they have only one thing on their mind.' At the time Philly heeded this warning; now she welcomed its implication.

The clock struck one. She rose from her bed, lit a candle and made her way along the dark corridors, until she reached Julek's room. She took a deep breath, turned the handle, and entered.

The room was small, intimate, and full of heavy furnishings. Julek was fast asleep in an oak cot. She walked up to it, held her candle high, and gazed upon him. He was naked, his smooth, hairless, exposed chest heaving, and one leg dangling over the edge. Suddenly, as if aware of the light above him, he woke.

His eyes alighted on an angel with a luxuriant mane of curly, honey-coloured hair, holding aloft a candle which reflected her enormous green eyes, making them sparkle like emeralds, who was standing over him. Her rich, full lips were parted. Suddenly, the angel's white gown slipped and became a white, silken pool at her feet, revealing a perfect body of burnt orange gold, gleaming in the flickering light of the amber flame. Her breasts were full and firm, and rose and fell in time to her breathing. Her free hand moved surreptitiously to the top of her thigh, and momentarily caressed against the soft, dark bush of hair before allowing it to hang free by her side. A dark, thin line, the remains of the gash sustained during the shipwreck, scarred her leg from just below where her hand hung to half way down her calf to dramatically erotic effect.

Julek looked at her hand, then followed the line of the scar and stared in wonder and amazement at the perfection of her ankle. A dream come true. True? Dream? Finally, he threw off his coverlet to reveal his full nakedness. Philly gazed, mesmerised, at the full measure of Julek's inflamed passion, and tried to swallow. She could not. She had not seen such a thing before. Wave upon wave of feelings she never knew existed froze her in a hot sweat, and she could not move. Julek rose from the bed, took the candle and placed it on the bedside table. He took her in his arms. The kiss was long and lingering, their bodies dripping with anticipation. He then gently lowered her, and himself, onto the bed –

*****

The Glorious Twelfth dawned, the cue for the 'killer squads' to arrive and, with the exception of Stefan and Jenny Sulechowski. for the young and the cultured to leave,

'So, you're deserting the realms of culture and exalted thoughts for the dubious delights of bagging braces of grice and peasants in revolt,' bantered Julek over a breakfast of porridge and fried kidneys and bacon, followed by toast and marmalade. Philly looked at him, hoping to catch his eye over the breakfast table. But Julek was not casting it. He kept his gaze well and truly away from her. Since he had despatched her back to her room just as the clock was striking two, he had not even acknowledged her existence. She had come down to breakfast, hoping to exchange meaningful looks that no one else would notice. She had hoped for some arrangements to be made for next time. She had hoped there would be a next time. Many next times. She had hoped at least for an acknowledgement of what had happened in the night. Arguably the most momentously exciting event that had ever befallen Philly in her life, it seemed to her, was not even worthy of mention in the cold light of day.

When everyone returned to their rooms to pack, Philly surreptitiously went to Julek's room.

'Hello, Philly,' he said. 'Have you finished packing?'

'Julek,' she said, 'about last night –'

Julek grinned. 'Yes. Fun, wasn't it? You never told me it was your first time. If only I had known.' He pulled away the coverlet on the bed. It was covered in blood. 'I got the impression you did this kind of thing often. That was quite an act. An angel in gold and amber at the moment of waking! It's what poets write about and men dream of.'

Philly froze, and her eyes opened wide. 'Quite an act? Is that how you see it? Julek, I – I came to say I meant it when I said I loved you, but you –'

Julek held her by the shoulders. 'Philly, dearest,' he said kindly, 'surely you must realise that last night was one glorious adventure, and nothing more? I love Claire. I thought you understood that?'

'You can't love Claire! She's a sour and serious Scotswoman, the daughter of a minister! You can do better than Claire, Julek!'

'How dare you!' Julek's brow darkened. 'How dare you even suggest such a thing? Please leave!'

Philly's disappointment turned to anger. 'If you love her, then why did you lead me on?' she sobbed, well on the verge of hysteria. 'You must have guessed how I felt about you! If you love someone, you do not make love to others!'

Julek assumed a look of resignation. 'Look, Philly,' he said kindly again, 'you're a lovely girl, very pretty, and you have a great personality and a beautiful body. I thought we were just having fun, like everyone else at country house parties. It's just one big Bosom of Aphrodite! Can't you see that?'

Philly burst into tears. 'To you it may be just a bit of fun, you heartless bastard, but to me it's my whole life! And you've ruined it for me! I hate you!'

She rushed out of Julek's room, straight into the arms of Charles, who had materialised at the door at that precise moment. 'Whoa!' he cried, holding her by the shoulders. Philly disentangled herself and ran down the corridor in floods of tears. Charles watched her go.

'Oh dear,' said Charles, taking one step into Julek's room. 'I just couldn't help overhearing –'

'Women!' muttered Julek, returning to his final packing.

'Oh, they're not so bad,' grinned Charles.

'What do you mean?' Julek stopped packing.

'Last night I nearly bumped into Phluffy Philly in the corridor.'

'She came to my room. But you knew that.'

'Oh yes,' Charles grinned. 'I was on my way to Flora's room!'

'You went to Flora's room?!' Julek's face lit up. 'And – did you – was there –?' He waved his hand at the bed, noticed the blood and hurriedly pulled the covers over it.

Charles' face fell. 'Well, no. But we talked. About opera.'

'Ah. You talked about opera,' Julek returned to his packing. 'No Bosom of Aphrodite, then?'

'There will be further occasions.' Charles, who had been standing all the while in the doorway, entered Julek's room. 'So it's still Claire,' he said.

'Yes.' Julek regretted saying that as he said it, and winced.

XIII

Julek saw no more of either Charles or Philly after his return to Edinburgh. The Ninth had done his concussion some good, even though he still suffered headaches. He also suffered some delayed pangs of guilt, along with feelings of euphoria, for the Philly affair, although not for Philly herself. He had decided that she had acted like a whore and had deserved what she got. But he genuinely felt guilty for having betrayed Claire's trust. 'I've been unfaithful,' he confided to Stanford the day after his return. They had been discussing their respective stints at the Bosom of Aphrodite over morning coffee in the drawing room.

'You can only be unfaithful if you're married,' said Stanford. 'You're still young and single. You have not formally embraced any obligations yet. You are entitled to explore what the world has to offer. And that includes the Bos – love.'

'I've made my mind up about Claire. I feel guilty at having betrayed her trust. It is her that I love.'

'Obviously not enough!'

Tavistock appeared, as if from nowhere, to take away the coffee tray. Julek momentarily imagined him, cloaked and with a scythe, and shuddered. He then looked at Stanford, and compared his friendship to that of Charles. He knew that Stanford would stick by him through thick and thin, and not pull his punches where opinion and advice were concerned. He also knew that he could rely absolutely on his loyalty. He was not so sure about Charles. He had, in one moment of lapsed concentration, let slip the very fact that he had so meticulously kept hidden from him over the whole of the summer. He wondered whether Charles would use the information in any way to stop his relationship with Claire.

'What if Charles spills the beans?' said Julek.

'My thoughts precisely, PK. If he did, it certainly would not be out of spite, or anything like that. I still think he has your best interests at heart. You must realise the dangerous waters you're sailing into.'

'Yes, but it's my choice. My life. My love. My future.'

'And Claire's.'

'She's with me all the way.'

'To Poland?'

Julek said nothing. He had not thought that far ahead. He still had a year to go before qualifying, and a year is a long time in a young man's life. But Stanford was, of course, quite right in spelling out the factor that he had not thitherto dared to contemplate. Now, for the first time, he found himself considering the bigger picture, and foresaw a further dimension to the problem that he decided not to face just yet. The image alighted on his mind of Claire as his wife, the Countess, the Lady of Sarenki, pillar of the community, the Church.

The Church.

'We shall see,' he said, finally. 'We still have a year at the Medical School. A great deal can happen in a year!' Beneath that confident, charming bluster, there was, it seemed, a good deal of his father in Julek.

It was Stanford's turn to say nothing.

*****

Events came to a head one twilit evening towards the end of August. It was a Monday. Dinner had just finished, and Tavistock was clearing away the dirty dishes. Sir Robert and Lady Sarah, Stewart, who was still bandaged up but able to get around,

Stanford and Julek were about to leave the table when there was a frantic ringing and loud banging on the front door.

Everyone looked up in surprise. 'Who on earth could that be, at this time of day,' said Sir Robert. Tavistock stopped what he was doing, and went to attend to the matter, while everyone went through to the drawing room for coffee. He returned a few moments later.

'Someone to see Mr Stanford, sir,' said Tavistock. 'The matter appears to be urgent.'

'Who is it, Tavistock?' said Lady Sarah. 'Very noisy, whoever it is.'

'He didn't leave a name, madam, only said it was a matter of considerable importance to Mr Stanford.' Before anyone could say anything, Tavistock had disappeared from the room, by which time Stanford had already preceded him at the double. He came back a few moments later.

'PK, you'd better come,' he said to Julek conspiratorially.

'What is it, Stanford?' said Lady Sarah. 'What's going on?'

But before anyone could answer, both Julek and Stanford were already out of the room.

'I'm going to see what's going on,' said Lady Sarah, getting up and following the two young men. In the open doorway stood Claire Fraser. She was wearing a travelling cloak with matching bonnet, and carried a small suitcase. Outside a buggy was just departing. She was in a state of considerable distress, and her eyes were puffed up, as though she had been crying. She was being held tightly by Julek.

'Please, Lady Sarah,' she sobbed, 'I'm so sorry to trouble you. I've left home. I've been travelling for four days. I've nowhere to go. I thought – perhaps –'

'Good heavens, child,' said Lady Sarah, pushing past Stanford and Julek, who were standing beside her, looking panic-stricken and indecisive. 'Come in, come in! Don't just stand there like a stuffed dummy, Stanford, ask her in!'

'Ask who in?' came Sir Robert's voice as he came into the hall. 'Good heavens! Claire! I thought we had made it quite clear –'

'Come on, Robert!' cried Lady Sarah, closing the door, 'can't you see Claire's in trouble? She needs our help!'

'I shall need help if word gets out! Julek, see Claire out! I'm sorry, Claire, surely you understand?'

'I'm so sorry, Sir Robert,' said Julek frantically, releasing Claire from his hold, 'I had no idea.'

'Can't you think about anything other than what people will say, father?' interrupted Stanford. 'Claire has come to ask for my help. My help, not Julek's. Not yours. And that is what I shall give her. Don't worry, father,' he added with a hint of sarcasm, 'we'll make sure no one gets to hear of her visit!'

Sir Robert relented. 'Very well,' he conceded. 'Do what you must do. But Claire can't stay here. We'll have the whole Church of Scotland besieging us if she does.' He stormed back into the drawing room.

'What are you going to do, Stanford?' said Lady Sarah, ushering Claire into the drawing room. Stewart was still there, in his favourite armchair, nursing his recovering ribcage. Once seated, he preferred to stay seated and still.

'Does your father know about Julek, Claire?' asked Stanford, sitting down.

'Yes,' sobbed Claire. She sat next to Julek on the sofa.

'Who told him?'

'I don't know,' said Claire. She had regained a certain measure of composure. 'But he did get a letter from Carnethie Castle about a week ago.'

Stanford pursed his lips. 'I somehow thought he would,' he muttered.

'Charles!' interpolated Lady Sarah. 'I told you not to trust Charles Carnethie, Julek!'

'He found out by accident,' said Julek. 'We went to a lot of trouble to put him on the wrong trail, but it all went wrong when –'

'So, he's thrown you out?' interrupted Stanford.

'I ran away.'

A chorus of 'You ran away?!'

'That puts a totally different complexion on things,' said Sir Robert, getting up. 'This is the first place her father will descend on. Claire must be taken elsewhere.'

'Ben Horlick!' said Stewart. All eyes turned to him. Until now Stewart had remained silent and aloof, as though the whole thing were none of his business. 'Ben Horlick will put her up. No one will find her there.'

'Who's Ben Horlick?' said Lady Sarah.

'He's the landlord of the Puffin's Nest tavern in Portobello,' said Stanford.

'A tavern?!' said Sir Robert in disgust.

'The Bosom of Aphrodite,' muttered Julek under his breath. Claire shot him a glance. It conveyed nothing. She took his hand in hers.

'The Bosom of who?' said Sir Robert.

'Just a manner of speaking, Sir Robert,' said Julek. 'It's the inn in Portobello where we were going to stay after the fishing trip.'

'Ben Horlick is a good man, father,' continued Stewart. 'I've known him for a very long time. He is very reasonable, and discreet.'

'Well, you should know!' said Julek pointedly.

'Then, common tavern or not, we shall have to enlist his services immediately,' said Sir Robert.

'I agree,' said Lady Sarah. 'But first, have you eaten, Claire? Perhaps Tavistock can come up with some cold lamb.' She raised her voice, 'Tavistock! Will you –'

But Tavistock was already in the room with a tray. Cold lamb, ham, rye bread, cheese, fruit cordial and jam tart. 'I took the liberty, madam,' he said, placing the tray before Claire, who smiled her thanks.

'I thought you said *he* didn't leave a name, Tavistock,' said Sir Robert quizzically.

'Just a manner of speaking, sir,' said Tavistock as he left the room, exchanging glances with Julek, who shuddered.

*****

Stanford sorted out the buggy with Julek's help, after which the three of them set off for Portobello in the gathering dark. Ben Horlick was already closing up, his last customers, a group of regular fishermen, having just left in deference to an early start in the morning. He was only too glad to let Claire have a room at the Puffin's Nest, even though it was late. The room was clean and comfortable, and a modest rent was agreed upon until further notice. Neither Claire, Stanford nor Julek considered it seemly, or advisable, for Julek to stay the night. While Julek helped Claire settle herself into her room, Stanford took a dram with Ben at the bar, and put him fully in the picture.

'So, if a Presbyterian minister comes looking for his lost daughter,' he said, pressing a gold sovereign into the innkeeper's palm, 'pretend you know nothing.'

'Dinna fear, Master Stanford, sir,' said Ben, 'I'll see nae harm comes to the lassie!'

Stanford set off for Queen Street in the sure knowledge that Claire was in good hands. It was past midnight when he reached home.

The following morning, Tuesday, the McWhirter house rose very early. Sir Robert had a business dinner engagement in Glasgow that evening, and Stewart had been invited by the old Wilberforces to spend a few days at Carne for some wholesome country air – and, of course, to be with Lady Jane. As Carne was on the way to Glasgow, Stanford had agreed to drive them in the family carriage, stop off at Carne to drop off Stewart and have lunch, then go on to Glasgow, where they were to put up at the Golden Lion. While his father attended his dinner engagement, Stanford had arranged to meet an old school friend and go out on the town together. Sir Robert and Stanford planned to return to Edinburgh the next day. They set off after a hearty breakfast, at which Julek's absence was noted.

'Where's Julek?' inquired Sir Robert.

'He got up early, father,' replied Stanford. 'He's borrowed the buggy and gone to Portobello.'

'Without breakfast?'

'He was in a hurry.'

'God save us!'

'Amen to that!'

With all the menfolk gone, Lady Sarah looked forward to a whole day of solitary splendour and blissful laziness. The Tavistocks, butler husband and cook-housekeeper wife, had been given the day off to visit their married daughter in Livingstone. She sprawled herself all over the sofa in the drawing room, a glass and a decanter of her favourite apple cordial by her side. She opened her book. *Ivanhoe*, by Sir Walter Scott. As if on cue, the doorbell rang. Lady Sarah dropped an oath as she rose to answer it. The caller, a tall, stately man with a noble face and a flowing mane of thick, white hair, introduced himself as the Reverend Menzies Fraser. He apologised profusely for the intrusion, and asked to see Count Julek Samojarski.

'Reverend Fraser,' said Lady Sarah politely, indicating the drawing room. 'Count Samojarski is not here at this moment. I am Lady Sarah McWhirter. Please come in. Some apple cordial, perhaps?'

'Thank you, Lady Sarah. It is good of you to see me.'

'What can I do for you, Reverend?'

'I will come straight to the point, Lady Sarah. I believe you know my daughter, Claire. She is studying at the Medical School.'

'Of course. She has dined here on a number of occasions.'

'In the company of the young Polish Count. Your lodger. Julek Samojarski.'

'Our guest, Reverend. We do not take lodgers. Count Samojarski is a close friend of the family. He and my son Stanford attended Almsbury together.'

'The Roman Catholic School in England?'

'Yes.'

'You are Roman Catholic, Lady Sarah?'

'Yes.'

'Yet your husband?'

'Is a Presbyterian, Reverend.'

'I see.' The Reverend Fraser's brow darkened. He said nothing more, and stared long and hard at the carpet. Lady Sarah poured two glasses of apple cordial. 'There was a time,' she continued, breaking the deafening silence, 'when Julek and Claire were friendly, but that was quite some time ago. I don't believe they have seen one another in recent months outside medical classes.'

'I have it on good authority, Lady Sarah, if you will be so kind as to bear with me, that their friendship continues. Thrives, even.'

'Good heavens, Reverend! This is the first time I hear such a thing! As far as I know, Julek's interest lies elsewhere, a young Roman Catholic lass.'

'Philomena Lonnegan.' The Reverend Frasers's brow darkened further, and his voice rose. 'A whore, Lady Sarah! A wicked, evil fornicating whore who has been set to entrap the young man and drag him from the paths of righteousness into the filth of Satan's moral mire! What chance has the young man of finding the True Path when they put such vile temptations of the flesh before him, and turn him into a fornicator himself!'

Lady Sarah's composure cracked, and she transfixed the Reverend Fraser with an icy glare. 'Just what are you getting at, Reverend Fraser? Have you come to my house to deliver a sermon, or is there something else I can do for you?'

The Reverend Fraser sighed. His body relaxed. 'My apologies, Lady Sarah,' he said quietly. 'I am in a very distraught state. Please forgive me. I have to inform you that Claire has left our home. She has run away, with the intention of eloping with Count Samojarski.'

'I don't believe it! How do you know this?'

'She has told me so herself. She has made threats.' Lady Sarah was beginning to find it hard to keep up the deception, and could only make a series of stuttering noises which might have sounded anything from aggressive to conciliatory. 'I am well aware that my Claire and the Count are in love,' continued the Reverend Fraser. 'But a union between their respective paths of righteousness is surely impossible. There is no compatibility, d'ye see. But I love my daughter dearly too. I would have her find true love and happiness in the Lord. I thought – perhaps – if I were to speak to the Count, man to man – to explain – to show him the True Path.'

Lady Sarah stopped and stared. 'You wish to convert Julek?' she said incredulously.

The Reverend lowered his eyes and his voice. 'Ay, Lady Sarah. That I do. If it can be done. If it will help. After all, God is Love, isn't it nae so? It is our duty to nurture and to foster Love. In whatever way we can.'

'Another glass of cordial, Reverend?'

XIV

At the Puffin's Nest Claire had slept only fitfully. By the time Julek had arrived as the early boats were putting out to sea, she had already been for a long walk along the seafront. Ben Horlick watched surreptitiously out of the corner of his eye as they embraced long and hard, and smiled. He had the distinct feeling that he was watching a romantic novel unfolding before his eyes: a dashing young Polish Count and a fair Scottish lassie from Skye! A Papist and a Presbyterian! A heady mixture indeed, yet doomed, perhaps, and destined for a tragic ending? 'Still 'tis early chapters yet,' he said to himself as he served them a breakfast fit for lovers: salted porridge, fried kippers, hot buttered toast and Dundee marmalade, all washed down with enormous quantities of sweet, milky tea. Ben watched them eat slowly, calmly, quietly, and wondered what tribulations lay ahead to test their love. They spoke in whispers, so there was no knowing what they spoke of, or what plans they were making.

During the course of the morning Ben bustled around, serving a plate of kippers here, a dram or two of whisky, there; a tankard or two of ale, or a pot of tea or coffee. The Puffin's Nest was a popular hostelry. Yet his lovers took no notice of all these comings and goings; they had eyes and words only for one another. By mid-morning, as Ben was wiping the tables and sweeping the flagstones after the early morning custom, they set off for a ride in the buggy that young Count Julek had arrived in. It belonged to the McWhirters. Nice lads, the

McWhirters. Many's the time they took rooms at the Puffin's Nest. Mrs Horlick liked to do for them, and they were always very appreciative. Always paid on the dot. Young Mr Stanford was a regular visitor, with his Miss Ann. Irish Roman Catholic, but a charming lassie nonetheless. As for Mr Stewart, he has not been for a while, on account of his broken ribs, poor man. Dreadful tragedy, the *Sally Jane*.

'Will ye take steak-and-kidney pudding?' said Ben when Julek and Claire returned from their ride along the coastline in the early afternoon. 'Mrs Horlick has a pot on the stove.'

Julek and Claire accepted gratefully, and washed the rich, steaming dish down with a tankard of Scottish ale. Most unusual, thought Ben, to find a lassie, especially from Skye, to take ale. 'Good on her,' he thought. 'Steak and ale: the second greatest combination known to Man!'

After Man and Woman, he reflected wryly, as the young lovers retired upstairs to Claire's room after lunch, and he saw no more of them until sunset.

*****

The Reverend Menzies Fraser declined Lady Sarah McWhirter's invitation to dinner. 'I've been invited to stay with the Reverend Robson at Warriston Crescent,' he said. 'He and I go back a long way, y'see. But I thank you all the same, Lady Sarah. It has been very kind of ye to see me. I am full of admiration for the way that you and Sir Robert have tackled the problems of religion. After all, there is only the One God. I'm fully confident that with the right guidance and understanding, we shall see the young people united in the Love of the Lord.'

After the Reverend Fraser had gone, Lady Sarah felt an enormous relief. Claire's father had come across as a very reasonable, kindly and humane man of character whose only concern was the happiness of his daughter – so long as it was under the auspices of the One True God's love. Absolutely no harm in that. What was more, she had impressed him with the example of her own marriage, which thrived under the auspices of the One True God's love.

She decided that she would speak to Julek about it in the morning. She spent the rest of the day with solitary splendour, blissful indolence regained and inroads into *Ivanhoe* achieved. After a supper of cold ham with mustard, rye bread and butter, and a slice of Mrs Tavistock's almond cake, she retired for an early night with a cup of hot chocolate, as she did not for one moment imagine Julek would be back until after she had retired.

She was right. Julek returned to Queen Street late that night, with his mind made up and his plan formulated and set in motion. He noticed that Lady Sarah had already gone to bed, and there was no sign of the Tavistocks. Perhaps they had not returned from their daughter's in Livingstone, and Sir Robert and Stanford would not be back before tomorrow afternoon. He crept up to his room as quietly as he could so as not to wake Lady Sarah.

First, he packed his belongings into his trunk. He left most of his clothes behind, reckoning that he would not be needing them where he was going. He did pack all his medical books, case notes, pamphlets, notebooks, illustrations and diagrams, as well as the literature about beneficial waters that Grant Burke had sent him from Bath. He then sat down and wrote four letters, to Sir Robert and Lady Sarah, to Stanford, to Mrs McIntyre and to the Principal of the Edinburgh Medical School. The gist of the letters was the same in each case: that for personal reasons he found himself forced to abort his studies, and return home to Poland forthwith. He added profuse apologies for his actions, along with expressions of thanks for friendships, kindnesses and hospitality, and hopes that when his personal problems were settled, he would be in a position to resume these friendships once again. He finished by begging for forgiveness for his actions and understanding of his personal dilemmas. He left the four letters, sealed and addressed, on the hall table. He then struggled to drag his trunk out of his room, along the landing, and to the top of the stairs, trying desperately not to make any noise that would wake Lady Sarah. It took him a very long time to manoeuvre the trunk down the stairs, across the hall and out into the chill night air of Queen Street.

The buggy was still parked where he had left it two hours previously. By the dim light of the gas lamps, he managed to hoist the trunk up onto the buggy, and climbed into the driving seat. He turned and cast a final glance at the house which had taken him to its bosom and gave him shelter and hospitality, where he had known some of the happiest days of his life, and was visited by a sharp pang of regret. He then took the reins, and the buggy moved forward, the sound of the wheels and clip-clop of hooves on the cobbles echoing eerily in the night.

Somewhere in Portobello a clock chimed three when Julek drew up outside the Puffin's Nest. Ben Horlick had been expecting him, and, hearing the discreet knocking on the pre-arranged ground floor window, rose from the chair in which he had fallen asleep, and let Julek in. Then, together they hauled the trunk into the tavern, and left it just inside the bar area. Then the landlord went outside, where he unharnessed and stabled the horse, and parked the buggy in the yard. When he had finished, he went back inside, where Julek was waiting for him. He was bleary eyed and looked exhausted.

'A wee dram afore ye retire, Master Julek?' he said.

'Why not, Ben?'

The landlord fetched two glasses and poured out two shots of best malt whisky. 'Are ye sure you ken what ye're doin', Master Julek?' he asked. 'It's one devil of a step into unknown territory ye're takin'.'

Julek looked at Ben over the rim of his glass, and felt unable to tell him that it was not his business to question his actions. It was, furthermore, the identical question that was foremost in his own mind.

'No, Ben,' he said. 'I'm not at all sure. It may well be the biggest mistake I shall ever make in my life. I'm walking out on my studies, walking into a new role as Lord of a Polish Manor, instigator and proprietor of a health centre in a land that I don't really understand, and husband of a girl brought up in a totally different culture, language and religion to me. So no, Ben, I don't think I'm at all sure that I know what I'm doing.'

'It's nae too late to change your mind.'

'It's made up, Ben. I have decided. There is no such thing as a wrong decision. There are only decisions, which lead to more decisions. Life is just a game of decisions and their consequences. The alternative is stagnation.'

'Does Miss Claire share your views, Master Julek?'

'Yes, Ben. She does.' The two men looked up. Standing at the foot of the stairs was Claire, wrapped in her travelling cloak against the night chill. She walked towards the table at which Julek and Ben were sitting, and joined them. Ben waved his hand at the whisky bottle, but Claire shook her head. 'We have both made the decision to elope, Ben.' She laid her hand on Julek's. 'Together. For better or worse, as they say in marriage vows. I cannot possibly live life according to my father's values, or his interpretation of the teachings of Jesus Christ. To me they're intrinsically wrong. But you're right. It may all be one monumental mistake. But we shall never know until we act on our instincts.'

'Or judgements?' said Ben.

'Indeed. A host of factors. But we have made our decision, and that is the path that is righteous for us at the present time.'

'The world, Ben, is our oyster, as they say. It's up to us to open it and make it work,' added Julek.

'Well. Master Julek, Miss Claire,' Ben drained his glass and rose, 'ye ken I wish ye the very best, all the happiness in the world, and may ye both spit in the eye of adversity! I bid ye a good night. I'll wake ye afore noon for your assignation.'

Julek and Claire fell asleep immediately, thinking longingly about the occasion when it would be right and proper to explore the joys of the Bosom of Aphrodite together.

It was past ten o'clock when they were rudely awoken, and Charles burst through Julek's door. Ben was hovering just behind, trying in vain to pacify him. 'Get up! Get up both of you!' he shouted, noticing that Julek was alone.

'Charles!' cried Julek, sitting up abruptly, 'what the devil do you mean by this intrusion?'

'I've come to drag you away from here and back to Edinburgh, and knock some sense into you! Get up!'

'You've no right to do anything of the sort,' shouted Julek. 'You've made life absolutely impossible for Claire and me, and we've had enough. We're going away together, and there's nothing you or anyone else can do to stop us!'

'We shall see about that!' replied Charles. 'You don't understand what's going on. I've just been to Queen Street, and Lady Sarah is worried out of her mind. She has had a visit from the Reverend Fraser!

'My father!' cried Claire. 'Where is he now?'

'He's staying with his friend, the Reverend Robson.'

'I knew it! He's followed me!'

'What in God's name do you expect?' cried Charles. 'But what you need to know is that he's in a conciliatory mood. He wants to talk to Julek.'

There was a pause before Julek spoke. 'Get Sir Charles out of here, Ben. We'll come downstairs.'

'This way, Sir Charles,' said Ben, raising his eyebrows at Julek and Claire before shutting the door.

'It's a ruse,' said Claire. She had a quiver in her voice. 'My father has never been conciliatory in his life!'

Ten minutes later Julek and Claire, both fully dressed and ready to depart, came down. Charles, who had been pacing nervously around the bar, rushed up to them. 'See sense, Claire!' he said. 'Your father and Lady Sarah have had a long conversation yesterday, and she has assured me that he wants to find a way for the two of you to be together.'

'How?' said Julek.

'He wants to convert you.'

'The Reverend is a jester!' Julek's laugh was totally mirthless.

'He's on your side!'

'Oh yes? He has a funny way of showing it!'

'And I'm on your side, too!'

'And you, too, have a funny way of showing it! Claire and I have spent the whole of the summer avoiding you, in case you tell on us!'

'You've been intolerably dishonest with me, PK. I thought I was your friend.'

'Some friend, who wrote to the Reverend Fraser telling him about us!'

'It was for your own good, Julek! I had to stop this madness! The two of you were heading for a disaster!'

'So you tried to split us up!'

'Yes!'

Julek's fist flew into Charles' face like lightning. Charles staggered back and fell against a table at which a sailor was seated, utterly immobile, with a tankard of ale in his hand. Only his eyes moved, going from Charles to Julek and back again. Charles fell onto the startled sailor, who did not see the physical attack coming. Julek leapt at him again, pushed the sailor out of the way, and continued to beat Charles across the face over and over again. Charles did not fight back. He did not retaliate in any way. He just took the punishment like a zombie, almost as though he were not yet aware that he was being beaten up.

Finally, Julek stopped, panting, his teeth set, his eyes ablaze as they transfixed his adversary with a look of pure hate. Charles lay still on the floor, his face a mass of blood and bruises. Claire bit her lip, and did not move. She had never seen Julek act with such a rage, and found the experience terrifying. She stared at him as if in a trance, and would have remained that way, frozen, had Julek not gone to her, taken her hand and ushered her outside. The buggy was there, loaded and ready for immediate departure, as had been previously arranged.

Ben, who had been standing behind his bar, listened to the clip-clop of hooves dying into the distance as he surveyed the battlefield that was his bar. A motley band of morning patrons were standing absolutely still with their backs to the walls, as though they had been trying to place themselves as far from the action as possible. The sailor who had borne the brunt of the fight had got himself up off the ground, and pulled himself back onto his chair, which had been overturned, and supported himself on the table, which was on its side. All the while his eyes were fixed on the prostrate body on the floor not one yard away from him.

*****

Half an hour later Lady Sarah arrived with the Reverend Fraser to find the Puffin's Nest a hive of activity, with people milling around and buggies jostling for positions in the street outside. Some men were carrying what looked like a body, and loading it onto a cart.

'Mr Ben Horlick?' said Lady Sarah, spotting the unmistakeable figure of the landlord. 'I am Lady Sarah McWhirter, and this is the Reverend Menzies Fraser. I understand that his daughter Claire has been staying with you.'

'That's right, Lady Sarah,' said Ben. 'And Count Julek Samojarski.'

'And where would they be now, Mr Horlick?' said the Reverend Fraser.

'On the high seas by now, I should imagine, Reverend. They hired the services of the captain of a Prussian vessel to take them overseas.'

'Where from?'

'Here. Portobello.'

'To where?' wailed Lady Sarah.

'They did not say, Lady Sarah.' Ben was obviously not saying any more. 'Truly I don't know.'

Two men pushed their way to Ben. 'Bad news, Ben,' said one.

'He's g-gone,' said the other, swallowing.

'My God!' cried Lady Sarah, looking round at the milling crowds, 'what has been happening around here?'

'There's – there's been a fight,' said Ben hesitatingly. 'An accident – a terrible accident, it seems.'

'It's that Polish Count,' said one of the men, 'he beat up Sir Charles Carnethie.'

'Killed him too,' said the other. The excited chattering stopped abruptly and everyone clustered round the body indecisively. One man pushed everyone aside, knelt down beside it, put his ear to his mouth for a good while and felt his pulse. He got up, looked intently at Ben, and shook his head.

'Bloody papist! Now he's escaped to sea, no way we can get him now!'

'Once again religion rears its ugly head and spreads death, destruction and misery all over this fucking world.' No one would have been expected to know, but the seemingly disinterested commentator was a Polish former 'bloody papist' by the name of Ząb, who had heard whispers, and had made a point of being around.

The Reverend Menzies Fraser closed his eyes and tried to pray to his God.

Coming out soon: Book 2 – Always Redemption